Praise for Paul Cleave's previous
international bestsellers

JOE VICTIM

Nominated for the 2014 Edgar Award
for Best Paperback Original

"Cleave pulls out all the stops in his seventh Christchurch noir. . . . [He] juggles all the elements with impressive ease. Darkly humorous references to horrific violence will resonate with Dexter fans."

—*Publishers Weekly* (starred)

"A little Hannibal Lecter. A little Richard von Krafft-Ebing. A lot of gore."

—*Kirkus Reviews*

"Cleave does his usual great job of threading two ongoing stories from two different serials into a single, closely knit unit and as usual, keeps the reader eager for more. It's hard not to empathize with Joe, even cheering for the bad guy is allowed, if for no other reason, we need to know what he will do next."

—*Suspense Magazine*

"Clever, compelling, and not for the faint hearted. Joe Middleton is the guiltiest 'innocent man' in crime fiction."

—Michael Robotham, internationally bestselling author of *Watching You*

THE LAUGHTERHOUSE

Finalist for the 2013 Ngaio Marsh Award for Crime Fiction

Suspense Magazine Best of 2012

"An intense adrenaline rush from start to finish, I read *The Laughterhouse* in one sitting. It'll have you up all night. Fantastic!"

—S. J. Watson, *New York Times* bestselling author of *Before I Go to Sleep*

"Cleave is a master of evoking the view askew; delving into the troubled psyches of conflicted characters. Former cop and convict Theo Tate, stumbling forward in search of some sort of redemption, returns to the scene of his first crime scene, hunting a killer and kidnapper set on revenge. Ferocious storytelling that makes you think and feel. A blood-stained high point in Cleave's already impressive oeuvre."

—*New Zealand Listener*, A Best Book of 2012

"This dark, gripping thriller, the latest in the Tate saga, is as hard-boiled as it gets. The surprise ending suspends all disbelief. Like a TV series that ends its season on a cliffhanger, you won't want to wait until next year. This will leave the reader clamoring for the next book in the series."

—*Suspense Magazine*

"Piano wire–taut plotting, Tate's heart-wrenching losses and forlorn hopes, and Cleave's unusually perceptive gaze into the maw of a killer's madness make this a standout chapter in his detective's rocky road to redemption."

—*Publishers Weekly* (starred)

ALSO BY PAUL CLEAVE

PAUL CLEAVE

FIVE MINUTES ALONE

A THRILLER

ATRIA PAPERBACK

New York London Toronto Sydney New Delhi

ATRIA PAPERBACK
A Division of Simon & Schuster, Inc.
1230 Avenue of the Americas
New York, NY 10020

First Atria Paperback edition October 2014

ATRIA PAPERBACK and colophon are trademarks of Simon & Schuster, Inc.

For information about special discounts for bulk purchases, please contact Simon & Schuster Special Sales at 1-866-506-1949 or business@simonandschuster.com.

The Simon & Schuster Speakers Bureau can bring authors to your live event. For more information or to book an event, contact the Simon & Schuster Speakers Bureau at 1-866-248-3049 or visit our website at www.simonspeakers.com.

Cover photographs by Getty Images and Arcangel Images

Manufactured in the United States of America

10 9 8 7 6 5 4 3 2 1

Library of Congress Cataloging-in-Publication Data

Cleave, Paul, date.
  Five minutes alone / by Paul Cleave.—First Atria paperback edition.
    pages cm
1. Private investigators—New Zealand—Fiction. 2. Rape victims—Fiction. I. Title.
  PR9639.4.C54F58 2014
  823'.92—dc23   2014011039

ISBN 978-1-4767-7915-7
ISBN 978-1-4767-7916-4 (ebook)

To my mum. I found a message just the other day she'd written into an old notebook of mine. She said, *How are you, Paul? Don't be so lazy—get up earlier (like me) and enjoy your day.* It made me smile. It reminded me of when she used to put lines through the swearwords in my manuscripts. We always laughed about that. Mum . . .you'd be happy to know I'm always up before lunchtime these days. And we miss you. And keep an eye out for Mogue . . .

FIVE
MINUTES
ALONE

CHAPTER ONE

Kelly Summers didn't like being out at night. She used to. Years ago she'd party all night and come home in the morning, sometimes only for a splash of deodorant and some fresh makeup, just enough time to change clothes and take a few shots of breath freshener before work. On weekends she'd hit the beach with her friends, maybe have a couple of beers and let the good times roll, but that was years and a different lifetime ago, back when she had more energy and less scars, back before the world shrunk to the building at work and the four walls of her house. Her best friend used to complain about how expensive town was, the drinks, the taxis, the shoes, and the skirts—they never could figure out why the shorter the skirt the more expensive it was—and back then life was pretty trivial.

Back then all changed five years ago when her world intersected with that of a man named Dwight Smith. The *Dwight* part of his name made him sound like a cowboy, like he should have been walking the streets wearing a ten-gallon hat and matching spurs to boot, like he should have been a do-gooding, all-round nice guy who'd say *howdy, ma'am* and sing sad songs. The *Smith* part made him sound like an Everyman, a last name like that could make him your doctor, your accountant, your neighbor. Or, in this case, it could also make him your rapist. She didn't know his name before their worlds intersected. Had seen him a few times, an acknowledged nod or raised hand that came with being neighborly as they drove past each other, because that's what he was—her neighbor.

Dwight had cut her. He'd cut her pretty bad. Cut her after he broke into her house, dragged her into the bedroom and cut her some more, then did some very unneighborly things to her. He had a hard-on for violence. That's what one of the cops told her after Dwight was sent to jail.

So now it's night and like every other night, and day too—let's be honest here folks—she's thinking about Dwight Smith. Her mind can't switch off from it. Doing dishes, taking inventory at work, mowing her lawn—Dwight Smith is always creep, creep, creeping around the corner of every thought. Tonight she's gotten caught late at work. One of the guys called in sick, and Jane just didn't show up, which was a typical thing for Jane these days, and the slack had to get taken up somewhere. It's just one of those things. That part has never changed no matter what the job. She used to work at the gym. She was a trainer. She had clients. They'd pay her and she'd torture them in the ways that would make them shed pounds and tighten flesh, and sometimes she'd have to work late there too.

After what she now considers "Dwight time," she didn't work for twelve months. She sat in her new home and she watched bad TV and ate bad food and instead of it making her fat it made her thin. Way too thin. Bad food isn't that bad when you're not eating much of it. It's just bad when it's all you're eating. Life, of course, moves on. It moves on at the exact same rate money runs out. She needed to get a job. What experience did she have? Well, there were two things she was good at—getting people fit and getting herself raped. She got a job in a supermarket, which involved neither of those things. She signs in deliveries and helps unpack them. In the summer the building is way too hot and in the winter it's way too cold, and it always smells of vegetables.

Her car is twenty yards away. Not far during the day. But pretty far when it's dark. There are lights flooding the parking lot, but still . . . there are plenty of shadows, the creep, creep, creeping shadows. She walks with her keys tight in her fist. She learned how to do a lot of damage with a car key in the self-defense classes she took once she started leaving the house again. Part of her always thinks about how empowering it'd be to kick the absolute shit out of somebody. Part of her knows that wouldn't happen, that she'd fall into a tight ball and let whatever was going to be done to her be done to her. *C'est la vie*. Isn't that what the French would say?

The twenty yards are eaten up quickly with long strides. Cowboy Dwight is nowhere in sight. And why the hell would he be? He's still in jail, hopefully getting done to him what was done to her. She wants him to rot in there. Wants him to die. Wants him to suffer. Every night she falls asleep breathing hatred for Dwight Smith and every morning she wakes breathing the same thing. She reaches her car and looks through the windows. It's paranoia, for sure, but paranoia has kept her world from intersecting with other Dwight Smiths. There is nobody inside.

The car is running low on gas. She hates getting gas. Hates the two or three minutes it takes to pump it, hates the small conversation with whoever comes out to help, hates the smell and the sense the whole place is one discarded cigarette away from becoming a fireball. But she gets gas and pays for it and doesn't get raped at the station or run off the road to be raped afterwards. She uses the remote to open her garage door. She drives in and watches in the mirror as the door closes behind her. Nobody rolls under it.

The lights are already on inside. She leaves them on during the day so she never has to come home to a dark house. She listens to the house for any kind of sound, but there's nothing. She strips off in the bathroom. She spends fifteen minutes in the shower. She dries herself down, puts on a robe, and opens the bathroom door to find Cowboy Dwight standing in her hallway.

Over the last few years she's seen Cowboy Dwight in the supermarket, at her sister's house, in the back of her car. Cowboy Dwight even made a brief appearance a few months ago playing the role of her optometrist. So this is nothing new. In fact her psychiatrist gave her something to make the visions disappear. Sometimes the pills work and sometimes they don't. She closes her eyes. All she has to do is count to five and Cowboy Dwight will be gone. He'll be back in jail serving his eleven years.

"You missed me?" he asks, and well now, this is new, because in the past the visions haven't spoken to her. She'd always wondered what they would say if they did. She figured on a few things—perhaps *I'm back to finish what I started,* or *I'm going to make you hurt.* Throw some expletives in there, perhaps a line or two of how he was going to do this to her and that, how he'd make her scream but *Really, really, you love it, don't you, bitch?* First time he showed up after her attack she ran out of the room and called the police. They found nothing. They assured her Dwight was in jail. They checked the windows and doors, and then she made them check with the prison to make sure he was still there. The second time she called them again. The third time a psychiatrist got involved.

She closes her eyes. Breathes in. Breathes out. Eyes open and Cowboy Dwight is still there. He's wearing gray pants and a gray shirt with a red logo on it, and it takes her a few seconds to recognize it—it's the logo of the gas station she just came from. He's also chewing gum. In the other visions he was always wearing the same jeans he wore when he originally broke into her house. He wore a stupid black shirt with orange flames coming up from the bottom hem, like his waist was on fire. And he never chewed gum.

Her heart starts to race. Something in her mind is slowly bending, bending.

She closes her eyes again. "One."

"I bet you did miss me," he says, and she can smell her vision—the gas on his clothes and his chewing-gum breath.

"Two."

"Bet you've thought of nothing else over the last five years. Well, truth be told—"

"Three."

"I've thought of very little else too." His fingers touch the side of her face, he trails them down the scar, that god-awful scar he gave her, and hey Mr. Psychiatrist, now that the visions are talking and touching her, she'll need her prescription updated.

"Four."

"You felt good, Kelly. Really good. I used to think, well, I used to think if I had just gone ahead and stuck that knife deep between those beautiful tits of yours, you would never have been able to tell, and I would never have gotten caught."

"Five," she says, and she keeps her eyes closed.

"Jail makes a man regret things," he says. "Some regret the crimes. Most just regret getting caught. That's what I regret, Kelly. I regret getting caught."

"Five!" she says, this time louder. She opens her eyes. The pills haven't worked because Cowboy Dwight is still here. She can see the blackhead pimples down the sides of his nose. She can see the creases around his eyes. He has a couple of eyebrow hairs sticking out much further than the others, curling down towards his eye.

"Go to Hell," she says, and the confidence she didn't think she would have, the skills she learned in those self-defense classes, in a heartbeat they all come back to her. She takes one step back and pushes her weight forward and swings her fist through the air.

Her vision of Dwight steps to the side. It swipes her punch off course with the back of its hand, then delivers one of its own. It gets her hard in the stomach. She staggers into the bathroom and into the side of the tub. She snatches at the shower curtain to balance herself, to stop from falling. It holds, it holds, then one of the plastic rings snaps. Then another, and they're snapping and flying around the room. She falls into the tub. Her head bounces into the wall but not hard enough to make the vision disappear and, unfortunately, not hard enough to knock her out. That means she's going to go along for the ride.

"Please," she says.

"This won't be like it was before," he tells her. "I mean, it'll start out the same. You're going to have to give me some of that good old-fashioned going-along-to-get-along cooperation, but it's going to end a whole lot different. Can't have you telling on me this time."

"Please," she says, and she's crying now. He leans down. He tugs at her robe and then it's gone and she's naked now, naked and exposed and vulnerable, too numb to fight back. Too scared. And why the hell can't she put up a fight, goddamn it? He drags her out of the tub and pushes her face down on the bathroom floor, right into a footstep puddle of water.

"Tell me you've missed me."

She can't answer him. Doesn't know what to say even if she could. He slaps her across the back of her thighs, hard, the sound echoing through the bathroom like a gunshot. Then he hits her again. She doesn't want to cry. He can take her body, he can end her life, but she's not going to give him any tears. It may not be much, but it's all she has. She. Will. Not. Cry.

She will. Be. Strong.

"Tell me," he says.

"No."

She hears his belt jingling and then his fly is being undone, and she won't survive it, not this time, and the truth is she doesn't even want to. *C'est la vie.* She closes her eyes and now the tears come. She sobs onto the tiles, the cold wet tiles that press against her, hoping her body can stay numb as the end comes.

CHAPTER TWO

I'm in the middle of a dream when my cell phone goes off. The dream is in an art museum. It's not one I've ever been to, but I've seen enough of them on TV and in movies where art gets stolen to know how they look. We're in a room with soft lighting, the sun diffused by frosted windows. I'm with Bridget and we're talking about how we don't get it. We just don't. We're looking at sculptures made from Band-Aids, from burlap sacks, we're looking at things that at other times we've seen dumped on the side of the road. That's the thing about modern art, Bridget is telling me. Some of it looks like it was constructed in ten minutes. Some of it looks like it took a year. You either like it or you don't, but at the very least you can talk about it.

One of the pieces is ringing. It's a cell phone that stands the height of a man, the body constructed from strips of roofing iron, the keys themselves are the old Bakelite phones we grew up with back when phones had dials and not buttons, back when people had to watch porn on videotape because the Internet was a thing of the future. These phones are bolted on, forming a three-by-four formation of twelve phones, and I can't tell which one is ringing. I pick them up one at a time, getting only dial tones, and each time I hang up the modern art world slips away, little by little, until there is only one phone left. My phone. My phone sitting on the bedside drawers of my bedroom that, at seven thirty on a Saturday morning, has no art and, at seven thirty on a Saturday morning, is already lit up thanks to the fact that we're a week short of December. That also puts us a week short of summer and one month short of Christmas. I guess at any given point we're always short of something.

Bridget is sleeping deeply. That's how she always sleeps these days. All twelve phones from my dream—thirteen if you include the large one they're stuck to—could be in here ringing and she wouldn't hear them. Every morning when I wake up before her, I wake worried she's found her way back to the vegetative state she was in for almost three years until, six months ago, something inside her came back to life.

I already know what the phone call is going to be about. Nobody rings early with good news. The caller display says it's Detective Inspector Rebecca Kent. My partner. We've been working together for the last four weeks, when we were both put back onto the force. I'd met Kent before, but never worked with her.

"I wake you?" Kent asks.

I sit up on the side of the bed. "I was dreaming about modern art."

"Is that what you like to dream about on your days off?" she asks.

"Among other things."

"You ever have a dream where you could afford to buy any?"

"I'm working my way up to it," I tell her.

"Next time you're asleep, take some bribes. Anyway, guess why I'm calling?"

I stretch back my shoulders, trying to loosen them. Something clicks. These days something always clicks. "To tell me to enjoy my weekend?"

"Strike one," she says.

"To tell me you'll be here in thirty minutes to pick me up?"

"Strike two," she says. "But you were close. Change *thirty* to *twenty*, and you got yourself a home run. We're on the team."

"What team?" I ask.

"The suicide team."

"We're killing ourselves today?" I ask.

She laughs. "Aren't we killing ourselves every day for this city?"

"True."

"And today isn't going to be any different. We've got a suicide to look at. Do you remember a guy by the name of Dwight Smith?"

I know I've heard the name, but it's too early in the morning to think back to when. Maybe if I had coffee or a better memory I'd get there. The memory has been a little patchy since the coma. I reach up to my head and feel the part of my skull that took the blow. Six months ago I was in the process of rejoining the police force when a severe head injury put me into an induced coma. I was tracking a serial killer who got the jump on me. He hit me in the head so hard with a glass jar that the jar smashed. That was the start. A month after that I took further blows, these from a different killer who disliked me equally as much. It was all those combined hits to the head that got me my ticket to Coma Town, where I spent a few months. Prior to the injury, I'd been off the force for three years.

"I'm not sure. But I'm guessing you're about to tell me all about him."

"You remember Kelly Summers?"

I think about it for a few seconds. "Vaguely."

She sums up Kelly Summers's past in a twenty-second blurb, and what Dwight Smith did to her five years ago, then tells me she'll see me soon. "I've got coffee," she says, which goes a small way to making the morning sound a little better. And it needs to get better too—because she also tells me the body is in a dozen pieces.

I walk into the bathroom. For the last few months I've been getting what I call *old man knees*. Every morning they're puffy and swollen and for half an hour or so a little sore when I walk around. I'll be forty next year, and the old man knees feel like a warning. I spend two minutes in the shower washing down the other old man body parts. When I get out I see that the bed is empty, and I can hear Bridget in the kitchen. I grab my suit out of the wardrobe wondering if I'll ever be able to afford one that's more than two hundred dollars, and figure that I can if I do what Kent suggested—take bribes in my dreams. I head to the kitchen and my heart breaks a little. Bridget is making breakfast. There are three bowls on the table. One for me, one for her, one for our daughter, Emily. Bridget has her hair tied back into a ponytail, where it touches just below her shoulders. It's just as blond as it was when we first met, and just as wavy, but she keeps it mostly tied up these days. At thirty-seven, she's two years younger than me, but has always seemed to age at a slightly slower rate than me, and even after all we've been through, all her body went through after the accident, she still only looks thirty. It's genetics, because her mom looks twenty years younger than she really is. She turns towards me and smiles, that room-warming smile of hers that I've seen disarm others, the smile where I've seen men glance to her hand to see if she's wearing a wedding ring. I imagine it's every man's dream to end up with a beautiful woman, and I'm living that dream.

Toast pops up and Bridget turns towards it, then moves it onto a tray, dropping the pieces quickly because they're hot. Then she starts buttering them, changing her grip every second. I walk over and put my arms around her from behind.

"Morning," I say, and I kiss her neck.

"Morning," she says, without turning around. "I'm guessing that was Schroder?" she asks.

Schroder. The bowl for Emily. This happened for the first time two weeks ago. "No," I tell her. "It was Detective Kent."

"Kent? I haven't met him."

"Her."

"She's new?"

"She got transferred from Auckland this year."

She keeps buttering the toast. "Is it bad? The body that's been found? That's why she called, right?"

I don't answer. I let her go and move over to the fridge and grab orange juice, then pour us each a glass. Bridget puts the knife down and turns towards me. "What's wrong? You look so sad all of a sudden."

"I don't work with Schroder anymore." I tell her the easy news, hoping she'll remember the rest without me needing to spell it out, but knowing that it's unlikely. When she came out of the vegetative state she spent four weeks not remembering a single thing, barely even knowing who she was. The day she came out was the same day I fell into a coma. We overlapped each other by only a few minutes. We were like ships passing in the night. Before I slipped into my own coma, I remember the doctor telling me Bridget had woken up, that there was a problem, and I don't remember anything else after that.

"You don't?" she asks.

"He left the force."

She frowns a little. "When was that?"

"Earlier this year."

"Why didn't you tell me? Did Kent replace him? Is she your new partner?"

"And you're making breakfast for Emily," I tell her, deciding not to update her on Schroder. He left the force because he was fired. He was fired because he had to make an impossible decision.

She shakes her head a little and gives me a slight smile. "Of course I'm making breakfast for her. I'm taking her to the movies later this morning. It's a shame you can't come along. But you're avoiding my question. Why didn't you tell me about Kent? Is she attractive?"

Four weeks after joining the land of the living, Bridget's memory came back. All of it—minus the few hours before and during the accident. Then two weeks ago the problems started. Small problems. Painful problems. My wife wakes up into the morning of the accident. She thinks that everything is as it was three years ago. It's the school holidays and she's taking Emily to the movies and Schroder is my partner and the world, to her, hasn't moved on.

Today is the third time it has happened.

I step forward and I grab hold of her hands. She tilts her head slightly and her forehead creases. "What is it you're about to tell me?" she asks.

"Emily isn't here anymore," I tell her.

Her forehead creases even more. The room smells of coffee and toast, and I can hear the clock on the kitchen wall ticking, each second dragging out longer than it should, tick . . . tick . . . tick.

"What do you mean? It's . . ." she says, and glances at the microwave, "it's seven forty. Where else would she . . . would she . . ."

she says, slowing down now. The cracks are about to appear. I can see her making the connection. "Oh, I'm doing one of those dumb things again," she says, and she turns away from me. She picks the knife back up and carries on buttering the toast. "I feel stupid," she says, her voice shaking a little.

"Bridget . . ."

She puts down the knife and carries the toast over to the table. She sits down. "She won't even be awake for another hour. She's never up before eight during school holidays. I don't know why I thought I would make her breakfast so early. I just wish . . . I just wish this'd stop happening, it's like these stupid black spots in my memory are always shifting around."

"Bridget," I say, and I sit down beside her and take her hands. I hold them tight. "Emily isn't here because Emily died. She died three years ago in the same accident that hurt you."

Her face tightens and she tries to pull her hands out of mine, but I keep hold of them. "That's not even funny," she says. "Why would you be so cruel? Why would—"

"Bridget—"

"Why would you say such a thing, Theodore?" she asks.

"Babe—"

"Why?" she asks, and she's starting to cry, the cracks are getting bigger. I pull her in closer to me. "Why," she says, and she starts sobbing, and she wraps her arms around my neck and sobs into me. "I miss her," she says, her tears running down my neck and soaking the top of my shirt. "I miss her so much."

"I know you do," I tell her. "I miss her too. I'm so sorry."

"It was my fault," she says. "I shouldn't have taken her, we should have stayed home, we should—"

"It wasn't your fault."

"I don't remember any of it," she says, and she never will. All she remembers is what we've told her, that a drunk driver was going through a parking lot at a shopping mall at the same time Emily and my wife were there. A drunk driver who had already been caught multiple times, who'd lost his license and paid numerous fines, a drunk driver that the court system kept putting back onto the street, like handing a loaded gun to a gangbanger and sending him on his merry way. That drunk driver's name was Quentin James, and he merryed his way directly into my wife and daughter.

She knows the man who did it disappeared, but she doesn't know I was the reason why. I dragged him out into the woods. I told her what I had done while she was in her vegetative state. I'd always told her about my days. I'd confessed my sins to her. But not now.

I hold her, and I'm still holding her when I hear a car pull up outside. Kent gives a brief toot. "I can stay," I tell her.

"No," she says. "I'm okay. I promise."

"I'm so sorry," I tell her.

"It's not your fault," she says, but somehow it feels like it is. I should have been able to protect my family. "I'll be okay. You go and save the world, Teddy," she says, and she's the only person ever to have called me that. Not even my mom. "Go out there and stop other girls like Emily from being hurt."

I kiss her good-bye and she walks me to the door. She waves at Detective Kent because now she remembers her, and Kent waves back.

"You look like hell," Kent says when I get into the car.

"Tough morning."

"It's about to get tougher," she says, and she puts the car into gear and Bridget is still waving at us as we pull away from the house.

CHAPTER THREE

The victim isn't in a dozen pieces, not quite, but it's close enough, Rebecca says, and probably doesn't make much difference when you're the one being put into separate bags. But that's in the future—it's twenty or thirty minutes away. Right now it's just a car ride through the suburbs. The car smells of coffee. I throw my jacket into the backseat on top of Rebecca's. For now there's sun and no blood. Cool air and no blood. Just two people taking a drive.

We're not quite close enough to summer for it to be warm at eight a.m., but we'll get there. Another month we'll be waking up and stepping into seventy-plus-degree mornings, warm winds, and after lunch skin-blistering sunshine. On the front side of December the mornings look warmer than they are. The sun is low but bright, the sky is blue, the temperature barely touching fifty. It's that annoying weather where it looks as though you don't need a jacket, and you're too warm when you're wearing one and too cold when you're not.

Rebecca is only a little shorter than me, but far more athletic-looking, the kind of body you couldn't stop yourself from staring at if she jogged by. Black shoulder-length hair, bright blue eyes, the kind of woman you'd follow into the pits of Hell just to see her smile. Five months ago an explosion took that away from her—explosions are well known for making pretty people a whole lot less pretty, and that's exactly what happened to Kent. Originally from Christchurch, she was posted in Auckland, where she spent ten years on the force, but was sent back earlier in the year to fight the good Christchurch fight and to replace one of our detectives who had fallen. Then that good Christchurch fight almost killed her. It was a car bomb that nearly tore her apart. It happened right at the beginning of the Christchurch Carver's trial. There had been a shooting in the parking lot of the court building where the Carver was being transported, and that was part one of the distraction. Part two came a few minutes later when C-four in Schroder's car was detonated, with Kent and Schroder running from it. Kent's chest was hit with bits of metal and glass, puncturing a lung; her left eardrum was ruptured; and she suffered two dislocated joints. Most of that is hidden away, either internally or by her outfits, but not the scar on her face. She wears that like a badge of honor. It's a quarter of an inch thick, and runs an S-shaped pattern from her right ear to the bottom of her jaw. It's a little ragged too. It looks like a fishing hook got caught just beneath her ear, and somebody just kept tugging it until it tore around her face and came loose.

Both of us are trying to get our feet under us again. Both of us are trying to move forward.

We don't make small talk. We've just spent five days working together, and now it looks like we might be working the weekend too. Kent gets right down to the details. Tells me what to expect. Tells me there isn't a complete set for the medical examiner to take a look at. I've seen bodies before that have been in pieces, bodies that have been scooped up into buckets, bodies with bits missing that were never seen again. I have a good idea of what's coming up.

On my lap is the Dwight Smith file. It makes for awful reading, but these things always do. Files on the Dwight Smiths of the world don't come with silver linings. It wasn't my case. I can remember aspects and have forgotten others. I remember it was the kind of case that made you want to put him into the ground. There were a lot of cases that made me feel that way—the Dwight Smiths of the world. Five years ago this particular Dwight Smith had a few shots of whiskey, smoked some weed, then dragged himself to his neighbor's house—one Kelly Summers—at eight p.m. on a Friday night and took all of his anger at the world out on her. He was angry because he'd lost his job. He was angry because his girlfriend had left him three days earlier. He was angry because the drugs he wanted to buy were no longer in his price range. He was angry

because he'd gotten a flat tire that morning, replaced it, and gotten
another flat in the afternoon. So he dragged that anger with him
three doors down the street and used it to brutally rape and almost
kill Kelly Summers. Something held him back from taking that
extra step. It couldn't have been a concern at crossing a line. You
don't rape somebody, cut them up, then worry about boundaries.
Smith wasn't a boundaries kind of guy. What Smith was, it turned
out, was a great-behavior kind of guy, and only served half his time.

There is a photograph of Kelly Summers, a look of surrender in
her eyes, the photograph taken the day after the attack. There is a
ragged scar down the left side of her face. It's swollen and purple and
the stitches holding it together look too big, like the stitches used
on a rag doll. Aside from being a good-behavior kind of guy, Smith
was also a biter. He left bite marks all over her neck and chest.

We hit the edge of the city. Gray streets stretch in straight
lines between the gray buildings, forming chessboard blocks. It's
an overcast morning. If you had to sum up Christchurch in one
word, you would go with *gray*. Different shades of it everywhere
you look. Except for the traffic and the people. Colorful cars, colorful outfits, the occasional splash of greenery when you pass the
occasional tree. We get through town and back out the other side
of it. We head west. Shops and outlet stores give way to service
stations and industrial buildings that soon give way to residential
areas, which then give way to paddocks and farms. We're heading
in the direction of the Christchurch prison, which always brings
up bad memories. I spent four months there last summer making
friends with the cinder-block walls, having been sent there after
I got drunk last winter, got into my car, and ran a red light. I was
working a case as a private investigator, one that was going badly,
one that made me start drinking and ultimately led me to crashing
my car into another one, almost killing the teenage girl driving it.
It was my lowest point. It was me becoming the same as the man
that had taken away my daughter. Even now I'm still ashamed by
it. The bad memories remain even as the prison comes and goes
and we keep driving.

Suicides are tough work. They're sad—not homicide sad, but a different kind of sad, the kind of sad I can relate to. Women often take pills, but men . . . men will do anything. I've seen men who have half cut their heads off with power saws, men who have stabbed themselves in the throat with screwdrivers, men who have smashed hammers into their heads over and over. In the world of suicides, the hardware stores are doing well. Three years ago when my daughter died, and my wife looked like she was going to die too, those same dark thoughts whispered to me too. *Come on, Tate*, they would say. *Do the world a favor. How about you, me, and that gun of yours all take a little walk on the wild side?*

Five minutes past the prison the GPS speaks up and tells Kent to take the next left. To our left and right are farms and not a hell of a lot else. Seems like a long way to drive to kill yourself. Unless sheep and cows and wheat were the last thing you wanted to see.

We take the left and two minutes later we come to the train tracks. There's the hustle and bustle that comes along with any train-related fatality—a bunch of police cars, an ambulance, people from the railway department. No media, at least not yet. Suicides aren't newsworthy unless there's a connection to somebody famous. Detective Inspector Hutton is up by the tracks. The scene is about five hundred yards from one end to the other. It's a big scene. It's cordoned off with tape. We get out of the car and the day warms up another degree and I put my jacket on and we make our way under the tape. In the past every red-blooded guy would be looking over at Kent and offering her some kind of smile, every red-blooded guy would be trying to figure out a way to ask her out on a date. But since the explosion she walks through them like a ghost, everybody trying hard to pretend they don't notice the scar on her face.

The train tracks make their way from east to west, or west to east if you're a glass-half-empty kind of guy. The grass leading up towards the stony bank is dry and thin and long and patchy, the kind of dry that looks dry no matter what the season, the kind of grass that isn't lawn, just weed, and the kind of weed that isn't looked after. It stops at the edge of the stones, which angle up-wards, elevating the tracks above everything else by three or four feet. Some stones have oil on them, some have grease, some have bird shit. Now some have blood on them too.

Detective Inspector Wilson Q. Hutton makes his way down the bank towards us, putting his arms out to his sides for balance. There are a few things that changed while I was slumbering away in a coma, but for the most part the world carried on the path that it was on, as worlds tend to do. But not everything was the same. Six months ago Hutton was close to a hundred and fifty pounds overweight, and he looked one cheeseburger away from his heart putting it and its neighboring organs out of their misery. He was given the ultimatum—lose weight, or lose your job. By the time I saw him again a month ago, he'd lost just over a hundred pounds, and he's still heading in the right direction. He smiles at us. He never used to smile. It suits him. And seeing him out here means there's more to this case than we first thought.

"There are two likely scenarios," he says. "The first is Dwight Smith sat down on the train tracks and let the train scatter him into the breeze."

I look around and, sure enough, there are pieces of what I'm guessing is Dwight Smith, each of them with a small red flag pinned into the ground marking the spot. A quick count shows there are nine. "And the second?" I ask.

"The second is somebody put him there. Our victim raped a woman five years ago, and he was released from prison two weeks ago. It looks like suicide, sure, but the time line is a problem."

"Because if Dwight Smith was going to kill himself, he would have done it when he entered the prison system, not when he came out," I say.

"Exactly." He starts playing with the waistband of his pants. They're a little loose. Maybe he lost weight on the drive over.

"And we're sure it's Smith?" Kent asks.

"The pay slip in his pocket suggests it's him, but we didn't find a wallet or any ID. The car," he says, nodding towards the abandoned car parked twenty yards away, "belongs to Ben Smith, which is Dwight Smith's younger brother."

"So it could be Ben Smith?" I ask.

Hutton shakes his head. "When Smith got released two weeks ago, he was given employment at a gas station," he says, "and the body we have here is wearing that uniform."

"So it could be anybody from the gas station."

"Could be," Hutton says, "if they had Smith's pay slip in their pocket and had borrowed or stolen his car. Anyway, we finger-printed the hand we could find and an officer is heading back into town as we speak. We'll know soon."

"The hand you could find?" I ask.

"We've got everything but his right hand," Hutton says, nod-ding out towards the red markers. "Either it's there, or some stray dog has run off with it."

"You've called the brother?" I ask.

"No. I'll leave that to you," he says, "but not until we've made a positive ID. Once we confirm it's Smith, we need to interview his family, his old cellmates, we need to chat to anybody who knew him. Killing yourself in jail makes sense, killing yourself out of jail is an anomaly. For the last two weeks Smith has been pumping gas for minimum wage. He's been keeping a low profile. Apparently the train driver didn't even see the body. Didn't even know he'd hit anything. It was a guy moving cows from there," he says, point-ing to a field on the other side of the tracks that we can't quite see because of the elevation, "to here," he says, pointing to what I imagine is the same kind of field, only on this side of the tracks, "that found it. Or at least he found the biggest part of it. Last train of the night was one thirty in the morning, a freight train heading into Christchurch. Medical examiner is on the way, and we've got a forensic team heading to check the front of the last few trains for blood so we can figure out which one hit him."

Another car pulls up. It's a guy in a suit and a bright green safety vest who must work for the railway. He gets out of the car and he looks flustered and stressed and he takes three seconds to scan the scene and to figure out who looks like they can make a decision. He heads towards us. He doesn't get far, as one of the police officers intercepts him. There's a brief discussion, and a moment later the man is being escorted towards us.

I climb the stones up to the tracks, my old man knees protesting along the way. The guy in the vest reaches Hutton and Kent, and soon they're arguing about trains and times and schedules, and of course the train line must have been shut down once the body was discovered. The guy in the vest wants to speed things along, he says the words *time is money* repeatedly, occasionally slapping the back of one hand into the palm of the other for added emphasis. "This is bullshit," Vest guy says. "You got some prick who jumps in front of a train and now I'm the one whose day is shot to hell? Tell me how that makes sense."

So Hutton tries to tell him how that makes sense, and I'm just pleased not to be part of the argument. Trains running late is just a part of life, just as people jumping out in front of them is a part of life—that's what I'd be saying. We used to call that spontaneous suicide. Catch the ten-oh-four from Why-the-Hell-Not to Oblivion. That could be why Dwight Smith drove out here. He came for one reason and stayed for another. Maybe Smith was a good-behavior and no-boundaries kind of guy, and Mr. Spontaneity too.

There are officers walking up and down the tracks looking for the missing hand. The point of impact is fairly obvious by the blood splatter. The train hit Smith at seventy or eighty miles per hour, and the result is that Smith's body was turned into a salvo of flesh projectiles, blood shooting in every direction, like hitting a water balloon with a baseball bat. On the tracks the blood looks like rust and on the thick wooden sleepers it looks like oil, and on the stones it looks like blood. The bits of Smith are all close by, the bulk of it his torso, which has both legs removed from above the knee and one arm removed too. It's covered in dirt and grease and a few broken dandelions have stuck to it, and most of it is wrapped in the uniform of the gas station he worked for. I feel sick looking at it.

I walk fifty yards along the tracks. I walk on the sleepers. The view ahead isn't much different from the view behind me. Weeds. Tracks. A road and farms and some tired-looking farmhouses in the distance. Only real difference is the direction of the shadows and the amount of body parts. I walk another fifty yards. No blood out here. I turn around and head back. Every twenty or thirty seconds I look over my shoulder in case a train is barreling towards me even though I'd feel it and hear it and people would start shouting warnings. I look anyway, the same way kids would throw glances behind them running through a graveyard at night. I think about Dwight Smith lying on the sleepers and the rails vibrating like they're being powered by a nuclear reactor. Instead of him going towards the light the light came towards him. Up ahead Kent and Hutton are taking a break from their conversation with the railway guy, and both Hutton and the railway guy are making phone calls while Kent stands there waiting, her hands stuffed in her pockets. I'm not sure why, but I give her a brief wave, she smiles, and gives a brief, small wave back. I smile back. What's it been? Two minutes since we last saw each other?

I angle off the tracks and take my old man knees down to the car Dwight was borrowing. It's a beat-up station wagon that, according to the registration sticker on the windshield, is fifteen years old. It looks like it was driven off the lot under the condition it must never be washed. There are scratches and dents all over the body-work, nicks in the paint from gravel, some chips in the windshield. The tires are balding and one has almost no tread on it at all. Even the fluffy dice hanging from the mirror are sun faded, some of the dots having disappeared.

I put on a pair of latex gloves. The driver's door is closed, but hasn't latched shut, so the interior light has remained on all night I imagine, and the battery will be dead, but I don't test my theory. The keys are in the ignition. Soon they will be dusted for prints. The whole car will be. The keys consist of a car key, a house key, and what I'm guessing is a padlock key. Later this morning the car will be towed into a forensics lab and people smarter than me will be able to figure out if Dwight Smith drove it last. In the glove compartment there's a map, a small torch, a pocketknife, some CD covers, and some loose CDs. Some country and western, some heavy metal, some rock from the seventies; some I like, some I hate, some I've never heard of. I check under the seats, behind the seats, all through the car. No blood. Doesn't look like it's been vacuumed clean. Just dirt and dust and bits of dried leaves.

On the passenger seat is a bottle of water. The label on it says *Water Bro*. It's part of a new range of products aimed at men. It started a few months ago with some aggressive advertising and some well-placed products in supermarkets. The Bro Range—or *Brange*. You can buy Chips Bro, Cola Bro, Salad Bro, Bread Bro—there are dozens of products available. I've been using the Shaving Foam Bro over the last month, but can't bring myself to try out the Clean Teeth Bro toothpaste. The brand has been so successful that six weeks ago they opened two fast-food restaurants in the city. The water bottle is half-full. I take off the lid and sniff the contents. A guy getting ready to jump in front of a train would be drinking something harder than water, I'd have thought, but not in this case. Could be Mr. Spontaneity didn't stop off for some gin on his way out here.

I close up the car. Hutton has gotten off the phone and is chatting to Kent. I head over to them. The railway guy is still in the process of his call, his free arm making big gestures in the air as if he's painting on an invisible canvas.

"What have I missed?" I ask.

"We've just made a positive ID on Smith," Hutton says. "Fingerprints were confirmed." He's nodding while he tells me, and Kent is nodding too, and it must be nodding Saturday because I find myself joining in.

"So what do you want us to do next?" I ask.

"Talk to his boss. Then talk to his brother and then go to his house and then speak to his probation officer. Get an idea of what Smith was up to, what his state of mind was. We don't want people thinking we didn't try to cover all the possibilities because we didn't like the guy. If we don't, then tomorrow's headline will be

accusing us of dismissing any crimes that involve unpleasant people being hurt. We may not like him, but we have to treat him the
same way we'd treat any other person who was killed."

"You have his address?"

"He lives in a boarding house in town—you know the one—it's
run by a guy who calls himself the Preacher."

I nod. I remember the house and the Preacher. Earlier this year
a private case I was working on led me there. It was the following
day that I had the glass jar crashed into the side of my head.

"Listen, Detectives," he says, lowering his voice. "It's important
we dot all the i's on this one. I'm sure Dwight Smith found some
reason to lay on the tracks to end his life, but . . . you remember
that case Schroder caught a few years back?" he asks, looking at
me. "The one with the train?"

"I remember it," I tell him, and suspect that's not just why we're
dotting our i's, but also crossing our t's too.

"What case was that?" Kent asks.

I let Hutton tell the story. A guy had been run over by accident.
The guy who did the running over had been drunk, and he figured
the way to hide what he had done would be to throw his victim
under a train, hoping it would be viewed as a suicide. It almost
worked.

"The impact of the train hid all the existing cuts and bruises.
The train couldn't hide the fact the killer had been seen doing it,"
he says, "but this . . . you know what I said before about the time
line?"

We both nod.

"Well, it's odd to kill yourself when you're out of jail, but why
kill yourself at the end of the working day? Why not at the beginning?"

"Maybe the news he got that made him want to kill himself
didn't arrive until late," Kent says.

Hutton nods. "Could be."

Just then one of the officers whistles out. We all turn in his direction. He's a hundred yards up the track and twenty yards out to

the side of it, and about twenty yards from all the other pieces. He's waving an arm. His own arm.

"That'll be the final piece," Hutton says. Then he puts his hand to his face, rests his chin on his palm, and uses his forefinger to start tapping his teeth. He does this for a few seconds. "Look," he says, and that word alone reminds me of Schroder, the way he used to open some of his conversations with me, a *Look, Tate, we don't want your help on this one,* and thinking of Schroder makes me realize I miss working with him. Hell, I even miss working at cross-purposes with him. "Truth be told," he says, but then he doesn't say, so the truth doesn't get told. He taps his teeth a few more times. "How do I say this," he says.

"You don't need to," Kent says.

And he doesn't need to. If it was a suicide, then fine—we can all sigh in relief that a really bad guy decided to hurt himself rather than somebody else. Case closed. Let's get back to the weekend we all had planned. But if it wasn't a suicide then we're still all feeling relief, because Dwight Smith seems like the kind of guy happy to take those bad things from his past and use them to build an even worse future. So the only difference between a suicide and a murder in Smith's case is who we have to thank.

That's what Hutton is thinking.

That's what Kent is thinking.

That's what I'm thinking.

Of course none of us say it.

"Hopefully you won't have to interview Kelly Summers. Hopefully she has nothing to do with it, but if this is more than a suicide then that will make her a suspect." He stares hard at me as he talks. "You can't go easy on her."

"Because of the i's and t's," I say.

"Exactly. I know you're thinking if Kelly Summers was a part of this, then society should let it slide. And truthfully, I'd agree. I think society owes her one. But it doesn't matter what we think— we have to follow this through. We're not judges. Are we on the same page here?" he asks.

"We are," I tell him.

"Good," he says, and nods. "We'll know more once the medical examiner has looked at him. Hopefully she's not going to give us some weird shit about him being dead already when the train hit, or find a bullet wound, but my gut instinct tells me it's not going to be that easy," he says, and I wonder if his gut instinct is smaller now that he's lost all that weight. "Go talk to those people. Hopefully they'll all tell us Smith kept saying how much he hated life. We get all that squared away without any kinks and I'll chalk this up as case closed," he says, but he doesn't believe it because his gut is telling him differently, and mine is telling me differently too. Things are never that easy. Not even a simple suicide.

CHAPTER FOUR

The man who saved Kelly Summers from Dwight Smith knows two things. The first is that the name he's come up with for himself is a good one. It's the type of name the media would give him if they knew the way his mind worked. It's the Five Minute Man. It has a ring to it. Over the last few years the city has had the Christchurch Carver, the Burial Killer, the Gran Reaper, even Melissa X. Every one of them a psychopath, a killer. The Five Minute Man is a superhero. People love superheroes. He used to love superheroes back when he knew how.

The second thing he knows is that later today the medical examiner will make the determination Dwight Smith was dead before being put on those train tracks. And that's a problem. He's bought them some time. Twenty-four, perhaps forty-eight hours, if the ME is backed up, in which to come up with a way to keep the police from suspecting Kelly Summers. And that's assuming Summers behaves the way he told her to behave when they interview her today—which he thinks they will. She just has to stick with the script—and he believes she will. After all, she's the one who killed Smith. She's the one who has the most to lose. She'll be fine—he knows it, because last night she experienced something she's dreamed about for five years: revenge.

Last night sparked something inside him that was lost. He's spent the last few months sitting in his lounge watching the sun climb one wall and descend the other. He's been tracking the progression of a spider who's building a life in one of the corners. Days pass where all he does is eat and sleep. Some days his wife drops by, but most days she doesn't, and on the days she does she doesn't bring the kids because he isn't their dad anymore, not really. The same way he isn't her husband or even himself. He knows there's more to life—only he doesn't care. His wife and children are part of the old life, and in that life hadn't he been happy? Working long hours, mowing lawns, taking his daughter to ballet practice, changing his son's diapers, paying the mortgage and taking out the trash—that was life. Looking back, he doesn't know if that made him happy, all he knows is that his new life makes it all feel irrelevant. He doesn't miss his family. He knows he should. He should miss them a lot. The truth is he doesn't care. That's the thing—the Old Him would have rebelled against the person he has become, would have fought and screamed to be heard, he would have gone to every doctor in the country to put things right, and if they couldn't then he would have searched the world. But the Old Him has gone, replaced by the New Him, and the New Him is all about acceptance. This is what he is. This is life. And that's fine. The New Him wasn't going to search for the Old Him. He skipped the first four stages of grief.

The New Him would slowly die in front of a TV he never turned on, on a couch he didn't like or dislike, in a house he didn't like or dislike, watching a spider that he had named Warren munching on the occasional unlucky fly. He isn't bored. When he shopped, he bought instant meals that could be heated in a microwave. The Old Him would have picked out foods he enjoyed, foods based on flavors and textures and scents and the fun of cooking and the memories those tastes and smells evoked. The New Him can't taste the difference. Chicken, ice cream, rice, tomatoes—there is only one flavor now. The doctor said there wasn't anything they could do about that. But he didn't care. Food was fuel. He ate it to live. And to be honest, he didn't care if he lived. Or died. But when he didn't eat he got hungry, and the hunger hurt, and that's why he ate. It's why he shopped. Warren would agree. Warren knew about hunger—sure he did.

Then came the conversation.

But a week before the conversation there was the referendum—or, more accurately, the result of such a referendum. The citizens of New Zealand were asked a month ago whether to keep the prime

minister they had, or vote on a new one. They were given that opportunity every three years. Personally, he never thought there was
much difference between politicians. Could they be trusted? No.
Did people know that? Yes. So who was the fool when a politician
let you down? He would vote Labour, he would vote National, he
would choose on the day. Who was the better of two evils? That
was the box he would tick. This time there was a second question
being asked, a question many were demanding to be asked. Should
the death penalty be brought back? The current prime minister
won by a landslide. But the death penalty was closer. Half of the
country voted yes. Half voted no. It was split down the middle.
A dead heat. So the votes needed to be counted. And recounted.
And recounted again. Which took two weeks. The votes weren't
split down the middle at all. They were separated by one hundred
and seventy-seven votes. They say every single vote counts. In this
case it was one hundred and seventy-six votes away from being
true.

The death penalty was coming back.

He didn't care.

It was what it was. It didn't affect him. It wasn't a big deal.

It was. Just. Life.

Then the conversation. It was three days ago. It wasn't just his
wife that came by. There were others. People he'd worked with.
People he knew. They felt bad about what had happened to him.
Of course they did. He didn't. It was. Just. Life. He was okay with it.
Didn't like it. Didn't hate it. He'd accepted it. People from his past
were showing up. They showed up without being invited. Sometimes with food. Sometimes with beer. He just sat and listened and
didn't much feel like contributing to the conversation—which, in
hindsight, meant he felt something, didn't it?

The conversation that changed everything was seemingly in-
consequential. There was the weather. It could rain or snow or the
sun could scorch the earth, and what would change? He'd sit in his
room and okay, maybe he'd put on a heater or open a window, but
life would go on. Other people. Names from his past were thrown

at him, this guy was doing that, that guy was doing this. World events. Oil was going up in price, somewhere was getting invaded, human rights were in jeopardy as they always were in some far corner, people being hacked to pieces a way of life the way ice creams on beaches in summer was a way of life in New Zealand. The referendum. The death penalty was on its way back and did he think it would change the level of violence in the country?

The Christchurch Carver—given name Joe Middleton—was a sick, twisted son of a bitch who for years had worked as a janitor at the police department during the day, but during the night was out there breaking into the houses of women who were alone, tying them up, and turning them into homicide statistics. The police arrested him late in the game, and a year later, on the day his trial was set to begin—the trial that would possibly send him to death row—Joe escaped. Even now he's roaming about freely, but nobody knows where.

And that did it. At the mention of the Carver he felt something stir inside him. It was like an old car that hadn't run in years was being started. Only the fuel was bad, the engine was half-seized, there was enough juice for the engine to try and turn over, but that was all, a hint of life and then nothing. So the New Him did care about something. It cared about the Carver, because back in the old life he had been on the task force that had failed for so long to catch him. He still felt the anger of the man's escape, but what could he do about it? Track the Carver down? No—because nobody has been able to. He cared . . . but then he didn't care. The anger just drained away. The Old Him—the Old Him would have fired up, would have topped the rev counter, would have exploded.

More of the conversation. The prime minister. Did he like the guy? He was fine. Fishing. They should go fishing sometime, like they used to. Did he remember that time the fishhook went through his ankle? The rugby season was over and had he seen any of the cricket? He should get out more, should try to get away, should try to do this and try to do that—and he nodded some of the time and some of the time he didn't, he just stared ahead, waiting to be alone. Travel. Gardening. New restaurants opening and old restaurants closing. A new mall was being built. Extensions to the prisons were almost complete. Dwight Smith was released two weeks ago.

Another jump start. Something inside sparked.

Did he remember Dwight Smith? Yes, he did, and wasn't it early for Dwight Smith to be released? Why yes, it was, six years too early. Why was that, he'd asked? Why was anything, he'd been told.

So something had sparked and it had caught. And why? Looking back, he thinks because Dwight Smith was somebody he could do something about. The Christchurch Carver—nobody knew where the hell he was, what he was doing, whether he was dead or alive or even still in the city. But Dwight Smith? Well now, Dwight was an entirely different kettle of spiders.

The conversation ended and he was alone again and on the couch he didn't like or dislike, and the motor was running. There were hiccups and moments where it almost stalled, but it was running.

Dwight Smith was free.

Dwight Smith was a dog who had tasted blood.

The Old Him had been about men like Dwight Smith. The Old Him had been about getting up every morning at seven a.m. and getting to work by eight, about fighting a never-ending fight, about dedicating himself to the cause. It had been about sitting at his desk with a coffee and catching up on paperwork, about taking orders, about giving orders, about often being somewhere in the middle of the chain of command. It had been about knocking on doors, interviewing shop owners and bank tellers and people whose homes had been broken into. It had been about interviewing family members and victims and suspects. It had been about seeing the good in people and the bad in people, but mostly about the bad. He would spend his days putting bad people away, and they would do their time and they would come back out and he would spend more days putting them away again. It was simply how the world worked. From eight o'clock to five o'clock, five days a week—that was his life, often with overtime. A never-ending cycle. Of course old age and karma caught up to some of those bad people so he never had to see them again, and occasionally they either gave up the life of crime or got so good at it they dropped off the radar, but there were always more being produced in the white-trash factories of the city, a production line of meth manufacturers and sociopaths and rapists and shoplifters and arsonists and people who just didn't give a shit. And of course the Old Him stopped being the Old Him because of people like Dwight Smith and the Christchurch Carver, and why should—

Why should.

There they were Two small words. *Why should,* and a future opened in front of him, just like that, a doorway to a world of possibilities. That was the moment he realized he was a man searching for something. That's what man did. If man didn't search, the world would not evolve. The world would not be explored. People would still be living in caves and killing lizards with rocks.

Why should a guy like Dwight Smith get a second chance at hurting people?

Why should Dwight Smith get to be happy? Should get to carry on? Should get to be free?

He didn't care. And at the same time he did care.

He didn't understand it.

What he did understand was Dwight Smith wasn't going to spend his life indoors staring at a goddamn spider in the corner of the room. Dwight Smith was a ticking time bomb who was going to cause a lot of pain.

Why should.

He was evolving. Why should Dwight Smith get to live a better life than him? Or that of the woman he had attacked?

Why should?

The answer was simple—he shouldn't.

CHAPTER FIVE

Our trip out to the railway line is reversed. Everything we saw on our way out we see on our way back, only from the other side of the road and heading the other way. There are some differences. The flow of traffic has increased a little, but not a lot. The sun has climbed a little, but not a lot. The temperature has raised another degree. There are more guys out in the fields raising sheep and cattle and turning seeds into vegetables. I couldn't do it. I figure I could work on a farm for five days at the most before catching the same train Smith caught.

Neither of us talk. We're both thinking our own things. Kent is motionless, staring straight ahead, her hands barely doing any work as we cruise at seventy miles an hour in a straight line.

Are we on the same page here?

Hutton's words keep coming back to me. Yes, I'm a cop again, yes I'm back on the force, yes I'm one of the team. But for the last three years, after killing the man who took my daughter away from me, I've been off the team. In that time I've developed some habits as a private investigator that don't mesh well with being on the same page. That's what Hutton is questioning. He's asking if my loyalty is to the job, or to doing the right thing. Or at least what I think the right thing is.

The service station Dwight Smith worked at is on the corner of a busy intersection with two separate entrances and two separate exits, one of each on a separate road, the intersection on this side of town, right where the farms end and the houses begin. There are a dozen pumps and half a dozen staff and a building in the middle of the forecourt that's like a small air-traffic tower overlooking it all, the building and signage painted the same yellows and blues

Dwight Smith was wearing, only the yellows and blues here aren't splashed with red and streaked with black. We park next to the building and lock the car because recently two police cars have been stolen, which caused a memo to go around at work reminding us to use some of that common sense we were all raised with.

The forecourt feels a few degrees hotter than the rest of the city. There are bags of charcoal for barbecues stacked up against one of the walls of the traffic tower, twenty-four packs of soft drink stacked next to them, and next to those are blackboards with special prices written on them, offering drink and chocolate bars for what I imagine is twice the price of a supermarket. We go inside. The guy behind the counter is between customers and is wiping up a coffee cup that's been knocked over. His hands are full of paper towels. We ask him for the manager. He picks up the phone and a minute later the manager comes out and we all shake hands. His name badge tells the world his name is Andrew Andrews, which suggests his parents were lazy. Andrew Andrews is clean-shaven but has missed a patch beneath his chin, and has busy eyebrows that would look more appropriate on a Muppet.

"Let me guess," he says. "You're here about Dwight Smith. That's why he's not at work, right? He's in custody for something, right?"

"You don't seem surprised," I tell him.

"Hey," he says, sounding cheerful, "every year we take on a couple of parolees, and every year they stop showing up for work, and every year somebody like you will come here and tell me why. But somebody has to hire these guys, right?" he says, still sounding cheerful, like hiring these guys can save the world. "What else you gonna do, just throw them into the streets and hope for the best?"

"Does Smith have a locker here?" I ask.

"Yeah. It's this way."

He leads us through a door and into a corridor with more of the company colors. On the walls are large photographs of the service station from over the years, starting with black-and-white images from fifty years ago, old cars and men in old-fashioned overalls, everybody smoking around the service bay, a guy sitting on a wooden crate drinking soda while squinting at the sun, a small boy playing beneath a jacked-up car. People weren't as much into health and safety back then, but the weather sure as hell was better. The air-traffic control building in the center of the forecourt only appears in the more recent pictures. I remember coming here with my dad, occasionally sipping a cola while somebody would wash the windshield and pump the gas, which was what, a quarter of the price back then?

"Dwight Smith worked here for two weeks," I tell him. "You must have gotten some impression of the man. What can you tell us about him?"

Andrew Andrews, the man who hires these men out of the goodness of his heart—and no doubt some tax breaks that come along with it—shrugs. "I don't know. He came in to work on time. He pumped gas. He kept himself to himself. Didn't make any waves. Didn't steal anything that I know of. What is it you're trying to get at? If you just tell me I might be able to help you a little more."

"He make any friends?" Kent asks.

Another shrug. "I don't think so. He seemed to fit in okay. He chatted to people if they chatted to him, but he hasn't been here long enough to build any friendships. Like I said, he kept himself to himself. So you going to tell me what he did?"

"He's dead," Kent says.

Andrew slowly nods. "So guess there's no need to fire him," he says, and he's still using the cheery voice, and I can't tell if he's being serious or if it's a bad joke.

We reach the lockers. There are a dozen of them, all with a range of padlocks, including Dwight Smith's, who has locker number ten. Smith's padlock is smaller than most of the others, as if he has less to hide.

"You were going to fire him for not showing up?" I ask.

"Listen," he says, turning his back to the lockers so he can face us. "We try to help these guys out, okay? But if they're not going to show up, what would you have me do? There are a hundred other guys coming out of jail who'd love to have his job."

"Do you know what he did?" Kent asks.

"What? You mean that got him arrested?"

She nods.

He shakes his head. "No. I mean, they send us people who don't have thieving on their rap sheet, but other than that we can't know. They don't tell us, and if they did, then we couldn't work with them. You know what I'm saying? If we all learned our new workmate was into hurting kids . . . Well, people don't get second chances in life if they're sharing their baggage with you."

"You think being in jail for rape or murder is baggage?" Kent asks.

Andrews shakes his head. "You know what I mean," he says, "and that's not it. It's just the way it has to be. What's the alternative? Let these guys live on the street? Then what? At least if they're working, they're not out there doing other stuff. So what happened? Somebody kill him? Or he kill himself?"

"Why? Do you think he'd kill himself?" Kent asks.

"I'm not thinking anything," Andrews says. "Just being curious. So you going to tell me?"

"We're not at liberty to say," I tell him. "You got a key for this?" I ask, pointing at the padlock.

"Yeah. All employees have to leave spares with us. Wait here a minute."

He leaves us alone. The lockers are part of a room that is attached to a couple of showers and bathrooms, none of which are currently in use. There's a bench running the length of the room in front of the lockers. It reminds me of the gym back when I was at school. There's a couple of car magazines sitting on the bench and somebody has left out a bag of sandwiches. Andrews makes it back. He hands us a key with a tag on it that says *Dwight Smith, #10*.

"Did he say or do anything out of character yesterday?" I ask. "Or did anybody come to see him?"

"Yesterday was my day off," Andrews says, "but I can find out for you."

"Okay, you do that," I say.

Andrews seems like he wants to stay to see what we find in the locker, but manages to last only a few seconds of me and Kent staring at him until he wanders off. We open the locker. There's a jacket hanging in there, it's brown and made from leather and looks beaten up and old—could be he bought it secondhand, could be it belongs to his brother, could be it's his from before he went to jail. Was last night warm? Not real warm. I wouldn't have gone out without a jacket. There's a cell phone that looks out of date. It's still on, the battery sitting at fifteen percent. There's no passcode required to switch it on. I check his call logs, his text messages, his address book. There's work, his brother, his parents, the Preacher from the halfway house.

Smith's wallet is here. There's a driver's license and two twenty-dollar notes and a photograph of a naked woman that, when I pull it out, shows it was torn from a magazine. There are no bank cards. There are no receipts. There's nothing else in the locker. I go through the jacket pockets. Empty.

"It's like he just decided to up and leave," Kent says. "Except for his keys."

"His keys he kept on him," I tell her. "This spare locker key looks identical to the one hanging out of the ignition of his car. He needed them to gain access to this stuff."

"Then why didn't he use it last night to gain access?" Kent asks. "Where would he go without needing his jacket, his wallet, or his phone?"

"You don't need any of that stuff if you're catching the front end of a train," I tell her, which is one of two logical explanations. The other one being he saw something that made him leave in a hurry. We put everything into evidence bags. We close up the locker and put the lock back into place.

My cell phone rings. It's Hutton. "How are you getting on there?" he asks.

I tell him about the cell phone, the jacket, and the wallet.

"So either something spooked him," Hutton says, "or the urge to kill himself came on so strongly he had to leave."

"There's a third possibility," I tell him because, after all, we're all on the same page here. "He might have seen somebody who fit whatever fantasy he was conjuring up next."

"The service station will have surveillance. See if they'll let you take a look at it, and if not we can get a warrant if things lead in that direction. The medical examiner just got here a few minutes ago. We're getting the body bagged up and she's hoping she'll have something for us by the end of the day. The car is getting towed by forensics right now as well, and we'll know more on that within an hour or two."

We hang up. Andrew Andrews is waiting for us just outside the locker room.

"Get what you need?" he asks.

"Almost," I tell him.

"Can I give the locker to somebody else?"

"Not yet," Kent tells him. "Not until we close the investigation."

"So what else do you want from me?"

"Surveillance footage from last night," I tell him. "And we still want to talk to somebody who worked yesterday with Smith."

"Not a problem on the second part," he says. "You can use my office."

"And the first part?"

He thinks about that for a few seconds. I can see the decision process taking place. Technically we need a warrant, and I can see him thinking that, and I hope he's also thinking that the world is full of technicalities that, if taken away, would make it an easier place to live. So he nods and tells us the video surveillance won't be a problem either.

He leads us through to his office. It smells of chicken and bacon and makes my stomach rumble. There are photographs of cars on the walls, some more nostalgia photos like those in the corridor. There's a seat behind his desk and two in front, and we rearrange them before he can come back with who turns out to be a guy by the name of Kevin McKay.

McKay is in his midthirties and, like always, I'm somewhat jealous of anybody younger than me. He looks tired and annoyed to be
here and I know the feeling. He sits down in the empty chair. We
introduce ourselves. We don't shake hands. I take out a notebook
and a pen.

"How long have you worked here?" I ask him.

"Three years."

"How often did you work with Smith?" I ask.

"Which Smith? There's always a Smith."

"Dwight Smith," I tell him.

"A bit," he says. "You know, not all of the time, but some of the
time. He's only been here two weeks, but our days overlapped. Four
days a week, for four hours a day. He started at four and finished at
midnight. I start at eight at night and finish at four in the morning."

"It's one thirty now," I tell him.

He glances at his watch. "It's also Saturday. Things are different
on the weekend. Dwight was supposed to start at seven this morning, but didn't show, you know? But coming off a Friday night and
getting here early Saturday is the toughest shift. That's why I'm
here, to cover it since Smith didn't show. It's Andrew's fault—but
don't tell him I said that. He just keeps hiring people nobody can
rely on. So this morning I got called in to cover Dwight's shift.
Which makes me tired and grumpy, so I'm sorry if it seems like I'm
being unhelpful here, but if there's a point you're trying to get to,
now would be a good time to make it."

"Did he leave early last night?" I ask.

"That's what you want to know?" he asks.

"That's what I want to know."

He shrugs. "I don't know. Maybe."

"Can you think about it a little bit more?" I ask him. "It's important."

He gives it some thought and comes back with a fresh answer.
"Yeah, he did leave early. It was annoying. Didn't even tell anybody. Just up and left."

"When?" I ask.

Another shrug. "I don't know exactly."

"How about not exactly?" Kent asks. "How about taking a guess?"

"I mean, he was there, then suddenly he wasn't there. I didn't notice until maybe around eleven, but I'm not sure when he actually left. Could have been nine or ten. I don't know."

I jot it down in the notebook. "Did you see him talking to anybody?"

"Yeah. A thousand people. It was a busy day."

"Anybody other than a customer?" I asked.

He shakes his head. "I don't know. Maybe."

"He seem any different yesterday?" Kent asks.

Another sigh, and this time he glances at his watch. "Different? How?"

"Different," I say. "Was he happier than normal? Was he angry? Was he bitching about something? Was he depressed?"

"Dwight never bitched about anything. He just did his job. Normal for him was to keep his mouth shut and pump gas and never get in the way, and in that respect I guess yesterday didn't seem any different, except for him disappearing early."

We spend another five minutes talking to McKay and don't learn anything new. When he's gone Andrews comes back in and fills the space McKay left behind. He drags the now empty seat over to his desk, leans across it, and angles the computer monitor so we can all see it. He plays around with the mouse and the view on the monitor changes from one of a spreadsheet to one of multiple camera angles and what looks like live footage from the service-station forecourt. There are cameras placed inside the shop and over the counters and over the tills and one in the doorway to the locker room, the quality as high as I've ever seen. Hiring guys coming out of prison means a place like this is probably being covered from every angle, and the way the economy is these days, people often fill up with gas knowing they can't afford to pay.

"Give me a time," Andrews says.

"Last night," I tell him. "McKay said Dwight Smith left early.

So I guess let's go back to eight o'clock and see if we can see him."

Andrews goes back to eight o'clock. We glance across the different camera angles, of which there are nine, and find him on the forecourt next to a car. He's pumping gas. After a minute he takes the nozzle out of the gas tank and hangs it up, disappears from that camera, and enters the range of another. Andrews skips forward half an hour. Then another hour. McKay is there. And the other staff. Customers coming and going. He keeps skipping forward and there's nothing here, it's just your typical rapist out on parole doing his job and keeping his head down.

Then that changes.

Because at ten o'clock Dwight Smith takes the nozzle out of a car to hang it up, but then comes to a complete stop during midstep, his mouth opening and his eyes widening. He is staring at a woman who is four pumps away, swiping her credit card to pay for gas. She plays with the buttons, then turns towards her car and puts the nozzle into the gas tank. She doesn't see Dwight Smith.

Smith's customer gets into his car and drives off. Smith disappears from that camera and into another. A moment later he is climbing in his car. At the same time, the woman hangs up the nozzle, replaces the gas cap, and climbs into her car.

She pulls away from the service station.

With Dwight Smith following her.

CHAPTER SIX

Andrew Andrews burns a copy of the surveillance footage to DVD, covering the angle of the woman filling her car with gas and leaving, and Dwight Smith freezing in time when he spots her, moving to his car, and pulling into the street behind her. Andrews promises to let us know if he thinks of anything else. As soon as we're outside Kent turns towards me. "Did you recognize her?" she asks.

Are we on the same page?

I slowly nod. "The lighting wasn't so great, and the angle wasn't so great, but . . . yeah . . . I think so. Plus it's been five years. If it's her, she's cut her hair a lot."

"It was Kelly Summers. She had the scar on her face," Kent says, and at the same time a finger goes up to her own scar and traces the S-shape curve. I've seen her do this a lot over the last few weeks. She puts her fingers up to remind herself things are as bad as she remembers them being.

We get into the car and use the police computer to look up the registration plate of the car the woman was filling. A few seconds later it's confirmed the car belongs to Kelly Summers.

"He followed her," she says.

"I know."

"Do you think he killed her?" she asks.

"I don't know. I . . . I don't know," I say. Five years ago Kelly Summers survived. By all accounts, Kelly Summers is a survivor. Did she survive last night? Did Dwight Smith end up on the tracks because of her?

Checking the car registration also has given us Summers's address. We put the sirens on and Kent drives there quickly, but we don't call for backup. There's no need. The man that followed her is dead. We're either going to find Kelly dead or alive or somewhere in between—and it's the in-between bit which is why we're speeding.

It takes us ten minutes from the service station. Four blocks out Kent cuts the sirens and slows down the pace. We don't know what to expect, but we don't want Kelly to know we're arriving—not if she's a suspect. It's ten thirty when we pull into the street. There are kids out on front lawns and on the street playing on bikes, and no doubt there are children inside in front of TVs with overflowing bowls of cereal and milk they poured themselves. Kent brings the car to a stop and we share a look where I tell her this case is going to take us to a bad place, and she shares one saying *bad* is what life is all about when you're in this line of work.

"I just hope . . . I just hope she's okay," Kent says, then she raises a hand up to the side of her face like she did earlier.

We walk the path to the front door. The house looks like it's been painted within the last few years. Red weatherboards, white trim windowsills, a black concrete tile roof that has moss growing along the edges. It looks cozy, but at the same time uninviting somehow, but I'm not sure if that's just my perception because of why we're here. There's a lot of color in the front garden. A silk tree in the corner, some rhododendrons spilling flowers onto the lawn, a row of roses leading up to the doorstep. It's that time of the year where one week your lawn is short, and the next it's around your ankles. Kelly Summers's lawn is short. There are strips in it that suggest a lawnmower passed this way within the last day or two. Sitting on the neighboring fence is a black cat with a white nose and eyes full of curiosity. I wonder what kind of things it's seen.

I wonder if it saw Dwight Smith last night.

Kent puts her finger on the bell. We hear it ringing inside. There are no broken windows, no blood, no kicked-in door, but that doesn't mean anything. We wait twenty seconds and then we ring it again. A few seconds later we hear movement from inside, then footsteps as a figure moves down the hall.

When Kelly Summers opens the door she looks surprised, she looks sleepy, and most of all she looks very much alive.

CHAPTER SEVEN

The Five Minute Man is listening to the radio. A body has been found hit by a train. No name, no details, not yet. The police will be covering the angles—they'll talk to people who knew Dwight Smith. They'll wonder why he went and sat on those train tracks. Then things will start to look odd. Things won't line up. Time of death, for a start. Dwight Smith's car for another.

He sits in the lounge on the couch he doesn't like or dislike, and he waits, and as he waits he thinks back to three days ago, two days ago, last night. The referendum, the conversation, the spark that started his evolution. Of course he thinks about it—he's thought about little else. The Old Him. The New Him. Both have evolved into the New New Him, and the way the New New Him sees it is like this—now that the death penalty has passed, he is allowed to kill people who deserve to die. Last night was the justice system in action at the beginning of a crime rather than at the end. Last night was putting a Band-Aid on your finger to stop the splinter from going in.

Dwight Smith was living in that god-awful halfway house in town, the one that housed a selection of ex–drug addicts, ex-rapists, and current crazy people. Fuckups from every walk of life. Even the building was a fuckup—a couple of stories of weatherboards covered in mold and flaky paint, a garden so dry it looked more likely to catch fire than the house. The place was run by an ex-junkie and ex-convict who was now clean and converted and who tried selling religion to those who came through his door.

He drove to that place two days ago. He was a man who didn't care but who found himself caring more the closer he got. Dwight Smith didn't deserve a second chance, because the Five Minute man wasn't getting one. It wasn't fair. Killing Dwight Smith was like giving the Old Him a gift, which was ironic because the Old Him would have hated the man he has become.

The house was how he recalled it. Warped weatherboards painted green, rusty guttering painted the same shade of red as the roof, a big wooden porch silvered in the sun. There were people sitting in the front yard drinking beer. A few cars up the driveway. He couldn't wait right outside the house, not with the beer drinkers classing up the neighborhood, so he drove around a little, passed by the same house a few times, then parked a couple of doors down. His persistence paid off. In the middle of the afternoon Dwight Smith climbed into one of those cars and the adventure started.

Smith was working at a service station. He started work at four p.m. and he finished at midnight. When he finished he visited a massage parlor, spent an hour upstairs, then reemerged a happier man. The Five Minute Man followed Smith back home, and he kept thinking *Why should.*

Why should life be okay for Dwight Smith?

Yesterday was looking a repeat of the day before, but then Kelly Summers showed up to get gas. Smith saw her purely by chance. Christchurch is like that—purely by chance happens a lot in small cities.

Smith walked off the forecourt, got into his car, and followed her home. The Five Minute Man, well, he followed them too, and in that time he was very aware of not calling the police, was very aware he could feel the engine inside him running, the hiccups were further apart, the fuel lines were clear, all systems were go— all he had to do was put his foot down. It was ten o'clock. It was dark. It was overcast. There was no natural light anywhere, only what was provided by streetlights and other houses. It was perfect breaking and entering and raping conditions. *A good night for getting what was owing to me*, which is what Smith said five years ago. Smith sat in his car for fifteen minutes doing nothing, maybe thinking, thinking the kind of thoughts a man like Smith would think. Then those thoughts led him out of his car and onto the property. He put his face against one window of Kelly Summers's house, stared inside, then moved on to the next. He made his way around to the back. He was carrying a crowbar.

He didn't come back.

The Five Minute man sat in his car only a few houses away with the car engine running, and the engine inside him running, and he knew what the right thing to do was. He needed to call the police. *Why should* had nothing to do with it anymore. A woman's life was on the line.

Only the police would never get there in time. He didn't have a weapon, but felt surprise would be a good enough one. He got out of his car and moved around to the back of the house. There was a gate. It was six feet high and the same height as the neighboring fence. It was closed and when he reached over to open it, he found it was locked. Smith must have climbed it. So he climbed it too. At the back of the house there was an open window. The wood around the lock was splintered away. Locks were strong, but window frames and door frames often weren't. He didn't know it then, but Summers hadn't heard the lock break because she had been in the shower.

The Five Minute Man went inside with a pretty good idea of what he was going to find, and he found exactly that—it was taking place in the bathroom. Kelly was face down on the floor. Smith was crouching behind her. They were both facing the other way.

Then Dwight sensed him. He twisted around and looked up. "Who the fuck," he said, but that was as far as he got. Those were his final words on this earth, not exactly words to be inscribed on a gravestone, but they were the ones he owned right before Death owned him too. A man is easier to subdue when he's naked with his dick in his hand. Smith was knocked unconscious and then dumped in the bathtub.

The woman had made her way into the corner of the bathroom. She was sitting on the floor and leaning against the wall. She was staring at him, her eyes wet, her hands were shaking, she was trying to cover herself.

"Are you okay?" he asked.

"Thank God," she answered. "Thank God you saved me," she said, and she was crying, and there was snot streaming down her face, and her cheeks were flushed and she was scared and confused and grateful and a whole bunch of other things he didn't know how to feel anymore.

He handed her her robe. She took it quickly and covered herself with it.

"I know you," she said. "I'm sure I know you." She did know him, only he looks different these days. He's lost weight. He's bald now, and there's a big scar on the side of his head, and she couldn't get there, couldn't put a name to the face. "You're a cop," she said.

"No," he said. "Not anymore."

"He was supposed to be in jail," she said, then she started to slowly shake her head. He knew what she was doing. She was doing the addition. She was trying to figure out how many years had gone by and the math was all out of whack. Then she started to look angry. Her face tightened and she clenched her jaw. The arithmetic and shock were giving way to the reality of what almost just happened.

"I'm going to call the police," he told her, and he meant it. He had wanted to kill Dwight Smith, but this would have to do. He couldn't kill this man in front of this woman. Smith would go to jail. In a few years he would be somebody else's problem. The engine was still running, but it had slowed down. Calling the police was the next move.

"Just who are you?" she asked again. "And why are you here?"

"I was following him."

"Why?" she asked.

"Why was anything," he said.

She didn't understand his answer. "You followed him here."

"Yes."

"You saved my life," she told him. "He was five seconds away from raping me."

He said nothing.

"None of it makes sense," she said. "I don't understand, I mean, he's supposed to be in jail, I'm sure of it, and why were you following him? How did you know he was going to come after me?"

"I didn't know."

"Then why were you following him?"

"Why was anything," he said again.

"I don't know what you mean by that."

"It's going to be okay," he said. "You're going to be okay."

She thanked him over and over as she sat in the corner of the bathroom. What had happened was sinking in. Then it came to her—who he was. It didn't make sense to her. Of course it didn't. Then she asked, "How long will he get in jail this time?"

He shrugged. Dwight Smith had broken into her house, he had assaulted her, but he hadn't raped her. The justice system was like a lottery sometimes. "I don't know. Two years. Five years. Ten. I don't know."

"Can I get cleaned up first? I don't . . . don't want to be naked when the police arrive."

"Of course," he said.

She would look at him and she would look at Smith, but mostly she would just look at the spot on the floor where, if things hadn't changed, she would now be pinned beneath a man and his knife. She didn't look like she was about to get up any time soon. She was nodding. She wasn't saying anything and she still kept looking at the floor, but she was nodding.

Then it came. A different question. Not too dissimilar to *Why should,* close enough, almost, to be related. She asked *What if.*

"What if we didn't call them right away?" Silence followed the question, and he let it hang there, allowing her to get her thoughts together. "What if . . . I mean, I mean, what if you gave me five minutes alone with him?" She looked up at him, and there were no more tears, all her tears had dried up and so had the snot, but her cheeks were still flushed. She looked angry. Only there was something else too. Something in her eyes. She was looking into the future. She was looking five minutes into the future and she was seeing what one human being was capable of doing to another, and she was liking it. And what did the New Him see? The New Him saw him evolving into a New New Him. The engine was redlining.

"Would you do that?" she asked.

It was a good question. An excellent question. It got him thinking. It got him thinking that in his twenty years as a cop he'd put away a lot of bad people, and in that time he'd had a lot of good people ask him that exact question. It was always five minutes. They wanted five minutes alone with the man that had hurt them or their family. It was never ten minutes. Or half an hour. Or an hour. Always five. He knew her five minutes probably weren't going to look like self-defense. He knew it could lead to problems.

"Yes," he said, because what did he care? Who was he to say no?

Even so, he knew he didn't want to go to jail. He didn't want her to go to jail either. He weighed that up against Dwight Smith's future—he had been released for good behavior, and he would be released again for the same.

"If you want five minutes, you can have them," he said, and he figured she deserved them. She had earned them.

"And then?" she asked.

"And then what happens happens," he said. "And we deal with it."

"I hate him," she said, looking at Dwight Smith. "I used to think of him as Cowboy Dwight. Even though he's been in jail all these years, he still keeps me awake. Sometimes I dream about what he did to me. Other times I dream about what I want to do to him. Will killing him help me sleep better?"

"It won't make you sleep any worse," he said, and he believed it.

"Then what? When the police come, will they arrest me? They'll know it wasn't self-defense."

"The police won't come," he said. "Dwight Smith will disappear. I promise you they'll never find him."

"Are you sure?"

"Yes," he said, but of course the car . . . the damn car would make a liar of him.

So he gave Kelly Summers her five minutes, in which Smith went from being unconscious to dead, then they got him loaded into the back of Smith's car, and everything was working fine until it wasn't. Ten minutes short of where he wanted to go, Dwight Smith's car broke down.

Will the police go to the service station where Smith worked? Yes, of course they will. Will there be surveillance footage? Yes, there will be. Nothing conclusive. That's what he told Kelly Summers. She just has to play her part when the police come. He told her that her bedroom window had been broken. He told her what to say. However it won't be enough. He has to make the police dismiss her as a suspect.

All those years . . . all those people asking the same question—he is beginning to think that is the answer to all of this. That's what will keep the police away from Kelly Summers. *When you find the guy who did this, just give me five minutes alone with them. Please. Please.*

His answer was always the same, a sorrowful sorry, but he couldn't do that, he understood their pain, but that wasn't the way justice was done.

No? What gives that guy/bastard/asshole/son of a bitch more rights than my dead daughter/son/brother/friend/sister/parent? My daughter/son/brother/friend/sister/parent will be in the ground forever, and the guy who put them there will be free in fifteen years to roam the earth. How does that make sense? Why should it be that way?

Why should anything.

He knows what he has to do.

CHAPTER EIGHT

Kelly Summers is twenty-eight years old, and on Christmas Day she will turn twenty-nine. My dad's birthday is on Christmas Day, and I know from experience that it makes shopping harder, but at least you don't have to do it twice a year. Kelly's hair is different from the photograph in the file, but the same as the surveillance footage. In the past it was blond and shoulder length. These days it's black and only finger length. Today it's sticking up in different directions because we've gotten her out of bed. She's wearing loose-fitting pajamas and the kind of robe my mother would wear. I get the feeling in an hour or two she'll look the same, that Kelly downplays how attractive she really is. She probably thinks her good looks played a part in Dwight Smith's selection process five years ago.

"Has something happened to my parents?" she asks, her words urgent.

We both shake our heads. "No," Kent says, and though Kelly won't know it, I can sense Kent's relief. The way things work out . . . we were both expecting to find Kelly Summers face down in a pool of blood. Is it possible this is one of those cases where everything turns out okay? Kelly is fine and Dwight is dead, and their worlds intersected at the service station last night, but then parted half a block later.

"What's happened?" Kelly asks.

"Can we come in?" I ask.

She nods slowly, her face changing as she figures something out. "You're here because of what happened to me five years ago," she says, the words are flat, but then her voice rises a little. "You're here because that sick son of a bitch is now saying he didn't do it, right? Do people believe him?"

"It's nothing like that," Kent says. "Please, can we come inside?"

Summers looks at Kent, and I see her eyes locking onto the damaged part of Kent's face, and as it does her hand goes up to the damage on her own. "Okay," she says, and she stands aside and lets us in. Then she closes the door behind her and locks it as, I imagine, is her habit.

She leads us into the lounge. It's warm in here. Warm colors, warm furniture. There's a stereo, but there's no TV. There's a large painting of a field of daises, a woman in a yellow dress walking through them with her back facing the artist, her head turned slightly sideways, not quite enough to get a good look at her, but enough to see an expression on her face that immediately makes me think of loss. Both her hands are reaching out and touching the flowers as she passes them.

"It's not my best work," Kelly says.

"You painted this?"

She shrugs. "Used to be a hobby."

"Used to?"

"I gave it up," she says, but the unspoken words are there—she gave it up after her life changed.

"It's beautiful," I tell her.

She gives another shrug, but she seems pleased with the compliment. This is a nice room. A happy room, and the painting, even though it's sad, contributes to that. Only thing that's missing is the smell of coffee. Offering to make coffee is a great way to make friends with a policeman, but Kelly doesn't seem keen to make friends.

I take my jacket off and rest it over the edge of the couch. Then I sit down on the couch next to it. Kent sits down on a chair that's at a ninety-degree angle to it, and Summers sits opposite us, forming three points of an equilateral triangle—give or take a handful of degrees. Kelly will have to look left and right to talk to us both.

"Dwight Smith was released from jail two weeks ago," Kent says.

Summers leans back and onto her side a little so she can pull her feet up to tuck them under her. She's wearing stripy socks that disappear into her pajamas. She becomes absolutely still as she stares at Kent, and after a few seconds of being a statue, she smiles, then shakes her head. Then her smile disappears for a few seconds, then comes back. She's trying to process something that doesn't fit. Her mind is banging a square into a round hole.

"I'm . . . I'm sorry," Summers says, and she's still smiling, "but you've got your facts wrong. He's still got six more years to serve."

"He was released early for good behavior," Kent says. "It was always a possibility."

The smile is still there on Summers's face. But it's the smile of somebody who isn't feeling any warmth, or experiencing any humor. It's how a person who doesn't know how to smile would smile if they'd just seen somebody doing it on TV.

"No," she says. The room goes quiet. We wait her out, knowing she'll fill in the silence. It becomes uncomfortable. Five seconds pass. Then ten. "Somebody must have put you wrong," she finally says. "Dwight Smith isn't capable of good behavior. This," she says, running her finger the length of her face that Smith sliced open with a fillet knife, "didn't come from somebody who knows what good behavior is. Therefore you've made a mistake. Therefore you didn't need to come here. Therefore somebody is wasting your time. Now, if there's nothing else, I have a big day planned." She uncurls her legs from beneath her and puts her stripy-socked feet onto the floor. She puts her hands on her knees and starts to push herself upwards.

"Kelly," I say.

She shakes her head. She settles back into the couch. "No," she says. "Don't you dare say it. He's in jail. They wouldn't let him out. You wouldn't let him out after what he did to me."

"Kelly," I say, "it's going to be okay. I promise."

"Of course it's going to be okay, but only for six more years," she says, "until he's let out of jail. I have six more years of freedom, and that's all. I know that. I know that for an absolute fact because if he had been released two weeks ago then you'd have come to see me two weeks ago to warn me. Anything less than that would have been putting me in danger. Anything less than that would make you an accessory if he'd hurt me."

"It doesn't work that way," I tell her.

"Six years," she repeats, shaking her head, and she looks close to tears. "That's how long I have until my freedom ends. Then we swap places. I turn my house into a jail, and he gets the world."

"People are released all the time without the public knowing about it," I tell her. "I didn't know about it. Detective Kent didn't know about it. We only both found out this morning. I'm so sorry."

"No," she says.

"There's more," Kent says.

"There's more? Well that's great news then, isn't it?" she asks, and now those tears are starting to spill. "Another psychopath out on the street? So now you're here to warn me because there's more. What more? What more could there possibly be? Are you giving him my new address? Do you have him out in the car with you right now so he can finish what he started?"

"Dwight Smith was found dead last night," I tell her, which I imagine is not just great news for her, but spectacular. I imagine there's not a piece of news we could deliver right now that would be any better.

"Was . . ." she starts, then stops, then searches for extra words, but doesn't find them. She stares at her hand as if the missing words are sitting there. She breathes out heavily. "He's dead? So you're saying . . . you're saying I'm free. You're telling me I'm free?"

"Yes," Kent says. "And that's why we're here. We're hoping you can help us figure out exactly what happened."

She nods. She's probably imagining what *exactly what happened* means in this sense, and she's probably hoping *exactly what happened* came with a huge dose of *the worst way possible*. "I hope he was murdered," she says, matter-of-factly. "I mean . . . it would be a great thing if he was. I hope somebody cut his balls off and stuffed them down his throat. Thank you for coming here to tell me this," she says, and the tears are falling freely now, tears of joy. She looks like she's about to jump up and dance, about to hug us tightly. Now she looks like a person who didn't learn to smile from watching it on TV, but a person raised by clowns. "I just wish I could have . . ." she says, then stops talking. "Well, you know."

Yes, we both know.

I can't tell if Summers is for real, or whether she already knew. I've been caught out on this kind of thing before. It feels genuine. The problem is we get by in society by being able to fake genuine when we need to.

"Has he tried to contact you?" I ask.

"No, not at all. I mean, like I said, I didn't even know he was out of jail. And he wouldn't have been allowed to contact me anyway, right? He . . ." she says, then slowly shakes her head. "I'm so stupid. I was going to say he wouldn't be allowed. Surely that was a condition of his release, right?"

"Right," I say, but those conditions don't do people much good when the person they're most afraid of comes back into their lives at three a.m.

"But it doesn't matter," she says, "because there's no way he could know where I live. He would have gone to my old house. Maybe you should check there."

"Tell us about last night," Kent says.

"Last night?" She nods slowly, thoughtfully. "He was killed last night," she says.

"Yes," Kent says.

"So really you're here because I'm a suspect, that's why, isn't it? You're here to see if I wanted him dead." She offers a small laugh. "I wanted him dead. Of course I did. But I didn't kill him. I didn't even know he was out of jail. None of my friends, none of my family, none of us knew. If I'd known he was out of jail I'd have bought a gun. Or I'd have left the country."

"Smith hurt you, so it only stands to reason that some people would think you'd want to hurt him," Kent says, with *some people* meaning us.

Kelly nods. "Should I get myself a lawyer?"

The words *That depends on whether you have something to hide* flash through my mind. No doubt they're in Kent's too. Words we've used plenty of times before. The words are a challenge. The words are saying *Just how good do you think you are?* But we don't use them. Not to a woman like Kelly.

"That's up to you," Kent says.

Kelly seems unsure, and again there's the pause as she thinks about her options. "Okay," she says. "I have nothing to hide. I just don't like the idea of . . . you know, being a victim once, and somehow being a victim again because somebody thinks I did something I didn't do."

"It doesn't work that way," I tell her, but of course sometimes it does.

"Well, last night was last night," she says. "Nothing different. I finished work and came straight home and, well, you know, nights can be tough for me. I don't like going out anywhere."

"Tough?" Kent asks, even though we know what the answer will be.

"Just tough, you know?" Kelly answers. "I got home and for some reason I was in a dark place, and when that happens I take the pills my doctor gave me, and sometimes those pills don't work so well unless there's some wine with them. So that's what I did last night. I had an entire bottle and that, well, that and the pills just knocked me out. I fell asleep on the couch and woke up around four a.m. and dragged myself to bed."

"What time did you finish work?" Kent asks.

"I don't know exactly, but around nine thirty."

"And you came straight home."

"I always do," she answers.

"You didn't go anywhere else?" Kent asks.

Kelly shakes her head. Then she nods. "Actually, yeah, I stopped off for gas."

"We know about the gas," Kent says, "because you went to the same gas station that Dwight Smith worked at."

"No," Kelly says. "I mean . . . what?"

"He's been working there since he got out of jail. We just came from there now. We saw surveillance footage of you using your credit card. Dwight Smith saw you too. He watched you, and then he followed you."

"I think I'm going to be sick," Kelly says, and she puts a hand to her mouth. "He followed me?"

"Yes," Kent says.

"He followed me home?"

"We don't know how far he followed you," Kent says, "but we're hoping you could let us look around to see if he was here."

"But he wasn't here," Kelly says, "at least he wasn't here inside."

"So we can look around?" Kent asks.

We wait for Kelly to think about it. If she says no, she's got something to hide. If she has something to hide, then we'll find it. Saying no will make her look like a suspect. And she should have no reason to say no.

"You want to look around my house?" she asks.

"Yes," I tell her.

"Sure, go ahead," she says. "I just . . . I can't believe he followed me."

I get up off the couch and Kent stays where she is. She will keep the conversation going while I look for any signs Dwight Smith was here. I walk around the lounge, not wanting to immediately disappear from Kelly's view. I listen in on the conversation. It's about work. Kelly tells Kent that most of the week she had to work late. I head to the kitchen. The conversation becomes murmurs to me. The kitchen is tidy, though not as tidy as the lounge, and standing in the kitchen reminds me of my conversation with my wife this morning, of her cooking breakfast for our dead daughter. Kelly Summers is a tidy person, but on the kitchen counter is an empty bottle of red wine, and sitting in the sink is an empty wine glass, empty except for about half an ounce.

The bathroom is clean and tidy and smells like lavender. There's a bright green shower curtain that doesn't fit with the rest of the décor and I imagine seeing a shower curtain like that every day would make me feel seasick. I check the medicine cabinet and find

different containers containing different pills, some names I recognize, some I don't. Probably pills to help Kelly Summers sleep,
others to help keep her numb when the dark thoughts come creeping her way.

From the hallway I take the doorway into the garage. Kelly
drives a dark blue two-door car ten years old. I pop the hatch and
the doors and can't see any signs of blood. I look around the garage,
but there isn't much in the way of tools. A hammer, a couple of
screwdrivers, and that's about it. None have any blood on them.
There's a recycling bin just inside the doorway. I lift the lid. It's
only a quarter full. There are other wine bottles in here, receipts,
scraps of cardboard, and paper.

I head back inside. One of the bedrooms has been turned into a
study, with a computer on a desk and bookshelves lining the wall.
I look through the titles. No crime fiction. No romance novels.
Mostly chick lit. The kind of books my wife reads. Books where
women are safe and children don't go missing.

The master bedroom has a painting that must also be one of
Kelly's as it matches the one in the lounge, different flowers and a
different woman, again she's just turned far enough away to make
her expression readable. Or perhaps to hide the scar. There's a
white duvet cover with light blue edges, most of it blank except
for a couple of flowers and leaves in the corners. The curtains are
drawn, and I pull them aside. The lock on one of the windows has
been torn out. I slide it open and can see pry marks on the opposite
side. Somebody dug a crowbar or a large screwdriver into it and
forced the window open.

Dwight Smith came here last night.

I bring to mind the photographs I saw of Kelly Summers a few
hours ago. I recall some of the facts that were in that file. He raped
her and bit her and cut her.

Are we on the same page?

I close the window and put the curtain back into place. In the
lounge the conversation is still going on. I lean in the doorway and
watch.

"When Smith was in jail, he never wrote to you? Never tried to call?" Kent asks.

"Not that I know of. Like I said, I moved five years ago. I couldn't go back into that place. Nothing ever got forwarded on, but come to think of it, I didn't leave a forwarding address, so maybe he did try writing." She looks up at me. "Can you tell me how he died?"

"Not at this stage," I tell her.

"Did he die badly?"

We don't know, so we can't tell her. We know he most likely did.

We wrap up the interview and Kelly Summers walks us to the door.

"For the first time in five years," she says, "I finally feel . . . not safe, no, *safe* is the wrong word, but I feel something. Relief, I suppose."

"Justice?" I ask her. "Do you feel a sense of justice?"

She smiles at me. "Thank you for coming by, detectives," she says, and the interview is over.

CHAPTER NINE

Kent starts the car and a cat rushes out from the bushes under the neighbor's house, across the road and past the front of us. "What did you think?" she asks.

Are we on the same page?

Yes, we are. Only we're not. Otherwise I'd be telling Kent about the window that was pried open. I'd be telling her about the recently purchased shower curtain with all the heavily creased fold lines. All depends on whether it was purchased before the train dismantled Dwight Smith, or after. Shower curtains are like rugs and drop cloths and tarpaulins—good for wrapping a body on the go.

"Hard to tell," I tell her.

"Something didn't feel right," she says. "It felt like everything was a performance. You know what I mean?"

Yes, I know what she means. Kelly's questions when she opened the door. The way her smile kept dropping away when we told her Dwight Smith had been released from jail. "Yeah, I do. That sums it up pretty well. But isn't that how genuine people behave too?"

"If she killed him she couldn't have done it by herself," Kent says. "Rage can be a great equalizer when it comes to strength, but I don't see it here. Way too much lifting and moving for somebody Kelly's size."

"They say you can lift a car if your baby is pinned beneath it."

"Yeah, and maybe that's true," she says, "but that's what, one second? Two? Say five seconds at the most. Pure adrenaline. But that's not what helps people transport and dump a body. That takes strength and determination."

"I agree," I say.

"Of course this could all be for nothing. For all we know Smith threw himself under that train. Maybe somebody threw him and it wasn't Kelly. But if it was, she had help."

I think about that. I can imagine if she'd gone looking for help a volunteer army made up of family and friends all would have put their hands up. At least in theory. What about when it came down to it? Would they be there for the messy bits?

"Let's go talk to Smith's brother," Kent says.

We hit the edge of town and a lot more traffic and Kent has to slow down. Over the next few weeks traffic will only get worse as Christmas gets closer. Already some shops have their decorations up. Santa is ready to take your hard-earned cash, Santa with a welcoming wave, Santa beating the economy. It's been four years since I last enjoyed Christmas. It was back when my daughter was alive. I remember running around trying to find some talking animal doll she had her heart set on, the problem was other kids all across the country had their hearts set on them too and they were sold out everywhere. The following two Christmases I went and visited my wife in her nursing home, and last Christmas I spent in jail.

As we drive I feel a ball of guilt in my stomach. If the investigation comes back to Kelly Summers, I can say I didn't notice the broken lock or the pry marks. Will the others believe me? Probably not. But what can they do?

I call Hutton and update him on everything except the broken lock and the new shower curtain. "There's something else," he tells me. "The car has been dusted for prints. All we've found are Smith's and his brother's, and also his brother's wife's. Nobody else had access to the vehicle, and it doesn't look like anybody else drove it. The seat is at the right distance from the pedals, so if Smith didn't drive the car himself then the driver was either the right height or slotted the seat back into place, and the driver must have worn gloves and not put his hands on the wheel where any normal driver would put them, that way he didn't smudge away Smith's prints. There are some foreign hairs around the footwell and pedals, the kind of hairs that get caught up in shoes and transferred, but we'll have to get a sample from Kelly Summers and compare them to rule her out."

"She's a suspect? Even though you're sure Smith drove the car out there himself?"

"He was following her," Hutton says. "And there's more. The car was out of gas."

I take a few seconds to absorb that fact, and I say it back to him. "Out of gas."

"The fuel indicator is one more thing that doesn't work on that car. It's stuck around halfway. My guess is Smith always figured how much gas there was by the odometer. So a stuck needle means no fuel warning. The car ran out of gas exactly where we found it."

"So Smith miscalculated," I say, "and he was on his way to somewhere else."

"Except Smith wouldn't miscalculate," Hutton says, "not driving that far out of the city. He'd have made sure he had enough gas. After all, he worked at a gas station and he could have topped up. You said there was forty dollars in his wallet, right?"

"Right," I say.

Hutton carries on. "That train track couldn't have been the destination he had in mind. It's possible, I suppose, he was going somewhere, forgot about the fuel because, as you say, he was distracted by seeing Kelly Summers. I think the next thing now is to wait until the medical examiner has taken a look. Why don't you go and see her now? I know it's early, but she might have something."

We change direction and drive to the hospital, and it's lunchtime by the time we get there. There is construction taking place, the same construction that's been taking place for almost the last two years. In fact construction has taken so long the mushroom cloud of dust around the hospital will probably take another week to settle once the machinery and workmen are gone. At the moment big machines are tearing into existing concrete and metal, and in ten years it'll happen all over again to make things even bigger. There's a dedicated parking space around the back for the police to use. There are a couple of nurses sharing a cigarette, standing so the sun falls on their faces. We step through a back entrance and have to sign a visitor log, and then catch an elevator that doesn't play any elevator music as it takes us down. I can't imagine a morgue being upstairs.

Tracey Walter, the medical examiner, meets us when the doors open. Her hair has been dyed red. Last time I saw her it was black, and the time before that it was brown. I guess she's searching for a look and can't quite decide what it is. Perhaps she's waiting for somebody to tell her. Like always she's looking lean and gaunt, a long-distance runner's body that looks ready to spring into action at any sign of a zombie uprising.

"How you doing, Rebecca?" she asks.

"I'm fine," Kent says, which is always what she says, and I know she's not *fine*, but I just hope she's at least a good percentage of that.

"And you, Theo? How's Bridget?"

"She's doing good. You know, not a hundred percent, but she's come a long way."

"That's good," she says. "But what's not so good is you guys are here about six hours ahead of schedule."

"I know." I try to look apologetic. "And I'm sorry. Have you managed to take a look?"

She sighs, and I've been through this with her before, just like every homicide detective has been through it with every medical examiner when they're in a hurry, the same way Captain Kirk would pester his chief engineer to work miracles in the least possible amount of time.

We move deeper into the morgue. I'm thankful to be wearing my jacket. The room has cinder-block walls, one of them dedicated to sliding drawers with square fridge doors on the front, bodies lying inside them. There are surfaces full of fluids and trays and sharp-looking tools. There are people lying on tables, people who have been victim to bad luck and bad health, people who have died for no other reason than their clock ran out. It's easy to tell Dwight Smith apart from these people. One look at him and the line *This was no boating accident* pops into my mind, followed up by *We need a bigger morgue*. The train made a jigsaw puzzle out of him. My stomach rolls a little and for a second, a brief second, I'm scared its contents are going to make an appearance.

The head has been separated from the body, a rough tear where the two once joined, bits of bone and flesh and muscle blending into a mess, topped off with grease and dirt and small leaves stuck to the blood and what looks like a dead moth. There's a wristwatch on the left wrist that will now be right only twice a day, only Dwight Smith isn't going to know when. The other arm is lying next to Dwight about where it would be if it were still attached, only it isn't, and the same goes for the hand. Same for the legs.

The hardest thing to look at is the head. It doesn't even look like a head. I don't know what the hell it looks like. There's blood and hair and flesh, but it doesn't look like it was ever human. It looks like one of the train wheels pushed it down, but instead of running right over it, it was pinched out into the air. It's partly separated, the skull cleaved open around the top, and inside is all the dark matter that once gave Dwight Smith some very sick thoughts. I can't see his eyes and don't know if they're in there somewhere, or whether they popped like grapes. I can make out the mouth only because I know where it ought to be. Kent keeps one arm folded across her chest while raising a hand to her face. She cups a fist over her mouth.

"Not hard to tell he was hit by a train," Tracey says.

I nod. I can't talk. I'm thinking Dwight Smith is going to replace my modern art dreams, or perhaps he will show up as an exhibit.

I take a few shallow breaths. "Was he dead before the train hit him?"

Tracey moves one of the severed arms a few inches, and it seems needless and I suspect she's doing it because she knows how I feel, and is punishing me for showing up early. The bloody stump makes a wet sucking sound as it peels away from the table. I keep expecting her to try and jam it into place, as if there's enough blood and goo to make it stick, as if she can pop it onto the nub of bone the same way I used to reattach the arms onto Emily's dolls.

"Like I told Hutton earlier, it'll be tonight. I'll call you later on today, okay?"

"We were really hoping—" I say.

She puts her hand up to interrupt me. "Don't," she says. "Okay? It'll get done when it'll get done. You've wasted your time coming here. Accept it, and move on."

So we accept it and we move on. We ride the elevator back up. It's another one of those trips I'm seeing in reverse. Same security guard. Same two nurses standing outside, only now they're no longer smoking. They're sitting on a bench, one sending a text message, the other reading a magazine. Compared to the morgue it feels like the day just warmed up forty degrees.

I call Hutton as Kent starts driving. He answers on the first ring. I update him, which isn't an update at all since we learned nothing.

"Okay," he says. "Listen, I've had an idea. Why don't you go and speak to Carl Schroder?"

I almost shake my head. I haven't seen Schroder in a while. He's different now. Difficult to talk to. Difficult to be around. After the explosion that almost killed Kent, Schroder tried tracking the Carver himself. He found him too—but for his efforts, Schroder took a bullet to the head and the Carver escaped. It almost killed him, and for a while we were both in comas at the same time. That's when the media called us the Coma Cops, even though Schroder wasn't technically a cop anymore.

"Schroder? Why?"

"He arrested Dwight Smith, and he's the one who helped Kelly Summers and, well, I want his take on this."

"His take?" I ask, but I can't imagine he'll have much of a take. These days he doesn't have much of a take on anything.

"Yeah. I want to know what he thinks Kelly Summers is capable of."

"I thought we were waiting to see what the medical examiner said."

"And we are. But like you just said, we won't know anything till later today. But you know what these things are like—there are things that happen that don't make it into the files."

He's right. There are things that don't make it into files. No doubt in this case among the things that didn't make it were the threats by Summers's family.

"Okay. I'll talk to him."

"I want you to go by yourself," he says. "We've had a report," he says, and goes on to tell me that a call has just come through—there's a report of a missing nine-year-old girl from one of the local malls. No details yet, just that of a security guard dealing with a hysterical woman whose well-behaved daughter has disappeared. It's the kind of call that makes your heart sink even though ninety-nine times out of a hundred it's nothing more than the girl having wandered off. But it's that other one time in a hundred we're all frightened of.

"It's the weekend and we're short on manpower with half the force still looking for the Christchurch Carver, and hell, to be honest, a missing nine-year-old girl is always going to trump a dead rapist, so I want you guys to split up. Drop Kent off at the mall, then go talk to Schroder."

We hang up and I explain the situation to Kent, who nods as she listens, then changes direction. We pull up at a set of lights. The light is green, but the traffic isn't moving. It's the same shade of green as the shower curtain in Kelly Summers's bathroom. There is one car ahead of us, and there are L-plates in the back window. The learner driver has stalled the car. After a few seconds he gets it started, the car hops forward a few feet, and then he stalls it again. He goes through this process one more time and then the light turns red. Then both doors open. A young teenager climbs out and moves around to the other side of the car, where his father is also climbing out. They swap places. The car starts up. The lights turn green. The car drives smoothly through the intersection then pulls over. We drive past.

Kent gets out at the mall and I walk around the car and climb into the driver's seat, offering an assurance I'll either join her later on the case, or pick her up.

"Good luck," I tell her.

"Hopefully I won't need it. Hopefully the little girl has just wandered off into a shop somewhere."

Hopefully the little girl has just wandered and hasn't been dragged. There's a world of difference between the two.

CHAPTER TEN

His house is beginning to fill with sunlight. It's above the trees and coming through the windows to the north. It's drawing a line across the carpet that moves a fraction with every passing minute. Warren has gone, his web empty this morning, and he wonders whether something bigger came along and ate him, or whether he evolved, that he needed more room to grow and become a better spider. It's lunchtime. He knows this because of the height of the sun and because he's hungry, but not from his watch. His watch is broken. He still wears it, but the face is cracked and the hands don't move. His watch died the same day the Old Him died.

He has work to do. But first he needs to eat. There's food in his house only he's not in the mood to cook. What he's in the mood for is eating.

Food will help him think.

He walks through to the garage. The garage has no tools in it, except for a lawn mower, which, he figures, isn't really a tool. The Old Him used to love mowing lawns. It was the only time he really felt at peace. He would move up and down the yard, emptying the catcher when it was full, and it really is the only thing in the world that would switch off his mind. At least he used to think that until he learned getting shot in the head works too.

He gets into his car and he drives with the stereo off. He doesn't listen to music anymore. Hasn't since the accident—not that it can really be called an accident. It's an accident in the same sense cancer can be an accident—in the sense you don't mean for it to happen. He used to love music. When he was fifteen he learned to play the guitar. He played it and it was just like the song said, he played it till his fingers bled, they'd hurt like hell but he stuck with it, thinking it was the kind of thing that would impress the girls. Only it didn't. Impressing girls took more than playing the guitar back then—you needed the right clothes and haircut and you had to be an intense, brooding asshole or have an easygoing, almost drifter-like personality, and if you didn't have either of those then you weren't a musician, you weren't an artist, you were just a guy with a guitar.

He heads to a drive-through diner called *Burger Bro* and orders a triple B—which is the Big Bro Burger. The guy at the counter is wearing a T-shirt that says *Bro's your uncle*, and when he turns around to grab the food he reveals the back of the T-shirt, on which is a picture of fries falling from the sky, a multicolored stripe cutting the horizon, and a pot at the bottom full of chicken nuggets. Beneath it the word *rainbro*, and for the first time in months, he almost smiles.

He's too hungry to drive anywhere, and he hates eating inside fast-food restaurants, so he sits in the parking lot and eats his triple B and thinks of last night and the mess Kelly Summers made. She had asked for five minutes, and five minutes hadn't been long enough, but ten was perfect. When she was finished, he realized he'd made a mistake. Dumping the body where nobody could find it was one thing, but they should have done the killing out there too. The only saving grace was it all happened in the bathroom. Bathrooms were easier to clean. With bathrooms you didn't have to tear up carpets.

So killing was a learning curve. He should have known that. And next time—

Next time?

Yes, *next time*. Another important pair of words. Like *Burger Bro* and *What if*. There was going to be a next time. And after tonight there will be more next times, right up until there is a last time.

He finishes his meal and balls up the mess and tosses it into a nearby bin. He turns on the radio and listens to the one o'clock news. The body on the train tracks is the third story and the facts are minimal.

He drives to the closest mall. You can drive for ten minutes in any direction in this city and find a mall. He buys the cheapest cell phone he can find. He uses cash. He already has a cell phone, but he wants a disposable one. Then he walks to a different phone store in the mall and buys a second prepay SIM card, then goes to the supermarket and buys a third. When he gets home he puts the phone on charge. With it still plugged in, he uses it to phone the prison where, until a few weeks ago, Dwight Smith was residing. It rings twice and then a woman answers.

"This is Detective Inspector Theodore Tate," he says. "I need to be transferred through to somebody who can help me out with some information on an ex-convict. More specifically I'm after the names of some cellmates."

"Just a moment," the woman says, and she puts him on hold, and it really is just a moment because two seconds into the hold music another woman comes on the line.

He introduces himself again, and he speaks confidently, like a man who has done this before—because he has. He tells her Dwight Smith has come up in an active investigation. What investigation, she asks? Well, he tells her, it's to do with the body found on the railway tracks.

"Was it Smith?" she asks.

"Yes."

"What can I help you with exactly, Detective . . . ?"

"Tate," he says. "Theodore Tate. I need to know who Smith's cellmates were over the last five years."

"Give me two minutes," she says, and she takes five, and when she returns she picks right up from where she left off. "He had three. The first was Eugene Walker. They shared a cell for twelve months, then Walker was released. He was replaced by Bevin Collard," she says, "and they were cellmates for nearly three years until Bevin was released. Then Smith had only a year with his third cellmate before Smith himself was released. Guy's name is Jamie Robertson."

"Bevin Collard," he says, and he remembers the case, and he remembers Collard had a brother. He writes the name down with a pencil. Using a pad and pencil is very old school. "You have known addresses for him?"

"No, but his parole officers will," she says, and she gives him the details. "Would you like me to send a copy to your department?"

"That would be great."

"Consider it done."

He considers it done then thanks her for her time. He uses his phone to go onto the Internet. He looks up Bevin Collard and refreshes his memory. Bevin, along with his brother Taylor, were sentenced nine years ago for raping a woman by the name of Linda Crowley. The case was assigned to Detective Inspector Bill Landry. Landry told him about it. It had happened at the victim's house. They had worn masks and they had come in on a Saturday morning while her husband was playing cricket. The brothers shaved Linda's head and broke both of her arms and raped her in front of her six-year-old daughter, Monica. Landry said every night for a week Peter Crowley would wait for Landry after work and beg him to have five minutes alone with the men who had done this. Landry kept giving him the same answer. No. It didn't work that way.

Bevin was released twelve months ago. His brother, Taylor, was released eighteen months ago. He rings the parole officer, identifies himself as Detective Inspector Theodore Tate. He asks for the last known address of Bevin Collard. One minute later he has it.

He taps his pencil against the pad. He's tired. He used to take caffeine tablets in his old life. Wake-E tablets. They used to help. Then they helped a little less and he had to keep taking more. The old life ended in June with a bullet. He was tracking the Christchurch Carver. He tracked him to a church, and there was a firefight. People died, including the serial cop killer Melissa X, but not before she shot him. The Carver got away, and the Old Him got a bullet in the head. It entered and never came out. It's still in there, lodged down deep. It's why, the doctors have told him, he can't taste anything anymore. It's why he can't feel anything. It's why he doesn't care. One day that bullet will switch off his lights and he'll be dead before he hits the ground. And that really doesn't bother him. Why should it? Not caring is the only advantage to having a bullet stuck in his head.

The doctors told him it will happen any day. Or in a year. Or ten years. Or twenty. Was there anything they could do? No. How high were the risks if they tried to remove it? Too high. The surgery would kill him—that was almost guaranteed. Almost? Well, if he survived the cutting he would lose so much brain function he would barely be alive anyway. It was a lose-lose situation. They told him to be careful. Don't get into a fight. Don't crash your car. Don't get drunk and fall over.

He reads more about Linda Crowley. Fourteen months after her attack, Linda Crowley took as many sleeping pills as she could get hold of, washed them down with a sixty-dollar bottle of red wine, and said good-bye to the world while her daughter was at school and her husband was at work. Landry told him Peter Crowley started coming to the station again after that, asking for his five minutes. He offered him money. Landry said one evening Crowley followed him home, knocked on his door, and handed him a briefcase with twenty-eight thousand, six hundred and eight dollars in it. *"It's all I have, but it's yours—just give me my five minutes."*

But Landry couldn't give them to him. He sent him home.

Landry may have said no, but the Five Minute Man can say yes.

He looks the husband up in the phone book and sees he's still living at the same house. He remembers the name of the street because he was with Landry when they attended to the suicide. It wasn't the same house the attack had taken place in. The Crowleys had sold that place.

He takes the SIM card out of the phone and snaps it in half, then replaces it with another. He hears a car pull up outside. He puts the pad away and moves to the door. *This is interesting,* he thinks, and for a moment wonders if this is about the phone call he just made, because he impersonated this very man, but no, of course not—how could it be?

He opens the door. Theodore Tate walks up the path towards him.

CHAPTER ELEVEN

Schroder has had a rough year. He split up with his wife a few months ago, and is currently on disability because he can't work. It's been a few weeks since I've seen him, and these days he isn't exactly what I'd call a talkative guy. He nods and, on occasion, he'll answer if you ask him a question directly, but he'll never take the conversation and run with it. Earlier this year he was forced to shoot a nasty old lady in cold blood to save an innocent girl. Taking a life was when Schroder stopped being Schroder. He lost his job, and I became a resident of Coma Land that same night. A few weeks later he started working for TV. He was the on-set consultant for a few crime shows, and he narrated and was in a reality show about a New Zealand psychic who looked for answers in unsolved crimes. Then the Christchurch Carver escaped and Melissa X, the Carver's girlfriend, shot Carl in the head, and then he joined me in Coma Land for a spell. When he came back to the world of the living the dark version of Carl became something else. I'm not sure what, exactly. Something empty. Something hollow. Something that made his wife leave him.

"Hey, Carl," I say, as I walk up the sidewalk to the front door. It's open and he's leaning against it.

"Hello, Theo," he says, and he hardly ever calls me Theo. It's always Tate. Or used to be. "Why are you here?"

"I need your help," I tell him, skipping over the pleasantries. Carl doesn't do pleasantries—not anymore.

He looks down at the file I'm carrying. Dwight Smith's file. "You may as well come in."

I follow him inside. The house is thirty or forty years old and doesn't have a lot of personality or a lot of furniture. There are no photos on the walls, no paintings. In the lounge there's a sofa and two matching chairs and a TV and nothing else, except dust on the floor and cobwebs in the corners. He doesn't offer me a drink. He sits on the sofa and I sit in one of the chairs facing him. He's bald these days, his head shaved when the doctors saved his life, hair unable to grow back on the scar tissue left from the gunshot, so now he keeps it shaved. The scar is awful, it's a shiny dime to the side of his head, small lines extending out from it like cracks in a mirror. It's an inch above his right eye and halfway between that and his ear. Then there are the scars from where the doctors went to work, thin white lines from cutting, holes where drills were used, those scars will fade, but not the bullet wound itself.

"How you been?" I ask him.

"The same," he says. "You?"

"Doing okay," I tell him. "How are the kids?"

"Why are you here, Theo?"

"You remember Wayne Beachwood?" I ask.

"Wayne Beachwood," he says, then he says nothing else for a few seconds, it's as if he's trying to access the memory, opening and closing drawers looking for the right file. "Yes, I remember him. The train guy. He's the guy who threw . . . what was his name . . . Russell Lighter onto the train tracks."

"Richard Lighter."

"Richard Lighter. Beachwood had been drinking and he ran Lighter over in his car. He picked him up and threw him on the train tracks, hoping to hide any evidence, but there was a witness," he says, all very monotone as if he's reading from the file he found. "You're here because of Beachwood?"

"Not quite." I hand the file out to him, but he doesn't take it. After a few seconds I lean further forward so I can toss it onto the couch next to him. "Do you remember Kelly Summers?"

"Yes."

"And Dwight Smith?"

"Yes. You still haven't told me why you are here."

"Dwight Smith is dead," I tell him.

"Okay," he says.

"Okay?"

He shrugs. "I can't imagine many people grieving for him. That still doesn't tell me why you're here, but my guess is it has something to do with Wayne Beachwood. Did Beachwood kill him in jail?"

"No," I tell him, then I fill him in on the last two weeks of Dwight Smith's life. His release from jail, his job pumping gas, his sudden departure from the gas station last night after spotting Kelly Summers.

"Kelly Summers is dead too?" he asks, and still without the emotion.

"Kelly is fine," I tell him.

"I'm pleased to hear that," he says, but he doesn't sound pleased. He doesn't sound anything. If anything he sounds bored.

"We think Dwight Smith was murdered," I say, and while most of us think that, I know it for a fact. I saw the window and the shower curtain. I don't tell him this. I'm here because Hutton wants me here.

"Okay," he says.

"Okay?"

"It still doesn't tell me why you're here."

"You were the investigating detective five years ago. I want to know what didn't make it into the file. I want to know what Kelly or her family is capable of. You got to know some of her friends and family. I want to know if you think she could have done this either alone or who would have helped her."

"So she's a suspect," he says.

"Possibly."

"Kelly Summers is a victim, Theo, she's not a killer. If Smith followed her to her house last night and forced his way inside, and she overpowered him, why not call the police?"

"Because—"

"Because what?" he asks. "There was nothing left out of the file, Theo. If Kelly killed him while defending herself, she would have called the police, you would have shown up, you would have taken a look at what had happened whether she'd hit him with a ceramic bowl or stabbed him with a pair of kitchen scissors, and you'd have concluded that Dwight Smith, ex-con and rapist, Dwight Smith who had just broken into her house and attacked her and had been fought off, well, that Dwight Smith would have gotten what was coming. I know you. I know you wouldn't have tried to see more to it than what was there if that's what you'd seen, and there's no reason Kelly Summers would suspect you'd see it any other way. There is no reason at all for Kelly Summers to have not called the police. There is no reason for her to try and hide it by putting Smith onto a set of train tracks."

"I don't think the train was part of the plan."

"I don't follow."

My phone starts vibrating in my pocket, but I ignore it. "Smith's car was used to transport him out there, but it ran out of gas. Whoever was driving was probably taking him somewhere to bury, where he'd never be found, but the plan changed."

"I see," he says.

"Does that change your opinion of Kelly Summers?"

"No," he says.

"No?" I ask, and my phone has gone quiet.

"It's the same thing, Theo. There's no reason Kelly would hide what would have been a clear case of self-defense. I'm not saying Dwight Smith wasn't murdered. It could be your theory all stacks up, but what I'm saying is something else must have happened between the gas station where Smith worked and his following of Kelly Summers. He couldn't have made it to her house. Have you considered he jumped in front of the train?"

"We're considering it," I tell him.

"What did forensics find in the car? Other prints on the wheel? Hairs in the headrest?"

"Nothing. In fact forensics is sure Smith was the last person to drive it."

"Well there you go," Schroder says. "Look, Theo, I know it seems unlikely he saw Kelly Summers then had the urge to kill himself, but to me it sounds like a simple case in which you're looking for a complicated answer. Does it look like Dwight Smith drove himself to those train tracks and jumped in front of it?"

"Yes," I say, admitting it, and I think about the window lock, the shower curtain with the fold lines. That was a brand-new curtain, and there was no packaging for it in the recycling bin. It's possible she bought it a week ago, just as it's possible she replaced it earlier this morning because last night she used her existing one to wrap a very dead Dwight Smith into. Just as it's possible that lock on her window was pried up a week ago or two weeks ago and she chose not to mention it. "Everything she said sounded rehearsed."

"It sounds to me she acted that way not because it was a performance, but because it was all genuine."

"Maybe," I say, and there's no need to keep pushing. I'm glad Schroder doesn't think she's capable of murder. Hopefully it means nobody else thinks so too. I want Dwight Smith to have killed himself and Kelly Summers to carry on with life. My phone starts vibrating again.

"Definitely," he says. "I hope this has been helpful." He stands up, and I follow his cue and stand up too.

"Thanks, Carl." I shake his hand. "I'll come back soon and we'll catch up some more, okay?"

"Whatever you say, Theo." He walks me to the door. "Hang on a second."

"Yeah?"

"The medical examiner. Who's working the case?"

"Tracey Walter."

"Okay," he says, slowly nodding. "What's she found?"

"She said she'll know something later on today."

"Keep me updated, would you? I'm curious."

I get out my phone as I walk to my car and see Kent has left two messages, no doubt about the missing girl, but before I can check them she calls me back.

"How you getting on?" I ask, scared of what her answer is going to be, hoping she'll lead with *wandering* and not *dragging*.

"Listen, Theo, there's no real easy way to say this," she says, which are never great words to hear from anybody, let alone another cop, especially when you're dealing with a missing child. In my mind I can see the little girl, a hand holding her arm tightly, a van door being opened, the girl crying as she's thrown inside, and I can't bear to think it through any further, but I do. Of course I do. It's my job.

"Just say it."

"The missing girl," she says. "Tate, the missing girl is your daughter."

CHAPTER TWELVE

The man who helped Kelly Summers, the man who tried to dispose of the body, the Five Minute Man as he thinks of himself—Detective Inspector Carl Schroder as other people used to see him (the Old Him), unemployable tragic Carl Schroder as they see him now (the New New Him)—sits back on his couch and looks up to the ceiling and sees that Warren has returned.

"I thought maybe you'd been eaten," he says.

Who would eat a spider? Warren answers and, for a moment, Carl Schroder thinks he has gone mad. Completely mad. But of course the spider didn't talk—they never do—and even if they were to start talking he doubts it would start with Warren.

"Tate has been a royal pain in the ass over the last few years," he says to Warren, but Warren is too small to tell if he's paying attention. "However, he's also proven himself a useful investigator. He has a way of getting the job done."

You're going to have to watch yourself, Warren says.

"I know. Kelly Summers may have put on an excellent performance at her house, but being questioned in your house and being questioned in an interrogation room is an entirely different thing."

Entirely, Warren agrees. *Just what in the hell happened?*

He leans back into his couch and sighs. "I was a hundred yards from the railway line when the car gave up. I pushed the car to within twenty. I was hoping the police wouldn't try too hard to figure out why a rapist got himself sliced and diced."

A good thought, Warren says. *So what, you took Smith out of the car and put him on the tracks?*

"Exactly. When the train hit, pieces of Dwight Smith flew everywhere. I'd tied a piece of rope onto the hand and reeled it in like a fish. I wrapped it in a piece of shower curtain to stop it dripping, then used it to leave prints around the steering wheel, the lever to move the car seat, and around the door handle."

That's clever, Warren says.

"And I'm talking to a spider," Schroder says.

No. You're talking to yourself.

He stops talking to himself. Last night he figured a walk back into town would take him five, six, maybe seven hours. He took his gloves off and he began. After twenty minutes he buried the shower curtain on the edge of a farm. He had to—because nobody walked down motorways carrying shower curtains. It would take him another twenty minutes to get to the end of the road that would then turn onto the motorway. Ten minutes into that walk a truck pulled over and a burly guy with thick forearms and a hair-cut that trailed down the back of his neck offered him a lift. He reminded Schroder of a guy he'd arrested years ago, a guy who was distributing child porn, a guy who on the car ride into the station had said the best part about child porn was the kids did it for free. Schroder wanted to shoot him. Of course that was the Old Him. The New New Him would have done it.

He was dropped off in town. He caught a taxi to within a mile of Kelly Summers's house. He paid in cash then walked the rest of the way.

Kelly had cleaned the bathroom. There was a plastic bag full of bloody rags, rags soaked in bleach, and the bathroom smelled like a hospital. She was sweating, but she was focused. She looked the same way he felt when he was mowing his lawns. He told her about the car. The plan was changing. He told her he would be back in twenty minutes. His clothes were clean—he'd been careful not to get blood on them. There was dirt on his hands, which took only a minute to clean up. He drove to the nearest twenty-four-hour supermarket. He bought a new shower curtain, and he bought some scented candles and some scented oils, and he bought some air freshener. When he got back they sprayed the room with the air freshener, set up the candles and oils to hide the smell of bleach, and hung the new curtain.

They sat in her lounge for three hours. He thought she would be nervous, but she wasn't. Cleaning the bathroom, she said, had felt cathartic. They rehearsed what she would say when the police showed up. He was sure she was going to be fine. Kelly Summers had a life ahead of her. She wanted that life. If she failed, the police would take her away. Dwight Smith would have beaten her, he said. Don't let him beat you.

He took her robe and the rags and the bleach and the shower curtain packaging. By the time he left the bathroom smelled like a Christmas tree. The only thing he couldn't do was fix the window, not in the time he had, but she would say she didn't know about it. It would be impossible for the police to know when it happened. Kelly Summers gave him a hug where he just kept his arms hanging down by his side. She whispered into his ear, her breath warm as she thanked him over and over. When she stepped back her hands found his hands, they interlocked, this very small human chain, this circle they made, and she smiled at him.

He dumped everything in separate locations.

He thinks about Theodore Tate, and wonders how much he really knows. That's the thing about Theo—you just never know.

He thinks about the Collard brothers, and about Peter Crowley, the man who asked Landry to have five minutes alone with them.

Tonight he is going to give that to Peter Crowley.

Tonight he sure as hell isn't going to run out of fuel.

Tonight the New New Him will continue to evolve.

CHAPTER THIRTEEN

I turn the sirens on even though it's not an emergency. Nobody is in danger. There are no lives on the line. So I turn them on to get traffic out of my way, but I don't put my foot down. I don't speed. Well not much. If I caused an accident I'd be toast.

I drive Kent's car into the parking lot where, three years ago, my daughter was killed. I can still remember every second of that day, getting the call, rushing to the hospital, praying to God while the surgeons played God with my wife. Of course there was nothing that could be done for my daughter. A day later I drove to this very parking lot. There was still police tape fluttering in the wind. Staring at it I knew my future—or more accurately, I knew the future of the man who had done this to my family. I find a parking space and make my way to the management offices inside. They're upstairs, a bunch of them leading from a corridor, and one of the doors to those offices opens and Kent comes wandering out.

"I saw you on the security camera," she says, and of course I look up and stare into the camera as if to confirm it. She gives me a smile, a slow, sad smile where she tries to tell me everything is going to be okay.

"Is Doctor Forster here yet?" I ask. Doctor Forster is Bridget's doctor, and when Kent was unable to get hold of me straightaway, she rang him.

"He got here about ten minutes ago. Listen, Theo, he had to sedate her. She's sleeping at the moment."

"What happened?"

So she tells me what happened. She walks through it step-by-step as best as she can, steps made up from eyewitness accounts, from the security guard that first tried to help her, and from Bridget's own accounts of what happened. There are a couple of seats in the corridor and I have to sit down as my legs threaten to collapse beneath me. Bridget had gone shopping. Nobody knows how she got here, but I imagine she caught the bus. She was walking past the cinema in the mall when she suddenly realized Emily was missing. She checked the theater, the bathrooms, the lobby, then sat on some stairs for a few minutes unsure of what to do. Then she got up and started asking people if they had seen her daughter—and showed a photograph of Emily. She was getting louder and more panicked, which drew the attention of a security guard, who then brought her to the management office. By this point she was visibly shaking, and the staff in the office along with the security guard assured her Emily was most likely wandering in the mall somewhere, and they paged her over the intercom.

Emily didn't show up. Then the first cracks in Bridget's story began to show. The movie she had taken Emily to was an animation that involved talking animals. And today there were no such movies like that. Still, her conviction at what had happened was strong, and obviously they were dealing with a situation that required the police, and so the police were called. When asked for my contact number, Bridget gave my cell phone, only I don't have the same number I had three years ago because that was a work number. So the number they were trying gave them only an automatic message saying it was out of service. Then she told them I worked for the police department and asked them to call me there. It was then that one of the managers recognized my name and, having worked here the day of the accident, realized what may be happening. Before she could decide what to do with the information, the first pair of officers arrived at the scene. She briefed them, and they quickly agreed what was happening here was something medical, was something weird, they were dealing with a woman who had snapped and not with a missing girl. Then Kent arrived and then everything was confirmed. I was talking to Schroder and not answering my phone, so they called Bridget's doctor.

Bridget didn't recognize Rebecca Kent because three years ago she didn't know her, and three years ago is where Bridget's mind was. She didn't recognize Doctor Forster for the same reasons. It was that cold Tuesday of the accident all over again.

I follow Rebecca back into the office. It's a big office, there are half a dozen desks in here and views out over the parking lot—and I can see the same spot where Emily was killed, and it would have been a horrific sight for whoever was up here that day. There's a bunch of people, a water cooler, there are half a dozen calendars hanging on the wall, a couple of clocks, some plants, lots of shelving with boxes and folders on them, and along one wall a couple of couches. It's on one of these couches that my wife is lying.

All the staff are standing, three of them have formed a semi-circle near my wife and are watching her, others have split off into pairs and are talking among themselves. Rebecca holds back and I move over to Bridget, crouch next to her, and take hold of her hand. It's warm. I stroke her hair off her forehead, then look up at Doctor Forster. He's a good-looking guy in his fifties, dark brown hair and designer glasses, and whenever I see him I keep thinking he looks more like a TV doctor than a real doctor.

"We always knew something like this could happen," he says.

"Is she going to be okay?"

"I think we may need to broaden our definition of what okay means," he says. "Is she going to wake and think it's still three years ago? I don't know. Probably not. Will it happen again? It's possible. This is the worst event, right?"

"Right," I tell him, unsure how I feel about what's happening being summed up as an *event*. "Every other time it's only taken a few minutes to convince her, I mean, remind her I suppose, of what's going on."

"And it only started two weeks ago?" he asks. I had called him after the first occurrence. He scheduled more tests, which are still two weeks away.

"That's right. She was fine up till then."

"My suggestion is that coming to the mall triggered a full-on break, and all these people are strangers so of course she wasn't going to believe or trust them. Do you know why she came down here?"

"No."

"She doesn't drive, does she?"

"Well, she used to, of course, but not now. . . . I don't know how she got here. I'm guessing she took a bus."

"Here's what I suggest. Take her home and keep a close eye on her for the rest of the weekend, then bring her in to see me on Monday. We'll do some tests. How does that sound?"

I nod eagerly. "We'll be there."

We decide the best course of action is to let her sleep upstairs for a while, rather than propping her up in the car or calling an ambulance. There's a stretcher in the nearby sick bay. We use it to carry her in there. We lay her down on the cot.

"Give her two or three hours," Forster says, and then he shakes my hand, tells me to *hang in there*, and reminds me to call him if there are any other problems. I tell him I will, that I'll see him on Monday, and then he's gone, leaving me and Kent alone with my wife in the sick bay.

CHAPTER FOURTEEN

I step into the corridor with Kent. We're the only people out here. She looks a little shaken, and I feel shaken, and I figure Elvis would know how to sum that up. I'm suddenly overcome with exhaustion, and I have to lean against the wall to stop myself from collapsing. Bridget was better. Life was going to be okay.

Kent puts her arms around me and embraces me. Her body is warm and smells slightly of perfume. "It's going to be okay," she says.

I don't know how to answer. The truth is her words make me want to cry, and I can feel the tears coming, they're almost here, and then they come. Nobody has hugged me like this in a very long time. The other truth is Rebecca doesn't know if Bridget is going to be okay—she's just doing what people do, saying what people are expected to say.

"It's okay," she says again as the tears spill down my face and onto her shoulder, and she keeps holding me, and the way she says it she sounds believable. We stay that way for the best part of a minute, then the tears stop falling and we pull away.

"It's so hard for her," I say.

"It's hard for you too, Theo."

I wipe at the tears. "I'm not the one who has to keep getting the news their daughter is dead. Every time I tell her, it's like it breaks her. It's so cruel."

"It may not be that way for much longer," she says. "Could be this is the last time it happens. You just have to stay hopeful. Five months ago she was in a vegetative state. Had you given up hope then?"

"No." Which isn't entirely true. "And I'm not giving up now. I just . . . I . . . I don't know. I just want her to be okay. I just want everything to be okay."

She reaches up and runs her fingers over the side of her ruined face. "I know what you mean."

"Thank you for helping her," I say, "and for calling her doctor."

She reaches out and squeezes my arm. I nod, as if receiving a message.

"So how did things go with Schroder?" she asks.

The conversation is such a shift in direction that for a moment I can't answer her. Schroder? Oh, that Schroder. Oh, we're working a suicide that's actually a homicide. I hadn't thought about it since getting here. I tell her what Schroder said, and she agrees with him. If Dwight had followed Kelly home and made his way inside, there would be no reason Kelly wouldn't have called the police if she had killed him in self-defense.

"You keep the car," she says. "I'll get an officer to give me a lift back to the station and check in with Hutton." We walk to the end of the corridor. "I guess it comes down to the ME," she says. "Unless Smith was dead before he hit those tracks, there's no reason not to call it how it looks. I'll get another car and head out and talk to the brother. I'll get Hutton to come with me. I'll give you a call and update you when I know more."

"Thanks, Rebecca."

She smiles again. "She's lucky to have you."

I watch her disappear into the crowd of people, thinking that Bridget was never the lucky one, that that was me. I was lucky to have Bridget. I head back into the sick bay. The room is twice the size of the prison cell I had last summer. There are two cots, each draped with gray blankets, one cot empty, the other has my wife lying on top. I pull a seat over to the bed and I hold her hand and I stare at her, remembering the times I used to do this when she was in the nursing home. The room smells of disinfectant and takes me back to when I used to go to school, the one or two occasions I felt sick and had to wait in the sick bay for my mom to come and get me.

"I've been thinking lately about how we met," I tell Bridget. "You remember?" I ask, sure that she would, but not as sure as I'd like to be. What if one day this thing that is wrong with her steals all of her memories? "I was a year out of police academy. Back then the biggest part of my job was walking the streets of town with a partner, watching out for bad things, mostly dealing with shoplifters, or if our shifts were at night, being called to break up drunken fights. The job wasn't as rewarding as I thought it was going to be. I don't know—I guess I had always figured people would appreciate us more for what we did, but instead everybody was unhappy. It just came down to degrees. There's something I've never told you about the morning we met."

I met Bridget at a coffee shop. I kept seeing her in there. Sometimes she'd be ahead of me in line, sometimes behind me, sometimes looking serious, sometimes happy, and after a few weeks we would start to exchange smiles. Then we'd make small talk. *Really* small talk. Things like *I promise I'm not following you*, and *I think I'm sixty percent coffee*. Then we introduced ourselves. At the same time the cappuccino machine was making a lot of noise and I didn't hear her name and, for some reason, I didn't ask right away for her to repeat herself. Later that day I saw her in town. I was in my police uniform talking to Schroder, and she came up beside me and said *Excuse me, officer, but do you drink anything other than coffee?*

I told her I did. She smiled, wrote her number down on a slip of paper, and handed it to me. *If you ever feel like getting a drink and not being alone when you're doing it, give me a call*, she said.

"The problem was," I tell her now, "is that I never heard your name when you gave it to me, and when you gave me your number, it was just your number. You didn't write your name down because you thought I already knew it. And from there it just became more awkward. I called you that night hoping you'd say your name when you answered the phone, but you didn't. We went and grabbed a drink that weekend. A few nights later we saw a movie. The following weekend we went out for dinner. I still didn't know your name, and because you were getting taxis to these places to meet me, I had no registration plate to check, and of course I didn't know where you lived. Not then. It was after our third date I came up with a solution. Do you remember when I started texting you in the third person as a joke? I said *Theo had a great time last night, and he was wondering if you would like to go out again this weekend?* You responded with *Bridget would love that.*"

Well, Theo would love it if she woke up and everything was the way it used to be. Theo would love it if we could be okay again. Meeting Bridget was the best thing that ever happened to him.

I smile at the memory. I remember laughing when the text came in. I never wanted her to know that story. I told Schroder, and other friends, but I never wanted Bridget to know, even though I'm sure she would have laughed.

I get myself a little more comfortable, adjust my position, keep holding her hand, and stare at her while waiting for things to get better.

CHAPTER FIFTEEN

Schroder checks the address he's written down against the address he's parked outside. It's a middle-of-the-road kind of neighborhood. Some lawns are a little long, some nice and lush and green, some too short and brown, others inundated with clover and weeds. Some fences are freshly painted, some in need of repair. Messy gardens, tidy gardens, no gardens. Nothing uniform, nothing overstyled.

He gets out of the car and heads for the house. There's a pile of weeds next to the path leading up to the doorstep, green on top with dirt clinging below. There are fresh patches of dirt in the garden from where they've been pulled. There are shrubs that look like they've just been planted, they still have the labels hanging from them, and there are more sitting in pots ready to occupy some of the holes that have been dug. Schroder loved mowing lawns, but he sure as hell hated gardening, and back in his old life he couldn't wait for his kids to grow enough to take care of the gardening for him.

Before he can reach the doorstep, the door opens and a young girl comes storming out. She's dressed completely in black. Her fingernails are black, and she's wearing big silver rings and silver bangles. She looks to be around fifteen, twice the age of Schroder's own daughter. She's got dark purple eye shadow on and black lipstick and he can already imagine the kind of arguments she has with her father.

Before either of them can say anything, Peter Crowley steps out of the door a few yards behind his daughter. "Damn it, Monica, I told you no," he says.

"Whatever," Monica says, which is a word Schroder knows all

kids grow into, along with *Fuck you* and *Can I borrow the car?* She looks at Schroder, dedicates two seconds of her time to look him up and down, then dismisses him. "I'll be back later."

"When later?" Peter asks.

"Later," she says, and then she's gone, a girl and her angst walking down the road.

Peter looks at Schroder, gives a small shrug, but the guy looks embarrassed. He also looks different from the last time Schroder saw him. All those years in between age a man anyway, but age one even more who's been through what Peter went through, losing his wife the way he did. His hair has gone gray, receding in the corners far more than the middle, and he's lost enough weight to look like a marathon runner.

"Teenage girls," Peter says—another pair of words that sum up the situation better than any others could. Two words, Schroder imagines, that make fathers go crazy. Schroder, even now, would tear apart the world to find his daughter or son if something ever happened to them. It's comforting to think part of him is still human. He shrugs in a way of agreement.

"What can I help you with?" Peter asks.

"My name is Carl Schroder," he says.

Peter nods. "One of the Coma Cops? I recognize the name."

"Yeah. One of the Coma Cops. Listen, can I have a few moments of your time?"

"What's this about?"

"Can we step inside?"

Peter gives him a suspicious look, as if Schroder is about to try and sell him something, maybe one of those cool comas he just came out of. Then he smiles. "Sure," he says. "Why not? Come on through."

Peter leads him into the house. There are photographs on the walls. Peter with a woman who isn't Linda Crowley. Peter with the girl who was outside a moment ago, but in those photographs the girl is a little younger, the black makeup and clothing still in the future. They sit down in the lounge and Peter offers him a drink and Schroder says no. There's a radio switched on, the volume just too low to hear what the DJs are talking about. He remembers the house from the last time he came here, though Peter Crowley doesn't seem to remember him from back then, just from the newspapers. The house is different now. Different colors, different furniture, different everything, a new stamp being put on the place by the woman in the photographs who replaced the one who had killed herself that day he came here. He looks into the corners of the ceiling and doesn't spot any Warrens.

"Is this about my wife?" Peter asks. "About Linda?"

"Yes."

"It's been almost ten years," he says. "Can you believe that?"

"Yes," Schroder says, and even though time heals all wounds, it doesn't wait, it doesn't pause, it just moves on dispassionately. In the last ten years Peter Crowley has moved on and started a new life for himself. In the last ten years Schroder has had two children and gotten shot in the head.

"Sometimes it seems like a lifetime ago, like some distant memory of a different time and a different family that wasn't even mine, like, I don't know, like it was a family I saw on TV. I know that doesn't make any sense, but . . . shit . . . I don't know, because other times it feels like it was only yesterday. I wake up expecting the woman in my bed to be Linda, only it's not, Linda is gone and she's been, I don't know, *replaced*, I guess, for lack of a better word, but you don't replace people, what you do is move on, and . . ." He smiles, then gives a brief, humorless laugh. "Listen to me, I'm sorry. I don't know where that came from."

"You've remarried?" Schroder asks, and he wonders what his own wife will do, whether she will replace him once she realizes he truly is lost.

Peter starts twirling his wedding ring. "Her name is Charlotte. Five years next February. We got married on Valentine's Day, which I thought people in their right mind never did. She's a great woman. I love her a lot. But I still . . . you know, I still miss Linda. We were . . ." he says, then lowers his voice and looks around the room in case somebody else is listening, "soul mates. We were meant to be together forever. We were going to have more children and we were going to . . . you know, we were going to live. We were going to have a great life. Now Linda is dead and our daughter does the opposite of anything I ever ask, and did you see the way she looks? If she woke up one day to find the world had run out of black clothing she'd kill herself."

"Where is Charlotte now?"

"She's out with her son. With my stepson."

"The men who did this to Linda, who did this to your family, they're out of jail now," Schroder says, and he has to be careful here.

Peter tightens his hands into fists, his jaw tightens, and a vain starts throbbing in his forehead. He doesn't say anything.

"Do you remember what you asked Detective Inspector Landry when your wife died?"

Peter nods. "I remember."

"You wanted five minutes alone with those men."

"I said I remember. And yes, I knew they were out of jail, but I promise you I haven't tried anything. I mean, I'd love to, I'd love to go and shoot those assholes in the head, but I haven't. So you don't need to come around and check on me. I've—"

"Moved on?"

"Yes. Isn't that what you want to hear?"

"No, Peter, it isn't."

Peter shifts in his seat, then leans forward a little. "Why are you here, Detective?"

"I'm no longer a policeman," Schroder says. "I was fired."

"And?"

"And Landry told me what you did, how you followed him home."

"It's his word against mine, no matter what he said," Peter says, "and Landry was killed earlier in the year, right?"

"Yes," Schroder says. Landry went rogue. Though, thinking about it, Landry really made the same set of decisions that Schroder is making now. Only Landry screwed up and for that he paid the ultimate price, whereas Schroder isn't going to mess up. Not again. When he and Landry used to work together, there were no shortcuts, each of them was very by the book. By the book ended for Landry in a forest after he was hit by multiple shotgun rounds, a situation of his own making, trying to do the right thing by doing the wrong thing. By the book ended in the messiest way possible. By the book ended for Schroder when he had to shoot that old woman earlier in the year. She was the mother of a killer, a mother who had tortured and tormented her son and turned him into a monster. Schroder shot her to save a young girl's life, and if you're going to stop going by the book, that was the way to do it, not just dipping in your toe, but diving right in. Of course it led to him losing his job, which led to him no longer being a cop when he chased down the Carver, which led to him entering a situation without backup, which lead to him getting shot in the head. He was lucky he wasn't arrested too.

"Landry told me you drew out your life's savings and put it into a briefcase. You offered it to him."

"That never happened."

"You begged him to let you kill the men who had hurt Linda."

"Is that what this is about?" Peter asks, his voice rising. "You want to blackmail me?"

Schroder shakes his head. "I don't want your money. I'm trying to help somebody. Somebody like Linda. Somebody who was beaten and sliced and raped, somebody who went to Hell and came back, somebody the justice system let down, somebody who is about to be in a whole lot of trouble unless I do the right thing."

Peter leans further forward. "I don't understand. This right thing," he says, "has something to do with my wife. This right thing—you need me to help you?"

"The right thing isn't always the legal thing," Schroder says. "And no. I don't need you to help me. I'm not here because I need your help, Peter. When Landry told me what you did, it really upset him. He took me to a bar and we had a few drinks, and he said he wished there was a way he could help you. You know what he said? He told me he was thinking of faking some evidence, trying to find a way to prove the men who hurt your wife were innocent. He said that way they'd be let out of jail, and that way you could have your five minutes. I told him he couldn't do that, and he said he knew, that he was just blowing off steam, that it's a path he'd never take," he says, and he wonders if that was the night Landry started thinking about different paths. "I can tell you I really think he was thinking about doing it. Landry never liked the way the world was, but he couldn't do anything about it. And he felt responsible for your wife taking her own life."

"Responsible? How?"

"Because if he had given you your five minutes, then you could have beaten the crap out of those two men. He thought if he had found a way to let you do that, to let your wife have those five minutes too, then she might have been able to move forward with her life. He thought it would have given her something to hold on to."

"I think you should leave," Peter says. "All you're doing is bringing up painful memories."

"You said you've moved on, but in my experience people don't move on from something like that. I'm not here because I need your help, Peter, I'm here because you need mine. I can't give you closure, but I can give you a step towards it. I'm here because you asked Landry if you could have five minutes with the men who attacked your wife, and I can give that to you. I can give that to you tonight and it's not going to cost you a single dime. Or have you moved on like you say you have?"

Peter doesn't answer. His face has tightened. It looks like it could explode. "What, exactly, are you saying?"

"I'm saying exactly what you think I'm saying."

"It's been a long time," Peter says, "but the anger, you know, the anger never goes away. It burns deep. I've often thought of trying to find where they live, but, you know, I was always a . . . a coward. Having five minutes in a room while these guys are handcuffed to chairs is one thing, but finding where they live and going to them . . . I hated myself for a long time for never being able to protect my wife. I hated myself for not being the man who brought those bastards to justice."

"I can change that," Schroder says. "All you have to do is come with me."

"Now?"

"It has to be now."

Peter says nothing for five seconds. Then ten. Then he shakes his head. "I can't. I'm sorry. I wish I was that man, but I'm not."

"Are you sure?"

"Yes."

"Then I'll be on my way." He stands up. "Promise me you won't tell anybody about this."

"Who would I tell?"

"You could tell the police."

"I won't call them," he says. "I promise."

"You won't need to call them. They will come here to speak to you."

"Why?"

"Because I'm going to kill those men for you tonight, and they're going to ask if you did it."

Schroder walks out of the lounge.

Peter catches up with him outside, just past the weeds and near the street. "If I helped you the police would come and arrest me."

"Would you care if they did?"

"No, I . . . I guess not."

Schroder looks up and down the street. It's deserted. "The police wouldn't arrest you. The police will be looking for somebody who doesn't exist. These two men, they will hurt other people. It's what men like that do. It's who they are."

"And what kind of men are we if we hunt them down?"

Schroder doesn't even have to think about it. "Men who do the right thing."

Peter starts nodding. "I have a new life. When I think about what those men did . . . I want to be sick. Sometimes I am sick.

Sometimes I have to rush into the bathroom to throw up in the sink, the images of what they did to her are so strong I can't escape them. I want my five minutes. I want them for myself, and most of all I want them for Linda, but I can't. I'm sorry."

"What about for your daughter?"

"What do you mean?"

"Your daughter saw the whole thing, didn't she?"

Peter doesn't answer right away. He starts breathing harder and faster. "You don't need to remind me of that," he says. "Everything that happened to Linda, I often wonder if it was worse for Monica having to watch. I often wonder if the worst part for Linda was knowing our daughter was right there watching and crying and asking those men to please stop hurting her mommy. She doesn't remember it, not really," he says, and he looks angry, as angry as Schroder has ever seen anybody. "I had to get her counseling, of course, and for years she would wake up screaming and asking for her mother, and that was only if she slept, which she hardly did."

Schroder says nothing. He doesn't need to. He knows what's coming.

"Are you sure you can give them to me? The five minutes?"

"Yes."

"Will it change me? Will it make me a different person?"

"Yes," Schroder says.

"What kind of person?"

"One who does the right thing."

"Okay," Peter says. "Okay. Let me lock up. I'm coming with you."

CHAPTER SIXTEEN

My wife ends up sleeping for three hours. A nurse drops in a couple of times to check on us, or to make sure we're not stealing all the supplies. I kill ten minutes by inflating a rubber glove, tying off the end of it, and drawing in a face with a Sharpie. I don't hear anything from Kent. Sometimes no news is good news, but other times no news is no news.

Bridget wakes up slowly. Her eyes open, she smiles at me, then the smile fades as she realizes the environment is different. "Teddy?"

"We're at the mall," I tell her. "Do you remember what happened? How you got here?"

She shakes her head, then nods a little. "It's coming back to me," she says. "I'm thirsty."

I hand her some water. "Why did you come here?" I ask, and I struggle to keep the edge out of my voice. She shouldn't have come here alone. Not yet.

She takes a mouthful of water and hangs on to the cup. "I got the bus," she says. "I wanted to go shopping. Somehow, somehow I thought that Emily was missing, but she's not missing, is she, Teddy. It's worse than that, isn't it."

"I'm sorry," I tell her.

"I feel so stupid. And embarrassed." She finishes the water. "I want to go home."

I help her get to her feet. She looks at the rubber glove and smiles, so I bring it with us. We head down the hallway and downstairs and through the mall. There are hundreds, maybe thousands of people still here, and I put my arm around Bridget and we weave between them out to the parking lot. I can tell she's holding back the tears. When we get into the car she puts on her seat belt and she looks over at me and puts a hand on my arm.

"I don't want to be this way," she says.

"You won't be. I promise," I say, breaking the cardinal rule about making promises you don't know you can keep. "We're going to see Doctor Forster on Monday."

"You killed him."

"What? No, I said we're going to see him. I didn't—"

She starts shaking her head. "Not Doctor Forster. The man who hurt Emily. I remember. You took him into the woods and you made him dig his grave, and you put a bullet in his head. You made him plead for his life."

I look at her, and I feel dumfounded. We stare at each other in silence for a few seconds. "Why would you say that?"

"It happened, didn't it."

"Who told you?"

"You did," she says. "I can't remember you telling me, but I know you did. I feel it. Am I right? I can see it as if I was there."

My heart is racing and I've never lied to my wife, but now seems a good time to start. "Bridget—"

"I know. You can't tell me, in case I black out and tell some-body what happened. But that would never happen, because when things go wrong with me I go back three years, I go back to before you ever killed him. So I would never tell anybody. I'd be unable to."

"Bridget—"

She carries on, talking quickly. "You said you used to come and see me all the time. You would hold my hand and you would tell me about your day. You thought none of it was making it through, but some of it must have. I know you've killed other people too. Bad people. I know the pain you've gone through over the last few years. But I know you've also done a lot of good. You're a good person, Teddy."

There are other people walking past the car on the way to their own. Most of them are carrying purchases. Some are smiling and some are arguing and none of them know they're walking past a car where a woman is telling her husband that she knows he's a murderer. "I don't . . . don't know what to tell you."

"The truth." She squeezes my arm. "Just tell me the truth. The idea that the man who killed Emily is still out there free, that hurts, Teddy. Knowing he's dead won't give me closure, and if anything I wish you'd just arrested him, but the idea he's out there . . . I can't handle that."

"Okay," I tell her.

"Okay?"

"Okay."

She stares at me, but I don't look at her, instead I grip the steering wheel and look ahead, out through the windshield, beyond the cars and the people and the asphalt, beyond the buildings and into the woods and back into the past. "It was two weeks after the accident. I made him dig his own grave. He didn't want to, but he, you know, he did it because he had to keep delaying the inevitable. When he was done he told me he was a different person, that there was Quentin James the drinker, and there was Quentin James the man in front of me then. It was Quentin the drinker that had killed Emily, and for that he would be punished, and he would get help, and he would never drink again. He promised. He begged for his life. He said over and over how sorry he was."

I look to Bridget. There are tears in her eyes, but they're not falling, not yet.

"I took him out to the woods knowing what I was going to do to him, and there was no second-guessing. It felt right. Not righteous, but right."

"And you shot him in the head."

"Both versions of him," I say, the conversation feeling very matter-of-fact now.

"And did you feel better, Teddy? Did it help?"

"It didn't bring Emily back. It didn't make you okay," I say.

"Did it help you?"

"I don't know." I look back to the windshield and all that lies beyond. "I used to think that it didn't, but now . . . now I think it helped me carry on," I say, but what I really think is that it helped keep me alive.

"I love you," she says.

I look back up at her. "Are you sure?"

"Of course."

"Even after what I've done?"

"I said it before and I'll say it again, Teddy. You're a good person. You did what you thought was right," she says, which is very different from her telling me I did the right thing.

I lean over and hug her and she hugs me back for a few seconds, then pulls away. "Let's go home," she says.

I start the car.

"But first I want you to take me there," she says.

"Take you where?"

"The grave."

"Emily's grave?"

She shakes her head. "Quentin James's grave."

I'm halfway to putting on my seat belt when she says that. I pause and turn back towards her. "Why?"

"Because I want to see it."

"I don't think that's a good idea." I click the buckle into place.

"Please, Teddy. I want to go there. You did what you had to do, and you had to go through it by yourself. I want to be part of it. I know you, I know it changed you, but I also know it's a burden you've had to carry. Let me take some of that from you. I want to see what you saw. I want to go where you went. I want to see where you left the man that killed our daughter."

"Bridget—"

"Please, Teddy," she says. "Please do this for me."

"When?"

"Now," she says.

"Now?"

"Is there a better time?"

"I still think this is a really bad idea," I tell her, but I put the car into gear. "Are you sure?"

"As sure as I've ever been of anything."

CHAPTER SEVENTEEN

They pass nice houses and awful houses. They pass nice cars parked on streets and falling-apart cars parked up on lawns. They enter areas where cars can be fieldstripped by neighborhood kids in just a few minutes. Then they pop out the other side of it. That's one of the things about Christchurch—there's not a lot of real estate between where east meets west meets rich meets poor. Their destination turns out to be a neighborhood of average houses, which surprises Schroder because he had expected Bevin and Taylor Collard to be living on a shittier street, the kind of place that wouldn't look any worse off, say, if a bomb hit it. They've driven past the house twice in the last hour, and are now waiting one block away near a park, waiting for it to get darker. They don't have a great view of the house from here, but they can see if any cars come or go.

"They stole her wedding ring," Peter says.

For the last twenty minutes neither of them have said a word.

"When they attacked her," Peter says. "They stole her wedding ring. The police never found it, and the brothers denied they took it, but they must have."

"Landry never mentioned it."

"Well they did. Do you think they still have it? They will, right? That's why they take things like that, right? Not to sell, but as a memento. I read about it. After the attack I read all I could about these kinds of guys. Can you imagine that?" Peter asks. "You're married, right? Can you imagine something that belongs to your wife in the drawer or pocket or cupboard of somebody who attacked her? Like a notch on a bedpost, a score, it's sick," he says. "This thing that happened is the worst thing possible, it's the worst memory my wife could have, a memory that made her kill herself, and these guys keep that ring as a souvenir. Can you imagine a little girl having to grow up knowing the men she saw rape her mother are keeping a memento? We should go in there now," he says. "Knock on the door and start swinging."

"What if somebody else answers?" Schroder asks. "What if there are other people in the house?"

"If somebody else answers, we just say we have the wrong house and walk away."

"And if the right person answers and we hear others in the house?"

"Then we improvise," Peter says. "I want to get this done."

"We'll get it—"

"In fact let's start improvising now," Peter says, "because that could be them."

There's a car backing out from further up the block. A dark blue sedan. It turns towards them, the lowering sun shining into the windshield, and both the driver and passenger are squinting against it. The car comes towards them, goes by them, then is gone.

"Was that them?" Schroder asks. "I couldn't tell."

"It was them," Peter says, and his voice has gone hard, and Schroder knows his anger has just kicked up a notch. "So now what do we do? Break into their house and wait? Or follow them?"

Schroder starts the car. "Let's see where they go. We can always come back."

He does a U-turn and goes left at the next intersection the same way the brothers did, keeping a hundred yards between them. He is aware he is deviating from the plan. Is this what happens when people are planning on killing? He thinks it may be what gets them caught. The ones who don't deviate are still out there free.

The route suggests after a few minutes that the pair is driving into town. Schroder keeps the same distance, letting other cars get between them. The drive is fifteen minutes long, and ends for the Collard brothers near a service alleyway near the heart of town, where they pull into a parking space. Schroder comes to a stop

twenty yards further away outside a bank. The bank is closed—
it would have closed at five o'clock. All the shops in town will
have closed around the same time. There aren't many people on
the streets, not much traffic, but in another hour or two that will
change. He watches in the mirror as the brothers climb out of the
car. The older one, the bigger one, is Bevin. The shorter one, the
one with no hair, is Taylor. Though they're brothers by name, the
older one was adopted. It was the classic scenario where two people
didn't think they could have a child, so they adopted, and soon
after found they were pregnant. It's hard on everybody. During the
rape trial, the brothers pointed out their parents wanted neither of
them at that point, and that their upbringing was one full of bruises
and sprains, of starvation and nights locked in closets. The parents
weren't able to defend themselves against the accusations, they'd
both died in their early sixties—one of a brain tumor, the other of
cancer. There were no neighbors, teachers, doctors, or friends who
ever saw any signs of abuse, and Landry told him he was sure it was
all bullshit.

Bevin walks to the back of the car, lifts the trunk, and at that
moment the view of him is obscured. Schroder can't see what he
takes out, but then it comes into view. It's a bag. The men both go
into the alleyway.

"So now what?" Peter asks. "We go back to their house and wait
for them?"

"Let's wait a bit," Schroder says, "and see what happens."

"What's down there?" Peter asks.

"Dumpsters. Rubbish. Back doors that lead into the shops and
bars. Mostly bars. Mostly it's for deliveries," he says, but they're also
places to buy sex, drugs, and weapons. It's all very rock and roll. Of
course it's not just rubbish and dumpsters and drugs found in places
like this—but dead junkies, dead dealers, dead hookers. He thinks
about the two times he's died over the last year. The first was just
before Christmas last year. He was held in a bathtub full of water by
a man named Edward Hunter, his head beneath the surface, water
flooding his lungs and then it was lights out—only he was revived

a few minutes later. He coughed and spluttered and life moved on. The second time was with the bullet back in June. As the doctors worked on him he was clinically dead at one point for ninety seconds. Then the coma, then coming out of the coma, and life again moved on—this time in a different direction. If anything happens to him down that alleyway he knows there'll be no coming back from a third. There'll be no hat trick. Dead is dead is the kind of thing that can happen in alleyways like this.

Peter's voice goes hard again. "Let's go down there and get this done."

"Not yet," Schroder says.

"Come on, there's hardly anybody around."

"We wait till dark."

"It's just that . . . shit, you know. I want to get this done."

Schroder can hear the unspoken words to follow. *Before I lose my nerve. Before I change my mind.*

"Just stay angry," Schroder says. "And patient. By the end of the night you'll have gotten what I promised."

CHAPTER EIGHTEEN

We go home first. We have to, because Bridget needs to change into better shoes for the woods. She changes outfits too. We both do. We wear jeans and shirts and light jackets. We look like weekenders who know nothing about hiking who are about to go hiking. Saturday is winding down. The malls are shutting and the fast-food restaurants are being flooded with people finishing work, and in a few hours' time the central city will be wall-to-wall partying. We also switch cars. I don't want to drive out there in a police car, so we use my car.

We head north and out of the city. Long open stretches of road with other traffic, long open paddocks, we pass roads promising to lead off to more of the same. I keep driving, remembering how it was last time, with Quentin James unconscious in the trunk—though he woke up at some point during the journey. With his arms and legs bound, he just couldn't do anything about it.

After thirty minutes we take a turnoff, and then another turnoff, and then we're heading towards the forest. I park up in a secluded area. By this stage last time Quentin James was so disoriented from the ride in the trunk that he couldn't walk straight for the first few minutes.

"Are you sure about this?" I ask.

She squeezes my hand. "Yes."

We get out of the car and I take Bridget's hand and I lead her into the trees where thousands of birds are chirping, and where on occasion something rustles in the foliage, sometimes a bird, sometimes a hedgehog, but most times something unseen. Last time I took this walk I was carrying a gun and Quentin James was carrying a shovel. This isn't the middle of nowhere—it's close—but it was always possible somebody could have come along three years ago and seen what was happening, or have heard the gunshot. Three years ago I cared about what happened to me—I didn't want to go to jail—but I cared more about killing Quentin James. That was what mattered the most. It was all that mattered.

Trees are trees and I'm no tracker, but I know exactly where we are and I know exactly how to get where we're going, the memory of three years ago working like a roadmap. We walk for ten minutes and then we come across a patch of earth that looks like any other.

"This is it," I tell her, and she tightens her grip on my hand.

Rocks, moss, dirt, tree roots, and lots of trees. "Are you sure?" she asks.

"I'm sure."

"So he's down there."

"He's there."

"Tell me about him."

"He begged for his life," I say. "He told me—"

She shakes her head. "No, I mean tell me about him. Was he married? What did he do for a living? What made him an alcoholic? Did he have children?"

Some of this stuff I've told her over the last few months. A lot of this stuff I didn't know when I dragged him out of his house, but I learned it last year. I was involved in a car accident of my own. It made me aware things aren't always as they seem. Back when I killed him, I didn't know Quentin James's story. Now I do.

"He was forty-eight years old. He was divorced. He had a twenty-five-year-old daughter. He used to own his own business. He was a mortgage broker, but then times were tight and he had to shut up shop. He couldn't get another job. Everything he used to be, everything he used to have, he drank away. The drinking started when his wife left him. The drinking and driving not long after that. Time after time the police would catch him, and time after time he was fined, kept his car, and set free. He was always going to kill somebody, it was just a matter of who, where, and when." I pause for a few seconds, letting that sink in. "We should go."

"Give me a minute," she says.

"Okay."

"I mean give me a minute alone."

I let go of her hand and walk back in the direction we came. After about twenty paces I stop. Bridget is kneeling next to the grave. She's saying something, but I can't hear what. I sit down on a fallen log and I stare in the distance in the direction of the car. I check my phone and see it has no signal out here. If Quentin James was still alive under the ground and his cell phone battery was still good, he'd still be unable to call for help. All the birds have stopped chirping. There is no breeze, no sound, the forest has gone quiet.

Then suddenly it all starts up again. The rustling, the natural sound of trees and wind and living things. I hear twigs breaking and footsteps and then Bridget is standing behind me with a hand on my shoulder.

"I'm okay," she tells me.

We walk back to the car, neither of us saying anything, neither of us needing to, Bridget thinking about our daughter, me thinking about her too, and I wonder what it was my wife said to the man beneath the earth. When we get back to the car the sun has almost gone, just the edge of it poking over the horizon. We're back into cell-phone range. There's a message from Kent, telling me to call her back.

"How's Bridget?" she asks, and Bridget is sitting in the car while I lean against it talking on the phone.

"She's back to normal. She knows what's going on."

"Good, that's good. And encouraging, right?"

I hear myself agreeing with her. "Yes, it's encouraging."

"We just got a call from the medical examiner. Want to have a guess as to what she said?"

"She thinks that Smith hated his job, couldn't see that ever changing, so drove out to the train tracks and laid himself down on them. She thinks he didn't kill himself in jail because back then he thought things were going to get better, and that his goal in life was to be killed by a train."

"I'm sure she thinks all kinds of things that are beyond the scope of her job," Kent says, "but she called us with what she knows."

"And what is it she knows?"

"She knows that Dwight Smith was dead before he found himself on those train tracks. She isn't sure for how long, not exactly, but she seems to think between an hour and two. That means we're now officially dealing with a murder investigation. And as much as I hate to say it, that also means Kelly Summers is going to be our number-one suspect. Hutton wants us to go and pick her up."

"What? Now?"

"No. It's the end of the day, and we all figure Kelly Summers isn't going anywhere. We'll go take a closer look at her house in the morning, and take her in for questioning. I don't want her to have done it, I really don't, but what else can we do?"

I don't answer her, and after a few seconds I realize the question isn't rhetorical. I think she really is asking me what else can we do. Only all we can do for Kelly Summers is hope that somebody else was involved, that somebody intercepted Dwight Smith before he got to her house. If that didn't happen, then Kelly Summers could end up going to jail for a very long time.

CHAPTER NINETEEN

The alleyway is near the center of the city, a few blocks away from Christchurch Cathedral, a church where Schroder once arrested a naked guy who had painted his genitals black, put a white collar around the base of his penis, and stood outside the main doors during lunch hour asking people to praise the Lord. When they got him back to the station, he tried to hang himself in his holding cell. They rushed him off to hospital where he was under care for two days, then put on suicide watch for a week, then on the way back to the station a guy in another vehicle was simultaneously having a heart attack and running a red light, and those events saw that guy plowing his car into the transport van and killing the suspect. Schroder always thought it was the equivalent of saving an injured seal and returning it to the ocean only to see it swallowed by a whale.

The city has gotten dark. It happened in degrees as they came up with different plans. Seven o'clock and the sky glowed red on the horizon, it reflected off the shop windows, it looked like lava. The eight o'clock shadows gave way to nine o'clock shadows. They were longer. The lava on the windows had cooled. Soon the shadows were gone, the sky a dirty blue, each passing minute turning it black. And still they waited.

By ten o'clock the only light is coming from the streetlights and from the bars around the corner. There are a few lights on inside the bank, and in some of the stores too, there for passersby to notice if somebody is breaking in. A few people walk past Schroder and Crowley, not many, though foot traffic at the end of the block is heavy because at the end of the block and around the corner are the bars the alleyway services.

The brothers are either still down there or they've gone through the back entrance to one of the bars. Nobody else has shown up. Nobody else has come out. Peter is always in a state of motion, his body one moment tight with anticipation, the next almost loose enough to slide under the door. Schroder should have done this alone, and he could have, but he wouldn't be much of a Five Minute Superhero if he didn't give people their five minutes.

"It's time," Schroder says.

"Finally."

"Two minutes," Schroder says. "Don't be late."

"I won't be."

Schroder gets out of his car. Before leaving Peter's house, he had filled one of the small, empty plant pots with some wet dirt. He now smears that dirt across both license plates, tosses the container back into the car, wipes his hands on his jeans, then crosses the road.

He can hear music coming from around the corner, the *beat-beat-beat* playing right alongside laughter and girls screaming in delight, a blast of foul language, the hubbub of life, guys yelling *hey bro* and *hey mate* over all of it. He walks to the alleyway, his hands deep in his pockets. When he gets there he's a guy now staggering a little. He's just a guy who's had too much to drink, a guy outside trying to clear his head, maybe looking for a dumpster he can take a piss behind.

On the left is the wall to a sporting store; the music store where, almost twenty-five years ago, his dad brought him to buy his guitar; and a bookstore. To the right are the back walls of the bars. There are stacks of flattened cardboard boxes everywhere. Bags of trash, most of them sealed, some of them torn apart by cats and mice, a large cardboard box lying on the ground with it's *this way up* arrows pointing the direction that Schroder is walking, making them *Head this way for trouble* arrows. It smells down here too, a combination of rotten food and wet dog, a gagging kind of smell, the kind of smell that requires a few showers to remove. He walks in and stops halfway, twenty-five yards of real estate behind him, twenty-five yards of it ahead, before the alleyway terminates. Either the brothers are further up, or they've gone through one of the doors, but he thinks they're further up. He has a pretty good idea why these men are down here. There are different types of music from the different bars, each competing to drown out the other, different beats, different tempos, some of the doors are ratting in their frames.

He moves forward. He counts off the seconds in his head. The back doors to the shops come and go. There's some light, but not much, and less the further the alleyway goes. Beneath the lights that aren't going are jagged bits of glass as rocks and bottles have been thrown at them. He stops ten yards later and turns back towards the street. He's in no-man's-land now. No wonder lots of bad shit happens in these kinds of places.

He is ten yards from the end of the alleyway when he first becomes aware somebody is following him. He stops. He turns. A bottle starts rolling across the ground from behind one of the dumpsters. He's walked right past somebody and not seen them hidden in the shadows.

He turns from the bottle. Up ahead a figure is standing at the end of the alleyway. There's a single, dim lightbulb overhead providing barely enough light to see him. A glance behind him shows the man he walked past is now picking up the bottle. Schroder turns towards the first figure he saw. The man is around six feet. Wearing black and with dark hair and a trail of tattoos from his hands leading under the sleeves of his jacket. Bevin Collard. He can hear the guy behind him getting closer too. The brother.

"What you looking for, buddy?" Bevin asks, and his voice is deep and gravelly and Schroder doesn't like it, not one bit. He's dealt with plenty of assholes in his day who all had similar voices.

"What are you selling?"

"Nothing. How about you just be on your way?"

Schroder shakes his head. "How about you give me what I'm asking for?"

"Only thing you're asking for is trouble," Bevin says.

There's a bag on the ground by Bevin's feet. Schroder points at it. "What will two hundred dollars get me?"

"Mugged, if you don't fuck off," Bevin says.

"Come on, guys, my money is good."

"Yeah, for getting mugged. You've seen too many movies, buddy, if you think we're drug dealers. How about you just be on your way and go back to your wife and kids and mortgage and your white picket fence, huh?"

He knows they're selling drugs. There's no other reason for them to be down here. He also knows that's why they're not going to hurt him. They can't. Because if they hurt him, then the police get involved, then they can't come back to their favorite spot for selling drugs to the people who frequent these clubs. He's still counting off the seconds. He's at ninety now.

"My wife left me," he says, "and I don't have a picket fence. I want what I came here for."

"Listen, mate, to me it seems like you've come here because you're looking for a bad place in town to be punished in, but this isn't it."

Schroder nods. "You're almost right," he says.

"Almost?"

"Yeah. Almost. Maybe a guy like me might come to a place like this because he wants to punish somebody else. You think of that?"

Nobody answers him. He can sense the guy behind him tensing up. So is the guy up front.

"Ah, geez, buddy, why'd you have to go and say something like that," Bevin says. Schroder doesn't answer. The two minutes are up. "See, that sounds like a threat. Sounds like you think you can take both of us on. Does that sound about right?" he asks, taking a step forward.

"Sounds about right, Bevin," Schroder says.

The question comes. It was always going to come. "How do you know my name?"

"I know it because I'm a concerned citizen. Lots of things concern me, or at least they used to. I used to care about global warming, about terrorism, about the economy. I should care that the bullet inside my skull is going to cross the finish line. But I don't. But what I do care about is getting Linda Crowley's wedding ring back."

"Who the hell are you?" Bevin asks.

Then, from behind Taylor, comes a set of headlights. The bright beams pointing at them, and all three are lifting hands to shield their eyes as the lights make their shadows stretch and dance across the walls. The car stops five yards short of Taylor. Then the driver, who leaves the lights on and the engine running, opens the door. He climbs out a little awkwardly because of the cricket bat he's keeping out of view.

"Hope I'm not interrupting anything, guys, but where the hell can I score some decent pussy around here?"

"You're in the wrong place, mister," Taylor says.

The driver stares at him, then turns slightly to his left and right. "You sure?"

"Positive," Taylor says.

"I don't know. This seems like the place," the man says, stepping forward. "I mean, I see a couple of pussies right here." He produces the cricket bat. He produces it in the same step that he takes towards Taylor, he raises it on his next step, and on his third he brings it around and smashes it into the side of Taylor's head. It's a one-swing deal. Taylor has gotten his arm up to stop it, but it's a useless effort, the bat most likely breaking it on the way through to a good, solid home run. A game-ending home run.

Taylor drops without understanding why, either dead before hitting the ground or one or two seconds after. Probably not a bad way to go out, Schroder thinks, compared to what is going to happen to his brother who, according to their interview statements, did ninety percent of the raping while Taylor did ninety percent of the watching.

When he turns back around Bevin is no longer facing him. He's looking for a way out. He's five yards from the end of the alley. Two. One. Then he's hard up against the wall. He tries the nearest door, but it's locked. He turns back towards Schroder, then reaches into his pocket and pulls out a knife.

"Put it down, Bevin," Schroder says. "Put it down and climb into the car and it'll go much easier. We just want to talk."

"Fuck you, man."

"We're going to get you into that car, Bevin, and we can do it the easy way or the hard way."

"Then it's going to be—"

The glass bottle whistles as it flies through the air, end over end, and it hits Bevin right in the middle of the forehead. He drops just as quickly as his brother. Schroder thinks that makes for pretty good symmetry.

"Nice shot," Schroder says.

"All those years playing cricket just paid off," Peter says. Then he looks down at the body by his feet. "I messed up. I didn't mean to hit the other guy so hard. I think he's dead already. I wanted my five minutes with him too."

"How about you take ten minutes with this one then?"

Peter nods. "I guess that works."

"Let's get them loaded into the car before somebody comes out of one of these doors. Oh, and make sure you grab the bottle. That's the only thing you touched, right?"

"Yeah."

"Good," Schroder says. "Come on, let's get this done."

CHAPTER TWENTY

Peter drives and Schroder gives directions. The brothers are stuffed into the trunk. A check by Peter for a pulse on Taylor confirmed Bevin is now an only child. As for Bevin, he's back there with his legs and arms tied up. Beneath them, keeping blood off the car, is a shower curtain.

"Are you sure you know the way?" Peter asks.

They've been driving for twenty minutes, most of that on the same road, then the turnoff, then the complicated maze of neglected roads without signposts, they go from tarmac to gravel and back and forth, never settling on one for too long. "I know it doesn't seem like it, but we're nearly there."

"I want to get started," Peter says.

"We've already started," Schroder says, and a moment later they're pulling into an entrance half-hidden and half-guarded by a pair of large oaks. The road goes from tarmac to gravel. Slimmer trees line the driveway to an abandoned building up ahead. It's an old mental institution by the name of Grover Hills, built almost a hundred years ago, abandoned for the last ten of those after the government took funding away from mental health institutions, penny-pinching to fund other schemes while simultaneously flooding the streets with a whole lot of crazies. The only thing climbing the walls these days are vines of ivy, they cling to the weatherboards, they wrap around the downpipes and thread themselves around the guttering. It looks like nature itself is doing its best to pull the building and the memories made here into the ground.

He brings the car up to the front entrance. This place was out of sight and out of mind for ten years until several months ago when one of the crazies came back. An ex-patient, homesick for the institution, started living here, along with a collection of people he began abducting. Schroder was still a cop then. Was still a family man and a by-the-book man. This isn't where he was going to bring Dwight Smith last night. It's similar—Grover Hills is one of three abandoned institutions out in these middle-of-nowhere parts, but this is the one he chose tonight because downstairs is a room perfect for their needs.

They get out of the car and it bounces and shifts on its springs and settles. Schroder stretches out his back and Peter does the same, some clicks and some pops and then they walk up to the front door. It has been padlocked closed, a chain running through the handles, but Schroder would never have been a very good cop if he didn't know how to pick a padlock. It takes him a couple of minutes, and then the chain is on the front step and the door hinges protest a little as he opens them, but then they're inside, the halls dark and unwelcoming, six patient rooms downstairs, a kitchen, a communal area for eating and TV, toilets, showers, offices, and upstairs another two dozen rooms all for patients. He can still remember the layout. Abandoned furniture, nothing worth more than what it would take to come out here and retrieve them, can be found in most of these rooms. And ghosts. If there are such things as ghosts, then this is where they would be. "It feels like people died out here, and that they suffered," Peter says, which reminds Schroder of Jonas Jones, the psychic he briefly worked with earlier in the year.

"They did," Schroder says, and not just earlier in the year with the crazy guy who thought he was returning home, but over the years this place operated. "Patients were tortured here. We found some of them buried out in the grounds."

"Jesus," Peter says.

"They say Jesus saves," Schroder says. "But He didn't save these people. Come on, it's this way." Schroder turns on a flashlight, the beam picking out the dust floating through the air, stirred up from the door opening. He leads them to a closed door. "This is it," he says, and swings it open to more protesting hinges. Behind the door are concrete stairs leading down into darkness. Schroder leads the way, the sound of his footsteps not echoing, but being swallowed up by the room. He moves the flashlight around, spotlighting an old couch, an old coffee table, an old bookcase. There's a wall forming a partition running left to right, in the middle of it a heavy iron door.

"This is where they died?" Peter asks.

"Patients used to call it the scream room," Schroder says.

Peter looks sick. "I can't believe there are things like this in this world."

"Really? After what was done to your wife, you don't think places like this exist?"

Peter doesn't answer.

They head outside. The cloud cover has broken up. Without any light pollution, they can see a thousand times as many stars. Tiny pinpricks, some flickering against the night sky, an endless amount of worlds. *It's beautiful*, he thinks, and for a moment, a brief moment, he thinks what it would be like to lie on the ground with his wife and stare up at them. It is, he realizes, the first time he's missed her.

The moment doesn't last. He pops open the trunk. Bevin has woken up, but the gag is keeping him quiet and the plastic ties are stopping any attempt of escape. Even so he's squashed so tightly in the trunk against his dead brother he couldn't have moved anyway. They pull him out and let him bounce off the bumper onto the ground, a grunt making it through the gag, then they pick him up and between them carry him to the scream room with the big iron door. They dump him on an old cot shoved against the wall. Collard straightens himself until he's sitting up with his feet on the ground. His hands are still bound behind him. There's blood dripping down them from where he's been struggling.

Schroder hands the flashlight towards Peter. It's solid and holds six batteries and is used by security guards to make shadows disappear and crack skulls.

"Now what?" Peter asks.

"Now you get your five minutes."

Peter reaches out and takes the flashlight. "It isn't how I thought it'd be."

"It never is."

"I mean—he looks so pathetic."

There is something different between last night and tonight. Last night Kelly Summers was chomping at the bit to have her five minutes. Last night Summers was angry because Smith had broken into her house. He was going to rape and kill her. She was running on fear and adrenaline and the need to see justice. Most of Peter's anger is still in the past, and any vengeance he wanted perhaps he got in the alleyway. He has to bring that anger forward.

"You're not angry enough," Schroder says.

"I'm angry," Peter says.

"No," Schroder says. "Nine years ago you were wild. Nine years ago if I'd brought you out here, you'd have made me pull over on the way just to break some of his bones and take a piss on him. I want you to do something for me."

"What?"

"I want you to close your eyes for a moment."

"Why?"

"Because it's important. Please, just for a moment."

Peter looks at him, then takes a few steps back from the room with Collard and closes his eyes.

"I want you to visualize what happened to your wife," Schroder says. "I want you to imagine her naked beneath this guy, with his sweaty hands all over her, with him fucking her, with your daughter close by watching and crying and asking them to stop. I want you to think about his brother egging him on, about your wife crying, her broken arms and shaved head, about—"

"Enough," Peter says. "What the hell is wrong with you?"

"He violated your wife, he laughed and grunted and—"

"Enough."

"Your wife prayed you would come home and save her and—"

"Enough!" Peter shouts, and this time he steps forward and

shoves Schroder in the chest, and he lets it happen, taking two steps back to absorb the impact. "Go and get me the cricket bat then leave me the hell alone."

Schroder leaves the flashlight with Peter. He takes the stairs out onto the veranda and takes another look up at the stars. The night has gotten chillier as it's gotten closer to midnight. They still have plenty of time, but he would like to get this done soon. The sooner the bodies are found, the sooner Tate will see a pattern forming that doesn't involve Kelly Summers. But for the pattern to stick, he'll need a third. One is unique, two is a coincidence, but three is a pattern. The sooner he is done with this, the sooner he can figure out who he'll choose for tomorrow night, then Kelly Summers and Peter Crowley won't look like suspects. He heads over to the car and grabs the bat and returns to the scream room where Peter is pacing in small circles, his hands clenching and unclenching. Schroder can feel the anger radiating off him. He hands him the bat and is ready to jump back in case Peter decides blood from one man isn't enough.

"Nobody can hear us, right?" Peter asks.

"That was one of the purposes of the room," he says. "Close that door and nobody is going to hear a thing, not that anybody would—there's nobody around for miles." Peter rests the flashlight on the coffee table so it lights up Bevin Collard. Urine is dripping off the edge of the mattress onto the floor, and he's crying. Peter takes the gag from his mouth.

"Please don't do this," Bevin says.

"You killed my wife."

"It wasn't me, it was Taylor. I tried to stop him, we just wanted to frighten her, that's all, but your wife hit Taylor and got him mad and things. . . . Please, I'm sorry, you have to believe me I'm so sorry. . . . Things just got out of control. Shit, I'm sorry, okay?"

"Sorry doesn't help."

"You're going to die here," Schroder tells him, a little worried Collard's act might change Peter's mind. He needs to get this back on track. "There's no escaping that fact. So ask yourself, do you want to die begging for your life, or do you want to die like a man?"

"Fuck you," Bevin says, looking at Schroder. Then he looks at Peter. "Please, man, please, think about this."

"You hurt her in front of our daughter," Peter says, and there are tears on his face, but there's rage there too. Mostly rage. "You raped my wife and you broke our daughter."

"Please—"

"You're a monster," Peter says.

"Please—"

Peter shakes his head. "You brought this on yourself," he says. "You're just lucky I didn't kill you ten years ago."

Bevin's screams follow Schroder up the stairs and out of the room, and they follow him onto the veranda where he sits and waits and stares out at the shapes in the darkness, and then they end when the iron door is closed. He sits down on the step and looks up at the stars. Then he looks out at the fields and the drive-way and then the car. All that darkness is broken up by a single light coming from the trunk of his car. They left it open after pulling Bevin out. The light is annoying him, and the last thing they need is for the battery to die. He gets up and moves over to the car to take care of that problem, only just like last night, things aren't going to plan.

Taylor Collard has gone.

CHAPTER TWENTY-ONE

I can't get to sleep. Bridget is. She's in bed lying on her back, both arms stretched over her head, her fingers interlocking, as if she's dreaming about throwing a hammer in the Olympics. For a while I sat in the room watching her, but now I'm out in the lounge watching TV. *Finding the Dead* is on, which is a New Zealand show about psychics who hunt out sad stories and capitalize on them. At least that's how some people see it. Others see it a different way—psychics helping where the police have failed. There are a few psychics on the show, the main one being Jonas Jones, and it's the show Schroder worked on too. For the show to be on this late at night means it's either a rerun or ratings are poor, but either way I find after thirty seconds of watching I feel queasy, as if Jones just entered my lounge and licked the back of my neck. I change channels, there's a movie on about a talking rodent, and for some reason the human race feels like it can always do with one more talking-rodent movie. Before I can change channels again, my cell phone starts ringing.

I look at the time. It's late.

"It's Sunday," I tell Kent.

"Only by five minutes," she says.

"I don't work Sundays, and I don't work after midnight."

"Nobody likes working on Sundays and nobody likes working after midnight, Tate. Including me. So we're on the same page here."

The same page. Are we?

"Okay. What have you got?"

"Drugs, blood, and a knife."

"No body?"

"No body, but a couple of witnesses said they saw one being loaded into the trunk of a car," she says.

I lean forward and pinch the bridge of my nose, my thumb and finger gently rubbing my eyes as I connect the dots. "Okay, and since you're calling me this late at night, it's connected to Kelly Summers somehow, right?"

"See? This is why you're a great detective."

"Give me the details."

"The report came in, and immediately a couple of officers were sent to the scene," she says. "A Saturday night—well, the report could be anything. Could be fake, could be some drunk kids got the details wrong, could be they saw some people overloading themselves into a car, or could be just a prank. But the cops go there and they find a knife and a bag full of cannabis, all bagged up into individual packets. The kind of thing nobody alive would leave behind."

"So why isn't this just some drug deal gone bad?"

"Because the drugs would have been taken. The two guys who called it in said they couldn't make out the registration plate of the car. They were pretty drunk—but not drunk enough to ignore what they had seen. We're lucky they even called it in. One of them is fifteen, the other sixteen, both should have been at home. They really do start young in this city, don't they," she says, and yes they do. Underage drinking and binge drinking are what Christchurch is becoming well known for. "So the natural thing is for the officers at the scene to get the knife fingerprinted."

"Don't tell me the prints belong to Dwight Smith?"

"I won't tell you that, because they don't. They belong to a guy by the name of Bevin Collard."

"Bevin Collard?" I stop rubbing at my eyes, but keep them closed. "I remember him. It was one of Landry's cases, right?"

"Right, so it's kind of ironic because the abduction took place behind Popular Consensus. That's the bar Landry's brother owns," she says, and I remember the brother and the bar because that's where the wake for Landry was held. "The alleyway runs behind that and a bunch of others. You get the connection now?"

I get it. A dead rapist last night, and one abducted tonight. I'm starting to think somebody last night was following Dwight Smith. I think he followed him to Kelly Summers's house, and after Dwight broke the lock on the window, but before he could go inside, he ended up being forced to drive out to the train tracks. He probably had a gun to his head or a knife to his throat the whole way. And that same person put Bevin Collard into the trunk of a car tonight.

Sometimes a shower curtain is just a shower curtain.

"Tate?"

"Yeah, I get it. So now the question is are we going to find Bevin Collard later on tonight beneath a train."

"Honestly, Theo, I think that's as good a place as any for him. I'll see you in a few minutes."

"I can't leave Bridget," I tell her.

"I know, that's why I'm coming to pick you up, and that's why I'm bringing my sister with me."

"What?"

"To look after Bridget in case she wakes up."

"You have a sister?"

"Two of them," she says. "And a brother. Get dressed. We're almost at your house."

I'm still dressed so I use what time I have to write Bridget a note in case she wakes while I'm gone, explaining that I'm gone and that Rebecca's sister will be out in the lounge watching TV. I also put on the kettle with the hope of making a coffee to help wake me up, but I don't get to make it before a car pulls up outside. I step out and pull the front door behind me, leaving it open about an inch. I walk down to the car where two women are climbing out. Rebecca's sister is a shorter and younger version of Rebecca, same shoulder-length dark hair, same big blue eyes, and no doubt turns the same amount of heads Rebecca would have before the explosion.

"This is Phillipa," Rebecca says, and I put out my hand and so does Phillipa. Her grip is warm and firm and her smile is warm and wide. I immediately like her.

"Glad you can help out," I tell her.

"Anytime."

"Phillipa used to be a nurse," Kent says, "so Bridget is in good hands."

Phillipa shrugs, dismissing the comment as if it's no big deal. I spend thirty seconds thanking her, and telling her to help herself to anything in the fridge, then Kent tells her we'll be back as soon as we can. Kent is in her own car, and I still have the unmarked police car at my house, so we leave hers parked on the side of the road and switch cars. Kent gets behind the wheel.

"Used to be a nurse?" I ask.

"It's a long story," Kent says.

"She wasn't putting her patients to sleep, was she?"

"No," she says, and doesn't elaborate.

It's a ten-minute drive into town and there's very little traffic. Sometimes on a Friday or Saturday night the streets can be congested with boy-racers in their souped-up cars, but not this Saturday. Maybe they're all off binging on Happy Meals and beer. We get into town where the atmosphere is electric, where there is so much body spray on the air that a lightning strike would ignite it. The streets are buzzing with energy. The alleyway has been cordoned off by two patrol cars and a station wagon, and on this side of the cordon people are taking time out from drinking and dancing to see what's going on, all the girls wearing very little and all the guys trying their best to look sharp in mainstream clothes. I immediately feel old. I'm a granddad to all these kids, I'm twice their age, I'm to them what people turning forty were to me twenty years ago, back when I had young man's knees. I am to them what eighty-year-old people are to me. How. The hell. Has time gone by?

We walk through the crowd. I can see people turning towards Rebecca for different reasons, on one side guys are staring at her beauty, on the other they're staring at her scarred face. She keeps looking straight ahead.

"Where's Hutton?" I ask the officer standing by the crime-scene tape.

"Back at the station. He's pulling information together about Bevin Collard."

"And the witnesses?"

He points his thumb in the direction of one of the patrol cars. "In the backseat," he says. "Let me show you what we have."

He walks into the alleyway and we follow. There are doors on the left and right, all of them servicing shops and bars and restaurants. From behind the ones on the right comes the base and beat as DJs deafen the crowds. There are bags of rubbish, there are dumpsters, there's a permanent chill and a sense that ten minutes down here would shrink your will to live. The officer points his flashlight towards some spots of blood about fifteen yards before the alleyway ends.

"Knife was over here," he says, then points the flashlight at the spot where it was found.

"Any blood on it?" I ask.

"Nothing. Just the prints," he says.

"Security cameras?" I ask, looking up outside the doors.

"Nothing," the officer says. "No cameras. Just the blood and the knife and the drugs and two drunk boys who saw part of it."

One of the doors opens and a couple of guys step outside, beers in one hand and cigarettes in the other. They look at us, then quickly go back inside. I walk over to the door, but it's already locked.

"They don't just come out for the weed," the officer says. The knife has been bagged and tagged, but not the drugs. They're still here. He crouches down beside the bag they're in and opens a side compartment. "Check this out." He holds up a couple of small zip-lock bags with pills inside them. "And look at this," he says, then pulls out a flare, the kind of flare you put at the scene of an accident to warn other traffic. "First sign of cops and this bag was getting torched, along with all the evidence inside it."

We head back towards the street. We cover half the distance and come to a stop next to a dumpster that somebody will go through soon enough. An officer is coming towards us, walking next to him a man I've only met once in my life: Bill Landry's brother. Kyle Landry puts his hand out and I shake it, and at the same time the officer tells us that Kyle here has information that might be useful. Kyle does look a lot like his brother. Same sharp features, same grim look of determination, he looks ready to blame the world for something.

"It's Theodore, right?" he asks.

"Right," I tell him.

"And Rebecca," he says, looking at Kent. "I remember you guys. Been a hell of a year for the four of you," he says, and by the four of us he means me, Schroder, Kent, and his brother. I figure it's a miracle only one of us is dead. The officer nods at us and I nod back, indicating we're okay to take it from here, then he wanders back towards the street.

"Your brother was a good cop," I tell him.

"I know," he says. "I also know he didn't like you much, though."

I'm not sure how to respond to that, so I don't, and he seems to hear what he just said then waves it away. "Don't worry about it," he says. "That was Bill. He often had a stick up his ass for the wrong reasons."

"Did you see something happen here?" Kent asks.

"Tonight? No. But I thought you guys might like to know this is a pretty popular place for selling drugs. People slip out of the back of the club, and of course it's not like we can chain those doors closed because they're fire exits, and we don't have the resources to hire bouncers just to keep an eye on them."

"You didn't call the police?"

"My brother was the cop in the family," he says, "not me. There have been people selling drugs down that alleyway for months and I just always figured somebody in the department must have heard about it by now, and just as equally figured nobody cared enough."

"You figured wrong," Kent says. "And I think drugs in the alleyway is good for business, right?"

"Like I said, my brother was the cop in the family, not me."

"You got any names?"

"What? You mean do I have the names of the people who would sometimes come along and sell drugs? No, no I don't. Listen, before we get too far down the path of you guys being pissed at me, I actually approached these guys a few months ago and told them to clear out. One of them pulled a knife on me and he told me if I ever spoke to either him or his brother again, they'd cut me up. Later that night after close of business somebody threw a rock through my window. After what happened to Bill, you know, I just figured I was best to mind my own business, and if these guys wanted to sell some weed and not stab me in the process, then who was I to say no? The body is a temple and all that crap, and if these kids want to come out here and poison themselves, then who am I to stop them?"

"You sure that's what he said?" I ask.

"Huh?"

"About him and his brother."

"That's what he said."

"You ever see one of these guys out here by themselves?"

"Always as a pair." He reaches into his pocket and pulls out a packet of cigarettes, then smiles sheepishly. "It's a family curse. Cigarettes were killing my brother, or would have if he'd lived another few months. Lung cancer got our father too. Sometimes you just can't escape genetics."

"Okay, hang around for bit, would you?" I ask. "We've got a detective on his way back with some information, including some photographs. Will you be able to identify these two guys if we show you?"

"I can identify the guys who sold drugs, yeah," he says, "but that doesn't mean it was the same guys out there tonight."

He walks back towards the cordon.

"It was both brothers who hurt that woman, right?" Kent says, and her hands are making gestures in the air as she talks. "How possible is it both Bevin and his brother were abducted from here?"

"I don't know. Twice as possible or half as possible as only one of them being abducted?"

"That doesn't even make sense," she says.

"Does any of this? How do you think he got here?" I ask Kent. "Bevin?"

She shrugs. "Maybe his brother dropped him off. Or if they came together, maybe they drove? Maybe both of them got stuffed into somebody else's trunk? "

"So where's their car?"

"Okay, I get your point," she says. "Give me a minute," she says, and gets out her phone.

We walk the rest of the way down the alleyway and into the growing number of people. I move ahead of Kent, clearing a pathway for us as Kent talks on her phone, somebody yells out *Here Piggy, Piggy,* and somebody else yells out *It's Babe the Pig! Only uglier! Show us some dance moves, Scarface Piggy!*

We get through the crowd and Kent looks calm and collected, but there's something in her eyes that betrays how she's really feeling. She's still holding the phone up to her ear, but at an angle that tells me she's waiting.

"You want me to go back in there and shoot them?" I ask.

"Would you? Or is that too much to ask?"

"Hmm . . ." I really look like I'm thinking about it. "Might be a bit extreme," I say.

"Maybe just shoot them in the kneecaps? Or better yet, slice their faces open and let them heal like mine," she says, and there is no humor in her words. Before I can answer, she puts her hand up to stop me and focuses on the phone call. I look into the back of the patrol cars and spot the one with the two kids who reported the crime. Kent nods and she says *okay* a few times, and then she writes something down on her pad. When she hangs up her mood has improved.

"I know what we're looking for," she says.

"And?"

"And it's right behind you," she says, and points to a car that is ten yards from where our car is parked. It's a dark blue four-door sedan with a bumper sticker with a picture of a chess piece on it that says *Bishop Takes Porn*. The car is locked. "Two, maybe three rapists in two nights. I get the feeling it's going to be a long night."

And I have the experience not to argue with her because she's right. I also have enough experience to tell me there is something else going on here.

I just can't figure out what.

CHAPTER TWENTY-TWO

Hopefully Taylor Collard is so badly hurt he's just wandering in a random direction and they'll find him soon. Schroder closes the trunk, then opens the door to the car. The keys are still in the ignition. If this is all about to go bad for him and Peter, he doesn't want these two assholes being able to drive home. Those assholes at the very least can walk. He hides the keys beneath the step leading up to the veranda. He can't feel any eyes on him. He moves inside. He knows his way around better than anybody else out here. There is no light coming from the basement, but that could just be because the iron door down there is shut.

He holds his arms out like a man who's woken from the dead and searching for brains, stumbling forward and letting his fingers brush against the wall. The air coming from the basement feels a few degrees cooler than the rest of the building. He reaches for his cell phone. If he uses the display for light, then the Collards are going to know where he is if they are down here. If he doesn't use it, he's going to trip on the stairs and break his neck. So he uses it, but the display is limited, he's lucky to see a foot in front of him. Slowly he makes his way down, ready to duck and react, but he gets there without any conflict. The cell door is open. Peter is lying facedown on the floor. He isn't moving.

Upstairs he hears floorboards squeaking, then the front door to the building is being slammed shut. He runs up the stairs in time to hear the chain being pulled through the handle. He bangs against it as the padlock latches into place.

"Fuck you, loser," Bevin Collard yells, his gravelly voice annoying Schroder more now than it did earlier. He rattles the doors, but it's useless.

He heads back into the basement. He's cautious going into the cell. If you're in there and the door is locked behind you, then there's no way out. Sure, the front door to the whole building is locked, but better two stories of patient rooms to move around in than a scream room the size of a jail cell. One side of Peter Crowley's skull has been dented in. The first blow probably killed him, only there was more than one blow because there's a line of blood on the ceiling, cast off from the second and third blow. Then he notices the beer bottle. Or pieces of it. The same one from the alleyway. Taylor must have brought it with him from the car. The first and second blow didn't smash it, but the third one did. One of the pieces of glass was probably used to cut the plastic ties securing Bevin.

Last night didn't go to plan, but compared to this, last night went like a dream.

He crouches next to Peter and puts a hand on his shoulder. The guy deserved his five minutes, he deserved his revenge, and this is his reward, his ultimate reward for having his wife raped, his wife dying, his reward for being angry about it.

"I'm sorry," he tells him, but Peter doesn't answer him. He just continues to lie facedown in a pool of his own blood. No amount of apologizing is going to undo this, but he gives it a shot. "I'm really, really sorry," he says, and he means it. He means it because he cares. Right now he is caring a lot, and right now he doesn't want these guys finding him and killing him. Nor does he want to go to jail.

"I'll make them pay, I promise," he says. "I hope that's at least some comfort."

He's not sure it is, but what he does know is it's all Peter has right now. For a man who a day ago couldn't feel anything, he sure as hell is feeling a lot of guilt, sorrow, and anger, all in generous quantities. He thinks about it a little more. "And, well, you were the one who checked for a pulse on Taylor," he says, and that helps alleviate some of the guilt. But not much, because why was he satisfied with Peter's assessment? What, did he suddenly think Peter was an expert on picking whether somebody was alive or dead? Pulses can be easy to miss, especially when you're flustered, when you've just killed a guy, when you think you're about to be caught. Pulses can be easy to miss even when you're none of that. He knows this. It was drummed into him years ago during first-aid courses.

He realizes he hasn't checked Peter for his pulse. He does that now, pushing two fingers into the guy's neck, nothing, nothing, he keeps searching, nothing, nothing, then something. Faint, but there. The guilt alleviates a little more.

"I'm going to get you out of here," he says, and he feels relief. "I promise," he adds, but he's been making a few promises lately he hasn't been able to keep.

With both the brothers injured, and with the car keys hidden, the two men aren't going anywhere. Unless they can hot-wire a car, which he figures they probably can. He wonders what their plan is, or even if they've figured one out yet. Hopefully they're just stumbling around out there. Hopefully one of them has stepped into a bear trap and the other fallen into a well.

He heads back upstairs. He starts going into the rooms as he passes them, looking at the iron bars over the windows and wishing he'd taken this show into the middle of the woods instead of the goddamn scream room. He finds the kitchen. He knows there's a door that leads from the back of the kitchen outside, but the damn thing won't budge. It's bolted closed or chained up, he can't tell. He puts his shoulder into it, he kicks at it, but nothing. He searches the kitchen, but there are no tools, no utensils, no cutlery—all that stuff was stripped away years ago. In the bedrooms there are beds he can hide under or take an uncomfortable nap on, but nothing else.

He moves into an office that looks out over the driveway. Something scuttles in the corner, making him jump, and when he turns his phone towards it he sees a possum staring at him, it's eyes reflecting the light from his phone back at him. It hisses, takes half a dozen steps towards him, then turns and runs into the corridor. Suddenly a beam of light comes through the window from outside and hits him in the face. He ducks down, but the light keeps com-

ing through the window and hits the wall behind him. It doesn't
follow him. It's the headlights from the car. There are no voices
and no sense of urgency. The brothers know he's locked in here.

He moves into the next office and stays low, then pokes his head
up to peek through the window. Both men are standing less than
twenty yards from him. The window is covered in grime and there's
a triangle section missing from the bottom, enough to put your fist
through if you had the urge to slice up the sides of your forearm.
He moves out of the office and into the first bedroom and gets the
same view, a dirty window, more ivy has twisted around more iron
bars, the two brothers beyond. This window is cracked, but there
don't seem to be any possums.

He goes through the ground floor, checking windows and
doors, but he's locked in here. And he has no weapon. He should
have picked up the damn knife Bevin pulled on them earlier. He
comes back to the office with the hole in the window. Taylor is
out there holding the flashlight, his left arm hanging limply from
the blow he took in the alleyway. Bevin is looking at something
in his hand. A moment later he lifts that something up to the
side of his head. A moment after that he talks into it.

They dumped the brother's cell phones in the alleyway. This
must be Peter's.

Shit.

He holds his breath and concentrates and does his best to listen
in, putting his ear up to the missing triangle of window. The words
carry on the still air.

"Matt? It's Bevin. Listen, I need your help. You heard of a place
called Grover Hills? Yeah, yeah that's it. You know where it is?
Well look it up on a map. Listen, I need you and . . . No, listen
to me, it's important. I need you and a couple of the . . . Yeah, I
know what the time is. . . . Uh huh, uh huh, well look, of course
it's important otherwise I wouldn't be calling. I need you guys to
come out here. And bring a couple of guns, okay? We're forming
a hunting party," he says. "Uh huh, yeah, I knew you'd like the
sound of that. Bring Buzzkill too. Oh, and some gas and a couple

of flares. Uh huh. Okay, sure, you can bring beer, but it's for when we're done, okay? Not before."

They're going to wait out there for him. Then they're going to burn the place down. Or they're going to come in looking for him. They're going to shoot him, probably torture him a little, then set him on fire. Then they're going to sit around popping open some beers and reliving the moment.

He figures he has fifteen or twenty minutes to figure a way out of here before Matt and Buzzkill arrive to turn him and Peter Crowley into ash and bone.

CHAPTER TWENTY-THREE

We talk to the two kids who phoned in the crime. At the same time we're waiting for Hutton, whose return has been delayed because now he needs a warrant for the car and also for the Collard house. It seems crazy because there's a crime in progress, but we're okay with crazy—we're okay with taking our time to get things right when it's people like Bevin Collard who's in trouble. We're happy to take the time to dot the i's and cross the t's, just like Hutton said out by the train tracks. If the Collards were the ones committing the crime, we'd have broken into their car already and ransacked their house.

The kids are nervous and seem to think we're going to arrest them. One kid's name is Danny and the other is Harry, and I wonder what their combined couple name would be, whether it'd be Darry or Hanny. Danny, the older one at fifteen, shrugs his shoulders at every question even when he knows the answer, and Harry can't keep himself from staring at Kent's chest. Their names make them sound like an IQ test, like *If Danny has half as much acne as Harry, and Harry has twice as much acne as Danny, then who's taller?* In this case, Harry is taller, and Harry has glasses he has to keep pushing up as if they're a little too loose, and Danny is wearing a leather bracelet he keeps fiddling with, and both kids are equally nervous.

"It's just like we keep saying," Danny says, "we didn't see much."

"And you saw just the one person being put in the trunk?" I ask.

Harry shakes his head, and Danny nods, two nervous boys on different pages.

"Okay. Let's try this again," I say. "Was it just the one person who got put into the trunk?"

"We didn't see a whole person," Danny says. "We just saw the bit at the end where we saw these two guys tucking somebody's legs—"

"The rest of them was already in there," Harry interrupts. "At least we think he was, unless the legs—"

"Were cut off," Danny finishes, "which they could have been. And there could have been a whole pile of body parts in there. Could have been two or three people."

"Or ten," Harry adds.

"Are you going to tell our parents we were drinking?" Danny asks.

"If you're helpful," I tell them, "I promise I won't say anything." Which is true. It'll be one of the officers here that will take these kids home, and they'll be the one to tell the parents. "You're not helpful, then we'll take you back to the station and put you in a holding cell for the night."

Both boys look petrified at that thought.

"What about the two men outside of the car?"

"We didn't see much of them," Danny says. "I mean, you're lucky we even saw any of it. It's pretty dark down there."

"How far down the alleyway were they?"

"Pretty far down the end."

"So how did you see them?" I ask.

"We were . . . I was, anyway, umm, going down there to take a leak, and so was Danny," Harry says, and Harry finally looks away from Rebecca's chest and it's all Danny can do to keep making eye contact with me.

"You were going down there to buy drugs, weren't you," I say.

"Look, we called the police, right?" Danny says. "We did the right thing. If we hadn't called, you'd never know we were even here. Please don't tell my mom and dad."

"Or mine," Harry says, looking up at us. He's starting to cry. "Please."

"I promise I won't tell them anything about it," I say, which is just as true as not telling them about the drinking. "Tell us what happened."

So they tell us. It was the classic case of each of their parents thinking their boy was at the other boy's house. It's classic because it works in the movies just as well as it works in real life. They caught the bus into town and there was a guy they knew, the older brother of a friend of theirs, who, for a ten-dollar fee, would buy them a six-pack of beer. This wasn't their first time into town at night, and each time here they learned something new, new friends who had older brothers who could help them out. Yesterday at school they heard about a couple of guys selling drugs. So that's why they came here. They thought it was exciting. They thought it would be an adventure. They got halfway down the alleyway when they heard the voices. Then they hid behind the dumpster and they saw the legs of somebody as he was stuffed into the trunk and the adventure was over. The best description they can give us of the car is it's a sedan, and that it's dark. The problem is the alleyway has such poor lighting that dark covers a bigger color spectrum than normal. It almost covers everything except white. Best description they can give of the two men is that one was bald and one wasn't, and that they were old.

"You know, like your age," Danny says.

We put the kids back into the patrol car. Soon they'll be taken down to the station to talk to a sketch artist, but first their parents will be called. I imagine those kids are going to find themselves grounded for six months. Hutton has shown up. He's brought along the Collard brothers' file, a warrant, and a slim piece of metal that's twenty inches long plus a hard triangle piece of foam that fits in the palm of his hand. He wedges the tip of the foam down the side of the window of the car to create a gap that widens the further down the foam goes.

"Breaking into a car always reminds me of Schroder," Hutton says.

"Schrodering the car," I say.

"What does that mean?" Kent asks.

"It's a case we worked on a few years ago," Hutton says, and he slides the thin piece of metal between the window and the door of Bevin Collard's car. "Schroder had gotten a warrant for a work premises. The suspect was a mechanic, so the premises was a work-shop. The warrant included all the cars that were parked there and being worked on. The problem was the workshop was next to an auto body shop, and between the two buildings was a driveway. The driveway belonged to the auto body shop, but he often let the mechanic use it to park cars. Schroder didn't realize the driveway belonged to the auto body guy. He opened the cars on it and found a pile of bloody clothes inside the back of the mechanic's car, who was the suspect, but technically the warrant didn't allow for the search. Our case was shot after that. The guy got away with it."

"Shit," Kent says. "Sounds tough."

"Tougher than some," Hutton says, still working with the piece of metal. Experts can pop a lock in five or ten seconds. Hutton isn't an expert. "And not as tough as others. But whenever there's a car involved we're extra careful. If not for that case, what was it, six years ago?" he asks me.

I nod. "Maybe a little longer."

"Well, if not for that case we probably would have opened this car," he says, nodding to Bevin Collard's car, "as soon as we saw it here. Maybe we'd already know where they are. But the law is the law, and if anybody tries to shortcut it and open a car without a warrant, we call it *Schrodering*."

"And how does Schroder feel about that name?"

"We never told him," Hutton says, "and we sure as hell never said it around him."

While he works on getting the car open, we show the photo-graphs from the files to Kyle Landry, who looks at the first one, nods, then looks at the second. He nods with that one too. "That's definitely them. I've never seen them apart."

Which means they probably weren't apart tonight, which means they're probably not apart right at the moment. At the same time we're showing him the photographs, four police officers are going through the dumpsters. It's an awful job, and one I've had to do in the past, and one that would make me retire early if I had to do it again. People throw all sorts of stuff into the garbage, from pus-soaked bandages to dead mice, sometimes you'll find a dead dog or a dead cat. Or worse.

Hutton gets the locks on the car to pop up. I've been at scenes like this before where cops have wagered on whether there's going to be a body in the trunk. We check that first. All that's in there are some plastic bags, a towing rope, and a set of jumper cables. In the front and under the seats are some soda cans and fast-food wrappers and nothing of any importance. Same for the glove compartment. Assuming the Collards don't come wandering out a bar later on tonight, the car will be towed away and searched more thoroughly by the guys who searched Dwight Smith's car.

"That was a waste of time," Kent says.

"Had to be done," I tell her.

"Go check their house," Hutton says, and hands Kent the warrant for the house. "See what you can see."

"Should we go speak to Peter Crowley first?" I ask.

Hutton nods as he thinks about it, then shakes his head. "No," he says. "We don't know the reason these guys were abducted, and if it is related to Dwight Smith, we don't know if Peter Crowley is involved. Go to their house first. For all we know they're sitting in front of their TV."

"You know what kind of men leave behind their stash of drugs, right?" Kent asks, as we walk back to the car when Hutton is out of earshot.

"Dead men," I tell her.

She nods. "What do you think the chances are of them sitting in front of their TV?"

"Zero," I say.

We reach the car. We stand next to our doors, but we don't climb in. We look at each other over the roof and carry on talking.

"Do you think that's the point?" Kent asks.

"I don't follow."

"Hutton is sending us to the Collards' house first, and not straight to Peter Crowley. Do you think he's doing that because he wants Peter to have a chance to finish what he's doing, if he's doing anything at all?"

"I hadn't thought about it like that," I say.

"I think like that all the time," she says, and she unlocks the door. "Come on, let's go fight the good fight and try to save these assholes."

CHAPTER TWENTY-FOUR

Schroder has two options. Find a weapon, or find a way out. Once out, he can walk through a bunch of paddocks and trees and find a road—but even that isn't a great option, especially with Peter Crowley draped over his shoulder. It means leaving his car here, and maybe Bevin and Taylor and Buzzkill have a way of figuring out who owns the car, or maybe they don't and they'll call the police and then the police will figure it out. These men were kidnapped and brought out here. They could call the police right now and the world would see them as heroes.

Which really means he has only one option.

He has to kill Bevin and Taylor before their backup arrives. Taylor with no doubt the world's biggest headache and perhaps a broken arm. Bevin with a headache too. Schroder thinks he could take them. He could walk out there and Taylor would be no match for him, and perhaps Bevin wouldn't be much of one either.

First he has to get out of here.

He thinks about what his doctor told him. Don't crash his car. Don't get into a fight. One lucky punch from somebody and the bullet camping in his brain is going to switch him off. And it doesn't even have to be that lucky a punch. He makes his way to the top floor, almost tripping on one of the stairs halfway up that's warped and lifted a few inches, and maybe it could all end there—tripping over, hitting his head, the bullet keeping his brain company calling it a day. He begins opening doors and he uses his phone to search the rooms and there's nothing, nothing but mattresses and beds and layers of dust. He moves to one of the windows where he can see his car and the two men.

Should he call Tate?

He considers it. What would he say? Come alone because he's gotten himself into a situation? There is no scenario where Tate wouldn't bring reinforcements. He will go to jail, but maybe jail won't be a big deal. Maybe he only has a few days or a few weeks left in this world anyway. Yes, jail might not be a big deal, but despite running short on his range of emotions, the idea of his wife and children knowing he went from Coma Cop to Killer Cop kills him.

He walks the corridor. More planks of wood groan beneath him. He chooses another room, picks up a mattress, and tosses it at the window. The sound of glass shattering is magnified in the calm air, magnified by the wide-open spaces of the countryside. He sweeps the mattress back and forth to clear the glass away, it snags and catches, but gets the job done, then he reaches through and grabs the iron bars. He pushes them. He pulls them. He tries rattling them. There is no movement. One of the brothers points the flashlight at him. He ducks out of the room.

Back to the stairs and the same pieces of wood groan beneath him, the same damaged step almost making him trip. Outside the view is the same—the two brothers waiting for their friends. For Buzzkill.

The back door. If he can break the hinges, or if he can rock the door back and forth enough something might give. Five seconds of trying to budge it tells him it's impossible, but he gives it another thirty seconds anyway. No good. The only way in and out is through the front door. Of course it is. This place was designed to keep crazy people inside.

The car that turns down the driveway a minute later is a white sedan. It comes to a stop next to his car. A guy topping six foot unfolds himself from the driver's seat. A guy just as big does the same from the passenger seat. They're both holding pistols.

Then one of them opens the back door, and who must surely be Buzzkill jumps out, lands on all fours, and starts barking as if its stumpy tail is on fire.

CHAPTER TWENTY-FIVE

A pair of officers follow us to the Collard house. On the way I read the file Hutton gave us, the file on what Bevin and Collard did nine years ago.

Bevin Collard had, according to him, been minding his own business while driving peacefully on the way to work. A car had cut him off. That car belonged to Peter Crowley. Bevin, according to him, honked his horn in frustration to which Peter, according to Bevin, wound down his window, gave him the finger, and called him a *fucktard*. Bevin who, according to Bevin, was insulted by the word and felt the word *tard* or *retard* was insensitive to the "special needs weirdoes you see when cousins bump uglies," wanted to teach Peter a lesson. So he followed him home. Then he went there the following morning with his brother, Taylor. Only Peter wasn't at home. It was Saturday and he was off playing cricket. A good way to teach Peter not to cut people off in traffic, the brothers thought, was to "make love" to his wife. That's how they put it. They each made love to her, and why not, they asked? She certainly was a fine piece of ass.

Their account of events makes me sick. I struggle to read it out to Rebecca, just as she struggles to listen to it, and I notice that she eases off the accelerator, not much, but enough to delay our approach.

"These guys were animals," she says.

"I know. But . . ." I say, then don't say anything else. I shrug, and somehow that gets the message across. What is there to say? These guys have rights? That it's our job to figure out what happened to them so we can protect them?

"I know," she says, hearing what I'm not saying. "They spent twelve minutes with her. Can you believe that? Within sixteen minutes they broke into her house, shaved her head and broke both her arms, and each raped her once, just leaving her on the hallway floor like a piece of garbage, like something they just used up. She couldn't even phone for help."

"I know," I say, and I can see it all unfolding. It's the policeman's curse—you see so much bad shit that when you hear about other bad shit you know exactly how it went down, from the pleading of the victim to the dirty facial expressions of the attacker.

"All of it in front of her daughter."

"I know," I say, and if I ever walked in on something like that happening to my family—well, what man doesn't think about what he would or wouldn't do? But Peter didn't walk in on it. The daughter would cry next to her mother for fifteen minutes before running to a neighbor for help.

The rest of the report doesn't read any better, but I read it anyway, feeling myself getting angry as I do so. In court they used the defense that it was Peter's actions that led them to attack his wife. The jury didn't buy it. It didn't help the brothers that the intersection where Peter had cut them off had a red-light camera, and the camera had caught Bevin talking on his cell phone while running the red light. It was Peter who braked hard and held his hand on the horn. It was Bevin who wound down his window and gave the finger.

"Let me ask you something," Kent says, and she doesn't glance at me, just keeps staring ahead at the road. She starts running a finger down the side of her face, touching the scars there, and I think it might be somewhat of a tell. I think she might do this when she's having dark thoughts. I think she'd be a great person to play poker against. "What's the outcome you want here?" she asks.

Are we on the same page?

"What do you mean?"

"I mean, let's say we're a week in the future and this case is closed, and we did everything right and found out exactly what happened, what result are you hoping to have had?"

"I'm just hoping we did the right thing." I tell her.

"That's not what I mean, and you know it."

"I do mean it. Why, what are you hoping for?"

"I'm hoping these guys killed themselves, just like Smith did."

"He didn't kill himself. We know that now."

"These two guys the boys saw in the alleyway stuffing Collard into the trunk, they're Kelly Summers's fairy godmother. They're who took Dwight Smith away last night, and tonight they're making the Collard brothers disappear. Summers wasn't involved, and I doubt Peter Crowley is involved. No reason for him to be following Smith, and no reason for Summers to go into an alleyway tonight to help Peter. It's somebody else. A pair of somebody else."

"The fairy godmother," I say.

"And his fairy friend," she says, then laughs and I laugh too.

"Be sure to call them that when we find these guys," I say.

She keeps laughing, and it's nice to hear her laugh. "I used to believe in fairies when I was growing up," she says. "Maybe it's time to start believing again."

We reach the house. Half the streetlights don't work, so all the houses just look like black holes against a slightly less black landscape. The Collard house is no different. We park outside and the patrol car parks behind us. The four of us walk up the pathway together, me and Kent unarmed, the two officers carrying handguns. There is no threat here—most likely just an empty house—but we still stay alert, the drugs the Collards were selling were made somewhere, and perhaps it was here. I knock on the front door figuring nobody is going to answer, and indeed nobody does.

We make our way inside, which is easy because the two officers have brought along a battering ram. The battering ram is a couple of feet long, made of steel, and can apply a few tons of kinetic energy to the lock it's being swung into. In this case, and as often is the case, the lock survives the impact, but the door frame doesn't, with chunks of it splintering away, wood cracking like a gunshot in the quiet street, bits of it left hanging sharp and ragged.

Nobody comes running out of any of the bedrooms. The two

officers go ahead of us, switching lights on as they go and pointing guns into the rooms. A minute later we've confirmed the house is empty.

We split up. Kent takes the lounge and one officer heads out to the garage while the other stays by the front door, keeping an eye on the street in case anybody else shows up. I take one of the other bedrooms. The house is impersonal. There's no art anywhere, there isn't a single photo on display, no pot plants, a mismatch of furniture and furnishings. I can't even tell who owns the bedroom I'm in. It has a TV mounted to the wall, and beneath it a set of drawers with a game console and a couple of remote controls on top. The bed hasn't been made, the sheets look like they need a wash, and the idea of touching them makes my skin crawl. I pull on a pair of latex gloves. I check under the bed. There's an old pair of sneakers and a pile of magazines full of naked women. I open the closet and check between the clothes, I check the floor to see if it can be lifted here— a favorite hiding space for drug dealers—but the floor doesn't budge. My heart isn't even in it, to be honest, and probably the best we can hope to find are drugs. I'm tired and I want to be home with my wife. I see Kent walk past the doorway and head into another of the bedrooms.

I start going through the drawers. Socks. Underwear. T-shirts. I pull them out and toss them onto the bed. Next drawer is more of the same. Some jeans too, some shorts, a few wifebeaters. Then a folder, maybe a quarter of an inch thick, full of newspaper articles.

"I've got something," Kent says, calling out from the bedroom across the hallway. I still don't know whose bedroom this is. I carry the folder through to her. "Check this out," she says.

She steps from the closet. The floorboards have been pried up. "It was already like this," she says. "There's nothing under there, but this will be where they hid their bag."

"What the hell is it with criminals and floorboards?" I ask.

"Well it's either that or the ceiling. You want to check the ceiling?" she asks.

"If there's anything up there it's probably just more drugs. Check this out," I say, and I stand next to her and start flicking through the articles in the folder. They're articles about the attack on Linda Crowley, all cut extremely neatly from the newspapers.

"Quite the collection," she says.

I keep flicking through, and then a small plastic bag falls out from between the articles and hits the floor. Kent scoops it up.

"It's a ring," she says, holding it up to the light. She twists the bag, studying the inside of it. "There's no inscription."

"Look at this," I say, and it's another newspaper article, only this one is much more recent. It's about a woman who was attacked in a park three months ago by two men. She was pulled into a bunch of bushes, had her top pulled off, but then a guy walking his dog heard the struggle and intervened. His dog chased the two men off. There are a few articles on the attack. People were warned to keep a lookout in the area and to phone the police if they saw anything suspicious. Nobody was ever caught.

We don't say anything to each other because there's no need. The articles speak for themselves. Then a different story, only this one doesn't have an intervening man with a dog. A woman was pulled into a car in a supermarket parking lot. She was driven a mile away to a park, raped, then left in the bushes. The men were wearing masks. Instead of calling the police she made her way back to the supermarket, got into her car, and drove home. She took a long hot shower, then a long hot bath, then one more long hot shower before crawling into bed. She would stay there and miss work and ignore her friends for a week until people started to come around and check on her. She told them what had happened. It was then that the police were called. By then there were no hairs, no DNA—and nobody to point the finger at.

"The Collards have been busy," she says.

I keep going through the articles, frightened of what else I'm going to find, or what they've escalated to. The attack in the supermarket was one week after the failed attempt in the park. But there are no other stories in here.

"I have a plan," Kent says, and she looks around to make sure neither of the officers can overhear her.

"Yeah?"

"How about I drop you off back home. It's late. Then I'll go home too. Then I'll pick you up at eight o'clock in the morning and we can go and talk to Peter Crowley then."

"And the Collards?"

"Fuck the Collards. None of this is going to help us find them, and even if we could, I'm not so sure I'd want to. Not yet. Tomorrow, maybe, but not now."

"Sounds like a plan," I tell her.

"But?"

"Does there have to be a *but*?" I ask.

"There is with you."

"But we can't do it," I tell her. "We have to do our jobs, even if we don't agree with it." I hear the words coming out and wonder where they're coming from, then I remember what Bridget said to me earlier. *You're a good person. You did what you thought was right.* I have to start being a better man for Bridget. When I lost Emily, and when I thought I had lost my wife too, then I didn't need to be a better man. I didn't have to answer to anybody. I had nobody I could let down. "We have to be better than the people we're investigating."

She looks at the ring. "If these people hurt your family, what would you do?"

"My job," I tell her. "That's what both of us have to do, no matter where it leads. Come on, let's go wake up Peter Crowley."

"And if he's not home?"

"Let's just hope he is," I say, because if he isn't then he was probably one of the two men in the alleyway, which would make him the fairy godmother's fairy friend.

CHAPTER TWENTY-SIX

A beam of light comes into the office. Somebody yells "Get 'em," and the dog, a rottweiler, sprints towards him. It covers the ground faster than any dog should, then leaps up, taller than any dog should be, its paws batting at and between the bars, thumping the window harder than any dog should. Suddenly it turns and runs to its left and picks something up. It's the possum from before—or a different one. The dog shakes its head from side to side, then uses its paw to hold the possum on the ground while tearing it apart.

"You're next," somebody yells.

Schroder runs for the basement door, then stops. It's a dead end, and he can't help Peter from in there. Even if he could somehow manage to lock them both inside the cell, then what? Sit there and be steam roasted as the building burns down around them? He shuts the door leading down the stairs so at least the dog won't run straight down there for Peter. There's banging at the front door. The padlock and chain are keeping them out. The guys who just showed up look like the sort to travel with a crowbar in the car.

Higher ground is the way to go, if for no other reason than it delays his death and the pain leading up to it. He trips on the damn warped step on the stairs to the upstairs landing and puts his hands out to break his fall, and his cell phone slips from his grip and sails down to the floor, hits hard and the light goes out. Ambient light is still coming in from the car outside. He can hear voices at the door, somebody is yelling at the dog to shut up. The phone is his lifeline. He gets back down the stairs, scoops it up, and drops it into his pocket, heads halfway up the stairs, then stops at the warped floorboard.

The floorboard is better than nothing.

He gets his fingers into the gap beneath it, tightens his muscles, and when he pulls it comes up easier than he would have thought, so easily he almost falls down the stairs. He gets his phone out and holds his finger on the power button hoping it's not damaged, that maybe the fall just disconnected the battery for a brief second internally, or some other weird random event that happens when you drop your phone, and he's relieved to see the welcome screen boot up. He looks at the floorboard. It's ten inches wide, two feet long, and has finger-length nails sticking out the end.

He runs to the end of the corridor. He uses the piece of wood to smash the window, then he grips the bars and tests for any movement, of which there is none, as good a job done upstairs as downstairs to secure them. However, this place has been abandoned for ten years, and in that time no maintenance has been done, and he imagines little was done before then too, so it's possible one set of bars could be only one good kick away from coming free, the bolts strong and unforgiving, but the wood they're bolted into tired and soft. He should head to the south side, where the shade helps grow mold, where hopefully some of the boards have absorbed enough water over the years to have started rotting.

He goes to a south-side bedroom. He smashes the glass. There is ivy twisted around the bars. When he tries pushing the bars off the house, he has no more luck than before. He smashes the glass in the next bedroom. Only this time when he puts his hands on the bar there's a gunshot and he feels something whizz past his face, and that same something smacks into the ceiling above him.

There is splintering from downstairs, then there's a gunshot from down there too, and then he can hear the doors being thrown open. He loads Tate's number up on the display of his phone. The dog downstairs is barking, he can hear it racing across the floor, its claws digging into the wood as it makes its way to the stairs. He wonders if it will go for his throat or for his balls, and isn't sure which is worse.

He presses send.

Tate will hear him being ripped apart. He just needs to hang on long enough to tell him by who and if he has time, he'll ask Tate to do him one last favor—to take care of these guys for him. To do to them what he did to Quentin James. He honestly doesn't know if Tate will agree to it. The Old Tate, the one from earlier in the year would have. But this New Tate is like the wood he's hoping to find the bars bolted to—tired and soft.

Only the phone doesn't dial. Where there's supposed to be signal bars there's a red X. The phone has gotten damaged in the fall. He can hear the dog coming up the stairs. He pockets the phone and tightens his grip on the floorboard. At the very least he should close the bedroom door and buy himself a few more seconds. If he's lucky, the four men will shoot him rather than set Buzzkill on him. He swings the door, but before it can latch, Buzzkill's snout and front paws appear in the gap. The dog is strong, too damn strong.

Schroder kicks the door, hoping to at least hurt the animal, which he must do, but the damn dog doesn't let it show, its pride and anger making it more savage as it barks and bangs at the door. Schroder knows he's losing a battle. He jumps back and tightens his grip on the floorboard. His eyes have adjusted slightly to the dark.

The door bangs open. Buzzkill pauses for one second, enough time to bark and snarl and figure out the best angle of attack, which it then decides is from the front, which it then puts into practice. It runs forward and leaps into the air, a mouth full of teeth, deciding the throat is the way to go.

CHAPTER TWENTY-SEVEN

It's almost three a.m. when we get to Peter Crowley's house. With this kind of news I don't think he'll mind being woken at this time of night—if he is home. We're still getting out of the car when Hutton calls us. Two cell phones have been found in one of the dumpsters from the alleyway.

"Phones were wiped down," Hutton says, "so no prints. But we do have a bunch of contacts. There are text messages too, which we think may be code, as there are lots of texts about books and shirts and DVDs, there are some locations that don't make sense—at least not to us, and at least not yet. I'm not sure if we're going to find anything on here that can lead to other drug busts, but hopefully it will," he says, and then we hang up.

There's a light on in the lounge of the Crowley house. I press my finger on the bell and can hear it ringing inside. We take a step back, wait half a minute, then ring it again.

"I'm coming," a woman says, and we see a hall light switch on, and through the frosted glass panels of the door we can make out the shape of somebody approaching. "I've told you not to leave your damn keys when you go to—" the woman says as she starts opening the door, and then she stops. She sees Kent and she sees me and we don't even need to tell her we're police, and already she's thinking a dozen things, all of them bad.

"Oh my God," she says, and she lifts her hands to her face, and they're shaking, and she takes a step back, then another, then her legs give way and she stumbles and falls.

"It's okay," Kent tells her, and takes a step forward.

"Is she . . . is she dead?" she asks.

She?

Both Kent and myself are shaking our heads. "No," Kent says. "We're here because we need to talk to Peter."

"So . . . So . . . Monica is okay? When she didn't come home I just thought . . ."

Monica. The daughter. A door opens into the hallway and a teen-age girl spills out of it. She's wearing a black T-shirt with a picture of a skull on it. The skull looks weird, and it takes me a moment to realize why—it has bone ears sticking out from the sides. The ears have earrings. "What's going on?" the girl asks. She sees who I'm guessing is her stepmother and helps her to her feet.

"You're home," the woman says. "I thought . . . Wait. . . . I fell asleep on the couch. . . . Where's Peter?" she asks. "Why wouldn't he wake me when he got home?"

"Is he home?" I ask.

"Of course he's home. Monica, go and get your father," she says, and Monica disappears. "Why do you need to talk to him?"

"We're hoping he can help us with a case we're—"

"He's not in bed," Monica says, calling from the bedroom.

The woman looks concerned. "He should have been back by now."

"Back from where?" Kent asks.

The woman straightens her pajamas. "He went out this after-noon. He left a note saying he had an emergency at work. He got called in. So . . . so you're not here to tell us something bad hap-pened to him?"

"No," Kent says.

I take a step towards the door. "Let's go inside so we can sit down and we can explain why we're here."

"I think that's a good idea," the woman says.

The woman walks ahead of us, and the girl, Monica, closes the door and follows us into the lounge. The woman introduces herself as Charlotte, Peter's wife. The girl is Peter's daughter. There is a boy here too, we're told, but the commotion hasn't woken him.

We explain we're following an active lead in a homicide inves-tigation, one that Peter may unknowingly have information for. Charlotte shakes her head as if she can't believe that's possible.

"What time did he leave for work?" I ask.

"I don't know. The note didn't say, and nobody was here."

"He was here when I left today," Monica says, "which was around two o'clock I guess, or maybe three. I was out the rest of the day and I snuck back inside about an hour ago."

"You were drinking, weren't you," Charlotte says. "We asked you not to—"

"I wasn't drinking!"

"No? Then what? Just hanging out? And smoking?"

"It was nothing like that."

"So where is Peter now?" I ask. "Where does he work?"

Monica shrugs, folds her arms, and stares at her stepmother. "You always think the worst," she says.

Charlotte ignores her. "He's on call. He's a plumber, but his van is still here so one of the other guys must have picked him up. He said there was a broken water main in an office complex in town, and not to wait up."

"I saw the guy who came to pick him up," Monica says, still keeping her arms folded.

"Who?" Charlotte asks.

"I don't know. I don't know everybody dad works with. Some bald guy."

Some bald guy. Just like it was some bald guy in the alleyway tonight.

"Sounds like Drew," Charlotte says.

"Can I have Peter's number?" I ask.

She reads it out to me and I tap the numbers into my cell phone. I press call and the line connects. It rings and after eight rings it goes through to voicemail.

"Is there a problem?" she asks.

I hang up. "He's not answering."

"Let me try." She disappears out of the room, leaving us alone with Monica.

"Why do you need to talk to my dad? Did he do something?"

"No," Kent says, "we're just hoping he can help us."

"Is this about mom?"

Kent looks at me and I look at Kent and we're not sure how to answer, but our lack of answer is an answer in itself.

"It is, isn't it. I don't remember any of it," she says. "I mean, I know what happened, and a few years ago I read about it, but I don't remember it. I don't know whether I even tried to help. All I know is that I sat there and watched it happen."

"I'm sorry about what happened," I hear myself saying, and I am, but the words don't change anything, they just sound hollow and empty, like saying *I'm sorry for your loss* to somebody you barely know.

"The men who hurt mom, will they ever get out of jail?"

Before I can answer, Charlotte comes back. She's holding a cell phone. "He's not answering me either."

"Okay. Can you give me Drew's number?"

"Something is wrong, isn't it," she says, and she sounds anxious now. "That's why you're here. Has Peter done something?"

"We just need to talk to him, that's all."

"At two in the morning? What aren't you telling us?"

"Please," I tell her. "Drew's number?"

"It's about mom," Monica says.

Charlotte looks at her and a small frown appears. "What? What could this possibly be to do with her?" Then she looks towards us. "Is this to do with the men that hurt her? Have they hurt him?"

"They're in jail," Monica says.

"Not anymore," Charlotte says.

Monica looks confused.

"They served their time," Charlotte says.

"No, that can't be, Dad would have told me."

"We didn't want you to know."

"Do you . . . Do you think they've hurt my dad?" Monica asks.

"Nothing like that," Kent says.

"Do you think . . . Do you think my dad is going to hurt them? I hope that's it," she says. "I hope he kills them."

"Monica, don't say such a thing," Charlotte snaps.

"Well I hope he does. If they'd never hurt my mother then I wouldn't have to listen to you," she says.

"Monica!"

Monica stands up. "This is bullshit," she says, looking towards me and Kent. "These guys kill my mom, and now you're here to treat my dad like he's the bad guy?"

"Monica!" Charlotte says.

"Whatever," Monica says, and storms off.

Charlotte sits back down on the couch. Her face has gone red. "I'm sorry about that, but she hates me because I can never be her real mother," she says, and she doesn't sound upset, if anything she just sounds used to it. "I can't imagine it's going to get any better. Here, let me find Drew's number for you."

She scrolls through her phone then reads it out. I dial it.

"Excuse me a minute," I say, and I step out of the lounge into the hallway, then decide to step outside instead. I have a feeling about what I'm going to hear.

"It's the middle of the night," Drew says, as a way of greeting.

"Is that Drew Fulton?"

"Yeah, it's Drew Fulton," he says, "and it's still the middle of the night."

"This is Detective Inspector Theodore Tate," I tell him.

There's movement, and I can tell he's pulling himself into a sitting position.

"The police?" he says. "Has something happened?"

"I wake you?" I ask, and I watch a guy get out of his car over the road, drop his keys, pick them up, fall over, and pick them up again.

"Yes."

"So you're not working," I say.

"What's this about?"

"Have you seen Peter Crowley tonight?" I ask, and the guy over the road is now staggering up to his front door the same way I play golf, with lots of lefts and rights and hitting the trees on the way. He drops his keys and belches loudly enough for me to hear him.

"Peter? What?" he asks, and he sounds concerned. "No, no, why?"

"He didn't help you with a broken water main in town?"

"What broken water main?"

"We're looking for Peter," I tell him, "and he left a note with his wife saying he had to work in town."

"If there's a broken water main I would have heard about it," he says.

"Thanks for your time, Mr. Fulton."

"Wait, has—"

But I don't wait. I thank him and hang up.

Peter lied to his wife.

Was the bald man that came to speak to him the same bald man Danny and Harry saw? I think it is. I think the bald man has pulled Peter into a whole world of trouble. Trouble that started nine years ago and took on new life in an alleyway in town, the kind of alleyway where bad things tend to happen. The question is—did Peter know the bald man before today? And if he did, did Kelly know him too?

CHAPTER TWENTY-EIGHT

Schroder jabs the end of the floorboard towards the dog's head. It bites down on it, opens its mouth, yelps, then takes another bite. It shakes its head furiously, saliva and blood spraying across Schroder as it bites onto the nails sticking from it. Schroder fights to keep the board in his hand, and the dog is driving him towards the window and across the shards of glass that bounced off the iron bars when he broke it. He pushes the floorboard. He pulls it. The dog keeps shaking its head like it's disagreeing with Schroder's desire to live. There are footsteps on the stairs, then somebody is swearing, yelling that they think they just broke their goddamn ankle because there's a goddamn stair missing.

The dog figures things out. It lets go of the floorboard and comes again for Schroder's throat. Schroder gets his forearm in the way, the dog's teeth latch on to it, and it doesn't hurt, not like he thought it would, but he suspects that's because adrenaline is flooding his system. The dog feels like it weighs a hundred pounds and the pressure in its mouth feels strong enough to jack up a car. He keeps waiting to hear something in his arm snap. He pivots, the dog's front paws swiping at his chest, its back paws tangoing across the floor. He beats the floorboard across the back of the dog's head, but he can't get enough leverage to make it hurt. The force becomes too much, his foot slips from beneath him as he steps on a piece of glass, and he loses balance. He falls on his back and he does all he can think to do—he pushes the dog up and over him as far as he can.

The momentum and the arc take the dog above him and into the window, then downwards, glass crashing around it. Its jaws open and let Schroder go. It becomes more furious. It growls louder. Schroder gets to his feet. The top half of Buzzkill's head has gone into a V in the glass, wedged in there and sinking deeper as it struggles, the glass angles sliding into its head. It struggles harder, already something has come loose as it tries wiggling its head side to side, an ear, perhaps, or something else. Its legs scramble as if it's on a treadmill that isn't there. Schroder grabs the piece of wood, turns it so the nails point downwards, and swings as hard as he can into the back of the dog's head, partly out of self-defense, mostly just to put the damn thing out of its misery.

The dog goes still.

He levers the nails out and takes the board over to the door. He closes the door and puts the board on a forty-five-degree angle, jams one end beneath the handle, then digs the opposite end into the floor. He kicks it, burying the nails partway into the floor. The door handle turns and then there's banging.

The only weapon he had is now the only thing keeping the others out.

There's a gunshot. He doesn't think the bullet makes it through the door because the door is too thick, but then there's another shot and a small hole appears in the wall next to the door, made obvious by the beam of light behind it. The wallboards are thinner than the door.

He moves to the window and puts his hands on the bars, and there's another gunshot, this one coming from outside, this one pinging off something only a few inches from him.

Another gunshot from behind. Another hole filled with light. The bullet smacks into the wall opposite. Another gunshot and another hole, then a foot appears down low. They can't open the door, but they can kick a hole in the wall next to it, reach in, and shift the plank. Or reach in and shoot him.

The foot disappears, then comes back. This time it twists, and instead of going out the way it came in, it gets caught up between the framework and the board.

Schroder grabs a hand-sized piece of glass off the floor, tears the perforated sleeve from his bloody shirt, and wraps it around the end to protect his fingers. The foot disappears. He waits for it to come back.

This time the foot kicks in a bigger section of the wall. Schroder grabs it, pulls upwards, then pushes the tip of the glass into the side of the calf. He drags the glass as hard as he can from left to right across the shin, and at the same time the owner of the leg starts to scream.

There's another gunshot, this one wild and he doesn't even think it's come into the room. Schroder keeps pulling upwards, trapping the foot against the beams in the wall. He moves the piece of glass to the back of the ankle. He feels it dig into something more solid then drags it with as much force as he can, hoping to slice right through the Achilles.

Another scream, this time louder. Schroder knows he can't keep doing this. He can't defend himself with a piece of glass. But he has bought himself a little more time. He lets go and moves back to the window. He picks up the dog and throws it as hard as he can against the bars. They shudder. He picks it back up for a second attempt. This time there is creaking and groaning and the bars tilt forward. There's a gunshot from outside, and he feels the impact of the slug going into the dead dog. The sense of hope that has come with the moving bars makes the dog feel lighter when he lifts it over his head again, and this time he throws it with even more force. This time the bars pull away from the top, they hinge downwards, the right side bottom breaks away, then it swings to the left, dragging across the wood and coming to a rest, hanging on by one final bolt at the bottom. Schroder throws the dog towards the figure shooting at him below. There's an impact and an *oomph* as the two shapes become one in the darkness.

It's too far to jump to the ground below and, anyway, the person down there is already starting to roll the dog off him. He climbs out the window, puts his foot on the corner of the dangling grate, and looks up. The roof is three feet higher than he can stretch and over-hangs the side of the building by a foot. There is ivy everywhere, so much that it looks like it's sprouting right out of the wood. It's thick in some places, weak in others, but he grabs a handful of it and starts climbing. The first handful is good, the second handful he's just pulling it away from the building, and he reaches further out and finds a thick branch of the stuff.

He climbs, and a few seconds later he's at the top of the wall. He stretches out and grabs the guttering. It feels strong enough to support him and, really, what option does he have other than try? He pulls his body weight up, and for a few seconds he's hanging from the roof, then he gets his fingers around the edge of a pole, a pole that he soon sees is the base of a TV antenna—he thanks God that mental people love TV—then a moment later he's scrambling onto the roof and thanking God he's even still alive. He's two sto-ries up. He rolls out of view from the ground then shimmies back until he can peer over the edge. The person he hit with the dog is on his feet, pointing the gun up at him, but there's no way the guy can see him, surely, and the proof of that is the guy doesn't take a shot.

The roof is made up of concrete tiles. He could pull up some roof tiles and crawl into the ceiling space, or he can try to climb down another wall. Either way he has more options than before, and one less dog in the world to worry about. He tugs at one of the roof tiles. It lifts, then there's some resistance because it's wired around a wooden slat beneath it, but he continues to pull and the wire unwinds itself. He pulls up two more. He figures he can send a few down to the ground. Why not? The tiles will be coming out of the dark, so the guy will never see them coming. The problem is the guy is two stories beneath him.

He decides he can afford to dedicate ten seconds of his life in the hope of getting lucky. Throw a few of them down there.

He gets lucky with the first tile.

He throws it so it spins sideways like a Frisbee, and it cuts through the air with a whistling sound and it's a direct hit, better than he could ever have hoped for, getting the guy somewhere in the middle of his face.

So he's down to one dead dog, one unconscious but most likely dead guy, another guy with a sliced Achilles, and two guys still fully mobile. Maybe he and Peter are going to get out of this after all.

CHAPTER TWENTY-NINE

Charlotte's first thought when I tell her that her husband lied is that he's having an affair.

"This notion he would be out there trying to hurt the people who hurt . . . his . . . dead wife," she says, avoiding the dead wife's name, "is ridiculous. Or, I suppose, he could be gambling. Come to think of it, gambling makes more sense than an affair. But out there looking for revenge? No, I don't think so. Peter is, well, not to sound mean, but Peter is Peter. He's a coward."

I don't tell her she's wrong. She'll come to that conclusion soon enough. "Have you ever heard him talking about Kelly Summers?"

She looks even more confused now. "Who? Are you trying to tell me he *is* having an affair?"

"No," Kent says. "This has nothing to do with anybody having any affair. Now, have you heard the name before?"

Charlotte shakes her head.

I carry on. "What about Dwight Smith?"

"Not him either," she says.

"What do you think Dad has done?" Monica asks, standing at the entry to the lounge. She's come back.

"This man who came to your house today, tell me about him," I say, looking at Monica.

She shrugs. "Like I said, he was bald. And white."

"Can you tell me more?"

"He was old. Like you," she says, and people need to stop telling me this. Closing in on forty means half the world sees me as old, and half sees me as young. "Like dad too," she says.

"Around forty?" I ask.

"I guess." She comes into the lounge and sits on the same couch as Charlotte, but there's a gap big enough to fit two more people. "Not granddad old, just, you know."

"Old."

"Exactly."

"What did this guy say?"

"Nothing. I mean, he was just arriving as I was leaving."

"Did your dad know him already? Or did he introduce himself?"

"I didn't hear."

"What was he wearing?"

She gives it a few seconds of thought. "Jeans, maybe. And a shirt. Maybe a jacket. Yeah, I think he was wearing a jacket. Black or blue."

"Okay," I say, "that's good, Monica. Really good," I say, but the truth is it's useless. I figure that if you're not under twenty and don't hate the world then you're invisible to a girl like Monica Crowley.

"Did this man pull into the driveway in a car?"

"No. I think it was parked out on the road."

"Did you see it?"

"Not really."

"Not really? So does that mean you kind of might have seen it?"

She shrugs. "Yeah, I guess it does kind of maybe mean that. It was like, dark blue, but I don't know cars, I couldn't tell you what type it was. It wasn't one of those four-wheel drives, though."

"So it was a sedan."

"What's that mean?"

"Four doors," I tell her. "Smaller than an SUV and not a sports car. Just a normal car."

"Then it was a sedan."

I stand up. "Was the bald guy taller than me?"

"Maybe," she says.

"Bigger than me?"

"I'm not sure."

"You really think he's out there looking for revenge?" Charlotte asks, the idea finally starting to take hold. "Is he in danger? This guy you're trying to get Monica to describe, you know him, don't you."

"No," Kent says. "Monica, please, this is important. Can you remember anything about the guy? Did he have any tattoos?"

"I don't think so, and I'm trying the best I can, but the guy was just average, you know? It's not like he was hot or anything."

I can feel fatigue and frustration kicking in. We still don't even know if Peter is involved in anything. He really could be fixing a busted water pipe, or he really could be having an affair at the casino.

"Does Peter have a study here?"

"Yeah he does," Charlotte says.

"Do you mind if I have a look through it?"

"Don't you need a warrant or something like that?" Monica asks.

"Monica," Charlotte says. "If it will help find—"

Monica starts shaking her head. "Don't you get it? If Dad is out there looking for revenge, then why should we help the police? Those guys who hurt Mom deserve to die."

"Monica—"

"But it's true," the girl says. "And if Dad has done something, why should we help the police send him to jail?" She looks right at me then carries on. "If you want to arrest my dad, then you're going to need to find enough evidence to do so. You're going to have to find the two bodies, you're going to have to find my dad's DNA and his fingerprints, and you're going to have to get a warrant."

"Listen to me," I say. "If your—"

She shakes her head. "No. Why should I listen to the people who let the men who killed my mother out of jail? The people who now want to put Dad in there?"

"Monica," I say. "We're trying to help your dad. We want to get to him before—"

She keeps shaking her head. "It's too late," she says.

"Mrs. Crowley," I say. "The study?"

But now Charlotte is shaking her head too. "Monica is right.

Not without a warrant. We don't know what my husband is doing out there, and I don't want him going to jail. If he's done something, we're not giving him up. You're going to have to prove it. This conversation is over."

"We're on your side," Kent says.

"Really? So if Peter is out there doing something wrong, you'll stand by him? You'll set him free?"

"We just don't want him getting hurt," I say.

She stands up and we stand up and she leads us back into the hallway. There are pictures on the walls of Monica and another boy, the one who's still asleep, of Charlotte and of Peter, of the four of them together, but there are none of Linda Crowley. Of course there aren't. Charlotte doesn't want to see her husband's dead wife every day.

I hand her my card. "Get him to call us when he gets in."

"I will," she says.

We get to the door. I turn towards Charlotte. "Whatever you're thinking of doing, you can't do it," I tell her.

"What does that mean?"

"You're going to go through your husband's study and you're going to try and hide anything that can link him to what he's doing. I want you to stay out of his study. Going in there is interfering with the investigation."

"It's our house," she says. "I can do whatever I want here."

"You can't hide evidence."

"Until you know for sure what happened, nothing here is evidence."

I step outside with Kent, and then we walk to the car. Charlotte and Monica stand in the doorway watching us. We climb in and Kent puts the keys in the ignition, but doesn't start it.

"We should get a couple of officers to keep an eye on the place," she says.

"I'll make the call."

"So now can we go home? No doubt there'll be a task force meeting early in the morning, but I don't know what else we can do tonight. These guys either show up or they don't, and as soon as Peter Crowley shows up we have the officers stay outside his house to babysit him. There's no way to know where they might be. There's no other angle here, not tonight. I'm tired and you're tired too, and if we're lucky those Collard brothers are never going to show up, and we'll never have to come back here and arrest Peter and destroy his family for the second time. What do you say?"

"I say we should see if we can run a trace on Peter Crowley's cell phone," I tell her, "and maybe we can find out exactly where he is."

CHAPTER THIRTY

Schroder hears the crash and the door to the bedroom banging into the wall. There are footsteps pounding. Then they're at the window. "What the . . ." but the guy doesn't finish his words. Schroder looks over the edge of the roof and can see a flashlight pointing down at the ground. It spotlights the dead dog, then a moment spotlights the body with the opened-up face, and from the clothes that guy is wearing he knows it's Taylor Collard. Then the light goes back to the dog.

"Buzzkill," somebody says. "The bastard killed my dog!"

"I can barely walk," the other guy says, and neither voice belongs to Bevin.

"Toughen up," the first guy says, and Schroder thinks of him as Dogman. Then Dogman adds, "He killed my dog!"

The light goes back to the body. Taylor Collard has had a bad night as far as head injuries go, but it looks like he's not going to have any more nights, good or bad. The center of his face has pressed in, the nose flattened to one side, a piece of scalp hanging over his forehead, the whole thing covered in blood. No need to check for a pulse this time.

"He's gotta be down there somewhere," the other guy says, and there is pain behind his words, and this guy Schroder thinks of as Achilles. Dogman is the one with the flashlight.

"We need to get the hell out of here. I need to get to a hospital before I lose my leg or bleed to death," Achilles says.

"We need to get Buzzkill to a vet," Dogman says.

A second light points at the ground now, stopping at the dog. "Your dog is dead, bro," Achilles says.

"Don't say that. Don't you say that."

"What is that, some kind of brick?" Achilles asks, changing the subject, most likely for his own safety.

"Where?"

"Where I'm pointing the flashlight."

The flashlight changes position. "No, it looks like . . . Shit," Dogman says, and an instant later the flashlight points upwards and hits Schroder in the face. He pulls away from the edge of the roof and hears a bullet catch the edge of the guttering where he was half a second earlier. For a moment his night vision is ruined and he has to blink away the bright spots of the flashlight floating in front of him.

He makes his way along to the chimney. Santa would have a pretty good escape plan from here. His heart is pounding and he needs to sit down and take a breath, perhaps lie down for a few minutes. He can't do any of that. He needs to get out of here before these guys call for more Buzzkills and more assholes to come and help, or before they decide to set fire to the place.

He moves around the chimney and positions himself so he can see out over the front of the grounds. He can see his car and their car and, as he watches, Bevin Collard walks up to his car and crouches beside the front wheel, stands up, and then moves down to the rear wheel. He can't hear it happen, but he knows he's just had both tires cut. Even if he could get the keys back and race to his car, there's no way he's leaving anywhere in a hurry.

He makes his way quietly towards the far end of the building. Ten yards short, just as the roof slopes back down, he braces himself and gets his fingers beneath a roof tile and pulls. This one comes away easier than the one he threw into Taylor Collard, the piece of wire supposed to be holding these things more securely isn't there. That's often the case with buildings of this age, where the tiles are held in place by the tiles around it, the builders missing the occasional piece of wire or just being too lazy. The next one also has no wire, the third one does, and so does the fourth, but not the next two. Within a minute he's made a hole in the roof. This next bit is going to be noisy, but he stomps on the wooden slats, they're thin and long and break easily, but they snap like kindling, the sound telling everybody where he is. He climbs into the roof. The air is thick and hot, and every movement he makes swirls up dust from the decaying insulation. He uses his cell phone for light and walks from beam to beam, there's enough head space so he can almost stand upright. There is no way of finding the manhole, but he doesn't need a manhole. All he has to do is step between the beams and he'll fall through the ceiling panels and into one of the bedrooms or, if he's really unlucky, onto the staircase, or, if he's really, really unlucky, he'll plummet straight down to the ground floor at the base of the stairs.

Construction hasn't changed much over the years or, more accurately, tradesman practices haven't changed much. There are scraps of wood, newspapers, empty insulation bags, and broken tiles that have been dumped up here. He sweeps his cell phone past it, looking for something he can use as a weapon.

"He's in the ceiling!"

The words come from somewhere beneath him, and he stops moving and turns the phone into his chest so no light can escape—not that they could see it anyway.

"I'm telling you, we should just burn the place down," Achilles says.

"He killed my dog," Dogman says. "I want to make him pay."

"Burning him alive will make him pay, and I have to get to a hospital."

"Burning him alive lets him off easy."

A moment later there's a gunshot. He hears a bullet come through. It cracks one of the roof tiles.

"What the hell? Don't do that," Dogman says.

Another gunshot.

"I said don't do that. What if you hit him?"

"I'm hoping to hit him. I gotta get this leg taken care of before I bleed to death."

"I just told you I want to make him pay. What if you get him in the head? No, shoot him if you see him, but only in the legs. Aim for his knees. Come on, let's find a way up there."

"He's probably listening to us," Achilles says.

"Then fine, let him listen. There's nowhere he can go."

Schroder moves along carefully, feeling a little safer that they're not planning on shooting him. What it means, though, is they're going to try and find a way into the ceiling. He finds a piece of rebar that's three feet long, but when he goes to pick it up it won't move. The damn thing is buried into a beam of wood, even though it doesn't seem to be doing anything. He tries to wiggle it, but it's no use. He picks up a broken roof tile. It's a diagonal, jagged piece of concrete shaped like a shark tooth that runs the length of his palm. There's an identical piece next to it.

He goes back the way he came. As soon as they start to come up here, he'll drop through the ceiling into the hallway or one of the bedrooms. Hopefully he can get back outside through the open front door. He makes it a few more yards when there's a sound coming from where he just was. Something is being dragged across the floor. One of the beds, probably. Which means they've found the manhole cover. He throws the roof tile, pitching it underhand into the distance where it crashes into the roof and then into the ceiling.

"He's getting further away," somebody says.

He moves carefully in the direction of the dragging sound, picks up the other half of the roof tile, crouches, and waits.

The dragging comes to a stop. There's the sound of the bed protesting against the weight, then only two feet away from him a crack of light appears as the manhole cover is lifted. The light gets bigger as the gap widens.

He stays still.

The cover opens a few more inches. Then a few more. Then it's tossed all the way up so it hinges over itself and lands on its back.

A hand appears, and then another hand with a flashlight, then the top of a head. A neck and shoulders facing away from him.

Schroder steps forward with the broken roof tile, but before he can swing it down he misplaces his foot, steps off the beam and directly onto the ceiling board, and a second later he's falling right through it, crashing to the ground below.

CHAPTER THIRTY-ONE

We sit in the car outside Peter Crowley's house and we make a call to the station to get them to trace Peter's number. We don't need a warrant. When somebody's life is on the line, we can call the service provider and get a telecommunications intercept. I give the number to the officer and he tells me it'll be a ten-minute call to the phone company, and from there hopefully they'll have a location within twenty minutes and he'll call me right back.

I can tell that Rebecca is grumpy with me, and to be fair I'm grumpy with me too. She wants to go home and I want to go home and instead the night keeps creeping closer to morning, and soon we'll be eating breakfast and sitting in a task-force room and Sunday will last forever.

Of course none of that has to happen. If we can find Peter Crowley, then maybe we can find the bald man too. Maybe all of this can end right now.

I tell this to Kent, who shakes her head.

"Bevin and Taylor were taken, what," she says, then looks at her watch, "almost five hours ago. You think they're still alive?"

"I don't know," I say. "It's possible."

"Okay," she says. "But here's the deal. We find Peter's location. If it turns out he's having an affair, or he's off gambling, then we go home, right? We go home and we just wait for the Collards to show up, either dead or alive."

"Deal," I tell her.

"And here's another deal. If we're going to kill thirty minutes, how about we go and grab some coffee?"

We head into town, back towards the alleyway the Collard brothers disappeared from, towards the drunks and the police sta-

tion, and we turn off a few blocks before all that and head to a line
of cafés, the average age here twenty years on top of the average age
of Popular Consensus and the bars around it. We choose a café and
sit at an outside table beneath a gas heater. We order coffees from
a waitress in a tight, black T-shirt with piercings in her ears, nose,
and tongue. We sit with a view out over the Avon River, a river
that winds around the heart of the city, its water dark and shallow,
home to ducks and beer cans. There are a dozen people at the café
doing the same thing as us. It's almost four a.m. and I guess some
of them have been out at clubs or bars and are now winding down,
while those half our age wind down stuffing their faces with burgers
at fast-food joints.

"So why did you join?" Kent asks me.

Our coffees have arrived and I'm still blowing on mine, trying to
get it to cool down. There's a stereo pumping music into the court-
yard, something easy listening that I don't recognize and could fall
asleep to.

"Sorry?"

"The police force. Did you join to fight the good fight?"

"Something like that," I tell her.

"Does something like that come with any other details?"

I shrug. "I guess so. I don't know. I mean, this city is my home,
right? I love it here. I know I bitch about it, but I'm allowed to
because it's my city, and I've just always wanted to make it a better
place. It deserves to be better than it is. I always thought I could
make a difference. That's really all it was. What about you? Why'd
you join?"

She smiles as if hitting on a happy memory, then blows on her
coffee. "Well, it was either that or be a baker."

"A biker?"

She laughs. "A *baker*. Can you imagine me as a *biker*?"

"Somehow it's easier to picture you as a biker than a baker."

She laughs again. "I joined the force because of my dad—you
know the cliché, girl becomes cop because dad is one. I kind of got
pushed into it, really, but I always have this dream of one day open-

ing up my own shop. I make the best muffins. I know that sounds silly, but I really do."

"You bake muffins?" I ask.

"Don't laugh," she says, but she's still laughing.

"I'm not laughing," I say, but I am. "When I try to imagine it, all I come up with is you wearing a chef's outfit along with a chef's hat covered in flour as you try putting out oven fires."

"I'll prove it to you," she says. "I'll make a bunch of muffins for you and Bridget and I'll bring them around on Monday and leave them on your doorstep for when you get back from the hospital."

At the mention of Bridget's name I stop laughing. I think about her trip to the mall, our excursion into the woods, about Monday's appointment.

"I'm sure it's going to be okay," Kent says, because she can tell where my mind has gone.

I manage to start drinking my coffee. "Do the guys at the station know about the baking?"

"No," she says, "and don't you dare tell them."

"Well, keep me in muffins and I promise to keep it a secret."

My phone rings. It's the station. They have a location on Peter's cell phone. It's west of the city, back in the direction of the train tracks where all of this started for us. But further. Three cell phone towers have been used to triangulate the signal. The location given is a farm, which, for all intents and purposes, is the middle of nowhere. We're told the cell phone is within a half-mile radius of that. We're told they'll update us if that signal moves.

"So whatever Peter Crowley is doing," Kent says, "he's still out there doing it."

"Seems that way."

"Okay. Good call on tracking the cell phone. Come on," she says, and quickly finishes her coffee, "let's go and arrest one of the good guys."

CHAPTER THIRTY-TWO

Schroder's fall is broken by Achilles, who for some reason has taken off his shirt. He lands on Achilles's head and shoulders, folding him into the ground. The broken roof tile is still clutched tightly in his grip.

The flashlight pointing into the roof now points down at him. Dogman is sitting on the edge of the crawl space. He starts to lower himself, then seems to think better of it and lowers his gun instead. At the same time Schroder swings the roof tile. He uses all of its weight and connects it as hard as he can into Dogman's knee. It tears into Dogman with a popping sound and though he can't be sure, it feels like he's levered most of the kneecap out to the side. He pulls the tile back out.

Dogman screams, then he's dropping onto the bed, rolling onto his back, and hitting the floor. Achilles reaches up, Schroder sees the movement, and turns towards it just in time to push the guy's hand away as he fires the gun. He uses the tile against the side of Achilles's face, clubbing him as hard as he can. It doesn't go in like it did to Dogman's leg, but it doesn't need to. Achilles is laid out flat. Schroder grabs the gun out of his hand just as Dogman is leaning up with his own gun. Schroder takes the shot before Dogman can, hitting him in the throat. For his part, Dogman is left with a very confused look on his face. All the pain and emotion and fear disappear from his features, and he slumps down and ends up sitting with his legs out ahead of him. He stares at Schroder, and now there is a crack of emotion, not much, but enough to see fear and confusion. Schroder keeps the gun pointed at him, and at the same time he watches Dogman struggle with the depths of what death is going to be like, then, with no real choice, he gives in to it.

He fires a shot into Dogman's head to make sure the same thing that happened with Taylor Collard earlier in the evening isn't going to happen again. Then he turns the gun towards Achilles and shoots him in the head too. He's seen too many horror movies to bother about thinking twice. He sits down hard on the floor and leans against the wall. He can feel his heart hammering inside his chest. All he can hear is the ringing sound of gunfire. It hurts. His throat is getting sore from breathing so heavily. Dusty insulation is falling like soft snow through the open hole in the ceiling. He wants to close his eyes and sit back and relax, to get some energy back, but there's still Bevin Collard to deal with. He looks at Achilles. The reason he's shirtless is because he's taken it off and tied it around the wound in his leg with his belt.

He looks at his hands. They're shaking. They're covered in scratches and insulation dust and dirt. The holes in his arm from Buzzkill look nasty, like a row of bloody eyes looking at him. He needs to get out of here. Needs to get Peter to safety. And the story? What will he tell the police? He doesn't know. For now they just need to get away from Grover Hills.

"What's going on up there?"

The voice comes from the ground floor, loud enough to be heard over his ringing ears. He's heard gunshots in close quarters before, and knows his ears will still be in pain for a few more minutes.

"Help," Schroder says, and he coughs as he says it and lowers his voice.

"Matt?"

"Help," he says again.

Footsteps on the stairs. Cautious. Schroder switches off the flashlight and stays in the doorway of the bedroom, wishing all of tonight could have been as easy as this moment is about to be. A moment later there's a beam of light, it plays across the walls and the floor and comes to a stop on the bodies.

"Oh sh—" is all Bevin Collard gets to say before Schroder pulls the trigger, aiming center mass. He's not sure where the bullet gets him, but Bevin is already taking a step backwards and the momentum takes him through the rail of the stairs. A second after that he crashes into the floor below. Schroder drags himself to his feet and steps into the hallway and points the flashlight down at the last victim. What was good enough for the others is good enough for Bevin, and the man's head twitches heavily to the side as Schroder fires a shot into it.

What a mess. A goddamn mess.

He gets Dogman's gun, then makes his way downstairs and picks up the gun Bevin Collard was using, giving him three guns. Outside he finds a fourth still clutched in Taylor Collard's very dead hand, but with life being a learning curve and on a curve where he learns from his mistakes, he fires a shot into Taylor's head too.

He goes down into the basement. Peter Crowley has rolled onto his side. His eyes are open and they watch Schroder as he crouches over him.

"What . . ." is all Peter can say, then he smacks his lips together a few times, then says, "water."

"I'm going to get you out of here," Schroder says.

It's not the best position for an injured man, but using a fireman's lift to pick Peter Crowley up is the only way to get him out of the basement. His arm hurts like a bitch as he carries him up the stairs, and it's hard work but not impossible, and a minute later he has Crowley outside and lays him on the lawn. He retrieves the keys for his car, then confirms two of his tires have been slashed.

"We're going to have to take Dogman's car," he says to Peter, crouching down beside him.

"The men . . ." Peter says, but nothing else. There is blood running out of his ear, and Schroder's hands have blood on them from picking him up.

Schroder puts his hand on Peter's shoulder and keeps it there. "They're dead. All of them. I got them for you. I know it wasn't supposed to be this way, but the men who hurt your wife are now rotting in Hell."

Peter smiles, reaches up, and puts his hand on top of Schroder's. "It's okay," he says.

"It's not okay," Schroder says.

"You killed them."

"Yes. I killed them."

"And I like ice cream," Peter says.

"What?"

"Chocolate is my favorite. Do you have any?"

"No," Schroder says.

"Chocolate is Linda's," he says, but then says nothing else, just stares ahead and releases his grip on Schroder's hand and lets his own hand hit the ground.

"I'm sorry," Schroder says, and he grips the dead man's shoulder and looks him in his open, unseeing eyes. "It wasn't supposed to be this way, but Linda would be proud of what you tried to do. I'm just sorry this is the way it went down."

It didn't have to be this way, not really. Things didn't work out because Schroder got caught up in the momentum of bad mistakes. That's what it came down to. He closes Peter's eyes, holds his fingers on them for ten seconds in the hope they won't pop open, and they don't. Then he wonders if he is going to cry, if the emotion of it will get to him, but no. Of course not. There are no tears for the New New Him.

There is still plenty of work to do.

He drags Taylor Collard to the stairs and lays him horizontal to them, then goes inside and drags the brother out and lays him on the first step, also horizontal. They help turn the stairs into a ramp, not a great ramp, more of a pyramid, but one good enough for Dogman's car to climb up without any real trouble, and Schroder does that now, parking as close as he can to the door. He moves to the back and pops the trunk. There are two metal containers, somewhere around fifty gallons of fuel in total, and two twelve packs of beer.

He takes out the spare wheel. In the cavity beneath the wheel is a plastic bag. He opens it and finds four silencers. He takes one out and confirms it fits his gun, then drops the gun and silencer into separate pockets. He rolls the spare wheel over to his car hoping it'll have the same stud pattern, and it does. It takes ten minutes to change it with one of his own, which is a few minutes longer than normal, which he puts down to the sore arm and fatigue. Then he switches the other damaged tire with his own spare wheel. He tosses both damaged wheels into the trunk of his car.

He empties the fifty gallons of fuel across the ground floor of the building, some around the car, a lot of it on the stairs. He can't imagine too many people will be upset with Grover Hills being burned down. If anything, most people will wonder why it wasn't torched months ago.

He can't find the flares Dogman was told to bring, but he finds a box of matches in the dead man's pocket. Since he's at it, he takes out the wallets of all the dead men and nets himself over seven hundred dollars in cash, most of it from Bevin Collard, and most of that he assumes is drug money. No need to see that burn. He looks at the driver's licenses. Matthew Roddick and Robin Walsh. Two unmemorable names. He wonders what kind of record they have.

He wipes down three of the guns, even though the flames will take care of any prints, then places them in the hands of three of the dead men—Roddick, Walsh, and Bevin Collard. The fourth he hangs on to. The shower curtain lining the trunk of his car he tosses onto the veranda.

The match lights on the very first try. He drops it into the puddle of fuel, it lights up blue and orange and races along the floor. It's only a matter of seconds before flames are leaping into the air. They reach for the stairs, the walls, they go into the shadows where the ghosts of Grover Hills are hiding. He picks up the roof tile he killed Taylor Collard with and tosses it into the fire, then drags Peter away from the flames. He doesn't want a good man to burn.

Schroder stands by his car and watches the flames, enjoying the warmth on his face, until after a few minutes it becomes too hot. All that wood—it's not going to take long until the entire thing collapses in on itself, all the DNA and fingerprints and the story of what happened here tonight burned away. He doesn't hang around to watch that happen.

CHAPTER THIRTY-THREE

I wonder what state Bevin and Taylor Collard are in, whether they're very much alive or very much dead, or some very much miserable state in between. I get the feeling it's the latter. I get the feeling Peter Crowley wants to make them suffer, and he's taken them well out of town for it. But they're just feelings, and in twenty minutes we'll know the facts.

For some of the journey it's the same as yesterday morning. We leave the edge of town. Onto the motorway. Houses petering out and farms petering in. The Christchurch prison is ahead, then we're alongside it, then it's behind us, traveling west, and I remember coming out here earlier this year and promising myself if another case ever brought me out here I was going to turn it down. We get a phone call from the station. The phone company has just reported that Peter Crowley's cell phone is no longer transmitting.

We're only a few minutes away from the location the phone company gave us when we see the glow on the horizon. Morning is on its way, and at first that's what we think it is, the lightening of the sky, but of course we're driving in the wrong direction for that. We're driving west and the sun is rising in the east. Then the glow becomes more yellow, more orange, it become stronger and we know we're not looking at some optical illusion as the sun reflects off the landscape. We're looking at a fire. I call it in, telling the fire service we'll have a more accurate address soon, but for now just to head west out of the city down the main highway and follow the flames. As we continue onwards it seems likely the location we're looking for and that orange glow are one and the same. Of course they are. And instead of going to the place the phone company told us, we drive towards the glow. We've turned off and are now heading north, through a maze of country roads, some sealed, some gravel, some just hard-packed dirt, and I now know exactly where we're heading, and a minute later it's confirmed.

We pull into the long driveway of Grover Hills, passing the big oaks guarding the entrance. Ahead the abandoned mental institution is a mass of black shapes covered in blankets of yellow and orange, the black shapes of walls and the roof all at right angles to each other, the yellows and oranges flowing over every surface. Windows crack, some pop, some explode, the sounds like gunfire in the night. As we watch, some of those right angles shift. Some grow and some shrink as beams inside twist and some start to fall. This is the mental institution where I tracked a serial killer earlier in the year. This is where I took the heavy blow to the head that was my golden ticket to Coma Land—come for the peace and quiet, stay for the dreams.

Kent gets on the phone and I jump out of the car and the air is hot, unbearably so, and looking at the fire is like staring into the sun. There's a body twenty yards from the entrance. I run over to it, and right away I can see the face of the man I saw in the photographs in the hallway when Charlotte Crowley was leading us to the door. I check for a pulse, but there's nothing there. The body is still warm, but that could just be because Grover Hills is burning. The side of his head has been caved in. Rebecca catches up to me.

"Who?" she asks.

"Crowley." I reach into his pockets. There's no cell phone, and maybe it's in the flames and that's why it's no longer working. I find a wallet and check the driver's license and it matches the dead guy.

"Is that a car?" Rebecca asks, and points towards the building.

At first I can't see it. The air is shimmering, there are sparks and flames and ash, and the building is in the throes of dying, and then through the flames I see it, a car parked up in the entrance of the building—it's climbed the steps and is almost right up against the door, pitched on an angle with the hand brake on. I can't tell if anybody is in it. We can't tell if anybody else is here.

"There must have been a second car," Kent says.

"Or somebody is still out here. Lock our car," I tell her, "and let's walk the perimeter."

She locks the car. It would be foolish to split up, and foolish to try and find a way in there. We would, if we really felt there was somebody in there to be saved. As it stands we're both sure if anybody is in there it's going to be the Collard brothers, and neither of us are going to go fire walking for those guys. We start left, the glow from the fire lighting the grounds in all directions, sparks jumping into the long grass and soon that will burn too. We start a loop, wide enough so we don't cook in the heat. Around the south side, about ten yards from the building, is a dead dog. The fire isn't as strong back here, but it will get there.

"A stray?" Rebecca asks.

I shake my head. "Looks like it has a collar."

I put my arm up to shield my face, and then I run to the dog, crouch down, and grab its collar. I start pulling, dragging the dog back from the building. Sweat is pouring down my face and back. I drag the dog twenty yards further from the flames. It's a rottweiler. Its head is a mess of blood and torn skin and one of its ears is missing. The collar doesn't have a dog tag on it.

We leave the dog and carry on. We don't find any other vehicles. No more dead dogs or dead people. We finish our loop.

"See that?" Kent asks, and points towards the burning car.

"See what?"

"I think there's a body beneath it."

I have to shield my eyes with my hand, but all I can see are flames, they're dancing back and forth, but then there's a gap, and I can see a head and shoulder with an arm pointing outwards from beneath the car and then the gap closes. "Want to go and drag it out?" I ask.

"After you," she says.

"Can you make out the registration plate?"

"I can't even make out the color."

There's a loud cracking sound, and we both jump as a section of roof collapses inwards. A new set of flames fills the space. They reach up and try to burn the morning sky. Ash and charcoal hang in the air, suspended in the moment as if hanging on wires.

"We need to move back," I tell Rebecca, "and we need to clear the drive for the fire trucks. We should drag Peter further back too."

"Let's photograph him first," she says, "for the medical examiner."

Rebecca drives the car out onto the road and returns with the camera. We snap some photographs of Crowley so the medical examiner can see what position we found him in, then we drag him to the guarding oak trees where there is no chance of being run over. If the fire trucks are getting close, we can't hear them as Grover Hills continues to eat itself, there's another crack, and another corner of the roof turns inwards, then part of the wall beneath it twists, balances, then falls inwards too. Sparks and fiery splinters of wood spray into the air, they catch on the light breeze and are taken away. I think about the scream room downstairs, the stories I heard of patients who used to be tortured down there by some of the staff, sometimes as punishment, sometimes just for kicks.

There is nothing more we can do as we wait for the fire trucks and for Hutton to show up, and soon we hear them, the sirens close enough to be heard above the splintering wood, four fire trucks in total, they enter the driveway and form a semicircle. Maybe twenty people spill out of them like circus clowns, and they get to work, and moments later water is being pumped into the heart of the fire from one truck, then another, then all four hoses are writhing like snakes across the ground as water fattens them up. We stay out of their way as all the evidence inside is torched first and then soaked with water. It seems like a war the firefighters can't win as the fire latches on to the landscape and tries to burn that too.

"I know who he is," Kent says. "The bald man."

I turn towards her because I think I know too. I've been think-

ing about it since seeing where the fire was burning. Grover Hills.
A bald man. I know one bald man that knows this place is out here.
But is it possible? No. Kelly Summers was his case, but not Linda
Crowley. But still . . .

"Who?" I ask.

"He's a victim. I think he's lost somebody close to him, the same
way Peter Crowley did. This bald guy, he's trying to help others like
himself. And if that's true, then he wouldn't have done anything to
hurt Peter, because they're on the same side, the same way he was
helping Kelly Summers."

I think about that, and it goes against what I've been thinking
since I got here, that somehow Schroder could be involved. I was
the one who tracked a killer out here months ago, but for the following week Schroder had to come out here every day, dealing with
the fallout, dealing with what we had learned about the history of
this place, what had been covered up here for so long, dealing with
those who spent days and nights in the scream room before being
buried in the ground. A lot of suffering happened inside these now-
burning walls, and a guy like Schroder knows a lot more suffering
could happen out here and nobody would ever know.

But Schroder is Schroder. At least he used to be. Not anymore. I
still can't see him being involved—of course not—it's just a coincidence he knows about this place, just as thousands of other people
know about it. After all, the case was covered in the news.

Kent carries on. "The train line where Dwight Smith was killed.
You draw a line between here and Kelly Summers's house, and that
train line is on it. Is this where they were coming before they ran
out of gas?"

"They?"

"If Peter was here tonight, only stands to reason Kelly would
have been here last night, don't you think?"

"There was no indication she had been in the car," I say, "and
if she had been following, then they could have dumped the body
into her car and carried on."

Kent thinks about that for a few moments. She runs the math, runs the scenarios, tries to get things to fit, but can't. "So maybe she wasn't involved. Maybe the bald guy was just doing this on his own. When the car ran out of gas he probably figured the best thing was to throw the body on the railway lines, hoping we would think it was a suicide. Then he walked back, or hitched a ride. Maybe he gave Kelly the option and she said no, and he gave Peter the option and he said yes."

A couple of police cars show up then. Hutton is among them. He sees us and comes over, and once again I think about how good he looks now he's lost all that weight.

"That's Peter Crowley?" he asks, nodding towards the body.

"Yeah."

"That's where you found him?"

"We had to move him," I tell Hutton, then explain why.

"Medical examiner is on her way," he says, "and she's not going to be too happy about that."

"She'll be happier than she would have been if we'd left him where he was."

"Any theories?" he asks.

I look at Kent. Kent shrugs, then shakes her head, and then says, "Nothing yet."

Hutton looks at his watch, then looks at the sky as if it confirms what his watch just said. "I want you guys to go back and talk to his wife."

"Now?"

Part of the building is no longer ablaze. It seems the war might actually be won by the firefighters. Not yet, but eventually. By the time it's over I can't imagine there's going to be a lot of the building left standing.

"I don't see any reason to put it off," he says. "Look, I know it's late. But give notification to the wife, and maybe now she'll let you take a look in her husband's study without a warrant, though at this point it's just a matter of semantics since we can get one anyway.

We've got a task-force meeting scheduled for nine, but I'll push it back to ten. I know it's not much, but it gives you time to grab some breakfast or try and get a quick nap beforehand. As soon as we can get a look at the car, we'll run the plates and see who it belongs to."

Right then one of the firefighters comes over and gives us an update. He expects they'll have the fire under control within the next thirty minutes, but then tells us not to hold out any hope of entering the building anytime soon. "If at all," he says. "You're apt to fall through the floor," he tells us, "or apt to have a wall fall on you. We'll send in a robot with a camera, but I'm telling you the best thing we can do is pull that car out of there, the bodies beneath it, then just knock the whole thing down."

"*Bodies?*" I ask.

"Yeah, there's two of them under there. We'll be able to get what's left of them, but not till the fire is out. Getting them out in one piece is going to be difficult. First of all, parts of those bodies are going to be stuck to the car, and if we tow the car out it's going to destroy what's under there, and I'm guessing you want them intact as much as possible."

"Yes," Hutton says.

"Okay. We'll get a crane down here. We'll figure a way to get the car lifted right up, and we'll do the best we can. But your medical examiner is going to have to keep in mind those bodies have already been burned and water-blasted, so there's not going to be much there anyway. Also, there's a dead dog around the south side."

"Yeah, we know about the dog," I tell him.

"Looks like somebody beat the hell out of it. I'll update you when we know more," he says, then walks back towards the fire, which is definitely dying down.

"A dead dog?" Hutton asks.

"Yeah," I say, then fill him in, and the whole time he's shaking his head.

"The guy who did all of this, he's not in there, is he," Hutton says.

I shake my head. "No."

"How can you guys be so sure?" Kent asks.

"Do you want to tell her or do you want me to?" Hutton asks.

"You go ahead," I tell him.

"Because nothing is ever that easy," he says.

CHAPTER THIRTY-FOUR

I can feel the heat on my back as we walk to Kent's car. When we're far enough away it actually feels pretty good. Then when we're too far away the night feels cool again. Not that it's night anymore—that's been and gone. Kent gets in the car and I get in and we stare out the windshield towards the flames.

"I'm not really up for this," she tells me.

"I feel the same way."

"I'll text my sister and let her know."

"I don't like the idea of Bridget waking up and me not being there. Seeing your sister is going to confuse her."

"It's after six," she says. "How about we swing by your place on the way and you can wake her up and tell her what's going on?"

So that's what we decide to do. Kent sends her sister a text message to tell her our plans. The drive back into town is a quick one, and after a while there's a glow on the horizon to the east. There isn't much in the way of life, just a couple of taxis, a couple of people walking home from clubs, a few women carrying their shoes. Some of these people probably didn't quite get the buzz they were wanting since the men behind the clubs they bought drugs from are out of business.

We get to my house and Kent waits out in the car. Her sister meets me on the path up to the door. She smiles at me. It's a little forced at this time in the morning, and I smile back, equally as forced, and she tells me everything is fine, that Bridget hasn't woken up. Then I go inside while she goes and chats to Rebecca.

Bridget is still asleep, and I tap her on the shoulder, then slowly shake her, then have to shake her even more to get her to stir.

"Morning," she says, and smiles up at me, and boy how I love that smile.

"Hey," I say.

Then she notices I'm dressed. "You're working today?"

"Yeah. I'm sorry," I tell her, "but I have to head out early."

"Teddy off to save the world," she says, and she still sounds asleep.

I tell her that I've been out during the night, and that Rebecca's sister is here to keep an eye on her.

"I don't need a babysitter," she says, now sounding awake.

"I know you don't," I tell her. "But I just want to make sure you're okay."

"So you're never going to leave me alone again?"

"No, it's—"

She smiles at me. "It's okay, Teddy. I'm just teasing," she says, but I'm sure there's some truth in there too. She's scared—and rightly so. She looks at the bedside clock. "You'll be gone most of the day?"

"Most of the morning," I tell her. "That's all I know for now."

"I'll call my mom and dad in a few hours and get them to come over, and then the babysitter can go home."

I give her a hug and then I'm heading back outside, and Rebecca's sister sees me and she climbs out of the car and we nod at each other, but don't say anything.

Fifteen minutes later we're pulling in behind the patrol car outside Peter Crowley's house. We are only a quarter of the way towards the front door of the house when it swings open and Charlotte Crowley, followed by her stepdaughter and her son, come spilling out onto the doorstep.

"Unless you have a warrant," Charlotte says, but then she stops. She knows. I don't know how she knows—both Kent and myself have done this before, and it's not written on our faces, but people just know. This is one of those occasions.

"Where is he?" she asks. "Why aren't you bringing him home?" she asks, but I recognize these questions for what they are—

delaying tactics. She knows her husband is dead, and if she can will it to be otherwise, then she'll give it a good shot.

"Can we come inside?" Kent asks.

"Who's he having an . . . an . . . affair with . . ." she says, but she runs out of steam, and there are tears there now. "Is it that woman you mentioned? Do you have a warrant?"

"We need to speak to you alone for a few minutes," Kent says to her.

"Where's Dad?" Monica asks. "Have you arrested—"

Charlotte turns towards her. "Go inside and wait for me."

"You can't tell me—"

"Monica! Please, for once in your goddamn life, will you please do what I ask of you?"

Monica looks shocked, but then she turns around and heads back inside, and a moment later her bedroom door slams.

"You too, honey," Charlotte says to her son, and he disappears without saying anything and then the three of us are alone.

"We're sorry to have to tell you this," I say, "but—"

"Then don't," Charlotte says, shaking her head.

"Unfortunately—" I say.

"Don't," Charlotte says. "Please, please, don't say it."

"I'm sorry," I say, slowly shaking my hand.

"I'm begging you," she says. "Please, I'm begging you, don't say it."

But I have to say it. It's why we're here. I have to tell this woman that her husband is dead, and no amount of begging is going to change that.

"Peter was found deceased an hour ago," Kent says.

Charlotte shakes her head, and she looks defiant, and she says simply, "No. No, you're wrong."

"Is there somebody we can call for you?" Kent asks.

"My husband. Perhaps I'll call Peter. Yes, I'll do that if you two don't mind just waiting outside. Peter will be able to sort this out."

"Mrs. Crowley," I say. "Can—"

"No," she says. "My answer to everything is no, not until Peter is home. Once he's home he'll be—"

Monica comes back outside. "He's dead," she says, and she says it calmly, and she's been listening in. "Don't you get that? They killed him just like they killed Mom."

"Who killed him?" Charlotte asks, and the question is for Monica as much as us.

"I hate this world," Monica says, her voice still calm, then she goes back inside and we hear a door close, this time it isn't slammed.

"Please, Mrs. Crowley, Charlotte," Kent says. "Let's go inside."

"Peter got called away yesterday," she says. "He's working on a broken water main, but he'll be home soon. We have to buy some more plants. We wanted to get the entire front garden done by the time the weekend ends." She starts pointing at the fresh plants in the garden alongside the pathway. "Peter kept saying we had enough, and I kept telling him that we didn't, and you can see . . . you can see . . ." she says, and her hands go up to her face. "Are you sure?"

"Yes," I tell her.

"Where?"

"An abandoned mental institution by the name of Grover Hills."

"The place that was in the news earlier in the year?"

"Yes," Kent says.

"Then it can't be Peter," she says, "because Peter would have no reason to go there. Or is that where the broken water main was?"

"This would be easier if we could go inside to talk," Kent says.

"Easier? No. Easier doesn't fit into this conversation at all." She turns, but then ends up sitting on the doorstep. The morning is quite light now, and soon the sun will be coming into view. "This is about the men that hurt Linda, isn't it."

"Yes," I tell her. "Did Peter talk much about them?"

"He used to, in the beginning," she says. "Not much. When I met him he was in a bit of a mess, but so was I. Robby wasn't even a year old and my husband had left me. I met Peter one day and, you know, that's what happens, right? People meet and they move on. I mean, it was hard for him not to talk about the men that attacked Linda, but when he did it felt like he was still living that life, and I always felt like I was trying to fill the shoes of the wife he left behind. You know? Nobody wants their husband to talk about their former wife, but when he did it hurt both of us, and it was unfair of me to be angry about it, you know? How can you be angry at somebody who was raped, then killed themselves? This is the house she killed herself in," she says. "I want him to sell it. I want us to move on, but he's always refused, at least he did until recently. I convinced him it'd be healthier for him and for me too, and probably also for Monica, though Monica says if we sell it she'll run away. I convinced Peter a month ago, and we're going to do it up first. It's why we're planting new shrubs. He just needs to . . ." she says, then shakes her head. "I can't believe this is happening. Those boys, did they do this to him? Did they take him out there and kill him?"

"It's looking like it was the other way around," I tell her. "There are two other bodies out there, which we haven't identified yet."

"You think it's them?"

"It's too soon to tell," Kent says. "But it's possible. It's possible Peter killed them, and it's likely he had help."

"Help? Who would help him do such a thing? The man that was here yesterday? You think Monica saw the man who got Peter killed?"

"We'll know soon," I say.

"So . . . does that mean . . ." she says, and then she starts to cry, and I know what's coming. It was always going to come. "If we had let you into Peter's study, if you had taken a look around, could you have . . . could you have stopped it?"

"We don't know," Rebecca says. "But if you let us look around in there now, we might be able to find the man who did all of this. This could have been something Peter was planning. Or it could be that yesterday was their first interaction."

"Did I help kill him? By not letting you look around?"

Kent shakes her head. "You didn't send him out there."

"But I could have stopped it."

"It's possible it was all over by the time we even came to see you."

"*Possible* also means *possibly not,*" Charlotte says.

"We need to talk to Monica again," I say. "We want her to come down to the station to give us a description of the man she saw."

"Okay, I'll get her ready," she says. "Give her a chance to get herself together, then I'll bring her in later this morning. I promise. But this bald man," she says, "you need to arrest him. He has to pay for what he's done, but at the same time you need to give him a medal too. If we had more people in the city like him doing your job for you, then people like Linda would never get hurt in the first place."

CHAPTER THIRTY-FIVE

If we had more people in the city like him doing your job for you, then people like Linda would never get hurt in the first place.

Charlotte's words stick with me as she leads us through to Peter's study. She sits in the lounge with the kids and talks to them in flat tones while we go through Peter's emails and bank accounts and anything else we can find, her words rattling around in my head, embedding themselves in there for good because she's right, of course she's right. And at the same time she's wrong. It would be anarchy. We look for forty-five minutes and find nothing. We tell her that as we leave, and it alleviates her guilt of not helping us earlier. Her life changed last night. Never could she have thought when she woke up on Saturday morning that by Sunday morning her husband would be dead and the world would be upside down. That's the way life works. Some people get to say good-bye—some don't.

"We got two and a half hours before our ten a.m. meeting," Kent says. "You want to grab a nap then meet for breakfast around nine thirty?"

"Waking up after an hour is going to hurt," I tell her, "but it'll hurt more if I don't."

"You want me to pick you up in the morning?"

"I'll meet you there."

She drives me back home. Her sister comes out and she smiles at me and tells me Bridget is still in the bedroom. I thank her for her help, and Kent drives away in the police car and the sister drives away in Kent's car. I go inside and lock the door to the world behind me. Bridget is sitting up in bed reading a novel.

"You solved the case already?" she asks.

"No, but I have an hour off to recharge."

I set the alarm and Bridget curls up next to me and I close my eyes, and the next thing I know my alarm is going off. I was right with what I told Rebecca earlier—it hurts.

Bridget isn't in bed with me. I've slept sixty minutes and the feeling I have reminds me of the hangovers I got last year when I would drink away the days and the nights, the alcohol an important tool to numb away the pain of all that I had lost. I climb out of bed. I'm still dressed. I head down to the kitchen. Bridget is making toast and there are only two plates on the table.

"What time is Rebecca coming by?"

Rebecca. Not Carl. Another good sign. I look at my watch. "She's not. I'm meeting her in town."

"Take a seat," she says.

She brings over two pieces of toast and a glass of orange juice and a cup of coffee. She brings over the same for herself. "You want to tell me about the case?"

Years ago I never would have. Years ago work stayed at work. It'd come home with me, it'd always be near the forefront of my thoughts, but I never shared it. I see no reason to change any of that. No reason to put bad images into Bridget's head.

"You don't want to know," I tell her, which is what I used to tell her.

"Yes, I do," she says, which is what she always used to say. "I want to be able to help you, Teddy," she says.

"It's fine. And, weirdly, it's not a bad case, if that makes sense. The people showing up dead are bad people," I say, and I take a mouthful of toast and then talk around it. "Except last night a good man died trying to hurt the men who hurt his wife."

She nods, staring at me. "Somebody is out there killing bad people, and now good people too?"

"Last night didn't go to plan," I say, and take another bite. "Somebody who thinks they're doing a good thing is doing a bad thing."

"What are you going to do when you find him?"

"Arrest him."

"And you think that's the right thing to do?"

I swallow the piece of toast. I look hard at my wife. "What do you mean?"

"I know you, Teddy. I know you must be conflicted on this. I just want to make sure whatever decision you make is one you can live with."

I let her words sink in. Before I can think of what to say, she carries on.

"Maybe we can go out tonight if you get back in time? A nice meal?"

"I'd like that."

Just before I go I give Bridget's parents a call and ask them to come over for the day while I'm at work. They ask me—like they always used to when they found out I was working on a weekend—why I'm working on a Sunday, and I give them the answer I always used to give them: because people die on weekends too. I tell them hopefully it'll only be half a day. Bridget promises me she'll be okay on her own until her folks show up.

I'm hungry again by the time I get into town. I meet Rebecca two blocks from the police station in a café called Froggies. I'm not sure what the owner's intent was, but within days of it opening it became the go-to place for cops, and at this time of the morning—at least on a weekday—it can be almost impossible to find somewhere to sit. There's a jukebox in the corner playing some seventies stuff—I know the songs, but can't name them. There's one spare booth along the back wall beneath a picture of a New York skyline, a black-and-white Empire State Building in the dead center of it. The café is warm and welcoming and smells like waffles and bacon and coffee, and what could be better? There are uniformed officers everywhere drinking coffee and trying to wake up for the morning shift, or who have finished their shift and are drinking coffee to wake up enough to drive home. There's laughter from some tables, intense debate from others, stories about criminals being shared the same way fishermen talk about the one that got away, or the big one they caught.

We pick up a couple of menus even though I already know what I'm going to eat. So does the cook. At this time in the morning they already have a bunch of big breakfast meals prepared out back for cops on the go. Which is what we are. We order one each and two minutes later we're eating bacon and eggs and mushrooms and tomato and hash browns and toast. I hate tomato so I pick it out and put it on Rebecca's plate, and the whole time I can't stop thinking about Schroder. Schroder the cop who arrested Dwight Smith. Schroder who years ago dealt with a man thrown on a set of train tracks to try and hide a crime. Schroder who knows all about Grover Hills.

Schroder the bald man.

Schroder who isn't Schroder anymore.

I want to run it past Kent. She never worked with him, not really, just for a day or two earlier in the year when she had just been transferred to Christchurch, back when Schroder was fired. And they were together when the car exploded and almost killed them both, but that wasn't working together, that was just being together. But she doesn't know him. I was in the academy with him, we were on the streets together, I was with Schroder when my daughter was killed. We used to hang out on weekends during the summer, there were barbecues and beers, and we'd talk the same way other officers in this café are talking—about the ones who got away, about the ones we caught. Our wives would hang out, my daughter would run around with his daughter, we would kick in doors and storm into houses together and we fought the good fight together.

Kent starts in on her bacon, chews it for a bit, then talks with her mouth half-full. "Maybe it's one of those *I'll scratch your back and you scratch mine*. Could be somebody was helping Peter, and Peter was supposed to help somebody. Or there's a bunch of them building an army."

"Do you think Kelly Summers was part of that army?"

She shrugs. "I'm just spitballing. When we know who that car belonged to at Grover Hills we'll be able to piece things together a little better. Come on, Tate, eat up, you're going to make us late."

I shovel what I can into my mouth, wanting to get my money's worth and knowing I may not get another chance to eat today. Then we drive to the station.

The fourth floor isn't any busier than normal. In fact it's slower, probably because it's a Sunday and I imagine a lot of detectives have "dead batteries" on their phones and haven't heard the news. We stand in the task-force room, about twenty of us, half of what I was expecting. Somebody has been working in here because up on the board are photographs of the Collard brothers and Peter Crowley. On another board are photographs of Kelly Summers and Dwight Smith. The two boards are far enough apart to make me wonder if that's because the cases are far apart—so far there's nothing to link them other than the timing.

We chat to Hutton for a few moments and update him on our talk with Charlotte Crowley and the search of her house. Then the meeting starts. Hutton stands at the front of the room and briefs us. The fire at Grover Hills has been put out. The car has been identified, and belongs to a man by the name of Matthew Roddick. A dog found at the scene didn't have a microchip implanted like we'd hoped and can't be traced. Police sent to speak to Matthew Roddick found an annoyed girlfriend and no Roddick, just information that he had gotten a call in the middle of the night and had left quickly, taking his dog with him. The dog's name is Buzzkill. The fire fighters still haven't gained access to the remains of the building, so as of yet there is no information as to whether there are more bodies inside. A crane is at the scene and the logistics are being worked out on how to move the car without the building collapsing around it and without pulling apart the two bodies beneath it.

Matthew Roddick has a record for assault, drug possession, and armed robbery. Over the last ten years he has been in and out of jail a total of four times, adding up to seven years. Nobody is going to build a statue to remember him.

"We've pulled Peter Crowley's phone records, and the call made to Matthew Roddick was made from his phone. We don't know who made the call, or how many people we're dealing with."

"What's the link between Matthew Roddick and Peter Crowley?" another detective asks, somewhere from behind me.

"That's the thing. It doesn't look like there's one."

"So why would he target Roddick?" the same person asks. "Why call him?"

"That's what you're going to figure out today," Hutton says. He pauses then, shakes his head a little, and tightens his face in the way a man will do when there's something on his mind he doesn't want to talk about, but has to. "Before we go any further, I need to address something I shouldn't need to, but seems I have to. I know what many of you are thinking. We've got a dead rapist confirmed—and we're probably looking at two more once those bodies beneath the car turn out to be the Collard brothers. Three dead rapists and Roddick is a bad guy too, and he's probably in that building somewhere, and you're all thinking that the world isn't going to mourn, and maybe you're right, but maybe you're wrong and there are brothers and sisters and parents and children out there who loved these men. It doesn't matter either way. It's our job to find who killed them, and if anybody here isn't up to that, then you should turn in your badge now."

Part of me expects a mass exodus, of people resigning on the spot and handing over their badge and ID. Part of me expects the shuffling sound of bodies as people squirm in their seats, looking at their hands or feet or towards the window, and that's the part of me that's proven correct. There's a room full of people staying employed, all of them unsure where to look.

Hutton carries on. "We all joined the force for noble causes, and by joining we all swore to do the right thing by the law. I know some of you are thinking three dead rapists is the right thing, and that somebody out there is doing us a favor, and you have the right to think that—but none of you have the right to act on it. We're dealing with a vigilante. The public cannot take the law into its own hands. We will find this person, and the courts will decide his fate, and we will do this before other Peter Crowleys are dragged into it. Were these bad men? Yes, they were. Are we glad they're dead? I'm sure some of you are. Will we drag our feet and fail to turn over every rock trying to figure out who killed them? No, we won't. Is there anybody in this room a little unsure of what I'm saying?"

It doesn't seem so. He lets five seconds turn into ten, ten into fifteen, and a year ago he would have been sitting down with the rest of us looking at his hands, but now he's in control and again I keep thinking about how it suits him. He reminds me a little of the way Schroder used to be, standing at the front and taking charge, not taking any shortcuts and always following the rules.

Hutton carries on. "Good. Now, we know Dwight Smith was dead before he ended up on those train tracks, and the medical examiner says she can't determine the cause of death. So the question is," he says, and he looks at one board and then the other, a yard between them, "are the two cases related?"

Nobody knows for sure, but I think about the pried-open window at Kelly Summers's house, the missing shower curtain, and most of all I think about Schroder. If I put my hand up and shared that with the class, then a third board would be added to the front of the room, this one sandwiched between the others with no room to spare, and on that board would be a photo of Schroder, taken from the last time he had his police ID updated.

"The two boys from the alleyway weren't helpful at all with their description," Hutton says, carrying on. "But we have another witness coming in this morning who saw a bald man at—"

"Must be Simon here," another cop says, then pats his partner, who has a drastically receding hairline, on the shoulder. The line gets more laughter than it deserves.

Hutton ignores it. "A bald man that came to pick up Peter Crowley yesterday. Now, we don't know this man is anything other than a friend who popped by, but Monica Crowley didn't recognize him. She'll be working with a sketch artist this morning, and then you can use that to canvass the neighborhood. Hopefully somebody else spotted him."

He tells us the fire department will be using a remote-control robot armed with a camera to look around inside Grover Hills. The car, once the bodies are stripped from beneath it, will be put on the back of a flatbed truck and driven to the lab to be examined. He says one of the bodies beneath the car had a gun in his hand or, more accurately, says the guy's hand had melted around the gun. Then he breaks down some tasks for us. Kent and myself are given the task of going back to talk to Kelly Summers. And then the conference is over and we're all pushing back from our chairs and desks.

"I've been thinking," Kent says. "If this bald guy was following Dwight Smith, then it's possible the gas station camera picked him up. We should check it out."

I think about it for a couple of seconds. "It's a good thought."

The footage from the gas station was burned onto a DVD for us. It's already been loaded up and viewed by others since yesterday, so viewing it on the computer is as simple as a few clicks of the mouse. We see Kelly Summers pull into the service station, we see Dwight Smith with the pause in his step towards hanging up a pump. We see Kelly leave and we see Smith follow, but that's all we see, and that's because the footage we burned is only from those angles and from that time.

"We need to widen the scope," Kent says.

"I agree. We need all the angles, and we need to go back further, and perhaps forward. We need to run the plates of all the cars and cross-reference them against criminal records and case files. If we're lucky we'll find a bald guy leaning against his car at the same time Kelly Summers appeared."

"Let's head back to the gas station," Kent says, standing up.

I stand up too. "Can you take care of this one by yourself? I want to check on Bridget. Just for an hour or so. How about I meet you at Kelly Summers's in an hour and a half?"

"Sure thing, Theo. I understand. Let me know if the plan changes and I can get somebody to cover for you."

"I'll be there."

We head outside and Kent drives off and I sit in one of the unmarked cars and get out a map and I look at the spot Dwight Smith was found, and I look at the address where Kelly Summers lives, then I run my finger slowly between them, transporting myself to those streets, trying to remember what's there. There are three malls within range of this route that include supermarkets, plus at least a half dozen stand-alone supermarkets, but as best as I can tell there are only two which operate twenty-four hours.

I tap my finger on the location of supermarket number one and figure it's as good a place as any to start.

CHAPTER THIRTY-SIX

Schroder hasn't slept well. For a guy who had his emotions switched off by a bullet, he feels—

Feels?

Feels he should have slept better. Only he's hardly slept at all. Every time he closed his eyes he would see Peter Crowley's broken-in skull, would feel his hand on his arm, would hear his final *chocolate ice cream* words. So he feels guilt and he also feels pain because his arm is throbbing consistently. That damn dog might have been carrying rabies or the plague or perhaps it was HIV positive or riddled with swine flu. Once he washed the blood and dirt away there were holes not as deep or as ragged as he'd feared, but they're still going to need treatment.

Four dead men. No, five dead men. That's three more than were supposed to die. The police will visit Peter Crowley's family. The daughter will remember seeing him, and she will give a description, but it won't be a good one. She looked through him as if he wasn't there. He doesn't think there were any witnesses from the alleyway, and if there were, what did they see? Two men in the dark and a car with an unreadable registration license.

The plan had been to dump the brothers where they could be found—he was thinking the beach—and then the police would assume a vigilante killer was working by himself, they wouldn't be thinking Kelly Summers and Peter Crowley were directly involved, they'd be thinking somebody was working from a list, somebody whose life had been altered by men like Dwight Smith and the Collard brothers, and they would never know where they had been killed.

They will think the same thing now—only a vigilante killer who is giving victims their five minutes. He wonders if Tate will think anything more than that, and suspects he will.

"What do you think?" he asks Warren.

If there's one thing I know, Warren says, or *would say* if he could, *is that flies taste really awful. No wonder you don't eat them.*

"And Tate? What about Tate?"

Tate always gets his man. You're going to go to jail.

"I wish I hadn't asked you a damn thing," Schroder says.

Warren says nothing. Of course he says nothing.

Schroder drives to the nearest shopping mall and goes into one of the two pharmacies in there. He buys iodine, some gauze and bandages, and then he buys a new cell phone to replace his broken one and he drives back home. He cleans the wound, splashes iodine all over it, applies some gauze, then wraps bandaging around it. He should get stitches. He should get a rabies shot. But who the hell ever gets rabies these days? He's never heard of it happening. He'll keep an eye on it for infection. He takes some codeine pills and after ten minutes the pain starts to fade. He puts his original SIM card into his new phone and charges it up and copies his contact list to it.

He is back out again when his new cell phone rings. He's at a tire store having his two tires replaced, a job that has taken fifteen minutes so far and still has another five to go, and a job that's going to cost him three hundred dollars. He gets out the phone and looks at the display and sees it's Tate. He moves away from the only other customer in the store, a young guy who keeps telling the man helping him that the most important feature he wants in his tires are that they look cool.

Is this it? Is Tate calling to tell him he's figured everything out? Have they taken Kelly Summers down to the station and has she confessed? It's possible. He told her if they took her into the station she was to say nothing except to ask for a lawyer. He told her the police have a way of trying to sweet-talk you around that. Then he realizes it's even probable she's told the police everything. And really, isn't that what he deserves for letting an innocent man die last night?

"Theo," he says.

"Carl, it's Bridget," Bridget says, and for a moment he's confused. Bridget? Bridget who? Theo's Bridget? Why would Theo's wife be calling him?

"How have you been?" he asks, because he knows that's what he is supposed to ask. He hopes she's okay—and with that thought he realizes he hasn't become a sociopath. Of course he hasn't. He hopes she's okay and he hopes Theo is okay too. Plus a sociopath wouldn't feel bad that Peter Crowley got killed. With those thoughts he realizes something else, something he thinks his mind has been trying to shield him from over the last day and a half—all of this has made him feel alive. All of this killing has made him *feel*.

"There's something wrong," she says. "With Teddy."

Teddy. He forgot she always used to call Theo Teddy. Personally he thinks it's stupid. "Tell me," he says.

"I woke up and he's left a note. It says that he's gone to work and there's a woman here to look after me, but . . . but . . . there's no woman and no reason I need looking after, and when I try his number it doesn't work. It says it's disconnected. I was going to call the police station but . . . Well, you're his friend, right?"

"Right," he tells her.

"I can't call him at work," she says.

"Why not?"

She doesn't answer him, but the line remains open. Is she still there? Did she fall asleep? Slip back into a vegetative state? "Bridget?"

"I'm still here," she says.

"What do you want from me?"

"Am I . . . how do I put this," she says, and spends a few more seconds not putting it any way at all, then finally she comes up with something. "Am I on the phone to Carl Schroder the cop, or am I on the phone to Carl Schroder our friend?"

You're on the phone to neither. "What's this about?"

"Please, Carl, just answer the question."

The question suggests something is wrong. It suggests she's in trouble, the kind of trouble that can't involve the police. Or Theo, for that matter—is that why she's calling him? "The friend," he says, which is the only answer he can give since he hasn't been a cop for some time now. *She knows this, doesn't she?*

"Are you sure?" she asks, and she sounds unsure.

"Yes."

"Can you help him?"

"Help him do what?"

"Not help him do something, but stop him from doing something. I think he's planning on . . . hurting somebody."

"Who?"

"I'll tell you all about it when you get here, but please, you need to hurry."

"Because we need to stop him from hurting somebody."

"Yes."

He doesn't have time for this. But he knows Bridget, and he knows she wouldn't be calling unless she really needed his help. He hasn't seen her since she was released from the nursing home. Last time he spoke to her Emily was still alive.

A lot has happened in that time.

"Please," she says. "You're the only one who can help."

"I'm on my way."

CHAPTER THIRTY-SEVEN

I drive to the supermarket. It's one of the city's biggest supermarkets and during the day it's busy, and during the day on a weekend it's even busier. I park on the edges of the parking lot, a few hundred cars between me and the front door. I maneuver my way around carts full of food, some with screaming kids sitting in them and some with parents making the kids quiet with pleas or threats or bargaining, others doing their best to pretend none of this is really happening. I remember Emily begging the same way. I used to hate shopping with her. She thought anything within reaching distance belonged to her, and the more colorful it was the more she needed it.

I use the signs hanging over the aisles to navigate my way through the supermarket, looking for the bathroom supplies. They don't have many shower curtains, just three styles to choose from, and within those styles a couple of different colors, but none of these match the curtain I saw in Kelly Summers's house.

When a guy working at the supermarket walks past, I ask him if they have any bright green shower curtains, and he looks at where I'm looking and says no, so then I'm a little more specific and ask him if they usually have them. Or ever have them. He says he doesn't know, and tells me to ask at the service desk.

I head up to the service desk where a woman with huge glasses helps me, her eyes magnified to look like golf balls, and one of those balls is slicing out to the right. She tells me the shower curtains I saw are the only curtains they have.

"No bright green ones?" I ask.

"Did you see any there?"

"No, but maybe somebody just bought the last one."

"Then you're out of luck," she says.

I show her my badge and she stares at it for a few seconds, then stares back at me, her golf-ball eyes taking it all in. "It's important," I tell her.

"Okay, Detective," she says, then turns her back to me and picks up a phone. Sixty seconds later she has an answer. "We don't sell green curtains," she says. "We might have, years ago, but nothing now."

I thank her for her time. I walk outside to find half a dozen free parking spaces all within twenty yards of the entrance. I walk across the parking lot to my car.

The next supermarket starts out with the same experience. Lots of traffic, not many spaces, and I end up parking on the edge of it all. Inside there are more screaming children, teenagers laughing loudly, elderly people will suddenly stop walking in front of me or change direction so I almost bowl a couple of them over. The lay-out of the supermarket is similar and I find the bathroom section, and this is where things between the last supermarket and this supermarket are different. There are only two shower curtains here to choose from. A bright green one, and a bright orange one. I pick up the bright green one. It's the same one I saw yesterday morning.

I carry it to the service desk. I have to wait behind a woman who's trying to return an empty bottle of wine because she didn't like the taste, while the woman behind the counter is telling her she must have liked the taste enough to have drunk it. The debate goes on, then carries on as a different woman comes over to ask if I need any help. I show her my badge, show her the curtain, and ask if she can access on her computer when the last few of these were sold.

"I can't," she says, "not from down here. Let me get the manager, I'm sure he'll be able to help."

The manager is indeed a helpful guy. He's in his midforties, but when he talks he sounds like a teenager, putting a raised inflection on the end of every sentence. He shakes my hand eagerly and then leads me upstairs and into his office. There are schedules and staff photos covering one wall, awards for best supermarket and safety and health and liquor certificates and licenses across the others. He uses his computer to punch in the barcode on the back of the shower curtain I'm carrying.

"It's not what I'd call a popular item," he says. "We've sold two in the last month."

I feel my heart skip a beat, and I suck down a deep breath and exhale calmly, not wanting my voice to break. *Please let one of them be Friday night—but is that really what I want? To see Kelly Summers buying it? Or the man that helped her? No, what I want is for Dwight Smith to have jumped in front of a train.*

"Let's see," he says, and a moment later he has his answer. "Friday night. Or, more accurately, early Saturday morning," he says, and bingo. It's showtime. "Here," he says, then taps the monitor, "they were sold just after four a.m. Both in the same purchase."

Now my heart is making up for the skipped beat. Now it's racing. So Dwight Smith not only pried open Kelly's window, he made it inside. Then what happened? Was she waiting for him? Or did the bald man follow him there? Why two shower curtains and not one?

"Can you pull up the receipt? What else was bought with them?"

"Hang on," he says.

This time it requires a few more minutes of work on his behalf, but then the receipt is displayed on the computer. "Air freshener, oils, and some scented candles. Looks like somebody was freshening up a couple of bathrooms," he says, and I remember the strong smell of lavender. "I'll print it out for you."

"Thanks. Was cash used? Credit card?"

"Hang on a sec. . . . Cash," he says.

"Okay, okay. Surveillance. You guys have cameras everywhere, right?"

"Not everywhere," he says, smiling up at me, "but yes, we'll have the person on camera who bought the curtain. Want to tell me what they did?"

"I can't," I tell him. "Can you get me footage?"

"Follow me," he says.

I follow him out of his office and into another room, this one has a security guard sitting in it and a wall full of monitors. The guard is staring intently at them. He introduces himself as Tony Langly and shakes my hand, and he squeezes too hard as if trying to compensate for the fact he's a security guard and not a cop. The manager tells him what we're looking for, and Tony tells us it won't be a problem. He loads up Friday night and takes us to within five minutes of the shower curtain being purchased. At this time of night there are only two people manning the checkouts, one person behind the service desk, and what looks like half a dozen customers at the most, all of them moving slowly. The time lines up with the receipt, revealing only one customer at the checkout.

"Is that your man?" the manager asks.

I shake my head. "No," I tell him. "I was hoping this was going to be the guy, but this is nobody. Sorry to have wasted your time," I tell them. "Sometimes things don't pan out how you'd like."

"Ain't that the truth," Tony says, and both he and the manager look deflated.

My hands are shaking by the time I get back to the car.

It wasn't Kelly Summers buying the shower curtains.

It was the bald man.

It was Carl Schroder.

CHAPTER THIRTY-EIGHT

Schroder hasn't been to Tate's house since the whole Coma Cop thing. The Coma Cop handle is one he imagines the Old Him would have hated. He'd have complained about it to his wife, maybe to some of the guys at the station, but of course the guys at the station would have mocked him for it. They'd have come up with a nickname, they'd have pasted newspaper articles of his story to every wall in the place.

When he came out of the coma, he saw what people had been saying about him. He was so caught up in the Christchurch Carver case that it had become personal to him, that he couldn't let it go, and ultimately it was costing him his life. Of course he was also the man who had brought down Melissa X. He was told there would be bits and pieces he would forget about that day, and in the beginning that was true, then after a few weeks of coming out of his coma it became less true. He can remember every little detail and, if he really thinks about it, he can remember the feeling of the bullet tunneling into his brain, a thud and a searing heat, he can remember the sound of a hole breaking open in his skull, the fractures from the impact radiating outwards, his head snapping back from the impact.

If he closes his eyes and sits in his quiet house, he can feel the bullet in there. He can feel it tugging at his brain, an itch he can't scratch, a humming sound he can't turn off, a glare he can't look away from. It's in there biding its time, this splinter that can't be pulled.

He walks up the driveway to Tate's house, feeling anxious as to what he's going to find inside. *Anxious?* Yes. He makes a mental note—that's another feeling that has returned. He doesn't get to the door before Bridget is swinging it open. This is the woman they all thought had been lost. And she has lost something, hasn't she? A bit of the spark she used to have? He can see that immediately. And some weight too—she's thinner than he remembers, her skin paler. She puts her arms around him and he does the same back, knowing that's what the Old Him would have done.

When she pulls back he sees her eyes are damp, but she doesn't look like she's been crying. "I woke up and . . ." she says, then she doesn't say anything else. A few moments pass and he lets them pass, knowing she'll carry on when she's ready. "You look different," she says.

"It's the new look," he says, brushing his hand over the top of his head. "Everybody is doing it."

"I'm not so sure it suits you," she says, "but it's not just that. You look, well, I was going to say older, but it's not that either. What happened to your head?" she asks, and taps her head in the same place he has his scar.

"War wound," he tells her, confused as to how she can't know this.

This seems to satisfy her. "Did you tell anybody at work you were coming here?"

"No," he says, because there is no work. There is just him sitting at home with Warren, and then of course there is him following people and ending their lives. And even though that's work, he knows that's not what *she* means by *work*.

"Where's your car?" she asks.

He turns back to the road and looks at the car parked there. "It's there," he says.

"That's your car?"

"It's all I can afford."

"Don't you drive an unmarked police car?"

"Sorry?"

"Don't you drive an unmarked police car?"

He shakes his head. "Not in a while."

"Oh," she says, and she's confused, and he's confused too.

"What's this about?" he asks.

She hands him a piece of paper. It's a message from Tate.

*Hey Babe, Kent is on her way to picking me up. Something
has happened in town—probably the usual bullshit. Hopefully
I'll be back before you read this. If I am, I might just read it to
you over breakfast, I'll look over your shoulder and read it out
loud while you're looking over the words—it'll be like being in
a movie. But if I'm not back before then, Kent's sister is here to
keep an eye on you. Love you!*

He reads the note again. Something has happened in town.
Something related to him? The alleyway?

"I don't—"

"Who's Kent?" she asks.

"Kent is his new partner."

"What?" She shakes her head. "But you're his partner."

"Not anymore," he says.

She's still shaking her head. "I don't understand. What happened? Did you have a falling out? Why wouldn't he tell me that?"

"We didn't have a falling out, no," he says. "I don't know why
he didn't tell you," he says, but what he really means is *I don't know
what's going on here*.

"He hasn't been telling me much since, well, since the accident," she says.

"It's been a tough time," he says.

"So why aren't you partners anymore? Something to do with
your war wound?"

"We're just moving in different directions, that's all."

"You've been promoted?"

"Something like that," he says, and suddenly he remembers the
last time he saw her back in their old lives. It had been his daughter's birthday and Tate and Bridget and their daughter had come to
the party. That day was full of smiles, and why wouldn't it be? Emily

was alive back then, her death and the accident were in the future, and so was the bullet that separated the Old Him from the New Him. He thinks about the day he first saw her, that day in town when she handed Tate her phone number, he remembers thinking how Tate was a lucky man. Then he thinks about the wedding, her beaming smile, then he thinks about how she looked in the hospital, a day after the surgery, bandages and stitches and bruises covering every surface, dislocations and tears and broken bones beneath the surface, Tate there holding her hand, his own heart breaking for Tate's loss, breaking for Bridget, this woman who had tried to save her daughter, but had failed. He remembers wanting her to wake up for Tate, and he remembers wanting her to never wake up for her own sake. "You said on the phone Theo is going to hurt somebody?"

"Are you sure you're not here as a cop?"

"I promise."

"Then, yes. I think Teddy is going to do something stupid. I can't lose him, Carl. I can't have Teddy go to jail."

"At least he's used to it," he says.

"What does that mean?" she asks.

Something definitely isn't right here. "Nothing. Who is Theo going to hurt?"

"The man who killed Emily," she says. "I think he's planning on . . . I can't say it," she says.

"If you want me to help you, Bridget, you need to tell me what's happening."

"He's going to kill him," she says. "I'm sure of it. He's going to take Quentin James into the woods and he's going to make him dig his own grave. Maybe he's just going to scare him, I don't know, but maybe it'll be more than that. I've been trying to ring him, but his number is disconnected."

"How did Theo find him after all this time?" he asks. Schroder, as well as many others, suspected Tate had killed him three years ago. So where has he been hiding?

"All this time? It's only been ten days," she says.

Now he's even more confused. Unless . . . "Bridget, how long ago was Emily's funeral?"

"What? Why would you ask that?"

"Please, it's important."

"It's been seven days," she says. "And I had to miss it because I was in the hospital."

Seven days. Suddenly it all makes sense. Bridget has gone back in time. Something to do with the head injury. She's trying to get hold of Tate on an old number. She still thinks Schroder is a cop. It's why he looks so different. He needs to get her inside.

But he's curious. Too curious to let this pass. And, really, as Warren would tell him, there's an opportunity here. "Do you know where Theo is taking him?"

"No. I mean . . . yes. Kind of," she says.

"Kind of?"

"It's . . . it's hard to explain. The woods. He's taking him into the woods."

"How do you know?"

"I . . . I just do."

"Do you know which set of woods?"

"No," she says. "I mean . . . maybe. I think so. I think I could drive there. I don't know how. I just don't understand why his phone isn't working. Can you try calling him?"

"Sure," he says, and he gets out his phone and he pushes the buttons, but doesn't hit send. He doesn't want the call to connect. He holds it up to his ear. He gives it ten seconds, then shakes his head. "Nothing. Do you think you could drive there now?"

She nods. "I think so."

"Let's take my car," he tells her. "I'll drive, you just tell me the way."

CHAPTER THIRTY-NINE

I sit in the car with my head spinning, and lots of different paths all lie out before me, lots of possible futures for Schroder. It doesn't make sense. Out of all the people . . . I mean . . . what the hell?

I try to think of it all as a coincidence. Schroder went shopping for a shower curtain in the small hours of the morning because he needed one, and that he bought a second as a spare. My guess is his tore his from the rings and he really wanted to take a shower at four a m , so he drove down to the supermarket to get a new curtain. What was the alternative? Get water all over the bathroom floor? That would just be stupid. And if you tore one, only makes sense to make sure you have a spare for the next time it happens. The other supplies weren't to hide the scent of bleach, but were to hide normal household smells. Maybe there was some meat that had gone off and he'd thrown it in the garbage. It makes sense. Perfect sense. After all, if you're going to buy a shower curtain, it has to be some time, doesn't it? Isn't the middle of the night just as good as the middle of the day? I can't imagine Schroder really doing well in big crowds, not since the shooting. He probably likes calm, quiet places. He probably likes—

"Damn it." I punch the steering wheel. "Goddamn it."

My cell phone rings. It's Hutton. I suddenly feel like I've been caught out, that he knows where I've just been, and that this is going to be a test. If I give up Schroder, then what? It becomes a simple chain of events. He gets arrested. If he denies it, there'll be a trial. If he pleads guilty, or is found guilty, then jail. And after that? With the new law coming into effect, is it possible the first person to be tried for the death penalty will be Schroder?

Yes. In fact it's more than possible—I think it's probable. I think

the prosecution will press for the death penalty to prove nobody
is above the law, that if you do the crime you will do the time
and perhaps swing for it. If they're prepared to hang a cop, then
they're prepared to hang anybody. It will make future cases easier to
plead out. Criminals are going to plead guilty and take twenty years
rather than risk the noose. And will it be a noose? That's what it
used to be, back before it was outlawed in the middle of the last
century. What about now? Technology may have advanced how
rope is made, but it'll still have the same effect. Will they come up
with something better?

I answer my phone. "Where are you?" Hutton asks.

"On my way to talk to Kelly Summers."

"Only now? Why so long?"

"We thought it'd be a good idea to check surveillance footage
from the gas station for the bald man. Maybe he was following
Summers, or following Smith."

"Did it pan out?"

"Not sure yet."

"Am I missing something here?" he asks.

"I'm just tired, that's all."

"You need to be your best, Tate. I don't want this falling apart
at trial."

I rub at my eyes. "I know."

"There's been a few developments," he says. "We sent a couple
of guys out to the prison this morning to get information on Smith
and the Collards. Turns out Dwight Smith and Bevin Collard were
cellmates for four years."

"So that's the connection?"

"Looks like it. There's something else. They said you called
them yesterday."

I try to get his words to make sense.

"Tate?"

"Yeah, I'm here. Who said I called who?"

"The prison fielded a call in the early afternoon from a man by
the name of Detective Inspector Theodore Tate."

"What?"

"That's what I'm telling you."

"I never called them."

"We know. The call was logged, along with the cell phone number the call came from. It's a disposable phone. Impossible to trace. The woman said Theodore Tate asked about Dwight Smith, then asked who his cellmates were. She gave him some options, and he thanked her for her time. She said she's dealt with plenty of cops before, and she was sure this guy was a cop. She never even thought twice about it, otherwise she'd never have given him the information. So then I called the probation officer for the Collard brothers, and he had the same Theodore Tate call him, and he thought the same thing and gave up the Collards' address."

"So somebody is impersonating me," I say, and a slip of the tongue here would be problematic, because I'm thinking not *somebody* is impersonating me, but *Schroder* is. I wonder if that amused him, if he thought it was payback for the times I've impersonated him, when I knew people on the phone would be more willing to cough up information to a cop rather than a private investigator.

"Looks that way. Smith also had a couple of other cellmates over the years, so we're in touch with their parole officers now. Could be they're also targets, or maybe even one of them is the other dead body we have at Grover Hills."

"Other dead body?"

"Firefighters have found two more bodies out there. They're still inside. Looks like they were upstairs, but they're on a section that collapsed onto the ground floor. Both of them were armed. Firefighters can see them, but can't get to them. Not yet anyway. Theory is we've got the two brothers, and now Matthew Roddick and another associate. Hopefully we can get to work on dental matches later on today. The car has been pulled from the building and is back at the lab. Nothing to report except the spare wheel is missing, and where it should have been was a plastic bag with three silencers in it. If there's any meaning to the missing wheel, then it's a mystery, and we don't even know it was in there to start with."

"Has Monica Crowley showed up?"

"About twenty minutes ago. I'll send through a composite when she's finished with the sketch artist."

I hang up thinking about how that sketch is going to look, and what that means for Schroder. I drive to Summers's house, and as I drive I picture Schroder calling the prison, then calling the parole officer. He called the prison to find out Smith's cellmate, and his next call to the parole officer suggests that's how he picked the Collards as targets.

There's not a lot of Sunday traffic, it'll come, but not until closer to lunchtime when some people will take advantage of whatever sales are on at the mall, while others will try to take advantage of what is going to be a pretty warm day. I think about the best way to tell Kent who our bald man is. I picture that conversation, her asking me *Are you sure?* multiple times, then being mad that I hadn't let her in on my shower curtain theory or told her about the window frame. I picture the conversation with Hutton, us driving back to the station and laying out the facts for him. Hutton shaking his head and saying *Are you sure, are you sure? I don't believe it,* only he does believe, they all do in the end. The idea of arresting Schroder fills me with a sense of horror, a sense of betrayal, like arresting Schroder makes me the bad guy.

I reach Summers's house and Kent is already here. She sees me pull up and she climbs out of her car and gets into mine.

"What's wrong?" she asks.

Guilt. Betrayal. Schroder is a killer. But he's also my friend. "Nothing," I tell her, and that's the first step into madness. I feel myself taking it, I try to talk myself out of it. There's still hope.

"You look like somebody walked over your grave," she says.

"It's nothing," I tell her, taking a second step. "I'm just anxious about the tests tomorrow," I tell her, taking steps three and four, and then I realize I took those steps on the phone to Hutton.

Are we on the same page here?

No, sir, we are not, otherwise I'd have told you everything I know.

Then what page are you on?

"You find anything in the surveillance?" I ask.

"Just other people filling their tanks with gas, and none of them are bald. If Smith was followed from the gas station, then it happened off camera. I'll run the plates I saw and check them out, but I'm not holding my breath. So how do you want to play this? With Summers?"

"We still don't know she's involved," I say, and I'm not just taking steps anymore, now I'm jumping. Now is the moment—right now—where I can fix this. There is still time. And if I don't? What happens if we break Kelly Summers, then she tells us the bald man bought the shower curtain? They'll retrace the same path I took earlier, they'll go to the supermarket, and then they'll see I already knew. What then?

Then I lose my job. Then there'll be questions.

But it's Schroder. Schroder who was with me the day my daughter died, who drove me to the hospital, who told me everything was going to be okay even though it wasn't. Schroder who stood beside me while my daughter was buried. Schroder who told me months ago he knew I killed Quentin James, but was always scared I would confess it to him. Schroder who put his life on the line for this city and who got booted from the force. Schroder with a bullet in his head. Schroder who will hang if he is found out.

Schroder.

I wish I'd never gone to the supermarket. Wish I'd never noticed the fold lines in Kelly Summers's shower curtain or the crowbar marks on her window frame. But ultimately the thing I wish for the most is that Schroder had hidden his tracks better.

CHAPTER FORTY

Bridget doesn't say much. She has one leg pulled upwards and her fingers interlocked around her ankle, with her chin resting on her knee. The only time she makes any conversation is when she's giving directions. The route they're taking—it's making him worry it's a wild-goose chase. Whatever part of her brain short-circuiting this morning never changes direction—it's left here or right there, and there's never any hesitation, never any *Oops I think it might have been that way*, no looping around and covering old ground.

They are north of the city. Long, straight roads for most of the journey, big paddocks and farm animals and long grasses, orchards and trees, and then a turnoff and similar roads, but slightly narrower, slightly less traveled, then there are houses and smaller farms, then back to stretches of long paddocks that look deserted to the left, and to the right a forest.

"We're close," she tells him.

It's secluded out here. Not the best place to shoot and bury somebody, but not the worst. After another fifteen minutes she tells him to slow down, and half a minute after that they're pulling into a spot twenty yards off the side of the road.

"Tate's car isn't here," he tells her. "Nobody is here."

"He's hidden it," she says, taking off her seat belt. "Or maybe he's not here yet."

"How far in?" he asks.

"About ten minutes," she says, "only . . . something isn't right," she adds. She has her eyes closed and her hands on the side of her head, she's applying pressure as if trying to pop her own skull. "I feel dizzy."

"Take a few deep breaths."

She takes a few deep breaths. "It's not helping. I feel sick."

"Let's get you outside."

"Not that kind of sick." She lets go of her head and she twists towards him. "The last thing I remember about that day," she says, "when Emily died, is that we were at the movies. I don't remember walking across the parking lot, but I know we must have, and because I can't remember it I can't even tell you what I could have done differently. Did I scream? Did I try to protect my daughter? Was it my fault? Had I not looked before stepping out? I don't know. I know what I was told. I was told I tried to push Emily out of the way, but what nobody ever tells me is that I should have done more. It was my job to protect her, and I failed."

"I'm sorry about what happened," he says, and he is. He remembers Tate getting the phone call. He remembers something else, something he'll never tell another soul. His first thought when he heard the news was *Thank God it wasn't my family.*

"We should hurry. I don't want Teddy to go to jail. Can you help him, Carl?"

He nods, and he has an image of the bullet in his skull going up and down inside him. "I can help him."

"He's through those trees," she says.

"Can you show me?"

She opens the door as a way of answering.

He follows her into the trees. The sun is still rising, the trees filtering the light, sometimes letting the warmth reach them for a few seconds at a time, then putting them into the shade. The ground is slightly damp. Moss sticks to their shoes and he feels his feet sink slightly into the dirt. Every direction looks the same. Fallen trees, rocks, a cropping of boulders here and another one there and, on occasion, two sets of footprints going in his direction and coming from the direction they're walking. Is it possible Tate and Quentin James were just out here? Bridget sees them too, but she says nothing, and he wonders what she makes of them, and figures she's thinking they're already too late.

"I hope he won't be mad," she says.

"Sorry?"

"Teddy. I hope he won't be mad at me. I know how much he wants to hurt the man who did this, but killing will change him, don't you think? Even if he gets away with it, he'll be broken, won't he? But will he hate me for stopping him?"

Schroder shakes his head. The footprints suggest they're already too late. "I've known Theo for twenty years," he says. "If there's one thing I know it's that he could never hate you. You're the world to him."

She starts to cry. She doesn't look at him. "I don't want him to kill for me and I don't want to lose him, Carl."

"Then let's make sure nothing happens."

She nods, then blots her eyes with the palms of her hands, and then they keep walking. He lets her set the pace. The other footprints tell him they're going the right way. After ten minutes the pace slows. There's a fallen log. He sees broken twigs and on the log moss has been scraped away. But there's no sign of overturned earth. Nothing to indicate Tate buried somebody earlier today.

"This is it," Bridget says.

And she's right, this is it. The footprints don't go further. They intersect each other, they form patterns in the dirt, and they head back the way they came. But they don't go any further.

He says nothing.

She looks at the ground, then slowly starts turning a circle, then she stops. She walks to one of the trees, a fir tree that has to be four, maybe five stories tall. She reaches to one of the lower branches. Hanging from it on a piece of string is a small, finger-sized wooden figure. She wraps her hand around it and pulls down, the branch bending downwards until the string snaps. She looks at the figure, angling it this way and that way so Schroder can see it too. It's a wooden bear. A smile comes to her face. "This was Emily's," she says. "My father carved it a year ago. It took him a month. It was a birthday present. Emily named the bear Henry. Dad's going to carve a different one for her every year, and he's already halfway through a . . . Oh," she says. Then she looks up at Schroder. "Oh."

"What's wrong?"

"We need to go."

"Bridget?"

"I shouldn't have brought you here," she says, talking quickly.

"What's here?" he asks, but he already knows.

"Please," she says, "I made a mistake. Something in here isn't right," she says, and taps the side of her head. "I've brought us into the middle of nowhere for no reason, and I don't know why I thought this belonged to Emily."

"It did belong to Emily," he says, "and you brought me out here because this is where Quentin James is buried."

She starts to cry.

"Your husband killed him three years ago, and recently he brought you here," he says, because one of the sets of footprints is smaller than the other, and it matches the steps Bridget has been leaving on the way in here today.

"Carl, please, you can't tell anybody. You can't. Nobody is supposed to know." She starts tapping the side of her head, softly at first, then with the palm of her hand, harder and harder. He reaches forward and takes hold of her hand. "What if it had been your daughter?"

"I promise I won't tell anybody."

She slowly nods and he lets go of her hand. She puts the wooden figure into her pocket, thinks on it for a few seconds, then hangs it where she found it. She ties the string over the branch, then steps away to watch the toy slowly sway from side to side.

"I feel so stupid," she says.

He says nothing.

"There's something wrong with me," she tells him, still watching the toy. "Something deep inside here," she says, and taps her head again, but this time gently. "It's getting worse. I haven't told Teddy, but I can sense it."

"It was the accident. The brain is a funny thing," he says, and how many times did his doctors tell him the same thing? "Just give it time."

"You know exactly what I mean, don't you," she says, and it's not a question but a statement. "I wake up sometimes a stranger to myself. I wake up one day thinking one thing, but it's another. The world is moving one way and I'm moving another. I think Emily is still alive, and those times are the best, because in those times there is nothing wrong, but then they turn into the worst when you re- member." She turns towards him. "If you take Teddy away from me then all is lost. I won't survive. I wouldn't even want to survive."

He doesn't mind repeating himself. Doesn't like it, doesn't hate it. "I won't tell anybody. I promise."

"Do you really?"

"Yes," he says.

"I'm pregnant. Teddy doesn't know. Yesterday I went to the mall. I wanted to buy a pregnancy test, only I had a . . . I don't know what to call it. An attack, maybe. My mind attacked itself and I went back to the day Emily disappeared. I spent yesterday afternoon thinking my daughter had been kidnapped. I still haven't bought the test, but I know I'm pregnant. Somehow I just know, the same way I know my brain is getting worse. My hope is that . . . is that I can stay myself for as long as it takes to have the baby. That's what I pray for. Did you know?" she asks, then nods towards the ground where three years ago her husband came out here and left a dead man behind. "What Teddy did to that man?"

He nods. "Yes. I just didn't know where."

"And?"

He shrugs. "And what? What Tate did," he says, and he's back to *Tate* now, not *Theo*, "was something most of us would have wanted to do. What he did took a lot of strength. It took a lot of courage."

She gives him a look he can't read. "Is that what you think? That what Teddy did was courageous?"

"It is," he says. "Don't you?"

"I think about it every day," she says, "and I'm still not sure."

CHAPTER FORTY-ONE

Kent pushes the doorbell and we step back. I turn my face towards the sun. It's going to be another nice day, and there will be more of them as we slide into summer, and then less of them as we slide back out. Summer has a way of always going too fast and never being what we want—either never hot enough or too hot, never as perfect as I remember them being when I was growing up.

Kent rings the bell again, then follows it with some knocking. Jammed between the door frame and the door is an envelope, the words *Mom and Dad* written on it. We stand back from the door and give it another minute.

"Now what?" Kent asks.

"Now we call her."

I have her cell phone number written in my notebook, and I punch it into the phone. It goes immediately to voice mail. I leave a message.

"Does she work Sundays?" I ask.

Kent shakes her head. "Doesn't mean she wasn't called in, though."

"Maybe she's just hiding from us."

"Is that really what you think?" she asks, nodding towards the envelope.

"That could be anything in there. Could be money, or a key, or a newspaper article."

"Could be any number of things," Kent agrees, "but there's one that sticks out more than any other," she says, and it's what we've both been thinking since we got here. Kelly Summers has packed her suitcases and gone. "I'm going to open it."

"You can't," I tell her. "It's not addressed to you."

"So what do you want to do? Come back later today? If she's on the run and this is her good-bye letter, then we're only letting her get further away. For all we know she's already caught a flight to the other side of the world. She's had twenty-four hours. She could be in Asia by now, or the US."

And if she is, then good luck to her. If she's there and not here, then we can't question her and she can't tell us about Schroder.

"Let me take a quick look around," I say.

I walk across the front lawn and around the corner of the house. There's a six-foot wooden gate and in the middle are two sets of shoe prints. People scaled this fence. Since it's locked, I scale it too. My old man knees have warmed up for the day and don't complain. My feet add to the scuff marks already on the timber. I drop alongside the attached garage. I look through the window. Kelly Summers's car is inside. I move to the back door and knock. No answer. It's locked. I walk the rest of the way around the house, passing the bedroom with the damaged window. The curtains are closed and I can't see inside. I come up against the fence again, this time on the other side of the house, this part without a gate in it. I scale the fence and drop into the front yard.

"Car's still in the garage," I tell Kent.

Kent has the envelope in her hand. "It's not sealed," she says.

I know what she's thinking. If it's not sealed, she can open it, read it, and put it back just how she found it. Whatever is inside might be relevant, or it might not be. She looks at me and I look back at her, and I know what she wants to see, and after a few seconds I give it to her. I nod.

Right then my phone starts ringing. It's my father-in-law. I walk into the middle of the yard and I watch Kent opening the envelope and I listen to my father-in-law as he asks me if I know where Bridget is, to which I reply she's still at home, to which he tells me that she isn't. He's there, his wife is there—but Bridget is missing. The first thing that comes to mind is what happened yesterday. She's going to be at the mall, or making her way to the mall on the bus, and soon she's going to be looking for Emily. Kent is reading the letter she pulled from the envelope. Her face becomes tight with concern. I suddenly have a very bad feeling the letter isn't the kind of good-bye we both first thought.

"I'm not real sure what you want us to do," my father-in-law says.

"I have an idea where she might be at," I tell him. "Hang tight, and I'll call you back in a few minutes, okay?"

"You shouldn't have been working today," he says, and he says it in a way that makes it obvious if anything bad has happened to Bridget then it's my fault. "You need to be taking care of her."

"I'm doing the best I can." I hang up. Kent is still reading the letter. I can tell from her expression it's bad news.

"Kick it in," she says.

"What?"

"The door," she says. "Kick it in."

I don't ask her why and I don't need to. I take a step back, put my hand on the handle to make sure it isn't unlocked—and it's not— and rather than kicking it, I ram my shoulder into it. It shudders in the frame, but holds. I keep holding the handle for balance, then pull myself into the door once again. It's solid, it hurts, but there's a slight crack. The third time doesn't work, but the crack is louder, then the fourth time the door splinters inwards. At the same time a voice calls out from behind us.

"What the hell are you doing?" We turn towards an elderly woman walking her dog. She's staring at us from the sidewalk. "I'm going to call the police."

I go inside. It's stuffy in here. Rebecca calls out to the woman that we are the police, and then she's a few footsteps behind. I hear the elderly lady call out, but I don't hear what she says. We move quickly through the house—the hallway past the kitchen, past the lounge, past the lavender smelling bathroom with the bright green shower curtain. One bedroom, two bedrooms, and it's bedroom three where we find Kelly Summers, lying on top of her bed in a pair of silk pajamas, her skin pale white, like she laid out under the moon all night and got bleached by it. I can hear Kent fumbling for her cell phone. I check for a pulse. Kelly Summers is cold. Very cold. She looks at peace. She looks and feels like she's been dead for most of, if not all of, the entire night.

"She almost looks happy," Kent says, and she's standing behind me, the phone down by her side, the call not made. "Look," she says, and nods towards the bedside dresser. There are three envelopes there. One is addressed to her mom and dad, another to all her friends, and a third to Detective Inspector Theodore Tate and Detective Inspector Rebecca Kent.

"What did the other note say?"

"It was a warning," she says, and she hands me the note while she picks up the letter addressed to us.

Hi Mom and Dad—
    This is going to be hard to read, but I've done something that's going to make you both really sad. I'm in the bedroom, but by the time you read this it'll be too late to save me. I've taken a bottle of pills and soon I will be at peace. I've left this note here so you know what to expect once you unlock the door. Perhaps you should call somebody first. I've left another note inside. I love you.

                                        Kelly xxx

I fold the note along the same creases Kelly folded. Rebecca is looking at me, a sad expression on her face, the letter to us is down by her side, but she hasn't read it yet. "Here," she says, and hands it to me. "You can read it first. I'm going to go and sit in the sun and call this in."

She leaves me with Kelly Summers and Kelly Summers's ghost and neither of them is in a talkative mood, but I am, so I do the talking.

"None of this is right," I tell her, "but it's the world we live in. I really hope you're in a better place," I say.

I open up the letter.

Detectives—

By now I'm guessing you've figured out what happened. I came home Friday night and within a few minutes Dwight Smith forced his way inside through the window. I used to call him Cowboy Dwight, is that on file anywhere? When I stepped out of my bathroom there he was. He pushed me back into the bathroom and pulled off my robe, and then he slipped on the wet floor and he hit his head on the edge of the bath. I didn't know if he was dead or alive, but I was too afraid to check. I was also too afraid to go for my phone in case he came to in the time before the police arrived. I reached up and grabbed the first thing I could—which was a ceramic soap dish. I only meant to hit Cowboy Dwight once in the head to make sure he would stay unconscious, but once I started I couldn't stop. I don't know how many times I hit him, but it was a lot. For what he had done to me, for the years I was a prisoner in my house, for taking from me the life I wanted to have, I made him pay. I could tell you I didn't mean for that to happen, but I think I did. I think I knew if I called the police you would come out, you would be sympathetic, but also you'd know there was a moment where I could have tried calling for help. I panicked. I dragged him out into his car. It was hard work. Heavy work. But I managed. I was determined. And the rest you know. I know what I did was wrong, but I'm glad I did it. It was like you asked me on the doorstep—you asked if I felt a sense of justice. The answer is yes. And the truth is I would have killed him over and over if I could.

Killing him isn't the reason I'm about to do what I'm going to do—or by now will have done. It's strange, but him being alive is the only thing that stopped me from killing myself years ago. I was too angry to die. Angry at Smith, angry at a world that allowed Smith to do that to me. I didn't know that anger was keeping me alive until I'd killed him. There's no reason to go on—I haven't been happy for five years, and that's never going to change, especially now that I'm facing jail for far longer than

Smith ever did, because that's what will have happened. You're probably reading this and shaking your head, but it's true, and you know it's true even if you don't like it. He rapes me and gets five years, I kill him and get twenty. Smith didn't kill me five years ago, and he didn't kill me last night, but he still took my life. I'm just glad I was able to take his, and I'm thankful to have the chance to take mine on my own terms.

Please don't think the worst of me.

Yours,
Kelly Summers

(P.S.—just how do you sign off a letter like this? Yours sincerely? Yours faithfully? Yours peacefully? Well, I'm going to die wondering. . . .)

I've lost count of how many suicides I've seen over the years. Some of them sad, some of them not, some of them simple, some of them not. Kelly's is one of the saddest. And what of Schroder? There is no mention of him in the note, and why?

Because he helped her. He saved her from the boogeyman. The letter isn't an accurate version of events. Kelly Summers came home, Dwight Smith broke into her house, and Carl Schroder saved her. She doesn't mention Smith's car running out of gas, or how she got back into town because that stuff didn't happen to her. She's taken the blame for it, and by doing so she's closed the case. Only four people on this earth will ever know what happened, and two of them are already dead.

Kent comes back inside. "Medical examiner is on the way," she says, "and so is Hutton. You read her letter?"

"Yeah," I say, and I hand it over to her.

"What about the other two?" she asks, and nods towards the table at the remaining letters.

I shake my head. "They're not for us."

"They could be important," she says.

"Could be, but everything we need to know is in there," I say, and point at the letter I just handed her.

"I'm going to head back outside. Is that okay?"

"I'll follow you in a minute."

I stay in the room with Kelly for a little while longer, and when I'm sure Kent is outside, I step into the hallway and make my way to the bathroom. The shower curtain doesn't look as new as it did yesterday. There are beads of water running the length of the hem, some caught in the creases. I touch the edge and I close my eyes and I picture Schroder in the supermarket paying for this in cash. When I open my eyes I notice the candles and air fresheners he bought are in here too. This is the room Dwight Smith died in, and then Kelly and Schroder cleaned it up.

Outside Kent is sitting on the front porch waiting patiently. The old lady with the dog is still watching us from the other side of the road, while the dog stares over at a nearby tree, probably thinking about chasing a cat up there or taking a leak against it. I sit down next to Kent and I put my arm around her and tell her that everything is going to be okay. We sit and we wait like that for the others to arrive.

CHAPTER FORTY-TWO

We are two minutes into our wait, my arm still around Rebecca and her leaning against me as she stares out across the yard, when I suddenly remember that Bridget is lost. I stand up and quickly update Rebecca, then I start pacing the yard while I dial the number of the mall, which I had written yesterday in my notebook. I end up speaking to one of the managers who helped yesterday. He tells me they'll keep an eye out for Bridget and call me as soon as they see her. I tell them I'll be down there soon.

Then I call my father-in-law. He answers after two rings.

"Should we go down there?" he asks.

"I'm going to head down there soon," I say.

"Soon? Why not now?"

"I—"

"Listen, Theo, I know this is hard, and I know you've done everything you can, and you know we love you, but this isn't good enough. Bridget can't be allowed to wander off like this."

"I know," I tell him, annoyed at him for telling me, annoyed at myself because I know he's right, annoyed to be having this exchange right now.

"Things have to change."

"I know. We'll figure something out."

"Good," he says. "I don't want to sound like a hard-ass, but . . . Wait, hang on a second. . . . Okay, she's pulling into the driveway now."

"She's driving?"

"No. There's somebody with . . . is that Carl? He looks different, but that's him. Everything is okay, Theo, she's getting out of the car. Tell you what, I'll call you back soon, or get her to call you soon, okay?"

"Wait? Carl is with her?"

"Yeah. I'll call you back," he says, then hangs up.

Carl? What in the hell is she doing with Carl? I drop the phone into my pocket.

"Everything okay?" Kent asks.

"No," I tell her. "I mean yes, she just showed up, but . . . but no."

"No?"

So I talk about it, filling in the ten minutes we have to wait for Hutton. Rebecca doesn't say much, just listens, and that's all I need her to do. When Hutton arrives he's trailed by a patrol car. We show him the two notes, and then he goes inside for a minute to look over the scene and comes back.

"You read the other two?" he asks.

Kent shakes her head, and I tell him no.

"There might be something important in there," he says.

"Everything relevant she already told us," I tell him.

He nods. "That's kind of what I figured too. Seems like there's no real reason to open them, but I'll talk to her family and see if they'll give us permission just so we know for sure."

The medical examiner shows up then. She gets out and we don't make a lot of conversation. She goes inside and I wait with Kent outside. The first media van arrives, a guy with big hair and chiseled features frames himself with the house as a backdrop. That means somebody has made a connection between the dead rapist and our suicide victim, and impressively quickly too, and it means Kelly's parents might find out from their TV before they find out from us that their daughter has died. Word will get out and soon there will be more vans, more reporters, more cameras. The story will pick up speed, and for the next two or three days it'll be the headlines. I can already see them—big block letters saying the justice system let Kelly Summers down, that it let out somebody who had attacked her and gave him the chance to finish the job, and why wouldn't it say that? That's what happened.

Tracey spends ten minutes with the body then comes out and tilts her face up to the sun and she's probably having the same *The world isn't fair* thoughts. "Everything looks how it should be," she says. "Certainly looks like a suicide, but I'll confirm it tomorrow."

"Tomorrow?" I ask.

She sighs. "I still have to make my way through the bodies from last night."

She disappears and a few minutes later a plain, white van shows up, and not long after that Kelly Summers is carried in a body bag into the back of it. We stand in a line between the front door and the van, not consciously, but it just happens, and we all stand silently and watch her carried, the body on a stretcher, the stretcher sagging in the middle. It's all sad. All so very, very sad. Even the old lady across the street looks sad as she stands with her dog watching us.

"I'll talk to her parents," Hutton says. "It's pretty clear-cut what happened here. The body's gone, you might as well wind down the scene. How are things coming along with identifying the man who visited Peter Crowley?"

"We're nowhere," Kent says.

"For all we know there is no bald man," I say. "I mean, we know there's a bald guy, but we don't know he's involved. Could have been a friend dropping by for five minutes. Could be a different bald guy from what the kids saw in the alleyway, or no bald guy at all. Eyewitnesses get that stuff wrong all the time. We just don't know. And going by the letter Summers left, the two incidents are unrelated," I say, and now that I'm committed to this path I can't back down.

"Somebody still called the prison saying they were you," Hutton says. "Somebody targeted those brothers, and they did it by asking about Dwight Smith, so the cases are related. I'm surprised you missed the window," he says, and is it me, or is he looking at me closer than he normally would? Is he looking for a sign I'm lying?

I look like I don't know what he's getting at. "The window?"

"That's how Smith broke in. The lock has been splintered away and there are crowbar marks in the wood," Hutton says.

"You missed that?" Kent asks me.

"Yeah, I missed it," I say. "I was looking around, but not as thoroughly as I should have."

"No," Hutton says, "I guess not. And if you had, all this could be different."

"Different how?" Kent asks.

"We'd have taken Kelly in for questioning. We would have found out what really happened, and right now she would still be alive," Hutton says.

I don't have an answer for that, and there's a reason his words hurt so much. They hurt because they're true.

"Canvass the neighborhood with the description Monica Crowley gave us," he says. "I have it in the car."

"You think he was here?" I ask.

"I think it's possible. I think that if he was, Kelly Summers sure as hell wasn't going to mention it in her letter. Head back to the station when you're done."

"Tate can't," Kent says.

"It's okay, I can—" I say.

"Why can't you?" Hutton says.

"His wife needs him," Kent says. "And tomorrow he's taking her to the specialist for tests, so he won't be in then either."

"I heard about that," Hutton asks, and his concern is genuine. Hutton, just like Schroder and just like Landry, they all used to know my wife, though Hutton and Landry never came around to any of my barbecues, but they would be at others we would be invited to. "Is she okay?"

"I don't know," I tell him.

"Okay, take the time you need and let me know, okay?"

He starts to walk back to the car, stares at the woman with the dog, joined by others now, then turns back towards us. "With all that's going on, I forgot to tell you," he says, "but we got some DNA from the dead dog."

"You took the dog's DNA?" I ask.

He shakes his head. "From its teeth. The vet found clothing fibers and blood. Looks like whoever attacked that dog last night was attacked first. If our guy has a record, we'll get a match."

"We should start checking hospitals and doctors," Kent says.

"Already being taken care of," Hutton says. "Faxes and emails will be sent to every doctor and hospital in the city, and I've sent a couple of guys to the hospital and every twenty-four-hour clinic to follow up. If the guy who got bitten isn't one of the men who got burned up and he goes looking for help, we'll get him."

He leaves us then, and Sunday morning rolls on as the van with Kelly Summers rolls out of the street, me thinking about what Hutton said, not just about the DNA, but about how Kelly Summers could still be alive if I had done the right thing.

The other right thing.

CHAPTER FORTY-THREE

The body in the woods changes everything and, for the first time since Friday night when things went wrong, things are now going right. Isn't that what Tate keeps saying? That the world is about balance?

Now Tate is going to help him. Tate is going to steer the investigation away from Kelly Summers. Tate isn't going to take her down to the station, because Tate is going to do what Schroder tells him to do.

He's back in his house, back in the lounge sitting in the couch he's starting to like a little more than he'd have thought, and he's thinking it through. He's in his thinking position—leaning back, one arm on the armrest, the other by his side. He's staring slightly at the wall and slightly at the window. Warren has ventured out from his web and is currently halfway towards the window. Is he leaving?

Schroder has the radio on. He's been listening to reports on and off during the day, trying to learn what he can about the fire at Grover Hills. The media is speculating that whatever happened there last night has something to do with the hospital's dark past. Then the reporter says something that Schroder hadn't thought of—that whoever is found to be responsible for the death of those last night may very well be the first person to face the death penalty.

The death penalty?

He tries to let that settle in. He doesn't want to be arrested—he's more certain of that than he was yesterday, but if he were arrested, would the death penalty scare him? Or does he not even care?

He doesn't know. Anyway, isn't he already on death row? Isn't that what all of this is about?

Yes, but it's more than that. It's about giving people their five minutes. It's about protecting Kelly Summers. With Peter Crowley dead at Grover Hills, the narrative he was trying to build has been destroyed. Tonight he would have targeted another rapist, and that would have led the police further away from Summers and Crowley—but there's no leading them away from Crowley now. That means they're going to take a closer look at Kelly Summers. That means he's really going to need Tate to play ball. And he will.

He reaches for the remote and turns up the volume when the story changes, heading away from Grover Hills and to Dwight Smith, and more accurately, to Kelly Summers. Kelly Summers found dead this morning in her own home. No suspicious circumstances. Police aren't looking for anybody.

Kelly Summers.

Saved on Friday night. Safe all day Saturday. Dead Sunday morning. Could he have done more? He suddenly feels deflated. What he does know is her suicide has made everything else pointless. He was trying to protect her, and all that's happened is other people have died. He wonders how she did it. When she did it. He wonders if her life was seeping away, sharing a moment in time when Peter Crowley's own life ended.

Kelly is dead. Peter is dead. All of it his fault.

This whole time they were on death row too.

What does it mean?

What in the hell does it all mean?

CHAPTER FORTY-FOUR

We don't spend much longer at the scene. We go through to the bedroom and we look at the window and Kent asks me again how I missed it, and I tell her I just don't know, that I didn't look at every single item or surface or shape inside the house. When we leave, we leave nothing behind to show we were even there. Kelly Summers has gone, she's left a hole in the world, but the world doesn't know it. Right now her parents are sitting on a couch getting the news, their faces in their hands, palms wet with tears, asking over and over why this had to happen. We lock the house and we take the note she left us.

I call Bridget. She answers right away. "Are you okay?"

"I'm fine," she says.

"You didn't have another episode?"

"Nothing like that."

"Why were you with Schroder?"

"He came looking for you," she says. "You know, just to catch up. I hadn't seen him in a while, and we figured we'd go out and grab some coffee. I should have left a note, I'm sorry, and I forgot that my parents were coming by."

"We thought something bad might have happened."

"I know. I'm really sorry, Teddy. It just . . . you know, just slipped my mind."

"It's okay," I tell her, and it is okay, because she's fine. That's all that matters. "So Schroder popped in just to check in on me?"

"That's what he said. And then we had coffee. He's a changed man, Teddy. I mean he's still Schroder, or at least it looks like Schroder, but it's not the same Schroder I used to know. But it was good talking to him because I . . . well, you know, I kind of know what he's going through. I'm not the same person I used to be either."

"You're getting better."

"We both know that isn't true."

"It is true," I tell her.

She doesn't answer me.

"Honey?"

"I'm here," she says.

"It's all going to work out, I promise," I say, just as I've told her before, just as people keep telling me.

"Okay, Teddy. I believe you," she says, but I don't think she does.

"I'll be home in ten minutes. Twenty at the most."

"It's okay, Teddy, there's no need. My parents are here, we're going to go out to lunch. Why don't you finish doing what you need to do?"

"I have finished," I tell her.

"I know you better than anybody, and I know there's always something else that needs chasing up. I'm fine, Teddy, I really am and, well, it'll be nice to have lunch with my parents. Mom's going to take me shopping, and there are some things I want to talk to them about. Just don't come home too late, okay?"

"I love you," I tell her.

"That's because you have great taste in women," she says.

When we hang up I update Kent on what's happening. Hutton has left us a copy of the sketch that Monica Crowley helped come up with. The bald man. Carl Schroder. Only it doesn't look like Schroder. It looks like Professor Xavier from X-Men. Monica hasn't mentioned the bullet-wound scar. I guess we're lucky she even noticed he was bald.

"Could be anybody," Kent says.

"Could be," I agree.

We take the sketch and go door-to-door. We get asked more

questions than we ask, nobody recognizing the bald man, a couple of people remembering seeing a car parked outside Kelly's house, but not being able to identify the make or model, let alone be certain of the color. We don't even know if it's Dwight Smith's car or the bald man's car. We find the woman with the dog who called out to us earlier this morning, and she tells us she saw two strange cars parked on the street on Friday night, one was there for half an hour, one for much longer. She gives us the colors, but not the makes or models.

"It's a real shame what happened to that girl," she says. "I never spoke to her, but I saw her occasionally and we'd wave hello every now and then. She always had this look about her like life tossed her into the mud and trod all over her, and I guess that's exactly what had happened. I'm eighty-two years old, I've survived two husbands, cancer, and once I got pneumonia on a boat and almost died, but compared to many my life has been easy. I feel so sorry for that poor girl."

It's heading towards four o'clock when we're done, the malls will be shutting down and some barbecues will be firing up.

"That's one neighborhood down," Kent says, "still Peter Crowley's to go."

I look at my watch. Then I look at Kent. "It's okay," she says, "I can take care of it myself. I'll update you tonight. She reaches out and touches me on the arm, then smiles at me. "Good luck with the tests tomorrow."

We pull out of the street and head in the same direction for about a minute before turning off separate ways. I drop the car back at the station and get back into my own. When I get home my in-laws are still here, and I go inside and talk to them for five minutes, then manage to talk to Bridget alone while they start putting together a meal in the kitchen. The smells and sounds make me hungry, and for a moment I don't want to think about death and loss. I don't want to think about Schroder. I just want to cling to the family that I have.

I ask Bridget about Schroder, and she tells me the same thing she told me on the phone earlier, that he just came by to see how I was doing. There's something in the way that she says it that makes me doubt her, only for a second, then I think about what Schroder said to me yesterday—that I'm always looking for things that aren't there.

"Well I might quickly go and see him," I tell her.

"What? Now?"

"Yeah. While your parents are still here. I need to talk to him."

"About what?"

"About this case I'm working on."

She looks unsure. "That's all?"

"What else is there?" I ask, and the nagging feeling is back that she's withholding something.

She shrugs. "I don't know. Just try not to be too long."

"Is there something you're not telling me?" I ask.

"Yes," she says.

"What?"

"It can wait," she says. "Don't worry, it's nothing bad. I'll tell you tonight, I promise." She kisses me on the cheek. "Try to come back soon, okay? We'll keep some dinner warm for you."

I head back outside. Four o'clock has become five o'clock, and it's Sunday so the mostly empty roads reflect that. There is still three, almost four hours of sunlight left. The entire drive I work on what I'm going to say to Schroder, and by the time I get there I still haven't narrowed down what I want to say. I sit in the car and his car is parked in the driveway, it's a dark blue sedan and of course it is, it's the car people kept on seeing. There is dirt smeared across the license plate, and I imagine DNA all through the trunk.

I step out of the car and I get most of the way to the front door and then he swings it open.

"Theo," he says. "What can I do for you?"

"I know," I tell him, then I exhale deeply, as if letting go of a giant weight, and all the things I'd thought of saying, all the different possibilities, they disappear. "I know you killed those people."

He looks at me, his face expressionless. "Then perhaps you should come inside."

CHAPTER FORTY-FIVE

Schroder leads Tate inside and he sits on the couch and Tate sits opposite him in the chair and he doesn't offer him a drink, even though part of him is telling him that's what he should do. A beer, he imagines, is probably the right kind of beverage for what's about to take place. But Tate doesn't drink anymore. He wonders what Warren is thinking.

"What people am I supposed to have killed?" he asks.

"The shower curtain," Tate says.

"What?"

"It was new. It still had the fold lines in it."

Schroder nods. They unfolded the curtain and hung it up and he took the packaging and the receipt with him. He knows where this is going.

"I couldn't stop thinking about the shower curtain. And in the end all that thinking led me to the supermarket it was purchased from. It was just a matter of searching for shower curtains that had been purchased in the middle of the night. I went there expecting to see either you or Kelly Summers."

"Why me?"

"You were the detective who arrested Dwight Smith. You knew about the Collard brothers. About how to try and hide a crime on a set of train tracks. You knew about Grover Hills. I suspected," Theo says, "but I didn't believe it. Not until this morning when I watched you on a security monitor buying the curtain now hanging in Kelly Summers's bathroom. You bought two of them. Did you use the second one last night?"

"I see," he says, not answering the question. He should have

used something other than a shower curtain. Or used nothing. He
did what he thought was the right thing at the time.

"That's it? That's all you have to say?"

"No," Schroder says. "There is more. First explain something to
me, because there's something I don't understand."

"What?"

"You saw the footage this morning. That is before you found
Kelly Summers dead, correct?"

"That's right."

"So you had this theory about the shower curtain yesterday. That
means you looked through Kelly Summers's house. That means you
would have seen the broken window latch. What that also means is
you knew immediately that Kelly Summers was involved, and yet
you didn't go to the supermarket right away. You didn't because you
didn't want to send Kelly Summers to jail. You were okay with the
fact that Dwight Smith was dead. Isn't that right?"

"I'm not okay with any of this," Tate says, and then he gets loud.
"What in the hell were you thinking, Carl?"

"It just happened," he says. "I was trying to help her."

"And now she's dead."

"So is that my fault for helping her?" he asks. "Or your fault for
trying to help her get away with it?"

"What the —"

"It's not either of those," Schroder says. "It's Dwight Smith's
fault. He's the one who hurt her. He's the reason she's dead now.
Not us. There's no need for you to beat yourself up about it, just as
there's no need for me."

"And Peter Crowley? Is there no need there too?"

"I wish that had also gone differently," he says.

Tate shakes his head. "You're unbelievable. I want you to tell me
what happened on Friday night."

"Do I need a lawyer?"

"Please, Carl, just tell me."

"What, as one friend to another?"

"As one cop to another," Tate says, and he looks ready to slam his hand onto the coffee table.

"I'm no longer a cop."

"But you think you are. Deep down, you do."

"Maybe," he says. "You're the only one who knows about this, aren't you."

Tate nods.

"Is it going to stay that way?"

"Just tell me what happened," Tate says.

"Are you here to arrest me?"

"Just tell me."

"Did Kelly leave a suicide note? Did she talk about Friday night and what happened?"

Tate nods. "Her version doesn't include you."

"I didn't want her to die. All of this was to save her. It's not essential that you believe that, but I would like you to. How did she do it? Pills?"

"Yes."

"Well it's better than what would have happened if I hadn't shown up."

"Is that what you think? That it makes it better?" Tate asks.

"That's exactly what I think, and I'm pretty sure that's what you think too, and I'm as sure as hell that Kelly thought the same thing," he says. "I saved her and she died on her own terms, and if I hadn't saved her she would have died horribly. You didn't see him, Theo, and I did. Dwight Smith was ten seconds away from putting his dick into her, and probably two minutes away from putting in a knife."

"Why didn't you call the police? Why were you even following him?"

"It was a gift to the Old Me," he says.

"To who?"

"To the Old Schroder."

So he tells Tate everything about the conversation. And the realization that Dwight Smith was going to live a better life than him. He tells him about Friday night. About following Dwight Smith to Kelly Summers's house. About climbing the fence and finding the bedroom window open and Kelly face down on the bathroom floor. "She asked me for her five minutes," he says, when he's done telling Tate, then sits in silence for Tate to work it out.

Only he doesn't work it out. "Her five minutes? What five minutes?"

"Think about it."

"I am thinking about it."

"How many times were we asked by somebody to give them five minutes alone with—" He stops talking when Tate's hand goes up in the air in a stopping gesture.

"I get it," Tate says. "So Kelly asked for her five minutes alone with Dwight."

"You can't sit there and tell me over the years you didn't wish you could have given that to people too. I think you'd have wanted your five minutes. In fact I'm pretty sure you've had them."

"I've told you a hundred times I had nothing to do with Quentin James disappearing."

"Whatever you say, Theo," he says, and that's okay, because Tate can believe what he wants for the moment. "The point is still the same—if you were offered five minutes with the man who hurt your family, you'd take it. That's what Kelly Summers wanted and I had no reason to deny her."

"So you helped her."

"To a point, yes."

"The same way you helped Peter Crowley?"

He sighs. He's getting annoyed at Tate, then wonders how a man who feels nothing can get annoyed. The answer is he's still evolving. Something inside has broken free, and though not all the emotions are there, some are. "Look, things with Peter didn't go to plan. And I'm sorry about that. But he made a mistake and he paid the price."

"He made a mistake because you put him into a situation you couldn't control."

"He wanted his five minutes."

"I'm sure he wanted to be alive at the end of them. You went to him, right? You phoned the prison and got Collard's information, and then went and wound Peter up. I just don't understand why."

"You're right. I did phone the prison, and I did go to Peter, and I was right because he did want his five minutes," he says, but he doesn't say that Peter needed convincing, that he needed reminding. "We drove them out to Grover Hills, but then the Collards got away and killed Peter, and then they phoned for help. It was me or them. It was self-defense."

"No, it's not, because you took the Collards out there. If anything, it was self-defense on their part."

"You can't have it both ways, Tate. You can't say it was self-defense for them when they had time to think about what they were doing, then not say it was self-defense for Kelly too. She wanted her five minutes and got it, and Peter wanted his and missed out, then those four men wanted their five minutes too. It's a miracle it's not me out there burned to a crisp. It was those guys that brought the dog and the gas and the guns. But you still haven't told me why you're here, Theo."

Theo leans forward. Schroder isn't sure if any of these answers are what his former colleague wants to hear. "And you haven't told me why the Collard brothers. Why did you call the prison to learn about Dwight Smith's cellmates?"

"Why does it matter? What is done is done."

"You could face the death penalty, don't you get that?"

"I know this is hard for you, Theo," he says, and it would have been hard for the Old Him too. He knows what the Old Him would be saying if he was sitting where Theo is sitting, and figures it wouldn't be that much different from what he's hearing anyway. "It's hard because you would have done the same thing."

"No. I would have called the police. I wouldn't have let Kelly deal with a man like Dwight Smith. You let it get out of hand."

"Like you did three years ago with Quentin James?"

"I told you already that—"

Now it's Schroder's turn to put up his hand. "That you had nothing to do with his disappearance, yes, I know."

"I didn't kill Quentin James," Tate says, "but I wanted to. But this—what you're doing, this is wrong. You're targeting people who have done nothing to you."

"So that's where you draw the line? If it's personal then it's okay?"

"That's . . . you're twisting my words," Tate says.

"And you're wasting our time. Look, Theo, like I said a minute ago, what is done is done. I did what I did last night to protect Kelly Summers. I didn't want her going to jail and no matter what you say, you know she didn't deserve to be locked away. I had her best interests at heart. I let her do what she needed to do, and then I needed to do what it took to cover it up. So I thought why not wipe out another couple of low-life degenerates and make it look like a vigilante was on the loose? It'd take the focus away from Kelly. Now it doesn't matter, right? Kelly is dead and Peter is dead and there are no more tracks to cover, and if you arrest me then it's hard for you to explain why you left it a day to investigate the shower curtain, and why you never told anybody this morning about the supermarket footage you saw."

Tate says nothing, but he can see the man thinking, can see possibilities come and go, then he leans further forward and starts talking. "You're wrong about that. I came here because I didn't want it to be true. I wanted you to tell me something that made you innocent of all of this."

"All I was trying to do was help Kelly Summers," he says.

"I know." Tate stands up. "Listen, Carl, you've been good to me over the last few years, really good. And . . . and I'm sorry about what happened to you, and sorry for the person you've become, but most of all I'm sorry for what I'm about to do. I'm going to have to take you down to the station. You're going to have to be accountable for what you've done. Given the circumstances—"

"Given the circumstances what, Theo? They'll let me off?"

"No. But—"

"But what?"

"I don't know. Goddamn it, Carl, why the hell did you have to put me in this situation?"

"So that's it? You're going to arrest me?"

"They have your DNA," Tate says.

"What?"

"The dog. It bit you, right?"

"Shit."

"You didn't think about that, did you?"

"It doesn't matter," he says. "They don't have my DNA on record."

"Not yet, but they'll come for it when they start to figure out what I figured out. I'm sorry, Carl, but I have no choice."

"Actually, Theo, you do. I think you need to sit back down for a minute because there's something else you ought to know."

CHAPTER FORTY-SIX

I feel like putting my fist through the side window of my car. I get in and put on my seat belt and then I start punching the steering wheel. Then I undo my seat belt, get back out, walk around the car unsure of where I'm going, only to complete a full circle and climb back in.

What. The hell. Am I going to do?

I reach into my pocket and pull out the small wooden toy Schroder gave me. It's the toy I hung over Quentin James's grave. I don't really know why I put it there. Maybe as a reminder to what that man had done. I don't know. I really don't. What I do know is I wish I hadn't.

I start the car. Schroder didn't tell me how he found the grave, but it must have something to do with Bridget. He says he's always known where the body was, and that today he went there to retrieve the small toy as proof, but I don't think so. I think Bridget took him there. I don't know why she would have done that, but I think she wasn't herself when she did it. I think she was some other version of Bridget, one whose brain chemistry is becoming more and more out of whack. I think that's what she is hiding from me. I think she promised Schroder not to say anything.

A different version of Schroder. A different version of Bridget. And me? Which version of Tate is going to deal with this? Drunk Tate? It's been a year since he and I have shot the breeze, but oh how I miss him.

Killer Tate?

I punch the steering wheel one more time for luck. Does Schroder feel any remorse over what happened? I should have told Kent about the shower curtain right away. We could have arrested Summers and Schroder yesterday. Peter Crowley would not have died. Bridget wouldn't have shown Schroder where Quentin James's body is. Kelly Summers would still be alive. I shouldn't be a cop. Shouldn't have been let back on the force. Being a cop is just getting people killed.

And now what? What if Schroder kills again?

Only he won't. He promised me it was over. He told me it's my job to lead the investigation in a different direction. To make sure he doesn't make a blip on anybody's radar. And if I can't do that, then I'll be going to jail right alongside him.

I don't drive back home for a shovel, instead I drive to a hardware store and buy a new one. I don't want to have to answer my wife's questions, and I don't want to face her right now, because I might just tell her what's happened and I don't want her to know. I don't want her to feel any guiltier than she must already be feeling. The store is open until eight p.m., which gives me twenty minutes. Normally I like hardware shopping. I think it's like shoe shopping for women. This time I spend less than five minutes and less than fifty dollars on a shovel and then I take the same route I took yesterday afternoon out to the woods. The sun is heading quickly for the horizon now, and in fifteen minutes it'll be gone, but it'll stay light until around nine.

I call Bridget on the way and tell her something has come up and that I'm going to be another two hours. She sounds disappointed. I tell her I'm sorry and she says that's okay, that her mom will stay because her dad wants to get back home because there's a movie on TV he really wants to see, which sounds like the kind of thing my own mom would say about my dad. I get to the woods and I park the car and I carry the flashlight and the shovel and walk for ten minutes and there are enough footprints in the dirt now to make it look like a walkway at an airport.

I reach the grave.

It's open.

Quentin James is gone.

CHAPTER FORTY-SEVEN

I put the shovel into the back of my car. I get in and put my seat belt on and I punch the steering wheel and I climb out and do the same loop I did earlier, only forty-five minutes later and twenty miles away.

You know what you have to do, don't you?

But Killer Tate doesn't want to go there. Not now.

Then when?

"Never."

I call Bridget and tell her I'm on my way, that things haven't panned out like I'd hoped, and she tells me she's looking forward to seeing me. For the next ten minutes I don't see a single car, then there are a few as I hit the highway, then more as I hit suburbia. I keep thinking about Quentin James and about what condition his body is in, how much evidence can be taken from it, how it can be linked back to me. Can it? Of course it can be. Nobody in the world had a bigger motive than me.

When I get home Bridget and her parents have eaten dinner—a pasta with pesto and salami. Bridget's dad has gone. My dinner is being kept warm in the oven, and the thought of eating doesn't help balance out the anger I feel towards Schroder, and actually eating doesn't help balance out the fear of what he's going to do.

"Are you okay?" Bridget asks, and her mom is in the lounge watching TV.

"Yeah. Just work stuff."

"Okay. Dad's on his way to come and pick mom up."

I finish my pasta and Bridget's dad shows up and we make small talk and they wish us the best of luck for tomorrow's tests and then they're gone. Bridget hangs out in the lounge while I clean up the kitchen. I spend some time standing by the sink staring out the window, watching the last of the light fade from the day, thinking about Schroder, thinking about Kent, thinking about tomorrow's tests, but most of all thinking about Quentin James and how he changed our lives. For the first time I regret what I did to him, not out of guilt, but out of fear for where it's going to lead. He's going to tear my family apart for the second time. The universe is resisting life getting back to normal. It gives with one hand and takes with the other. My wife is out of her vegetative state and life is good, but life is still cruel because it deceives her and tricks her with the past. I've been deceived and tricked by Schroder too, but then again I'm not the same man I was three years ago. In some ways I think Schroder is acting out a darker, harder version of me. Is this where I was heading? If Bridget had not come back to me, would I be doing what Schroder is doing?

When my phone rings I see it's Kent. I spend a few seconds considering whether or not I should answer it. For now I just want the rest of the world to disappear. Especially Kent and Schroder and all that they represent.

"I quit," I tell her when I answer it.

"Well, before you run off to sculpt your first modern art piece, I thought I'd tell you I've been doing some homework," she says, "on Smith's other cellmates."

"And?"

"He had two other cellmates at various times during his stay there. A guy by the name of Jamie Robertson, and a guy by the name of Eugene Walker."

"What are these guys in for?"

"Robertson was in for armed robbery," she says, "but it's Eugene Walker that we need to focus on. You don't remember him?"

"No."

"The tax guy," she says.

"Oh shit, that guy?" I say, remembering the case and the stories that made the news and the stories that didn't. Walker worked for the Inland Revenue Department. He would target women who had recently become single. He would use his resources to look up their address, and knowing they were now living alone, he would target them and sexually assault them. He chose only woman with babies, and he would tell them after the attack that if they went to the police he would kill their child. For three years he did that, and nobody ever went to the police. There was a serial rapist in the city and nobody knew. Then one day he tried to attack a woman being investigated for tax fraud. A tax inspector was following the woman and was parked outside her house when he saw Walker forcing his way inside. The police never found out how many women he hurt—four came forward after his arrest, but we always suspected more.

"That was when, ten years ago? Fifteen? Must be fifteen—I hadn't been on the force long."

"Fifteen," she says.

"Where is he now?"

"He got out a few years ago," she says. "I'm still trying to get hold of his parole officer. If prison is the connection, and cellmates are connected, then it stands to reason Walker could be next. We'll have to have officers babysit the guy. What a waste of manpower."

"It is what it is," I tell her, but what I really want to tell her is that what it is is a waste of time too.

"Also, Hutton is still convinced the bald guy may have been at Kelly Summers's house. It makes sense that Kelly couldn't have lifted that body alone, and there's no trace of her in Smith's car. He wants us to fingerprint her place."

I suddenly become light-headed. "What?"

"Yeah. I know we'll probably only find her prints and family member's fingerprints, but if somebody did help her, and it is this bald guy, then he might have touched a bunch of surfaces."

"I don't know," I tell her. "It seems pretty thin."

"Maybe," she says. "But it's worth a shot, right? I think we should fingerprint Peter Crowley's house too."

"I don't think his family will be too thrilled with that."

"Nothing to lose," she says. "I'll send a fingerprint team out to get it done."

"When?"

"First thing in the morning. You want me to keep you updated?"

I think about Schroder's prints all over the shower curtain, over the windowsill, all over everything. He would have wiped everything down, wouldn't he? Yes—but it only takes one print.

"Tate? You still there?"

"I'm here."

"Want me to keep you updated?"

"Yeah. Of course."

"Good luck for tomorrow," she says, and I'm thinking the same thing.

I go back to staring out the window, thinking about life, about the paths I've taken. I think about all the hard work, about getting Bridget back, and I think about how easily it will disappear if they find Schroder's prints all through Kelly Summers's house. Somehow I have to stop that from happening.

CHAPTER FORTY-EIGHT

Schroder is sitting at his kitchen table. It's thirty or forty years old, has a hard varnish top and metal curved legs and a bunch of scratches. It cost him fifteen dollars and came with two chairs even though one is all he needs. He has a supermarket pizza, which on one bite he can't taste, and on another he thinks there might be a hint of flavor, but then thinks it's his memory fooling him because the third bite is back to nothing. Beside him is a piece of paper on which he's listing his returning emotions. On the top of the list is *curiosity*, and even though he's not really sure that can be included as an emotion, he figures there's nobody here to argue. If he wants curiosity to be an emotion, then it's an emotion. Beneath curiosity he has written *guilt*. Guilt is one emotion that has definitely returned. He has written *passion*, but has crossed it back out. He was confusing his desire to protect Kelly Summers as something he was passionate about, but really it was closer to guilt than passion—or more accurately, to the guilt he would have felt if he hadn't protected her. Which he feels now.

Anger? No. *Happiness?* No. *Sadness?* He writes *sadness* down and puts a ring around it—he isn't sure. *Love?* No. *Hope?* No. *Joy?* No. *Disgust?* Yes. *Anticipation?* Yes. He writes that down too. *Fear?* Yes—he has a fear of being caught. Of going to jail.

Desire?

Desire. He puts a ring around it. Then underlines it. Then sits at the table tapping his pen against the pad while staring at the word. *Desire.* Yes, he feels desire.

He comes back to *fear*. He puts a line under that one too. It's not just a fear of being caught, but a fear of not making a difference. A fear of moving on from this world and being forgotten and, really, hasn't he invested too much of himself into this city for that to happen? A fear of dying. He doesn't want to die, but it's happening. Melissa X took care of that. If he were to die tomorrow, how would people view him in six months' time? What would they say? That he died a hero? That he died cleaning up a city? What about in ten years? A hundred years from now nobody will be talking about him at all, and he figures when you're dead a hundred years will go by pretty quick. A hundred years is a heartbeat compared to eternity for a dead guy. He writes *anger* back down on the page and puts a ring around it, somewhat surprised he dismissed it earlier on.

He wonders if there is anything he can do about the guilt, and decides there is. It's all about balance, in the same way a hundred years or a thousand years can slip by unnoticed by the dead, unnoticed by oceans and landscapes. He thinks that his guilt can go unnoticed if he can flood his system with whatever the opposite of guilt is. Legally, the opposite of guilty is not guilty, but in this case the opposite of guilt is going out there, tracking down some really bad people, and killing them. The opposite of guilt is giving others their five minutes with those who have hurt them, and making sure nothing goes wrong. And nothing will go wrong, because if it does, he has Tate in his corner to help him out. Tate with his own personal demons and definitions of what justice is. Tate who feels he can judge even though he took the man who killed his daughter into the woods and killed him. Tate who two hours ago sat opposite him, getting angrier and angrier as he held the small wooden toy Schroder gave him. They had been friends once, but two hours ago all that turned to dust. And what did a dying man need with friends anyway?

Enjoyment. He writes it down.

If, for the moment, he removed Kelly Summers's death and Peter Crowley's death from the guilt equation, then if he had to label what was left, wouldn't he call that *enjoyment*? He puts a line through it, then writes *fulfillment* beneath it. He puts a ring around it, then a tick next to it. Fulfillment is the answer, not enjoyment. He is a man with a time bomb inside his head who two days ago wasn't searching for anything, didn't care about anything. He was a man who was leaving the world to its own devices. The New New Him is all about fulfillment.

He will give others their five minutes.

There is no need to target other cellmates, or other people Dwight Smith knew—that ruse is over. Any other names he got from the prison officer are useless anyway as the police will now be keeping an eye on them.

So who?

Who does he target next?

He closes his eyes and starts thinking back over the years and he waits for a name to jump out from his past.

CHAPTER FORTY-NINE

We go to bed and we sit up for a while and read. Bridget is reading a novel about a boy who runs away from home to find his missing dog, and I'm reading a novel about a boy who runs away from home because his dad used to beat him up, and now he's joined the circus and learning how to be a knife thrower while his dad comes looking for him. I can figure out where it's going. However I can't get into it. I'm too distracted. By life. By Schroder. By the tests tomorrow. The world is closing in on me. Even if I can somehow take care of Schroder's fingerprints, then what? Something else will come up, of course it will. Two or three somethings. A whole handful of them. We lie in bed and we don't talk about the tests, this unspoken thing between us, as if mentioning them will jinx them. The thing Bridget wanted to tell me today has now been put off for tomorrow, and that's okay by me—I have enough things on my mind.

When the lights are off and we're trying to fall asleep, all I can see is Schroder telling me he knows where Quentin James is, that from now on I answer to him, that if I didn't want to end up in jail alongside him then I have to keep the police from knocking on his door. Then he told me he was done anyway, he had saved who he wanted to save, and that soon none of it would matter anyway. The bullet in his head, he told me, would solve all our problems soon enough.

Bridget starts snoring softly, which is something she never used to do, but it's part of who she is now. I watch the numbers on the clock roll on, each one bringing me closer to either dealing with Schroder or helping Schroder, which is the same as me going to prison or not going to prison. By the time six a.m. comes around,

I've slept on and off during the night for three hours. I feel exhausted. I climb out of bed and sit on the edge with my face in my hands, thinking this could be my last day as a free man.

When six thirty comes around, I shake my wife awake. She smiles at me, and then that smile turns into a frown when she sees I'm wearing the same suit I wore yesterday. The suit I wear to save the world.

"You're going to work?"

"Just for an hour, maybe a little longer."

She looks at the clock, and then looks at me. "Are you serious?"

"It's something I have to do."

"Let somebody else do it. Today is our day, Teddy."

"I'll be back in time for our appointment. I promise. Hopefully I'll even be back in time for breakfast."

Her usual smile and her *Teddy off to save the world* response isn't there. She looks annoyed. "Why do I always feel like your job is more important than me?"

"You shouldn't feel that way," I tell her, "because it isn't."

"You worked all day yesterday."

"It's just this morning. I promise, okay? There's something I have to do."

"You can't call my parents this early," she says.

"I know," I tell her.

"You want to leave me alone," she says.

"It won't be for long. I don't have a choice. If there was any other way I'd find it, but there's not. I don't want to go, but it's important."

"More important than me?" she asks.

I shake my head. "I'm doing this for you," I tell her. "For us."

She nods. "Want to explain how?"

"I can't. I'm sorry."

"Okay, Teddy, but don't be late, okay?"

I lean in and kiss her on her cheek and thankfully she doesn't pull away. "I won't be. I promise."

I feel like a complete bastard as I leave my wife, but that's a better feeling than being in jail for ten years. Then, as I drive, a new thought hits me—under the new law I could actually face the death penalty. Would they do that to me? Would they make an example of what I have done? They'd see why I did what I did . . . but still . . . I killed a man in cold blood. The *why* doesn't matter. It's the outcome that matters. I put a man in the ground. The *when* doesn't matter either. There's talk that soon an offer will be made to every person out there wanted for murder. Turn yourself in before the end of the year. Anybody arrested after the end of the year, whether it's for a current murder, a recent murder, or a cold case, no matter when the crime was committed, you may face the death penalty.

A few months ago me and Schroder were called the Coma Cops.

What will they call us when we're both hanging from our necks?

It's ten to seven when I get to Schroder's house. The street is quiet. I knock loudly enough for him to hear, but not too loudly for the sound to wake everybody on the street. It takes him a minute to come to the door. He looks tired.

"Kill anybody else last night?" I ask him.

"What do you want, Theo?"

"I want to know how many fingerprints you left at Kelly Summers's house, and at Peter Crowley's house too."

He nods. "None at Peter Crowley's. I was careful not to touch anything. I cleaned down Kelly Summers's house too, but it could be a problem. Are the police going to print it?"

"Yes."

"The intent was for Dwight Smith to disappear," he says. "I wasn't wearing gloves. There was never meant to be a reason for them to question her, and certainly no reason for them to print the place. We cleaned up really good, but it's impossible to know for sure. You need to figure out a way to stop the police from printing it."

"And how do you suppose I do that?"

"You're the cop," he says. "It's your job to figure that kind of thing out."

I shake my head. "Actually, Carl, it's your job to figure it out. You're the killer. You're the one who's not meant to leave anything behind."

"If you don't want to end up in jail, Theo, you'll figure out a way to stop them."

"Well it's your lucky day, Carl, because I already have figured it out. Put on a shirt and tie. We're going for a ride."

CHAPTER FIFTY

The painting of the woman in the field of daises is Kelly Summers. I didn't notice that before. Her head is turned slightly sideways, but the expression of loss I saw in her features on Saturday is now an expression of peace.

"She painted that?" Schroder asks.

"Yeah."

"It's amazing," he says. "Who do you think the woman is? Do you think that's Summers?"

"I don't know."

"I tried to help her, you know. I really did."

"I know."

"Do you think I could have it?"

"What?"

"The painting. I would like to have it. It speaks to me somehow."

"I don't think so."

"You don't think it speaks to me?" he asks.

"No. I mean I don't think you can have it. I'm sure her parents will want it."

"You're probably right." He walks around the lounge. "We sat in here. She sat there, and I sat there," he says, pointing to the couch and the chair. "I told her everything was going to be okay as long as she did what I told her to do."

We go through to the bedroom. He uses a handkerchief to open up the window, and then he wipes all the places he and Smith might have touched it, and the windowsill too, even though, as he says, he did this already.

It's eight o'clock when Rebecca Kent arrives. She takes a second look at my car and I can see her trying to figure out why I'm here, then she looks even more confused when she steps inside and sees Schroder. Following her are two officers carrying fingerprinting tools. She tells them to start in the bedroom, then tells me that Hutton has called in sick today, and that she's taking lead.

"How you doing, Carl?" she asks, and she reaches forward and embraces him. He hugs her back. They hold each other tight, and even though they barely worked together, the explosion they were in has bonded them.

"I'm surviving," he says.

"I'm sorry I haven't been to see you," she says.

They make small talk for a minute, the question hanging between us, and then Rebecca finally asks it. "So why are you here?"

"I was thinking about what you said last night," I say, answering for him, "about Kelly Summers having help."

"And?"

"And it was Carl's case."

"And you spoke to Carl already," she says.

"I know. I figured it would be a good idea to bring him here to take a look around."

"In case something sparked a memory," Schroder says.

"A memory?"

"Theo thought I might see something that could help. Something that might make me go *ah*, and then give him a name. I told him it was a stupid idea."

"And was it stupid?" she asks. "Or have you seen something?"

"It was stupid," I tell her. "We looked around the house, but he didn't see anything that could help."

Rebecca stares at me, and then she stares at Schroder, and then she looks at Schroder's hands. I'm pretty sure she's noticing he's not wearing any gloves, and that means his prints are now going to be on some surfaces.

"Your watch is broken," she says to him.

"I don't really have much of a use for time," he says.

"It got broken in the explosion, didn't it," she says, and she holds a hand up to her face.

"Yeah."

"Why do you still wear it?"

"Probably for the same reason you haven't had your face fixed. It's a reminder. It's a piece of me now."

Rebecca slowly nods. "I never thanked you for what you did."

"Thanked me?"

"You promised me you would get them," she says.

"I failed by half," he says.

"You succeeded by half." She stops touching her face and gives a small shrug, as if none of it really matters, not in the big scheme of life. "Well, I guess in theory it could have been a good thought," she says, "you coming down here to look around."

"That's what police work is sometimes," Schroder says. "Theories that don't pan out."

"I'm going to take another look around. Don't you have somewhere else you need to be, Theo?"

I look at my watch. "Yeah, you're right."

"You've seen the papers today?"

"No."

"Check them out," she says. "It was good seeing you again, Carl. I hope things get better for you."

They hug again, and then we head out to the car. It's not until we're driving that Schroder starts talking again.

"Do you think she knows?" he asks.

"What, Rebecca? No. How could she?"

"Because she's a good cop. And because you shouldn't have figured it out, and yet here we are."

"And if I hadn't, then your fingerprints would be coming up this morning and we'd be on our way to arresting you."

"It would have been easier for you that way, wouldn't it?"

He's right. "Would you still have told the police about Quentin James?"

"No. There would have been no need. It would have been over for me and there would never have been anything you could have done. What are you going to do about Rebecca if she figures it out?"

I pull over and turn towards him. "What the hell does that mean?"

"It doesn't mean what you think it means. All of this," he says, "is about second chances. These guys do horrible things and they go to jail, and then they come back and are allowed a second life. But not me. I don't get a second chance. I give my life to this city, and what is my reward? I lose my job and I get shot in the head and then I lose my family. If I'd raped and killed some woman fifteen years ago, I'd be in a better position than I am in today. It's not fair, not to me, and not to the guy I used to be. These guys don't deserve a second chance, but you know who does? Me. That's who. But that's not going to happen."

"Is that what all this is about? You're pissed off?"

"Damn right I'm pissed off," he says, and for a moment there's some emotion there, not much, but a little bit, a bit of the Old Schroder. "But not pissed off enough to hurt people who don't need hurting. You have to keep Rebecca heading down the wrong path. That's all I'm saying. I would never hurt her, because of all the people who deserve second chances, she's one of them. And so are you. You killed a guy and got to move on. Your wife came back. You're back on the force. You're a second-chance guy, Theo. Hell, you're the king of second chances. Me, I'm a one-chance guy, and I've had it, and now I'm fucked."

I look out the windshield and stare at the road. Up ahead a seagull is nudging a flattened hedgehog. "I'm sorry about what happened to you, I really am. And you're right, it's not fair, it really isn't, but you can't do this. You can't take on the role of judge and executioner because the wrong people are getting hurt."

"I'm learning," he says.

"Learning?" I turn back towards him. "That makes it sound like it's not over."

He doesn't say anything. He turns and stares out the windshield beyond the hedgehog and at a road of possibilities.

"Is it over?" I ask him.

"I have nothing else. My family has gone, and I'm okay with

that. I have no future, and I've accepted that. I have nothing to offer. This . . . doing this, it's something. I can make a difference."

"Your family hasn't gone," I tell him. "You just have to start talking to them."

"I think I might walk from here, Theo," he says, and he opens the car door.

"Carl . . . Hey, Carl," I say, but he's climbing out of the car. I climb out too and lean across the roof to talk to him. "I can't let you do this."

"Do what?"

"Carry on what you're doing. You told me yesterday it was over."

"A lot has changed since yesterday."

"Nothing has changed."

"I'll let you know when I need your help, and you will help me, Theo."

"No. This ends now."

"You're a good man, I know that, but you've had enough second chances, and now the way you've made up your own rules over the last couple of years is finally coming back to bite you in the ass. You're either going to help me or shoot me. The way I see it, you don't really have any other choice."

CHAPTER FIFTY-ONE

It's a ten-minute drive to his house, but an hour walk, and that's okay. It gives him time to clear his head. He stops on the way to get coffee. He used to drink a lot of coffee in his old life, back when he could taste it, and this morning he decides to give it a go, a *Who knows?* going through his head, the *Who knows maybe today will be different?* He is, after all, feeling different, so he waits in line and he listens to other people ordering kinds of coffee that sound completely alien to him, and he looks at them and he thinks *You are who I am dying for? People ordering hazelnut half mocha half bullshit no sugar soy lattes?* Yes, he took a bullet for these people.

He orders a black coffee that costs five times what it should, and probably tastes half as good, and the bullet in his brain makes things process a little differently these days, but he figures that means he's drinking a coffee worth ten percent of what he paid. There are half a dozen complimentary newspapers and none are being read as every other person in here is texting or emailing or writing a novel. He sits and looks at the front page where a half-page picture of a bald man that doesn't look like him looks out at him. The headline is *The Five Minute Man.*

For a moment his heart freezes. The café darkens a little.

In smaller print beneath the title, a byline. *Christchurch's serial killer only wants five minutes of your time.*

What the hell? How could they know what he's calling himself? Then he realizes they don't, that when he came up with the name he thought how the media would come up with something similar—well, it's not just similar, it's exactly the same.

He reads the article. It's about Peter Crowley. The reporter has spoken to Charlotte Crowley, and he wonders how that conversation went to make this interview happen so quickly. Charlotte talks about her husband, about what a good man he was, about how, when they met, he used to tell her about his wife. He had told her he used to ask the police for five minutes alone with the men that hurt her.

"*He didn't get it back then,*" Charlotte is quoted as saying, "*but somebody gave it to him on Saturday. Or at least they tried to. Peter had always wanted his five minutes, and in the end it killed him. I just wish there had been another way. I just wish that at the time the police really could have given him his five minutes. He could have gotten a lot of it out of his system. Can you imagine how life would be? If the victims were allowed their revenge in a controlled environment? Then none of this would have had to happen. Maybe it would even help prevent crime. I guess that's what they're hoping the death penalty is going to do, right? But the death penalty is the government executing a bad guy. Don't you think that belongs to the victim if they want it? I think the victim should be given the chance to pull the lever.*"

When asked if she thought the Five Minute Man was doing a good thing, she answered "*A very good thing. I just wish he'd been better at it.*"

Peter Crowley is dead, but the man's wife isn't blaming Schroder for it. She's blaming society. She's blaming the Collard brothers. She's blaming the justice system for letting them out, and she's blaming the police for not doing a better job.

"*Do you hate the man who did this? Would you want five minutes alone with him if you could get them?*"

"*I don't know,*" she says. "*Ask me after I've buried my husband.*"

He thinks about ways the police could have done a better job over the years. It's true, what Charlotte Crowley said. There are cases that didn't make it to court. Cases where the police didn't have enough evidence to convict who they knew was guilty, or cases where evidence was dismissed. Cases where men kill and don't need a second chance because they haven't used up their first.

It gets Schroder thinking. Maybe this isn't about looking up people who are out of jail and on a second chance, maybe this is about those who got away. That's what the Five Minute Man needs to do now, and if Charlotte Crowley were here she would agree with him. She would thank him for what he was trying, and she would ask him to do a better job next time, and if she were here he would tell her that's exactly what he's going to do.

CHAPTER FIFTY-TWO

When I get back home Bridget is happy to see me. Whatever argument we were heading towards this morning is forgotten because I'm back when I said I would be. I haven't gone running off to save the world or even just our small corner of it.

Our appointment is for eleven o'clock. We do what we did last night and not talk about it. We sit out on the porch and she reads the same book she was reading last night and I read the newspaper, the front page calling Schroder *the Five Minute Man*, and I wonder what Schroder's take on that is. Earlier this year I worked a case where a man begged me to give him five minutes with the man who kidnapped his daughter. So I get the principle. Just like I did every time over the years, different victims and different killers, men asking me for five minutes with the man who had done this to their families, some of them just token words, some of them meaning it, some of them I don't know what would have happened if they'd been given their time. Perhaps they'd have used it. Perhaps they'd have sat in a corner and cried.

Schroder is right. I had my five minutes with the man who killed my daughter, and then I was given a second chance. Who am I to stop other people from wanting the same?

At ten thirty we drive to the hospital. It's another of those days where you don't know whether to go in a T-shirt or take a jacket. We find a space in the parking lot and feed the meter and head into the lobby then take the elevator up to the third floor.

We introduce ourselves to the nurse at the appointment window who has a set of symmetrical moles on her cheeks, one with a black hair, one with a gray one, and then we wait. I figure an appointment at eleven o'clock means we'll be going in closer to eleven thirty, but we actually get called in at eleven twenty. I figure that puts us ten minutes ahead for the day, and I wonder what we can do with that. I wonder if it's all going to be good news from here on out.

Doctor Forster shakes my hand and gives Bridget a small hug. Then we sit down and he sits down behind his desk, and the first thing he does is tell Bridget that she is looking well.

"I don't feel that well," she says.

"In what way?"

She shrugs, and then she looks at me, and then she shrugs again.

"Bridget?" Doctor Forster says, and he looks concerned.

I tighten my grip on her hand, and she tightens her grip on mine. Then she looks at Forster, and as she talks she won't look at me at all.

"I'm changing," she says. "I can feel it. It's like I'm losing a little bit of myself every day."

"It's only normal you—"

She interrupts him. "I know, and maybe you're right, and I hope you're right, and I'm grateful not to be in the vegetative state anymore, I really am, but it feels like this is just a holiday from that. It feels like I'm heading back there. I don't mean soon, not tomorrow, not next week, but I'll be lucky to see another year."

"We—"

She interrupts him again and shakes her head. "I can feel it happening. I know it's happening."

"I know you're scared," Forster says. "The brain, it's a funny thing. We know so little about it. But the fact that you're back with us, Bridget, that's a medical mystery. We have you back, and we're not going to let you go. We're going to figure out what's going on," he says, which in some ways contradicts what he said about the brain being a mystery. It means there are no guarantees.

We chat for a little while longer, and then we all stand up and he asks a nurse to lead us into an examination room. He tells us he'll be with us in another hour. The examination room has lots of posters on the walls, of brains and skeletons and organs, and in here they look like a wonder of science, but these same posters on a wall in some kid's bedroom would probably turn him into a serial killer. The nurse has a girl-next-door smile and a great bedside manner, and she uses both of these things in full force as she draws blood. She takes four vials, smiling the whole time, chatting about Christmas decorations her husband is putting up at home. When she's finished, she hands Bridget a urine-sample jar, gives her directions to the bathroom, and asks her to fill it up.

When she's done, she's handed a hospital gown and asked to change, and to remove all her jewelry. Then a different nurse takes us down another corridor, and then another, and I would hate to try to get anywhere in a hurry in a place like this. Or lost. Then we're heading into another room, this one not as brightly lit as the others. A giant metal tube is in the middle of the room. A narrow table is at the end of it, the open tube looking like a mouth and the table its tongue. I remember being in this same room after the accident, Bridget lying on that table as it slid into the machine, the CT scan taken in thirty minutes, me sitting outside the door praying she would be okay, and hoping my prayers would be heard. They weren't. At least not back then.

I stand back as a nurse and a technician prep Bridget. They lay her down on the machine, pads holding her head and neck still, and she's asked not to move.

"Can I stay in the room with her?" I ask, and last time they said no, and this time they say no too.

"It's okay, Teddy," Bridget says. "But can you give me a few minutes alone with the nurse? I need to discuss something with her."

"Maybe I should—"

She smiles. "It's okay, Teddy, it really is. I'll see you on the other side."

It makes me laugh when she says that, and I squeeze her hand, and then I head out into the corridor and make myself comfortable for thirty minutes. When it's all done, the nurse comes out to let me know, then I head back in as Bridget is getting to her feet. She looks calm, and she tells me that everything went okay, and then we're led back to the examination room where she gave blood and we get to wait in there for ten minutes by ourselves, and then Doctor Forster shows up.

"How are things looking?" I ask.

"There's still more testing to go," he says.

For the next hour he runs through a series of tests, hearing and speech. He checks her eyes, he checks her coordination, the whole time jotting down notes. He starts tapping her with a reflex hammer, which is something I've only ever seen on medical dramas, and until today wasn't even a hundred percent sure they really existed. Many of these tests, including the CT scan, Bridget had when coming out of her vegetative state a few months ago, back when I was in my coma, which gives the doctor a benchmark.

Then it gets worse. He asks Bridget to lie on her side on the examination table, and a nurse comes in, and together they prepare for a lumbar puncture. I can barely watch the anesthetic needle being put in, let alone the spinal needle he slips between her vertebrae a few minutes later. Bridget's face tightens during the process, and she clenches her hands a few times, but she braves it out and from start to finish the procedure takes thirty minutes, and results in about an ounce and a half of fluid. By the time the needle is out, Bridget has a headache. Forster tells her to stay put for another half an hour, and then he leaves us again. I sit on a seat next to the table and think about drawing a face on an inflated rubber glove, but decide against it. We barely speak. Bridget lies with her eyes closed with a small frown on her face, the headache fading, but still there. After half an hour the same nurse who took the blood earlier comes in and tells Bridget she can get dressed, and then tells us to head down to Doctor Forster's office when we're ready. By the time we sit back down in his office, the circle of tests having brought us back to where we started, four hours have passed.

"First of all, there are going to be no quick answers here," he says. "As much as I'd like to be able to take a look at these results and give you some peace of mind right now, I can't. I have to decipher what we have and wait for the labs. But I have put a rush on it, and I am hoping to have more within twenty-four hours."

"That's fine," Bridget says. "I'm just grateful you're trying."

She sounds a little defeated, and that breaks my heart, and I reach out and squeeze her hand.

"We're going to do more than try," Forster says. "We're going to do our best."

We talk for another ten minutes, and we probe away at him, and I feel the same way I feel sometimes when I'm sitting across the table from a suspect trying to learn what I can, but in the end we leave with a pair of handshakes and promises he will be in touch tomorrow, or Wednesday at the latest.

When we get back out to the car there's a ticket on the windshield because the meter ran out two hours ago. I fold it up and pocket it, pretty sure I can find somebody to make it go away. We don't talk much on the way home, each of us thinking our own thoughts, probably sharing some in common. I don't think much about Schroder, I just think about the future, about Bridget, about how it's all going to be okay.

Just like people keep saying.

CHAPTER FIFTY-THREE

Ron McDonald—no relation to the clown, as he said the day they came to arrest him—is a man who got away with murder. The clown joke is something he used on his doorstep, again at the station, and again in front of his lawyer, and for Schroder the joke went from being not funny, to really not funny, to making him want to toss Ron out the ninth-story window.

Cops can be like fishermen, reeling in criminals, sometimes letting the smaller ones go in order to catch the bigger ones, and the bigger ones they'll take photos of and put up on display. And of course there is always going to be the one that got away. For Schroder, the one that got away was the Christchurch Carver. But he's not the only big fish to have gotten free.

Ron McDonald murdered his wife.

It was seven years ago. McDonald had been working late. He was a mechanic who owned his own workshop. He finished installing a secondhand gearbox in a twenty-year-old Honda, cleaned up, locked the shop, then drove home to find his wife of eight years, Hailey, lying on the kitchen floor in a pool of her own blood. Taken from the house were jewelry and cash. It was a high-risk killing for not a lot of gain, but these things happened, and Schroder knew there were many people who would kill for less. Sometimes crimes evolve. For example, a guy breaks into a house thinking it's empty, but it's not. He sees a good-looking woman in her thirties who, on any other day, wouldn't even give him the time, but on this day she's in a house he thought was empty and he thinks to himself *Why not?* The two big words right up there with *What if?* and *Why should?*

So he attacks her. He thinks she'll do whatever he asks, only she doesn't do that at all, and then there's a struggle and then before he knows it he's stabbed her once, twice, a dozen times because she really, really shouldn't have said *no* like that.

That is the scene Ron McDonald came home to. A scene where the blood had reached the edge of the room on one side, where it was pooling in the grouting between the tiles everywhere else. He screamed. His neighbors heard him scream, and one of them came rushing over. Ron was on his knees in the blood trying to stop what was still inside Hailey's body from leaking out, but it was too late. When the police arrived he couldn't speak. They escorted him into another room and an officer helped him out of his bloody clothes and into new ones, and the entire time Ron just stared ahead, something inside of him having snapped.

The case was assigned to Schroder. It was a horrific scene, and he pictured himself coming through the door. A *Hi honey, I'm home* then seeing his wife's blood everywhere. Most scenes he pictured the victim as somebody he loved. He couldn't help it. The other thing he couldn't help was thinking right off the bat that McDonald was guilty. He thought that because of probability. Because of statistics. Statistics dictated that nine times out of ten a dead woman in a house was dead because of somebody else who lived there, or somebody she was involved with. This looked random, yes, especially because all the missing cash and the jewelry. However, he also knew that making planned look random didn't take a lot of work. Random happened a lot in this city, but so did planned.

When McDonald came around enough to talk, he told them what happened. He was a mechanic. The secondhand gearbox. The drive home. What he found here. It wasn't long into their talk that McDonald told Schroder that, when he found the man or men who had done this, he wanted five minutes alone with them. Schroder slowly shook his head, apologized, and said as much as he would love to do that, the world didn't work that way.

The following morning he started working on McDonald's alibi. Did he have one? No, he didn't, because there was nobody at work to verify he had been there. There was a record that the alarm was set at nine p.m., but he could have driven home, killed his wife, driven back to work, and set the alarm. He began to dig deeper. McDonald and his wife weren't happy. Often they argued. *She was afraid of him*, her father had told Schroder.

Did you ever see him display any behavior that was scary? Or abusive?

No.

Did she?

She didn't say it, not like that, but I could tell.

If she was that scared, or you were that worried for her, why not contact the police when it first started happening?

I wish I had, he'd said. *I just thought I was being a silly old man for thinking those things, but now look at me. I've become the stupidest old man in the world because I did nothing. When you find the guy who did this, can you do me a favor?*

There was nothing at the house to suggest McDonald was a guilty man. The blood on him was explained by trying to help his wife, but even then the blood was only on his hands and knees and feet, all parts that came into contact with the ground and his wife. There weren't splatters and arcs across his chest and neck. If he killed her, he didn't do it in the clothes they found him in. If he killed her and drove back to his work, he could have disposed of his clothes along the way.

They interviewed McDonald's staff. Had they seen anything suspicious? No, none of them had. But then they found out that one of the men had come back to work at eight p.m. because he'd left his cell phone there. *The alarm wasn't set, and Ron's car wasn't there, but the work stereo was on and his tools were out. It looked like he'd just popped out for a few minutes. He'd do that occasionally. We all would if we were hungry. There's a service station about two minutes away. Nobody is going to break into the shop and steal all the tools in only a few minutes*, he'd said, which Schroder knew wasn't as unlikely as the guy seemed to think. People steal things much quicker than other people think possible, because they practice, practice, practice.

So Ron McDonald hadn't been at his work when he'd said, and when questioned where he had been, he said he'd been at the service station getting a snack. Did he have a receipt? No. How did he pay? Cash. What time was he there? He couldn't be sure. Sometime around eight, maybe. How long was he gone? Five minutes at the absolute most. Or maybe ten. Who served him? He couldn't remember. What did he buy? A can of Coke and some bags of crisps, plus a couple of heated sausage rolls. Did he drive or walk? He drove. It wasn't far, but he didn't feel like walking.

So they went to the service station. There was surveillance footage. They checked it. They watched it around eight p.m. They went forward an hour. They went back an hour. They went forward two hours. They went back to that morning. They found McDonald there in the morning, they saw other staff there on and off, but nobody in the evening.

He spoke to McDonald again. This time McDonald wanted a lawyer. He was informed about what they had found. McDonald shook his head, then had a twenty-second conversation with his lawyer in hushed tones, his lawyer shook his head once, then nodded twice, then it was over. *The fact is my client hasn't been completely open with you,* the lawyer said. *For the last month my client has been having an affair, and this is where he was on the night his wife was killed.*

They followed up the affair story, of course they did, but this was a story they had heard before with other suspects and other crimes, and one they would hear again. The problem was it was a good alibi. They couldn't shake it.

Still, there was a case against McDonald and it was building. A neighbor had seen him park his car a block away, then walk the rest of the way to his house around eight p.m., where he spent fifteen minutes and then walked back to his car. How good a look did the neighbor get? A good look. But it was eight o'clock, it was the middle of winter, it was dark. Could it have been anybody? No. It was Ron. Most definitely Ron.

Then they got a warrant for the workshop. Schroder took a team of people to tear the place apart. It was in Ron's car that they found the clothes he had been wearing. They were soaked in blood. They had been balled up into a black rubbish bag and they had been stuffed into the trunk beneath the spare wheel.

They arrested Ron. They stood up before a judge. And it was dismissed before it even got to trial. There wasn't enough evidence. Not without the bloody clothes. The bloody clothes weren't evidence. And why? Because the warrant had been for the workshop and the cars parked on the premises, and Ron's car had been in a driveway owned by the neighboring auto repair shop. It was a technicality. That was all. But the law is built on technicalities. In the future, other detectives would call this *Schrodering*. They never thought he knew, but he did know, and it pissed him off, more so that he had messed up than the name they gave it.

The police would have to come up with more.

Only there wasn't any more, and other people were dying in the city, other people were running free and, somehow, Hailey McDonald and her killer husband slipped through the cracks.

Until now.

"I didn't kill her," Ronald says, and he's bleeding from the right side of his abdomen where Schroder shot him less than a minute ago. He's crying too. Big fat tears streaming down his face.

Schroder keeps the gun pointed at him. "Yes you did. I know you did."

"You're making a mistake!"

"You lied to us."

McDonald is on his knees. He's looking up at Schroder. "I was just trying to hide that I was having an affair," he says, clutching at the wound, then poking a finger into it as if that will stop the blood from leaving and the Reaper from coming. His face is going pale.

"And you were seen entering your house."

McDonald shakes his head. "That wasn't me."

"Do you remember what you asked me?"

"Please don't do this."

"Answer the question."

McDonald is still shaking his head. "What? What question?"

"I asked if you remember what you asked me."

"What? I don't know. What are you talking about?"

"The night we first met. You asked me if you could have five minutes alone with the person who killed your wife," Schroder says. "Well, consider this getting exactly what you asked for."

CHAPTER FIFTY-FOUR

We get back from the hospital and there's a basket on the front doorstep. There's a red-and-white checked cloth over the top of it, and I lift it to find an assortment of muffins, a dozen of them maybe. I show them to Bridget, who looks happy at the gesture, then a little less happy when I tell her they're from Rebecca.

We're eating dinner when my cell phone rings. It's the third time it's rung, and the last two times I reached down and ended the call without answering. I'm in the process of doing it again when Bridget tells me that it's okay, that it may be important.

"It doesn't matter," I tell her.

"Just answer the phone, Teddy."

So I pick up the phone and see it's Rebecca, and I'm still tempted not to answer it, but then I'm always tempted not to answer it.

"Hey," I say. "You calling about the newspaper article or about the fingerprints?"

"Neither," she says. "I've got some bad news."

My first thought is *Schroder*. Schroder has done today what he's done the last two days, and we've got another crime scene.

"Another dead rapist?" I ask.

"I said bad news," she says. "It's Hutton."

"What about him?"

"He had a heart attack this afternoon. The doctors seem to think it's to do with all his weight loss and dieting and running that he's been doing."

"Shit, is he going to be okay?" I ask, and Bridget stops eating and looks up at me.

"No," she says. "He didn't make . . . He died, Theo." She starts to cry. "He died half an hour ago."

"Oh shit," I say, and the world sways a little and I can feel my dinner moving around in my stomach, ready to leap north. "Where are you now? At the hospital?"

"I'm at home. His wife is with him at the hospital, but I just got the call from the superintendent to tell me what happened. He said he's been trying to get hold of you. I can't . . . you know, I can't . . ."

"Believe it?" I ask, and I rest my elbow on the table and hide my face in my palm, eyes closed, and there I can see Hutton as I saw him last as we stood outside Kelly Summers's house.

"We just saw him yesterday. How can people just leave the world like that?" she asks. It's a naive question coming from somebody in Kent's position, but it's still a good question despite that. It happens every day.

"What happened?" I ask.

"I don't know. He rang in sick this morning, remember? I guess . . . I don't know. I just don't know. But he's gone, Theo. He was a good guy. A really good guy."

"He was a good guy," I say, and Bridget is looking at me with concern. She knows somebody has died.

"He has a couple of kids," she says.

"I know."

"I feel like I need to do something, you know? Like if I can just figure out what to do we can change what happened. Like he's dead right now, but by the time we go into work tomorrow it'll all be okay, and he'll be there."

"It's always like that," I tell her.

"The case is yours," she says.

"What?"

"That's why the superintendent has been calling you. To tell you you're leading the case now."

"Me?"

"Yeah. You. He thinks you're up to it. He also agrees the bald man is the real deal. He walked away from Grover Hills, and we think he helped Summers. We got a list of Roddick's known associates and compared dental records. We got a name on the fourth body at Grover Hills. Robin Walsh. He was a known associate of Matthew Roddick. He picked the wrong night to try and help out his buddy. The Five Minute Man picked them all off. You like the name the media gave him?"

"Not really," I say, but it's better than calling him *Carl Schroder*.

"The medical examiner retrieved bullets from the bodies. They're out being tested, and three handguns have all been found at Grover Hills. Something will match up," she says.

"Bound to."

"I still can't believe Hutton is gone," she says.

"What happened with Kelly Summers's house? You find any prints?"

"Plenty."

"And Dwight Smith's?"

"No. But what we did find were a lot of clean surfaces. I mean, there were no prints on the windowsill. There were hardly any in the bathroom. Somebody cleaned up."

"Kelly looked like a tidy woman."

"Nobody is that tidy," she says. "But, you know, there's nothing there now to suggest it went any other way than what Kelly said in her letter, and now that you're leading the case I guess it's up to you what we do next."

She asks how Bridget is, and I update her, and then we hang up. I break the news to Bridget about Hutton and she cries, and I feel like crying too. She knew Hutton—not as well as she knew Schroder, but enough to feel the impact of his loss. Here one moment and gone the next. Life. Sunday we were working overtime together. Today he's sick. Later in the week we'll be going to his funeral.

When my phone rings again I know it's going to be either Kent or Superintendent Dominic Stevens, and for a moment—just a brief moment—I think they're ringing to update me on news, there's been a miracle, hallelujah, and Hutton isn't dead after all. But it's neither of those. It's Schroder.

"I need your help," he tells me.

"No," I tell him, and then I hang up.

"Who was that?" Bridget asks.

"Somebody I'm trying to avoid," I tell her.

My phone starts ringing again. I give it a few seconds, and then I tell Bridget to give me a minute and I walk into the lounge and take the call. This time I don't say anything. I just let him speak.

"You're going to get a call soon. There's been another body," he says. "You remember Ron McDonald? He was the guy who kept laughing about not being related to the clown, the guy who—"

"I remember him."

"Well he's dead now, and there's a problem. This is the second case now that I was lead detective on, and that means there are going to be questions. You need to keep me out of it."

I'm pacing the lounge, my grip so firm on the phone that if I did right now what Hutton did today, they'd never be able to pry it out of my hand. They'd have to bury me with it.

"Jesus Christ, Carl. You've totally lost it."

"We're in this together now, Theo."

"Hutton died today," I tell him.

"What? How?"

"He had a heart attack. Just came out of nowhere."

"That guy has been a walking heart attack for the last ten years."

"You could at least feel sorry for him."

"I wish I could. But if it helps I do feel something. I know that it's a shame. And I also know that you're going to do what I ask unless you want to risk jail or the death penalty. Are you replacing Hutton as the lead?"

"Yes."

"Then this should be simple for you," he says. "Now, Theo, this is very important. I left something behind."

"What are you talking about?"

"I left one of my cell phones behind when I killed McDonald. There shouldn't be any prints on it, but there may be a print on the SIM card. It must have come out of my pocket during the struggle, which means it's probably on the floor. I need you to take care of that for me."

"Why don't you take care of it yourself?"

"Because I can't go back there. It's too big a risk," he says.

I sit on the couch and hang my head and stare at the carpet. "So you want me to wipe down the SIM card?"

"No, Theo, I need you to retrieve the phone and bring it back to me."

"How about I just turn us both in instead?" I ask, and I mean it. I think. "I have to stop you, you do understand that, right?" The voice from earlier comes back, and it says *What about now? Now do you want to think about what you don't want to think about?* No. No I don't.

"No. You won't, Theo. I know you won't. Has your wife given you the news?"

"What news?"

"Then she hasn't. And when she does you'll know you'll never turn yourself in. Hell, if I wanted to I could make you come along with me next time, and you know what? Maybe I'll do just that."

"You're losing control," I tell him.

"No. I'm finally in control. Don't you see that? For the first time since wanting to make a difference in this city, I finally can."

CHAPTER FIFTY-FIVE

Bridget asks why I'm looking concerned. I tell her I'm worried about heading up the case. A few months ago I was in a coma, and before that I wasn't even a cop. I'm sure it's not going to be a popular decision. Others on the force have worked hard and longer and are better suited. But being given the case is not a promotion. It doesn't come with more money or a better job title. It just means doing exactly what I was doing plus more, and getting all the stress that comes along with it.

"You still haven't told me what you wanted to tell me yesterday," I tell her.

"It can wait," she says.

I shake my head. "No, it can't wait," I say, a little firmer than I should.

"Teddy—"

I put up my hand. "I'm sorry. I didn't mean that to sound like I was snapping. It's just that . . . well . . . with Hutton gone there's going to be more to do at work until this case is wrapped up, and the last thing I want to do is put in more hours there and less here, and . . . and, well, I don't really know what I'm trying to say," I say, which isn't true. I know exactly what I'm trying to say. I'm trying to say *Schroder tells me you know something that he can use to blackmail me.*

She reaches out and grabs my hand. "The reason I went to the mall yesterday," she says, "was to buy a pregnancy test."

I try to answer, but don't know how.

"I didn't get one then, but my mom took me back yesterday. I took the test, Teddy. I'm pregnant. That's what I had to tell the nurse today before the CT scan. Six weeks pregnant. We're going to have a baby."

The news is so different from anything I could have imagined her saying, and when I try to say something I still find that I can't.

"Teddy?"

A baby? Sleepless nights. Changing nappies. A toddler walking like a drunken Bambi as they search for balance, first words, play dates, going to school, getting hit by a car and burying them before their life gets under way. But then I backtrack because that's not going to happen, not this time, this time everything is going to be okay. So I think of playing in the backyard, of getting a cat, buying teddy bears and reading school report cards. I think of watching her playing sport at school, of pigtails, of freckles, and of one of her hands in mine as we walk down the beach, a bucket and spade in her other hand. We build sand castles and eat fish and chips and yell at the seagulls to leave us alone. I think of her friends coming around, of smiles with missing teeth, bribing her with junk food, telling her about Santa and putting crayon-scrawled pictures of cats and trees on the fridge. I think of her growing up, leaving school and going to university, of becoming her own person, making a difference in the world, I think about her being whatever it is she wants to be and her being happy doing it.

"Teddy, it's going to be okay," she says. "Nothing is going to happen to her."

"Her?"

"It's a girl," she says, and I realize I've been thinking of her as a girl too.

"You've—" I say, but she's already shaking her head.

"No, I haven't been to a doctor, and it's too early to tell, but I can tell."

"A girl," I say, and if I don't do what Schroder wants me to do, how old will my daughter be when I'm executed by the government? All those things I imagine doing with her I won't be able to do. She'll grow up, her daddy in the newspapers for killing the man who took away the sister she never got to meet, her daddy in a court of law, her daddy being escorted by two guards and a priest on his way to the end.

"Are you happy?" Bridget asks.

I move in and hug her. I hug her tight. It's life giving me another second chance, because I am the king of second chances. "Of course I'm happy," I tell her. "I feel unbelievably happy."

"It's going to be amazing," she says.

"I know."

"And we'll make sure nothing bad ever happens to her," she says.

"I know." And it will be amazing and we will make sure nothing bad happens to her. But already I'm scared. I'm scared of the future and all the unknown things that are out there in the world, things always searching for a way to take away the second chances I've been given because I didn't deserve them.

We are still hugging when my phone rings. I don't want to answer it, but I have to. I have to because Schroder has killed somebody and I have to clean it up, and if I can't then the life Bridget and I are dreaming about isn't going to happen.

Before I can apologize to Bridget she tells me to go ahead and answer it. She says it's been an eventful day, and with the loss of Hutton she knows the next few days are going to be tough.

I look at the display and see that it's Superintendent Dominic Stevens. Stevens is one of the reasons I got back onto the force. When I was fighting to become a cop again, he's the one who gave me a chance. It's because of him I'm not busking in malls or selling bits of my liver for cash.

"I've been trying to get hold of you," he tells me. "I have some bad news."

"I heard," I tell him. "Rebecca called earlier."

"He was a good man and he was a good cop, and over the last few months he was reaching his potential. It's a shame," he says, "such a shame."

"It still doesn't seem real," I say, and I want to add more, but right now I can't think what else to say.

"True, and as much as I hate doing this, and I know Hutton

would understand what I'm about to say, but we still have work to do. There's been another homicide."

"You're saying we have to move on," I tell him, because it has, after all, been five minutes.

"He'd understand," Stevens says. "And the alternative is what?"

"I get your point," I tell him. "What have we got?"

So he tells me. Ron McDonald. Did I remember him? Yes. Did I remember the details of the case? Mostly. That Schroder screwed up the warrant? Yes, I remembered that, and of course it made sense to me why McDonald was picked.

"Schroder was lead detective on two out of our three cases the Five Minute Man has targeted," he says. "The second was Landry's case. Do you think somebody is picking victims because of who investigated them?" he asks, and I wait for him to add *Is Schroder doing this?* but he doesn't, and that's because Schroder isn't a suspect, Schroder is Schroder, he was one of us, one of the good guys.

"I don't know," I tell him.

"Get hold of Detective Kent and meet her down at the scene."

"Who's there at the moment?"

"A couple of officers and the guy who found the body, but that's about to change."

I look at my watch. It's eight p.m. "Okay, look, before we get half the police force down there tramping all across the scene, let me meet Kent down there first. Let us have the scene to ourselves for half an hour. Call the officers down there and tell them to wait outside."

He says nothing.

"It might not help, but it might. Just let us spend thirty minutes looking around in some peace and quiet without other officers and forensics moving and shifting everything."

"Okay," he says. "It's your call. I don't see how giving you time down there alone is going to hurt, and maybe you will see something you wouldn't otherwise see," he says, and I think *hopefully the cell phone.*

"I'll call Kent and then I'll head right there."

There is a workshop on the edge of town, a place McDonald owned and operated and where he employed half a dozen staff. Business for Ron McDonald was good—but businesses that rely on bad things happening to other people are always good. Lawyers, dentists, doctors, mechanics, and cops all share that in common. It takes fifteen minutes to get there, but before I leave I call Bridget's parents and tell them that one of my colleagues has died, and that I need to go into work. There is no argument from them—of course there isn't—not when I've lost a friend.

I meet Kent out front. There are two patrol cars, one has two officers sitting in it, the other is empty. The scene is being lit up by the cars, which have their lights on and the engines still running. Standing near the main entrance are two more officers, and sitting in a white sports car is a guy talking animatedly on his cell phone, who must be the man who found the body.

We chat to the officers and get the rundown on how the body was found. We learn that the man in the sports car is Chris Watkins. We learn one of the officers stepped into the pool of blood we're about to see to check the victim for a pulse. He holds up a plastic evidence bag with his shoe in it.

"I took it off right away, as to not risk contaminating the scene," he says. "I hope nobody is too pissed at me for stepping in the blood, but I had to do it in case the guy could still be saved."

"The guy in the car is who called it in?" I ask.

"He's one of the staff here," the officer says. "McDonald's wife said Ron was due home around six, and when he didn't show up she tried calling him and didn't get an answer," he says, glancing down at his notepad. "She rang Chris and asked if he knew anything, and he said he didn't, but he would come down and check it out."

"Did he call the wife?" I ask.

"Watkins called the police right away," he says, "but he says he didn't call the wife because he didn't want to be the one breaking the news."

"Well he's breaking the news to somebody right now," Kent says, glancing over towards the car. "He's probably already phoned a dozen people."

"We don't have the right to take his cell phone off him," the officer asks.

"Did you at least ask him for it?"

"No. I guess I should have."

"Well go and ask for it now before the news of Ron McDonald's death reaches his wife before we reach her, okay?" Kent says.

"Sure thing, Detective," he says, and walks over to the car, walking with a slight limp because of the missing shoe.

I head inside with Kent. We have to walk through the office to get to the workshop. The office is full of photographs of cars and of men working on cars, of men in overalls laughing, of them sitting outside and smoking. It reminds me of the photographs at the service station Dwight Smith worked in. The staff look like a close-knit bunch. There are a couple of them on a fishing boat hooking something big, some of them standing in an army hunting pose, the kind of pose you see of men who have just brought down a big bear, only these guys are holding paintball guns, another of them go-carting.

The workshop is like any other male-dominated world I've had to visit where cars are the center of that world. The office with its paintball and fishing photographs is for the public, but behind that in the work area are calendars of half-naked women, large posters of rally cars and sport cars, pictures of women sitting in or draping over performance cars, pictures of women in bikinis waving checkered flags. There are large hydraulic lifts, two of them—one empty, the other with a car on top. There are long tables full of tools, tools everywhere and then even more tools, and in the middle of it all is Ron McDonald, lying on his back with his eyes open taking in none of the sights, the half-naked women maybe one of the last things he ever saw, and I figure there are worse things to see when you're checking out.

There is a lot of blood around the dead man. He was probably still alive when he went from standing to lying, and he was probably still alive for some time after that too. The epicenter of all that mess seems to be McDonald's abdomen. There's a hole in the dead man's overalls. It looks like a bullet hole. There's a single footprint in the blood.

"So who exactly is this guy?" Kent asks.

"His name is Ron McDonald, and a while back we were pretty sure he killed his wife."

"But?"

"But we couldn't prove it. There was a problem with the investigation and in the end it didn't even make it to trial. We found bloody clothes in his car, but we couldn't use it because there was a problem with the warrant."

"*Schrodering?*" she asks.

I nod. "Yeah, that's where the term came from," I say, and then I fill in the details. The arrest, the alibi, the lying, the affair. After the clothes were ruled out as evidence, the case stalled, then became cold, then became dead.

"Not dead for the Five Minute Man," she says. "Because that's who did this, right?"

"We don't know that yet."

She tucks her hands into her pockets and bounces slightly on her feet. She's staring at me. "You know what I think?"

"Tell me."

"I think we might be looking at a cop."

"What?"

She looks around to make sure we're alone, and we are, except for Ron McDonald who isn't taking any notes. "It fits, right? It's why he's always ahead of us. It's gotta be somebody who has access to this kind of information, and don't forget the woman at the prison said she was sure she was talking to a cop on the phone when you were being impersonated."

"I don't know," I say. "I don't see it."

She takes her hands out of her pocket and tilts her palms upwards. "Why?"

Why? Yes, Tate, why exactly? "Because we work with these people. Because they're good people. I just don't see it."

"Yes, we do work with good people, but this guy thinks he's doing a good thing. McDonald here got away with murder, but the Five Minute Man fixed that. It sounds like a cop kind of thing to do."

"Then why now? Why not back when Hailey McDonald was murdered?"

"And that's the question, right? Why not back then? Come on, let's take a look around before we let everybody else in."

"Why don't we start with the obvious," I say. "Go check the office and see if anybody was due to pick up a car or drop one off. We don't know for a fact this case is related to the others. The guy, after all, was a mechanic. I'm sure lots of people have wanted to kill their mechanic."

Rebecca walks back through to the office. I spend a few seconds standing by the pool of blood and I stare down at McDonald and I wonder how it all unfolded. It's possible he didn't know who he was talking to, that Schroder was a customer, a guy he didn't recognize, and the next thing he knew he was being shot. There are no drops of blood leading to or from the body, so he was hurt where he fell, so the struggle took place here. I don't see Schroder's phone, and that could be because it's not here, but it could also be because McDonald is lying on top of it.

Only it isn't under McDonald at all. It's about ten feet away against the wheel of a two-door Toyota. I turn towards the office. There is no line of sight to Rebecca. I walk over to the phone and the angle between me and the office becomes even narrower, but not narrow enough. If Rebecca looks through the doorway she'll see me. I use my foot to slide the phone behind the wheel, and then I carry on walking around the garage floor, looking for clues, looking for a weapon, trying to figure out who has done this by being a good policeman, by being on the same page, and I am on the same page—but not out of Hutton's book, and Hutton is gone now anyway.

"Found anything?" Rebecca asks, coming back out.

"Nothing."

"I looked through the receipts and the quotes, but nothing stands out, and there's nothing from tonight anyway. I just heard the medical examiner is here. You happy to let her in or do you want to keep the scene to just us at the moment?"

"Go and tell her she can come in," I tell her. "In fact tell everybody they can come in."

"It wasn't a stupid idea," she says, "wanting to come here before all the others."

I shrug, like it kind of was and kind of wasn't. Rebecca moves back into the office to head outside, and as soon she does I reach beneath the Toyota and pick up the phone. I tuck it safely into my pocket, where I can feel it burning, where it will scar my skin and set fire to my jacket and fall out in front of everybody, exposing me for what I am now—an accomplice to murder.

CHAPTER FIFTY-SIX

Because it's an industrial area, and because all the workshops and buildings closed around five or six o'clock, we can't do any canvassing. There is nobody to ask any questions. I talk to Chris Watkins, the man who found the body. He looks shaken up, but he also looks hyped up, the way anybody would be when their boss has just been murdered. He's wearing a T-shirt that says *Uncle Badtouch wants a kiss*, and he's wearing jeans that have to be about forty percent torn, as if the production line included the lion's den at the zoo. He's in his midthirties and has an army buzz haircut and a couple of fingernail-sized moles on the side of his face.

"I don't know what I was expecting," he says, and he's talking quickly, eager to get out the words, "but it sure as hell wasn't this. I just figured he was working late and had his phone turned off, but then I also thought you know that maybe there'd been an accident, you know, things happen and all that especially when you're around all these tools and all these cars and things have a way of going wrong. They hadn't, not here, but that only meant it was more likely, you know? That our time was coming. Geez, poor Ron. First his wife—I mean his first wife, and now him. They must have been cursed somehow."

"You're the guy who came back to get his phone the night Hailey McDonald was killed, right?"

"Yeah. Yeah, that's right," he says, and I know it's right because a few minutes ago I read what I could about that night and the days that followed, the bigger pieces I could remember, but not the smaller details. "I'm always forgetting my cell phone, well, you know, not always, but a lot. I've lost a few over the years, which means I can never buy a nice phone, you know what I mean? Like my dad used to tell me, the more expensive something is, the more likely somebody is going to take it from you. Or, in my case, the more likely I am to lose it."

"And tonight?"

"Yeah, yeah, tonight Naomi calls me about—"

"Naomi Williams?"

"Yeah, well no, it's Naomi McDonald, but it used to be Williams, sure."

"So Ron married the woman he was having an affair with?"

"Yeah, about two years ago. They're madly in love, have been since the moment they met. Or . . . or were, I guess, now that he's dead."

"Okay, talk me through tonight," I tell him.

He tells me about tonight, about the phone call from Naomi, and the whole time I can feel Schroder's cell phone burning hotter and hotter in my pocket. Hell, I didn't even check to see if the damn thing was switched on. It'll be just my luck that it'll start ringing. I reach into my pocket and fumble with it while Watkins talks, and I'm able to dig my thumbnail into the small release in the back and pop out the battery. By now there are two dozen police at the scene, and the workshop looks like an eighties Wall Street party with all the white fingerprinting powder everywhere. Kent is going through the dead man's car, and the medical examiner is going through the dead man's pockets, and soon she'll be going through the dead man. I finish up with Watkins and go back inside and talk to Kent, who's holding up a set of car keys she found in McDonald's pocket.

"Apparently this is the same car he used to own back when his wife died," she says. "Kind of weird. I'd have thought he'd have sold it or, better yet, a guy in his position could have torn it apart and used the parts."

"Yeah, I know what you're saying," I tell her. "A big piece of evidence like that, you'd think he'd want to get rid of it. That's not the only thing. The woman he was having an affair with who gave him the alibi? They're married now."

"Married?"

"Yeah. And happily, according to Watkins out there."

"So . . ." she says, then pauses to think about it.

I run with it. "So if there was any doubt in her mind that McDonald killed his wife, then I don't see her marrying him. If anything I see her never wanting to see him again."

"Unless she was involved in what happened."

"There is that," I say. "Which means one of two things. Either she wasn't lying about the alibi because they really were together, or she was lying about the alibi because she knew exactly what he was doing."

"If she wasn't lying about the alibi, then does that mean McDonald was innocent all along?" Before I can answer, she carries on. "Back then I'm guessing the general consensus was she lied for him, but believed without a doubt he was innocent."

"Pretty much, yeah."

"And you? What did you think?"

"I thought the same thing."

We start to walk back outside. I think about the original case. I worked the case, but I wasn't the lead. In fact I hardly contributed. I remember canvassing the neighborhood. I remember finding a witness who said they saw McDonald park his car a block away and walk to his house, then walk back. Only she used the word *sneak*, because she thought that's what we all wanted to hear. And it was what we wanted.

"Well, I guess it's all irrelevant," Kent says, and we reach McDonald's car and I don't recognize it from all those years ago because I've seen a lot of cars between then and now. She pops the trunk and carries on talking. "Doesn't matter what you believed and it doesn't matter what you could prove. At least one person was adamant Ron McDonald was a guilty man."

"Yeah, but you're a step ahead of yourself," I say. "We still don't know this has anything to do with that case. It could be—"

"A disgruntled customer," she says. "Yeah, you said that already."

"Or a disgruntled husband. If he was cheating on his wife back then, it's possible he was cheating on his current wife now. It could be somebody found out."

The trunk is empty and Kent pulls up the carpet to reveal the spare wheel. There's a bolt going through it to hold it in place. She starts undoing it. "Chris Watkins said they were madly in love, right? From the moment they met?"

I nod. "Right."

"So that means Chris knew her early on when the affair was happening. If he's a guy who knows those kinds of things, then if you're right it's possible he'd know if McDonald was having an affair now."

"Yeah, good idea," I say. "You want to go ask him?"

"You want to take over here?"

"No problem."

She goes and talks to Watkins, and I get the bolt out and then the spare wheel and there are no bloody clothes under it, not like last time. While I'm waiting for Kent, I call Bridget and tell her I'm still going to be another couple of hours. She tells me she'll go to bed soon, and that her mom will sleep on the couch and her dad will head home. We have a spare bed in the house—the bedroom Emily used to have—but neither of us suggests Bridget's mother sleeps there. That room will always be Emily's. Although soon I guess it will belong to another little girl. For a moment I can feel the pride and excitement of being a dad again, and I think of birthday cakes and ice cream.

"You're smiling, aren't you," Bridget says.

"How can you tell?"

"I can almost hear it. It suits you," she says. "Take care of the case, get it wrapped up, and when you're done we'll switch your phone off and then you're mine for a few days, deal?"

"Deal."

I hang up and Kent comes back out and shakes her head. "Watkins has no idea if McDonald was cheating on his wife, but he said he seriously doubts it. I guess he gave me the same speech he gave you about the two of them being deeply, madly in love."

"Let's look through the car, then go talk to the wife."

"Yeah, that's going to go a lot like seeing Peter Crowley's wife."

"If he was having an affair, it could be she knew about it. Or suspected. Could be she's the one who killed him."

"You seem really stuck on this affair theory."

I shrug. "Just a theory," I say. "I don't want to attribute this one to the Five Minute Man until that's what the evidence says," I say, but of course the evidence is burning a hole through the pocket of my jacket, trying to expose me.

CHAPTER FIFTY-SEVEN

We're both parked out on the street, with Kent parked behind me. I'm about to climb into my car when she puts a hand on my shoulder to stop me.

"I need to say something," she says, and my heart drops and I know what's coming. I reach into my pocket and put my hand over the cell phone, as if I can hide it even further.

"Yeah?"

"This morning at Kelly Summers's house," she says, and I almost breathe a sigh of relief. But I don't because this could still be going somewhere bad.

"Yeah?"

"I wanted to say something at the time, but there were too many people around, and then it's not like I could call you, not with you taking Bridget to the hospital today, then when you asked about the prints before Hutton had just died, and right then I decided I would let it go, but, well, suddenly I can't."

"You want to tell me what's on your mind?"

"You took Schroder to a crime scene. Look, I understand why you did it. He was the primary detective on her case five years ago and Hutton is the one who asked you to get in touch with him a few days ago, and sure, maybe he'd spot something, maybe not—it seemed a long shot, a hell of a long shot because I don't really know what it is you were expecting him to see, but sometimes long shots pay off. But come on, Tate, no gloves? You know better than that. Neither of you were wearing them."

"You're right," I tell her. "I'm sorry. With all that's going on with Bridget . . . I don't know. I guess I was distracted," I say, feeling sick in the stomach that I'm using my wife as an excuse. "I know that's no excuse, and I'll make sure it doesn't happen again."

"Schroder should have known better too."

"Well if it helps I don't think we touched anything," I tell her.

"No, that doesn't help. His prints showed up, so he touched some things."

I don't ask where. "Look, I'm really sorry."

"I know. I just wanted to point it out because next time—"

"There won't be a next time."

"Next time it could have been somebody else noticing. If the superintendent had been there this morning he'd probably have put you on suspension and he probably would have kicked Carl in the balls. Anyway, I've said my piece, so how about we draw a line under it and move on?"

We move on, with me leading the way and Kent following. It's a ten-minute drive to Ron McDonald's house, but a lot of places in Christchurch are only a ten-minute drive—that's one of the best things about Christchurch. I think about teaching my daughter to drive and wonder how many cars will be on the roads then, what they'll look like, or if we'll be driving around like George Jetson.

When we get to the address the door opens before we're even halfway up the path, and an attractive dark-haired woman in a robe is coming towards us at a pace between a walk and a jog. She's holding a phone in her left hand, and her right is being used to hold her robe closed.

"Is it true?" she asks, and somebody Chris Watkins spoke to has spoken to somebody else, maybe a chain of somebodies, and Naomi McDonald has just become a link in that chain.

"We're sorry to have to tell you that we found your husband deceased," Kent says.

"No," Naomi says, and her mouth is trembling, and she drops the phone and lets go of her robe and both her hands go up to her mouth. "No." Then she takes a few small steps backwards, then she stumbles, then she's on the ground and crying into the grass. "No!"

It becomes routine then. We help her up and lead her inside and we ask if there's anybody she would like us to call, and she tells us that there is, that she wants her parents, and she gives Kent the number, and while Kent calls them she also puts the kettle on and starts making cups of tea while Naomi sobs and sits on the couch and asks me over and over if I'm sure that it's him, that it's her husband that's dead, and I tell her we're sure, and she asks how it happened. I tell her I'm still not sure yet.

"When Chris went to look for him and didn't call back and he ignored my calls, I knew something bad had happened, and now, just a minute ago . . ." she says, and she takes a deep breath and looks up at the ceiling and tries to calm herself. "She said he was dead," she says. "On the phone, Chris's wife, she just called and I didn't want to believe her, but I knew."

Kent finishes with the phone call and making the tea and then she sits next to Naomi and opposite me and we tell her how sorry we are, and then we apologize for what's about to come next—but we need to ask her questions. We tell her we understand the timing is hard for her, that she's in shock and in pain, but the quicker we can understand what happened the quicker we can find who did this.

"Was it the Five Minute Man?" she asks, clutching her cup of tea.

"Why do you ask that?" I ask.

"Because of what happened to Ron's first wife."

"Are you saying he killed her?" I ask.

She shakes her head, a sad smile on her face. "No, but that's the thing, right? Nobody ever believed he was really innocent, but he was. You people think I made up that alibi for him, but I didn't. The night Hailey was murdered he was with me. He'd been with me for two hours and he told her he was working on a car, but he wasn't, you know? He was here, and the time of death your experts gave proved that, only none of you would listen. But the weird thing is this morning I saw the newspaper and I rang Ron and I told him about the article. This guy is out there killing people, and this woman in the newspaper thinks that's a great thing, and you know what my husband says to me? He says he better watch his back. But it was a joke, you know, a dumb joke about how he could," she says, and she's struggling to hang on, "could be next, but he didn't think it, at least he didn't, but when he said it I thought *Hey, hey, maybe he's got something there, maybe he really should watch his back*, but I didn't say it, you know? And the thing, the really stupid, dumb, crazy thing is that when I hung up, I thought *Great, you know, great this guy is out there because maybe he'll get the guy who really killed Hailey*. I mean it wasn't Ron, of course it wasn't, and if I thought it was possible I'd never have married him, but he didn't do it, couldn't have done it, and that means the guy who did do it is still out there."

I'm not quite sure what to say after that, and it seems Kent isn't either. Naomi is staring into her cup of tea. She's holding it, but not drinking from it.

"I know what you're both thinking," she says. "But what you should have been thinking all those years is who put those clothes into his car?"

"We don't know that this has anything to do with what happened to Naomi," Kent says. "We don't know he was targeted by the man you read about in the newspaper."

"It could have been a customer," I say. "It could have been somebody trying to rob the place. They might have thought it was empty and forced their way inside and suddenly there was confrontation. Did your husband talk about any problems at work? Was there anybody he had been arguing with?"

"I thought cops weren't supposed to believe in coincidences," she says.

"We have to explore all angles," I say.

Naomi shakes her head. "Well, there was nothing like you're suggesting. Ron never argued. I mean, sure, he did with his first wife, but those two fell out of love a long time ago. That's why he was with me, and it's not like it was a secret. I mean, sure, he kept it from you guys because he knew how it would look, and that only made it worse, but Hailey knew all about me. She didn't know who I was, but she knew I existed. She'd known for about a week. She didn't care. Not in the least."

"I remember," I say. The problem was that made it seem even more likely. The wife finds out, and despite what Naomi here thinks, she does care, they argue on and off for a week, and then the argument gets out of control. The same way Schroder has gotten out of control.

"I'm sure you do," she says, "and that made him look even guiltier. Look, this is all history and really painful stuff. You guys really screwed Ron over and he didn't deserve that, and somehow, somewhere, maybe you guys will pay for messing up, but right now that doesn't help find who hurt him tonight, does it. So ask what you need to ask. I know you're capable of thinking just about anything, so let's get on with this."

I lean forward and soften my voice. "Is it possible he was having an affair?"

"What? No, never," she says. "Ron's not that kind of . . ." she says, then stops as she hears the irony in what she's about to say. "I mean, not with me. He loved me and I loved him. It was different to what he had last time. Back then he was trying to leave a loveless marriage. That's nothing like what we have."

"If he was cheating on you," I say, and I feel bad for saying it, I feel like a complete bastard, but even if Schroder wasn't holding me over a barrel I'd still have to push the point . . . though perhaps not as hard, "then it's possible whoever he was seeing was also married. It's possible he upset the wrong person."

Before I even finish saying this she's shaking her head. "No," she says, "and if this is anything like last time, you're going to focus all your attention on the wrong person. There is no *other woman*, and there is no other woman's pissed off husband. What there is is a crazy person who thinks he's doing the world a favor, but all he's doing is getting good people killed. I don't know how to tell you any more clearly, but my husband wasn't cheating on me."

"Would you mind if we went through his personal belongings?" Kent asks. "Emails, files, bank statements, that kind of thing."

"You won't find any receipts for hotel rooms, if that's what you're thinking."

"It's not what we're thinking," Kent says, "but we have to allow for the fact that your husband may have known the person who attacked him. If that's the case, we need to talk to everybody he knew. We need to know exactly what was going on in his life."

"Nothing was going on in his life, except for the fact the police thought he murdered his wife and because they never found who really did do that, people were always so sure he'd done it. The first few years were the hardest. We'd go to the supermarket, or we'd go to the movies, and people would stare and point. And then after a few months they stopped pointing. They'd turn slightly to each other and whisper, and we knew, we always knew what they were saying. All because you gave up on finding out what really happened. So no, nothing was going on in his life except for the fact somebody out there decided not only was he guilty, but that he needed to be dealt with. I get what this guy is doing, and on some level I want to agree with it, because right now I'd love to get my hands on the person who hurt my husband, but don't you see that the blame is not his alone? It's also yours. And it's the person who killed Hailey. You and he are—"

"Please, Mrs. McDonald," Kent says.

"Let me finish," she says, and puts up her hand, "and then you can go through our house and his computer and through every scrap of paper you can find. But you and the man that killed Hailey are equally to blame for what happened tonight. The actions of a madman and the actions of a narrow-sighted police department got my husband killed."

A car pulls up in the driveway, two doors open and close, and then the sound of quickly approaching footsteps. "My parents are here," Naomi says, and a moment later the front door opens and a man and a woman both in their sixties come bursting into the lounge. Naomi tries to stand up to hug them, but she can't make it, her mother slides in next to her and wraps her arms around her, and then Ron McDonald's widow bursts into tears. Her father looks at us, a sad look on his face, but at least he isn't looking at us as if we're the enemy.

"Perhaps we can talk outside," he says.

We follow him out to the front yard. He keeps reaching up and scratching at the moustache that's warming the base of his nose. His hair, still mostly black, is combed to the side, the edges of it gray. He introduces himself and puts out his hand. "Bob Williams," he says.

I introduce myself and then Kent.

"Are you sure?" he asks. "That it's him?"

"Yes," I tell him.

"Jesus," he says.

"This is tough," I tell him, "but we need to ask some questions."

"I understand," he says.

"Can we be frank?" I ask. "The sooner we know what's going on, the sooner we can find out who killed Ron."

"I'd prefer it if you were," he says.

"Is it possible Ron was having an affair?"

"Possible?" He shrugs, and doesn't need to give it much thought. "Sure. He'd done it before, right? I hated that my daughter got involved with a married man. But probable? No. I don't see it."

"You knew about the relationship before Hailey McDonald was murdered?"

He nods, then crosses his arms. "Yeah, I knew. But that's love for you, right? Makes you do stupid things, but in some ways that's the best part about it."

"Did you like him?"

"Ron? Sure, he's a likeable guy. Always been great to Naomi, always been polite to us. Respectful, helpful, exactly what you want in the guy your daughter is involved with, but . . ." he says, then doesn't add to it.

"But?" Kent asks.

"But no father wants their daughter involved with somebody accused of murder."

"So you thought he did it," I say.

He shrugs again. "Look, I'm no cop, but I did work security for thirty years, and twenty of those I was out at night patrolling areas with nothing more than a kick-ass flashlight and a radio for backup, but I have seen some pretty nasty shit. I know how the world works. I do. People break into buildings all the time. They smash windows or pry open doors and spend a minute inside while the alarm is going off taking what they can because they don't give a shit about other people. Where Ron works, I used to work that area. In fact that's how they met. I knew him. I knew him because I worked security on his building, and he was a good mechanic, and when Naomi's car broke down I spoke to him about it. I even took her in there. So for me I always think that if Ron did kill his wife, then it started that day he met my daughter. It started then because he fell in love with her and out of love with the wife he had, and that can be a messy thing. Like I said, love can make you do stupid things. But murder? I didn't know back then and I still don't know now. Back then me and Camilla, that's my wife, we figured he was going to jail so we didn't have to try and talk any sense into Naomi, but then the arrest got screwed up and he didn't even make it to trial. When it became obvious he was going to be a free man we begged her to leave him and she refused. Ron was a nice guy, sure, but could I trust him? I wanted to. I really did, because I trusted my daughter, and if she said she was with him that night then she was with him, I don't doubt that, but still . . . I couldn't trust him. I couldn't be *sure*. Not one hundred percent, and that's what you want when it comes to family. Does any of this have to do with what happened tonight?"

"We're not sure," Kent says, "but it's possible."

"Just like it's possible Ron worked on some guy's car and that guy didn't like the fact the fuel pump had to be replaced. Or possible he was having an affair. Or possible this madman I read about in the papers today is . . . Oh, shit," he says. "That's what you think, isn't it?"

"It's possible," Kent says again.

"*Possible*. I guess that means I don't get to ask any questions."

We go through the usual questions with him then. The *Do you know of any problems he was having at work? Was he fighting with anybody?* All the kinds of things that somebody like Bob here would sum up as *getting the real measure of the man*.

"There is one thing I'll tell you, though."

"Yeah?"

"Two years ago Ron came to me. He came to do the traditional thing and ask if it was okay if he married my daughter. I could tell he thought I was going to say no, and I probably would have, but then he said something. He said after the case got dismissed he tried to convince his lawyer to have the, hell, I don't know the legal terms, but he wanted the ruling that the evidence that was dismissed be allowed to be used."

"What?" I ask.

"Yeah. See, he had this theory. He knew he hadn't done it. So that meant somebody had, right? And those were his clothes in the back of that car. He didn't deny that, but he thought somebody else must have worn them. So he had this idea that if the clothes could be used as evidence, then the police could send them away and get them tested for DNA. He said his would be on there because they were his clothes, but that somebody else's would be on there too. Whoever wore them. His lawyer told him it was a stupid idea, and maybe that's because his lawyer didn't believe him the same way nobody else seemed to. He told Ron that he was a free man, and if he let the police use that evidence then they would use it against him. The proof was in the way they were already treating him. And even if the clothes were planted, then what if the guy who planted them was careful? What then? No, that gesture would come back to bite him in the ass. That car being searched like that, that mistake, right in that moment it was keeping him out of jail. That's what the lawyer said. But Ron, he said that mistake made him a guilty man in the eyes of the public. It makes you think, doesn't it? Makes you think that Ron might have been innocent all along."

CHAPTER FIFTY-EIGHT

It feels like Sunday morning all over again, going through Peter Crowley's stuff, the physical motions of searching, the same sense another good man has been killed. We get a call from the medical examiner who tells us she'll work on the body tomorrow, that she's still working on the four men found at Grover Hills, but what she will do tonight is retrieve the bullet inside Ron McDonald for ballistics.

"What do you think?" Kent asks me.

"The wife was convincing."

"Really convincing," she says. "If I'd been on this case back then, I think I would have bought her story."

"And perhaps the jury would have too. The question is, is that all that is? A story?"

She shakes her head. "Not to her. To her it's real. To her Ron McDonald was an innocent man. I really believe she would never have married him if she even had any doubts, and she didn't strike me as somebody who could have been involved. We should talk to his lawyer and see if that's true about him wanting the evidence tested."

We agree to schedule a task-force meeting in the morning, and then we're both in our cars and heading home. I call the station on the way and arrange for memos to be sent to the other detectives involved with the deaths over the last few days that we're all going to be meeting at ten a.m.

The next call I make is to Schroder.

"Did you get my phone?" he asks.

"Yeah, I found it."

"And nobody saw you?"

"Of course not. You'll get it back, but right now I'm tired and am heading home. It's been a long day, and that's thanks to you."

"If you let me do what I've started doing, your days can get shorter, Theo. There'll be less bad guys around."

"It doesn't work that way."

"No. I suppose it doesn't. You can keep the phone," he says. "Hell, it doesn't even work."

I think about that for a few seconds, and then it all slips into place. "Does the phone really have your fingerprints on it?"

"No."

"You didn't drop it in the struggle, did you."

"There was no struggle. You put it there deliberately. You wanted to see whether or not I would pick it up and do as you asked."

"That's very pessimistic of you, Theo."

"Am I right?"

"Yes, you are. You're going to do a great job, Theo, and now that we're in this together we can really make a difference in this city. I'll give you some time to steer the investigation in a different direction, and in a few days' time I'll choose somebody else for us."

"I'm hanging up now."

"Good night, Theo."

"Fuck you, Carl."

CHAPTER FIFTY-NINE

The following morning everything goes to plan. I wake up at eight o'clock and my wife wakes up at the same time and we eat breakfast together, and then she promises me she's going to be okay and I believe her and head to work, but on the way I call her parents anyway and ask them to give her a call every now and then to check in on her.

"I think she wants to go shopping for baby clothes," her mother says. "She's convinced it's going to be a girl, but you know what? I have the feeling it's going to be a boy."

A boy. I realize I'd just taken Bridget's word for the fact the baby would be a girl, even though it was nothing more than a feeling, nothing scientific at all. For the first time I consider having a son. I imagine all the cool things we can do together. I can teach him to throw a rugby ball and how to kick tires on a car.

"Have you told your parents yet?" she asks.

"Not yet," I say, "but I will. Soon."

I get to work at nine thirty and I already feel like I need a nap. I hide Schroder's cell phone under the seat of my car. No official decision has been made as to whether last night's homicide has anything to do with the weekend's events.

"First of all," I say, when I stand up in front of the room of people, the smell of shower gel mixing with coffee, Kent in the front row, Superintendent Dominic Stevens next to her, "I want to say what we're all thinking, that losing Hutton is a hell of a loss. He was a good man and a good cop, and he will be missed. Sorely missed. The funeral is on Friday afternoon, and I think he'd really appreciate it if we can figure out what in the hell is going on and bring it to a stop before then."

There's a general murmur of agreement, and I remember Landry's funeral earlier in the year, all these same people getting drunk at the wake, then the call came through of a homicide and everybody here staggered into taxis and showed up at the scene.

"Right, so Ron McDonald. I know some of you worked on the case back when his wife was murdered, and some of you didn't. The decision is we're going to take another run at the original case."

More general murmurs that don't sound positive or negative.

"We discovered a few things last night that put doubt on what happened seven years ago."

"Like what?" somebody from the back row asks.

I update the room on the conversations we had with Naomi and her father. Some people in the room are slowly shaking their heads, and some are slowly nodding. I make it sound convincing, and why not? We were convinced.

"So here's how things are going to work. Seven years ago the clothes were never tested because they weren't considered evidence. We still have the clothes in our possession, or we did because thirty minutes ago they were shipped from our evidence warehouse to the DNA lab. It'll take at least a month to match a DNA profile if we have that profile on record, but as you also all know it'll only take between twenty-four and forty-eight hours to see how many DNA sources are on that shirt. They'll be swabbing the armpits, the back of the collar. They'll be swabbing the whole damn thing. If somebody else was wearing that shirt then we'll know in the next day or two. So here's what I want us to find out today. I want a list of people who had access to the car seven years ago. I also want a list of people who had access to the house. If somebody else was wearing those clothes, then how did they get them?"

"And then what?" somebody else asks, and it's Detective Travers, a guy I've worked with a few times over the years. Travers is the best dressed out of all of us, often making the rest of us look like our outfits cost about five dollars. "If we find DNA on the shirt, we can't run it against any suspects. And if you run the profile and we find a match and find a suspect, what happens in court when we're asked what pointed us in the direction of our suspect?"

"I know it's complicated," I tell the room, "and that's why we're not running the shirt to try and match a profile. I know it would help, and I know it seems counterproductive, but if we do find a match the case will be thrown out before it even begins. Let's be clear, here. We're running the shirt to see if there is more than one type of DNA on it, and nothing more. It's to tell us if we're on the right path. Remember, we're looking for somebody who either believed Ron was at work that night, or knew he was having an affair and therefore wouldn't be home. The medical examiner said there were no defensive wounds on the wife, so she was with somebody she knew and trusted. While some of us are focusing on that, some of us will talk to McDonald's friends and family and the staff and try to figure out what happened last night," I say, and then I tell them our affair theory. I tell them that of course we can't rule the Five Minute Man out of the equation, but equally we can't become narrow-minded and focus only on him. "If we do then we risk making the same mistakes we made seven years ago."

"We don't even know we made mistakes back then," Travers says. "The clothes were his and this DNA test is going to prove that."

I stare out at the room for a few seconds until the silence becomes a little uncomfortable. "I know some of you think this is a waste of time, but I really don't think it is. We should talk to family and friends of Hailey McDonald. Find the transcripts from the interviews, go through them, then go and re-interview these people. Last time we asked those questions we were thinking her husband was a guilty man. This time ask them as if he's innocent. And, while you're asking them, ask yourself who would want to hurt her and frame him? Who hated her enough to see her dead, and him enough to see him in jail? Which one of those two things was the driving factor to what happened that night?

"Look, I know it seems like a lot of work, I know it seems like we're focusing on the wrong case here, but the two are linked. We'll be hearing from ballistics later on this morning—that will hopefully give us a better understanding of what took place at Grover Hills, and we'll know if McDonald was shot last night with the same gun. We're also hoping the dead dog might help us out. The dog has traces of DNA and clothing fibers in its teeth. It bit somebody before it died, and if that somebody has a record, then we'll get a match."

"But not before Christmas," somebody else says, and it's true.

I swap places with the superintendent who gets up and picks up where I left off. He goes through my points almost in reverse order, and comes back to the first point I made about what a loss the death of Detective Hutton is. By now everybody is nodding, and later this week it will be the second police funeral of the year.

When he's done I get back up and assign the tasks. There are a dozen detectives who are split up into pairs and sent out into the streets, some to talk to people who knew Ron McDonald, some to canvass the area where he was killed, some to interview the staff. More officers will be sent into the streets to canvass the neighborhoods of Crowley, McDonald, and Summers. McDonald's staff have all been contacted this morning—there are eight of them—and been updated on the situation, and then asked to come down to the station for interviews, the eight of them being staggered across the day. We're working two cases now. I tell Kent I want to interview the woman I spoke to seven years ago who identified Ron McDonald outside his house the night his wife died.

"You want to work on the old case, and not the new one?" Kent asks, when the meeting is over.

"No," I tell her. "But I want to talk to her first because that was my part in the investigation back then, and I want to know if I did everything right."

"For your peace of mind," she says.

"I'm sure as hell going to need some if we messed up back then. First we have to see if she even still lives there."

We're looking up her address on a computer when Superintendent Dominic Stevens comes and finds me. "A word," he says, then
turns around and heads back to his office.

I follow him in there, and he nods towards the door, the meaning is clear, so I shut it. He sits down behind his desk. Opposite him
is an officer, and it takes me a few seconds to realize it's one of the
officers from last night, the one who took off his shoe.

"This here is Officer Jim Williams," he says, and that's two Wil-
liamses in two days and if there are any more I'm going to lose
track. "Why don't you tell Detective Tate here what you just told
me?"

"Yes, sir," Williams says. He turns towards me. He is standing at
attention with his hands behind him. "I was one of the officers who
got the call out last night. When we got there the door was open
and the lights were on, and we went through the office and the first
thing we saw was the body."

"And you took your shoe off to check for a pulse," I tell him.
"That was smart to take it off and put it into the bag. I know all
this."

He nods, but I can tell he's happy with the compliment.

"After we called it in, we went back outside and guarded the
building, which is what we were doing when you arrived. The
thing is," he says, and then he looks at Stevens who nods at him
to carry on, "the thing is the blood and the body wasn't the only
thing I saw."

"Meaning?"

"I had to sit down to get my shoe off because I had to remove it
carefully. When I was taking it off I saw a cell phone on the ground.
I figured it probably belonged to the victim and that it had gotten
kicked over there in the struggle. Later, when everything was being
logged into evidence, I saw it wasn't there. I checked back inside,
but it was gone."

"Gone?"

"There's no mention of it."

I shake my head. "I don't understand," I say, and I can feel my heart start to beat a little harder, and am I sweating? Is my heart hammering a heart shape into my shirt, the way it would in a cartoon? The shape extending out half a foot? No. No? But I think it's about to. Schroder's stupid test to make sure we're both on the same page . . . Goddamn him.

"He's saying somebody stole evidence," Stevens says. "You're dismissed," he says to the officer. "And don't breathe a word of this to anybody, you understand me?"

"I won't," he says. "That's why I came straight to you. Nobody else knows."

"Let's keep it that way."

"Yes, sir," Williams says, and then he opens the door and closes it behind him.

Stevens leans back in his chair. He puts his elbows on the armrests, steeples his fingers, and touches them to his chin. "Shit, Tate, what a mess."

I keep shaking my head. "I still don't see it."

"No? You think he's lying?"

"No, it's not that. There are plenty of reasons it could have gone missing—if it was even there in the first place."

"So you think he's mistaken then."

I shrug. "It's possible. More possible than one of us stealing it. Hell, if one of us were going to steal something, we wouldn't choose something important to the scene. Stealing something from the office, or some tools, I mean, even that's a stretch, but I can see that happening. Stealing a piece of crucial evidence because somebody wants a new cell phone? No." I shake my head. "I don't see it."

He nods. "I'm inclined to agree with you. Things get stolen from crime scenes, Detective, but you're right—it's from the opposite end of the house because an officer sees a fifty-dollar note on the dresser or a camera and it's four rooms and a hallway away from the crime, but stealing a key piece of evidence? That's reckless and stupid. Which makes this even worse."

"How so?"

"Because nobody on your team is that reckless or stupid. The phone wasn't stolen because somebody wanted a new phone, Detective. It was stolen because somebody wanted to hide evidence."

I'm still shaking my head. "That would mean they're involved in the killing. It has to be a mistake."

He swivels slightly in his chair, left to right, right to left, just a few degrees. "Okay. Here's what's going to happen. I'll look into the chain of evidence. Maybe it was picked up and is sitting in the bottom of another box all forgotten about, and somebody forgot to write it down. But you're going to do the same thing that Officer Williams is going to do, and that's to tell nobody about this. Not even Kent. I'll refer this internally. If the evidence was lost, then that's sloppy police work and somebody will be reprimanded or suspended. But if somebody took it to hide what happened, well, you know what that means."

"I know," I say.

"If the Five Minute Man is responsible for Ron McDonald's death, then he could be the very person who removed that phone. You're going to have to start keeping an eye on your team, Tate. It's possible our Five Minute Man is a cop."

"I think you should let me talk to Kent about it. I mean, she was with me on Saturday night from the alleyway to Grover Hills—there's no way it could be her."

He taps his finger to his chin while he thinks about. "Okay," he says. "Okay, I can let you do that because the last few days are set in stone, and everything you and Kent did will be examined in detail, so if she is somehow involved we'll find out."

"And me? Why are you telling me?"

"Because you're leading this investigation, Detective, and that means I trust you and your abilities. I wouldn't have given you the responsibility if I didn't think you were up to it. Schroder always vouched for you, as did Hutton, and I've seen what you can do. In saying that, I also know you can walk a pretty fine line. Do you think these bad men deserve what they're getting? Yes, I'm sure you do. But could you be the one hurting them? I don't see it and, as you pointed out, both you and Rebecca were working when the Grover Hills fire was set. Innocent people are being hurt, and despite what some people think you may be capable of, I know you would never allow that. So for now you and Detective Kent keep this to yourselves while you and your team are investigated, and bring me this bald-headed bastard before the media turns him into some kind of superhero vigilante."

CHAPTER SIXTY

I step out into the corridor and Kent is waiting for me. "What was all that about?" she asks.

"Just being reminded where my place is in the scheme of things," I tell her, "and being told not to mess it all up."

"Is that all?"

"No, it's not all. Let's go grab a coffee."

We walk two minutes to a nearby café. We order drinks and sit outside with a view of the Avon River ahead of us, the dark water reflecting the sun. There are some ducks sitting idly on the bank sunning themselves, a couple of glue-sniffers doing the same thing. Summer is doing an impressive job of letting us know that it's almost here.

I tell Kent about the meeting with Stevens. She starts shaking her head halfway through the story, and says *I don't believe it* twice before I'm done. But then she does believe it.

"It confirms what I was saying yesterday," she says. "We're looking for a cop."

I take the last mouthful of coffee. "I don't know what to think."

We head back to the station to get the car. On the way I get a call from a guy by the name of Chuck Langly. Chuck is the only guy I've ever met with the name Chuck, and Chuck works in ballistics, which means, if this was an IQ test, I could safely say that all Chucks work with bullets.

"I got something for you," he says. "In fact a whole lot of somethings."

"Shoot," I tell him.

"That's funny," he says. "So we got four bodies from Grover Hills, right?"

"Right."

"And there were three guns recovered from the scene."

"Right."

"Well none of the bullets in the four victims at Grover Hills came from any of those guns."

"So we're looking for a fourth gun," I say.

"Exactly. And that fourth gun got used on all the victims at Grover Hills, and was also used to kill Ron McDonald."

"That at least proves those two cases are related. Thanks, Chuck. Get that typed up and circulated, huh?"

"Will do."

We get to the station and get the car and Kent drives and I ride shotgun and I tell her about what Chuck had to say. We drive to the neighborhood Ron McDonald used to live in until he or somebody pretending to be him killed his wife. We have no idea who's moved into the place since then, but there's a car parked up the driveway and in one window we can see a small statue of the Eiffel Tower, and in another one is a foot-high plushy Smurf. It's the house opposite that we've come to visit, and we walk up to the door and the same woman who answered it seven years ago answers it now.

"I remember you," Julianne Cross says, once we're inside and sitting down in the lounge, cups of coffee in our hands. We're surrounded by photographs of children and grandchildren, none of them hers, she tells us, but all of them children she helped raise. Julianne was a nanny for over forty years and could never have children of her own—she tells us this, just like she had told me before. "You're the one who interviewed me back then. I heard on the news this morning that karma can be a pretty horrible thing," she says.

"It can be," I tell her.

"I read a lot," she says. "And I watch a lot of TV. At my age, sometimes it's all I feel like doing, especially when winter kicks in. Do you want to ask me what I read?"

"What do you read?" I ask.

"Crime novels, young man. And a lot of them. Both me and Barney—Barney's my husband who passed away—used to spend two hours a night reading before we'd go to sleep, and after we retired we'd spend two hours reading in the morning too. So I know why you're here. You're here because seven years ago I saw Ron McDonald going into his house where he stayed for fifteen minutes and then I saw him sneaking back to his car. You want to know if any of that has changed."

"And has it?" I ask.

"No, not in the least, sonny."

"Can you talk me through it again?"

She talks me through it again. It's almost the same, word for word. Julianne Cross has an excellent memory.

"How good a look at his face did you get?" I ask.

"It was good enough," she says.

"Good enough?" Kent asks.

"It was him, if that's what you're asking. And just why are you asking?" she asks. "Why are you here? Something must have come up for you to be covering old ground," she says, and then her crime-reading mind kicks in. "Are you saying he didn't do it?"

"We think it's possible somebody else was wearing his clothes."

She starts nodding. "One thing that comes with old age is stubbornness," she says. "I'm as stubborn as an ox. But the other thing that comes is wisdom, and I'm not so stubborn that I won't admit when I'm wrong, not like most people who make it to eighty. Did I see his face? It was dark. Of course it was dark, and the streetlights lit him up every few yards, and he was wearing a hat, a baseball hat like people wear when they're trying to look cool or hide a bad hairline. But yes, he was wearing Ron's clothes and he looked like Ron. Yes, yes, I would still say it was him."

"The car he parked a block away, how good a look did you get at it?" Kent asks.

"It was too far away to see a license plate, and I'm not good with cars. The best I could do back then was tell you it was dark, and that's the best I can do now."

I take a sip of coffee. It's better than the stuff we had in town, but I just don't have the room for it. "How well did you know Hailey?"

"Well enough. I've been in this house for nearly fifty years," she says, "and I've seen other families come and go. She lived there with her husband for six or seven years before what happened happened. So I knew her in a neighborly way. We'd chat in the street, one year she helped me with my Christmas decorations. If they were having a barbecue they'd sometimes ask me and Barney over if we weren't doing anything. They were a nice couple. After Barney died they often checked in on me. They were nice, but were they happy? I think so. There never seemed to be any chemistry there, if you know what I mean, but we never heard them fighting. They were a couple just going through the motions. It all came as a shock when he killed her."

"So it's safe to say you knew her fairly well," Kent says.

"As well as a neighbor can, dear."

"We spoke to Naomi McDonald last night. She's the woman who—"

"Yes, I know who she is, dear."

"She said the wife knew about the affair, and that she didn't care. Not in the least. Did Hailey seem like the kind of person who wouldn't care?"

She shakes her head. "No, of course not. She would have cared a lot. Unless . . ."

"Unless?" Kent asks.

She smiles at us then, takes a sip of coffee, then sets it down neatly on the table next to her. "Well, it seems to me what you're asking is this—is it possible for a woman not to care in the least that her husband is cheating on her? Well, let's say just for the moment that it is possible. Now, if it's possible, then you need to ask a different question. You need to ask yourself what kind of woman wouldn't care?"

"One who doesn't love him," Kent says.

"There's that, but there's more," Julianne says.

"One that was in the marriage for a whole different set of reasons," I say.

PAUL CLEAVE

"No," she says. "But one that has moved on. One that knows the marriage is over, one who knows that they are separating, and one that has already moved on emotionally and, perhaps, physically."

"Was Hailey McDonald having an affair?" I ask.

"If she was, then it wouldn't really be an affair, would it? Not in the traditional sense. Both husband and wife were separating, they were both moving on. In a way they weren't even cheating on each other."

I look at Kent and Kent is looking right back at me. "If it's true," Kent says, "then whoever she was seeing could be who killed her."

"And if she was seeing him at their house while Ron was at work or seeing his own new girlfriend, that would give him access to the clothes."

I stare at my coffee, taking on board the information. Does it fit? It seems to.

"We need to talk to Hailey McDonald's friends," I say. "If she was seeing somebody, then maybe they knew."

"Wouldn't they have come forward and told the police?" Kent asks.

"Not necessarily," Julianne says, and we both look at her, and maybe with all the books she's read we should have her on the force as a consultant. "I mean, if I had known she was having an affair, I wouldn't have come forward. The way the courts work these days, often it's the victim who's put on trial. It's disgusting. If I had known, I'd have said nothing. What would be the point? The man who killed her was in custody, and I helped put him there because I saw him. They were going to charge him with murder, they found bloody clothes in the back of his car, so why risk Hailey's reputation when you already caught who did it? I know why he was let go, some technicality with the warrant, but that didn't make him innocent, it just made him lucky. No need to go to the police and say *By the way, his wife was stepping out on him and let's have the newspapers call her a whore.*"

"Can you do something for me?" I ask.

"Sure thing, sonny."

"Think about that night. Think about it in the context that you know now. Back then Ron was a murder suspect, and that's the narrative you saw him in when you gave your statement. Think about him now as the victim. Think about his wife having an affair, and think about it being that man that killed her while Ron was ten miles away. Think about it, and if you remember anything differently give me a call."

"I'll do just that," she says, and offers us more coffee when we stand up to leave. We say thanks but no thanks.

"She really was a nice young woman," she says as she follows us to the door. "It's true what they say, and I know this because I'm old enough to have lived it, but you just never know what's waiting for you around the corner. One day you're here, and the next day you're gone. Just like that," she says, and she clicks her fingers, only it's a very soft click, and I get the idea she was lucky not to have broken something.

We get outside and stand on the sidewalk and face each other.

"The cap never made sense," I tell Kent.

"What cap?"

"Mrs. Cross said the man she saw was wearing a baseball cap, and she said that seven years ago too and it'll be in the statement. When Schroder found those clothes in the car, it was a shirt, pants, and shoes. No socks, no underwear, and certainly no cap. The socks and underwear wouldn't have gotten blood on them, but the cap would have. Why discard the cap separately?"

"And you never found it?"

"No. Ron had a couple of baseball caps that he hardly ever wore, and they were both tucked away in his wardrobe, but neither had blood on them. First of all, it makes no sense he would leave the bloody clothes in his car without the cap. Why discard that separately? Same goes for the murder weapon. We never did find it, but why not keep it with the bloody clothes?"

"You didn't ask yourself this last time?"

"We did, and we figured he liked the hat and wanted to hang on to it, and that he managed to dump the knife before he dumped the clothes. We didn't question his stupidity at keeping his clothes in the back of his car—I mean, we tried to ask him, but his lawyer was present and by then the warrant was under question so we never got any further with it."

"And now you think whoever it was wore a cap to try and hide their face."

"It does seem that way, doesn't it?"

"I'll admit, it all does seem convincing," she says. "The problem is it means some poor police work was done seven years ago. Where to now?"

"Let's head back to the station and go through the original materials, and the evidence that was stored away will be there now too. We'll make up a list of people we can speak to about Hailey. If she was having an affair, somebody might have known."

CHAPTER SIXTY-ONE

The dog bite has gotten infected. Each hole in Schroder's arm is bright red, but dark in the middle, greenish dark blood caught under the skin, yellow pus bubbling over the sides when he squeezes it, and he should stop squeezing it because every time he does he feels a wave of nausea come over him. His entire arm hurts like hell.

At the moment he is outside the emergency entrance to the hospital. Last night he couldn't sleep. He sat talking to Warren about how things have gotten out of hand, asking Warren if he thought that Tate was right with his assessment. Is it possible he really is out of control? No. Yes. No. Warren was also unsure.

The doors open and a young boy with a cast on his arm walks out, alongside his dad, the boy saying he can't wait for his friends at school to sign it. The world sways for a second, then another second, just long enough to think *This is it, this is the bullet finishing what it started*, only it's not that at all. He hasn't eaten in twenty-four hours and the infection is burning through him. He is about to step through the still open doors when it comes to him. The mistake he is about to make.

When he burned down Grover Hills, he should have thrown the dog in there too. The damn thing bit him. The police know it bit him. They will have alerted the hospitals and every doctor across the city. He can't go in there. He's on his own with this one.

And if he does have rabies?

He just has to hope that he doesn't.

When he gets home he spends fifteen minutes in the bathroom poking and prodding the wound, making a fist while he squeezes the green and yellow holes. He wipes away anything that comes out, and then squeezes it some more. When he's done, he splashes iodine on it before bandaging it tightly. He opens his medicine cabinet. He needs antibiotics, but can't get them without a prescription. He has the painkillers he was prescribed for the headaches, and he takes those, hoping they'll at least help.

He heads into the lounge and sits back on the couch that he is really starting to like now, and he holds his arm out in front of him to study the bandaging, and so Warren can see it too, and Warren doesn't seem concerned by it.

"It's going to slow me down," Schroder says.

You need slowing down, Warren says. *You've seen this before. You try taking care of everything in one or two nights, you're going to make a mistake. You'll be like the last guy you ever arrested. Remember him? In fact you've already made mistakes. Two innocent people have died, and not putting that dog on the fire . . . well, that was about as dumb as dumb can be. And this is coming from somebody who eats flies. Sure, Tate is on your side, but there's only so much you can do. You're not really going to take him along when you kill somebody, are you?*

"No. Of course not. I was just saying that."

You say things you don't mean? Warren asks.

"Of course. You don't?"

No, it's not the spidering way. If you get caught, will you show the police where you hid Quentin James's body?

"No."

You won't tell them about him at all?

"No."

So you didn't mean that either when you told your friend you would turn him in if he didn't help you.

"No, I supposed I didn't."

People are complicated, Warren says, before scurrying along the wall to chase shadows.

Schroder lies down on the couch. Warren moves out of his field of vision, and then out of his thoughts. It's been a long weekend of killing bad people, and he sees no reason he can't take a few days off before killing again. Let the arm settle down. Let the infection work its way out of his system. That gives him a few days to think over old cases and pick somebody else. Somebody he's never met. Somebody just out of jail seems like a good option. Somebody who is doing well, somebody who has a second chance and is now living a better life than Schroder has, a better life built on the ashes of the pain and destruction they caused.

There's no point in burning himself out over the next week killing people, and even if he could, how many would he get through? Five or six? He needs to think about the long term. He needs to space things out and do his homework better, otherwise there will be more dog bites and more suicides. He's done with the five-minute thing, at least done in the sense of offering it to people. Last night was the start of that. He could have gone to Hailey McDonald's father and asked if he wanted five minutes with Ron. And the New New Him would have, but the New New Him is in the past, and now he is the Evolved Him. The Evolved Him has learned from the mistakes all the past Hims made. These people ask for their five minutes, but they don't really want them. They like the idea of it, just not the reality. Kelly Summers liked it because she was in the moment. Smith was attacking her and she was angry. Crowley thought he wanted them, but Schroder had to push him into it.

Things will be different now. He will do all the dirty work. He's still the Five Minute Man, only now he's giving these people their five minutes by proxy. He can live with that, and they can live with that, and that way there are no secrets and nobody innocent can get hurt.

It's a win-win situation. And when his arm is healed he'll start winning again, slower than before, maybe once a week, maybe once a month, but it'll be winning all the same. Long-term winning, and that gives him something to live for.

CHAPTER SIXTY-TWO

We have a list of names. People who knew Hailey McDonald. People she was friends with who could know if she was having an affair. There is momentum building. A call is patched into the task-force room and I take it. The caller identifies himself as Jerry Williams. It's another Williams this week, and in a thousand years' time will the rest of us have been bred into extinction? Jerry is from the DNA lab where the clothes were delivered by an officer earlier.

"You've run the clothes already?" I ask.

"Not yet, but it should be tomorrow."

"Should?"

"I know," Jerry says, "everything is a priority, and that's the problem. But I'm actually calling to help you out. I may have something for you. We found some hairs in the clothing. We've got three types."

"Three?"

"That's what I said. What I need from you are some exemplars of the victim and the suspect so I can do some comparisons and then I can tell you which of the three is the anomaly."

"Okay, we have samples from the victim, but not from the suspect."

"The suspect have short hair?" he asks.

"Yeah."

"He have short hair seven years ago when this happened?"

"Yes. Short and black with some gray in the sides."

"We got short and black in here," he says. "But just the one. It's buried in the collar around the back. Anywhere else on the shirt and I'd say it was transfer, maybe even from one of the officers at the scene, maybe even from you if you have black hair and were there. But buried into the collar like that, well, that's where you find them when you wear a shirt. Only I'd expect to find more. Because we did find more. Of the other two. So maybe this black one got stuck in there and didn't come out in the wash. The other two are both long and both blond."

"From two different women?"

"From two different people. Hair comes in all kinds of thicknesses and I can't tell you if these are from a male or a female, not yet, but a couple of them have the roots and we'll be able to run DNA and then I'll be able to tell you for sure. Send me the victim's hair and I'll run it against what we have. And this short hair, you have more we can test against?"

"That won't be a problem, Jim," I say, and think about Ron McDonald somewhere in the morgue. "These two other strands, can you photograph them and email them to us right now?"

"It's Jerry," he says, "not Jim, and yes, I can do that. But it's more than two strands. We've got eight in total, five from what I'm guessing are the victim's since they're on the front and some caught up in the blood, and three in the collar around the back with the other hair we found. Give me your email and I'll get something to you within the next few minutes."

I give him my work email and then we hang up, and I explain everything to Kent, and then I log in to one of the computers and a minute later an email appears in my inbox. I open it up. There are four photographs, and in two of them a plastic ruler measures the lengths of the hairs.

One is twenty-four inches long. The other is fifteen.

The other two photographs are zoomed in much closer, the hair photographed through a microscope. The longer hair has been dyed blond, Jerry has written. The shorter one is natural, more of a brown than a blond.

"Do you think another woman wore these clothes?" I ask Kent.

"Or a man with long hair."

"What color hair did Naomi have back then?"

"Black, the same as now. These aren't hers, but we'll get a sample from her too to confirm. There's another possibility. Ron could have been cheating on both his wife and his girlfriend, and that's who the hair belongs to. We need to widen our scope," I tell her. "We should start with Chris Watkins. He said he knew Ron was having an affair. If Ron was having a second affair, he might know about that too."

"We should head back to the workplace," she says. "I think it'll be good for both cases. If he was still sleeping around we might find evidence of it, and we might find something that was overlooked seven years ago."

We update the superintendent and I organize for an officer to take hair from McDonald's body to the lab, and another officer to go and get a sample from Naomi McDonald, and then we're heading downstairs and driving to Ron McDonald's workshop. There are some media vans, but the reporters are all chatting among themselves, no cameras pointing anywhere, everybody a little bored as if knowing the next break in this story isn't going to happen here, but is happening somewhere unknown to somebody unknown. At least for now. Ron's car is still parked outside.

There is music coming from nearby buildings, the sounds of machinery, people at work, things getting made and things getting repaired. The sounds of life carrying on. We park on the street. There are officers walking the area talking to people who work nearby, showing pictures of the bald man and asking what these people saw. The entire scene looks different from last night, the morning sun highlighting different angles and glaring off different surfaces, just a normal Tuesday morning with the addition of black and yellow crime-scene tape.

We head into the office where one detective is going through the computer and another is flicking through receipts and files and another is reading everything else he can get his hands on.

"The car McDonald was working on last night is a two-door Toyota," Detective Watts says, and Watts is the other guy beside Travers who was calling things out this morning during the briefing. Watts has been on the force far longer than any of us, and is only a year or two away from retiring. What hair he has left has been gray since I met him twenty years ago. "It's parked up in there," he says, nodding towards the workroom.

"I remember seeing it," I tell him, because it's the same car Schroder's cell phone was placed against.

"It belongs to a guy by the name of Stephen Becker, and at the moment Becker is using a loaner car."

"You called him?"

"Actually he called us. He heard about it on the news and is worried the repair on his car is going to be delayed. He asked if it could be returned to him today. The guy said he would get a lawyer involved if we couldn't comply. I told him he could call all the lawyers he wants to, but he's not getting that car back until we're done with the scene."

"Have forensics found any sign of forced entry?" I ask.

He shakes his head. "Either the door was left unlocked, or our victim let his killer inside either as a customer or because he knew him."

I head into the workshop with Kent where there is a pool of dried blood that isn't as dark as some of the oil stains in various locations across the floor, but will start to get there unless it's cleaned up. The Toyota is exactly where it was last night, and for a brief moment I can see the ghost of the cell phone down there, haunting and mocking me.

We look around, Kent looking for what happened last night, me hoping she won't find it. Whatever happened seven years ago there won't be any evidence of it here. Staring at tools and a blood-stained floor isn't going to solve this—we need to talk to the people who worked here. The people who knew Hailey and Ron McDonald the best.

We walk back through the office. The detectives are still doing what they were doing. The big fishing and paintballing and go-carting photographs look over the scene, happier men in happier times, and I take a moment to look at these people, at Ron McDonald, and I think about how his actions brought death into his life.

I look at the paintballing photograph. Six men are in it, perhaps some of them still work here, perhaps some of them don't. Arms around each other and paintball rifles pointing into the air, Ron in the middle. On the right-hand side of Ron with half his face towards the camera is Chris Watkins. Chris with his army buzz-cut hair is laughing and holding his rifle high, a man who looks victorious. I take the photograph down from the wall. I turn it over and there's a date on the back. This picture was taken eight years ago. A year before Hailey was murdered.

I close my eyes and pinch the top of my nose with my thumb and middle finger, and tap my index finger against my forehead, over and over and over.

"Tate?"

I think it through. The long hairs. Access to the car. To clothes. Hailey McDonald having an affair.

"Tate, what is it?" Kent asks.

"Take a look," I say, and I hand her the photograph.

"Take a look at what, exactly?"

She doesn't see it. And then she does. She cocks her head slightly as if letting the thoughts inside jumble around, letting them shift into position as she thinks the same things I'm thinking. Which she does, because a moment later we're both rushing out to the car and back to the station.

CHAPTER SIXTY-THREE

There is that buzz I hear sometimes, the pumping of adrenaline through my body when I know I'm close to wrapping up a case.

"We don't know anything for sure," Kent says, and she moves in and around traffic.

"I know that."

"It's just circumstantial," she says.

"I know that too."

"Really this interview might rule him out just as equally as make him guilty."

"I know. I know all this, Rebecca."

"I know you do. I just don't want you to get your hopes up. And remember, the hair found in the back of the shirt worn when Hailey McDonald was killed isn't evidence. It can only tell us so much, but if we build any kind of case on it, it will be thrown out before it even reaches court."

"True, but he doesn't know that," I say, and *he* is Chris Watkins, the man I spoke to last night, the man who seven years ago said he went into work to retrieve his cell phone and saw that Ron McDonald wasn't there. Chris Watkins in the photograph with the army buzz cut, all except around the back where a rattail hangs down between his shoulders. Long blond hair, just like in the email earlier. Chris Watkins had access to Ron McDonald's car.

"It's still not getting us any closer to what happened last night," Kent says.

"Yes it is."

"How?"

"Because if it's the Five Minute Man who did this, it changes everything."

"In what way?"

"Because he's out there thinking he's doing good, right? He thinks he's saving the people of this city from the people of this city. How do you think he's going to react when he learns he's killed an innocent man?"

She pauses to consider this. "That's been your thinking all along," she says.

"Pretty much."

"That's good," she says. "You think rather than catching this guy, we can appeal to him to turn himself in."

"Exactly," I say, the word summing up how opposite that is to the truth—exactly opposite.

"Like I say it's good, but you should have said something earlier," she says. "We're a team, remember?"

"Of course I remember. It's like Hutton said—we're on the same page."

"Sometimes it doesn't feel like it."

My cell phone starts ringing. Kent keeps driving and I take the call. It's Julianne Cross, the crime novel–reading witness we spoke to this morning.

"I'm very upset," she says, and she sounds it. "I did what you asked me to do. I started going over everything I saw that night. And do you know what happened?"

"Tell me."

"Everything changed. I began to convince myself of different things. As soon as you left I sat down and I saw it all just as I remembered, but then I saw something new too, something that felt real in that moment, but then less real the more I thought about it. The harder I thought about it, the more things from that night became something else, and now I don't know what's real. I'm upset because I'm worried I tried to put an innocent man in jail, and a bad man is still walking free."

"What is it you remembered differently?" I ask. "Before you concentrated too hard and everything shifted."

"It's such a small thing," she says. "But Ron, and I'm still sure it was Ron, well, when he got to the house he didn't let himself in. He knocked."

"He knocked?"

"Yes. On the front door, and his wife let him in."

"Why didn't you tell me this before?"

"When I close my eyes I can see it as plain as day. Ron walking from his parked car one block away with his hat pulled down and then knocking on the front door. Yes, yes, I'm sure he knocked. I can remember him knocking. Why would he need to knock on his own door? I suppose, maybe if he'd forgotten his keys, but he had just driven there so his keys were on him. If it really was Ron, he would have let himself in, wouldn't he?"

"Yes," I tell her. "Most likely he would have."

"I made a mistake, didn't I," she says.

"A lot of us did. Thanks for calling me back, Mrs. Cross."

I fill Rebecca in.

"Even if it's not this Watkins guy, it really doesn't look as though Ron did it," she says.

"For seven years everybody thought he was guilty," I say, feeling sick at the thought.

"And it took getting murdered to clear his name," she says. "He was just trying to move on with his life."

We reach the station. If things are going to schedule, then the Chris Watkins interview would have started only a few minutes ago. He'll be answering a standard set of questions, and then any other questions the two detectives talking to him send his way. *How long did you know the victim? Were you friends? Were there people who hated him? Was he a good boss? What was his relationship like with the rest of the staff? Where were you last night and can somebody verify that?* He's not a suspect, and because Chris Watkins didn't kill Ron McDonald he won't feel like one. He won't be in there asking for a lawyer. He'll be in there shooting the breeze, drinking coffee or soft drinks and feeling laid-back. He'll talk about the phone call he got from Naomi McDonald last night asking if he knew where her husband was.

We get up to the fourth floor and we confirm Watkins is in the building and is talking to two of our guys. We figure out a plan for our interview, and we take twenty minutes to put together what we need. Then we tell Superintendent Stevens about the hairs in the shirt, the interview with Julianne Cross, and then we show him the photograph from the workshop.

"This is what you have?" he asks. "A photograph of a man with long hair? And you don't even know the hair found on the shirt comes from a man."

"The rest of it fits."

"Even if we could get a warrant for a hair sample," he says, "we can't run it against that shirt. That shirt was ruled out."

I tell him the same thing I told Kent. We know that, but Watkins doesn't.

"You think you can get him to confess?"

"No."

"Then what?"

I look at Kent, and she nods slightly at me, and then I look back at Stevens. "We think we can get him to lead us to the murder weapon."

"How?"

"By using the clothes as leverage."

He starts tapping his chin, nodding at the same time. "You think you can trick him?"

"I spoke to the guy last night. He didn't seem like a criminal mastermind."

"Clever enough to have gotten away with it if you're right about what you're saying."

"Maybe. Or just lucky. If we'd tested those clothes seven years ago we might have found his DNA all over them. And if that's true, then he's not that clever at all."

"So when did he place the bloody clothes into Ron's car?"

"My guess is when Ron was at his girlfriend's. The car was out on the street. It was dark. He took the opportunity."

"And why not the knife?"

"Maybe the knife belonged to him. Maybe his fingerprints and DNA were all over it and he was worried it could be traced to him."

"If you go in there now and get nothing out of him and he becomes suspicious, you'll never get another chance without his lawyer present."

"We know."

He keeps nodding. "Okay, Detective, it's your call. This is why you're running the case. But play it easy, okay? What about Ron McDonald?"

"If we can prove Ron was an innocent man," Kent says, "then that might change the Five Minute Man's outlook on things."

"You think he might turn himself in?" Stevens asks.

"Hopefully," I say, but really what I want from Schroder is just to stop what he's doing. We don't have to catch him. An innocent man has died, but Schroder will pay for that soon enough anyway—the bullet in his head will see to that.

"Okay. This is good work, detectives. I hope you're on the right path here. Keep me updated. And don't screw this up."

CHAPTER SIXTY-FOUR

We take another ten minutes to prepare, and then I knock on the door to the interview room and open it up. No detective likes being interrupted during an interrogation, but this isn't an interrogation—at least not yet—and one of these guys got a text message ten minutes ago to prepare them for this.

"Sorry to interrupt," I say, "but we just got a call from your wife," I say to one of the two detectives. "She's just gone into labor."

"Oh shit," he says, and he stands up quickly, responding to the code we've used in the past if we need to switch detectives in front of somebody who has just become a suspect without warning that very suspect.

"I'll drive you," his partner says, also standing up, and then to us he asks, "can you two take over here? It's all basic stuff."

"Ah, yeah, I guess," I say, then look towards Rebecca who is in the hall behind me. "That okay with you?"

"I was about to grab something to eat."

"Should just take a few minutes," the detective tells us.

"In that case, sure, why not?"

"Good luck with the baby," Chris says, as the other two detectives rush out of the room where, no doubt, Stevens will update them on the situation and where, no doubt, they'll be annoyed they weren't given the chance to conduct the interview.

"Right, right," I say, and I'm carrying a cup of coffee that I put down on the table in front of me, a little bit of it spilling over the edge. I wipe my hand on my shirt, then I put down the folder I'm carrying too, then I sit down and look over the notes the detectives left behind. "Chris, right?"

"Right," he says.

"Hang on a second," I say, "just let me see . . . so . . . so it says here you work, or worked, for McDonald."

"Yeah, that's right."

I keep looking at the notes, scrolling through them with my finger. "And . . . and it says here . . . oh, you were the one who called it in."

"I spoke to you last night, remember?"

I look up at him. I tilt my head slightly. "That was you?"

"Yeah," he says, smiling. "Long night, huh?"

"It's why God invented coffee," I say, and sip at mine. "Yeah, yeah, of course it was you. At the crime scene, right?"

"Right."

"I'm Theo," I say, and reach out and shake his hand, "and this here is Rebecca."

"Hey," Rebecca says, and she sounds bored. Then she glances at her watch. Then she yawns. Then she leans back in her chair.

"Must have been a hell of a thing, going inside like that and seeing Ron that way. A hell of a thing."

He nods.

"You want something else to drink?" Rebecca asks.

"I'm all good," he says, and holds up a can of Coke and shakes it so we can hear it's half-full.

"Well if you need anything let us know," she says. "I know spending your day in the police station isn't any fun, but we'll try to make this quick for your sake as much as mine. If I don't eat something soon I'm going to go crazy."

"I know you guys are just doing your job," he says, "and anything I can say that might help find who did this . . . well, you know. Ron was a good guy. A really good guy. You know when people die and other people say the world won't be the same without him? That's what it's like with Ron. Even years ago, when you lot were adamant he killed his wife, nobody who knew him really believed that. And me, hell, I'm the guy who had to tell you that I had gone into his work and he wasn't there. It was because of me you figured he was lying, and you know what? When he was let go I thought the first thing he would do would be to fire me. He took me into his office and said I'd done the right thing, that I was only saying what I had seen and my job was still mine if I wanted it. I told him of course I wanted it."

"You never thought he was guilty?" I ask.

"Never."

"Just guilty of having an affair," I say.

He leans forward. "Ron was a good guy," he says, "so let's not go there, huh?"

I lean back. "Go where?"

"Go back to you blaming him for what happened to Hailey."

"Fair enough," I say, moving on, but of course we'll move back soon enough. "So the last few years, things have been good at work?"

"I suppose," he says. "I mean, we're always busy."

We ask him about that. We engage him in five minutes of conversation about how work was, how many hours they were putting in, what the customers were like.

"The notes here say you were with your wife last night when Naomi called you, is that right?"

"Yeah. Her parents were around and we had made dinner for them. They can all tell you I was there," he says, "if that's what you're getting at," he says, and adds a smile.

I laugh. "Nothing like that. We're just trying to build up the time line. You left work at five o'clock, is that right?"

"We all did, except for Ron. He had this dickhead of a customer he was trying to help out, some guy who had blown up the gearbox in his Toyota."

"Is that this Stephen Becker I've heard about?"

"That's him."

"Things were argumentative between them?"

"No. Just, you know, the guy was a dick, and Ron, and I don't know why Ron felt this way, but he wanted to help the guy out. He figured he'd put in an extra hour at the most. He said he was going to leave around six."

"Making him the last person there?"

"Yeah."

"Would the workshop door the cars are brought through have been open or closed by then?"

"I closed it before I left."

"And the office door?"

"Ron would have locked that. Nobody ever works there alone with the door unlocked. Often you're making noise and you'd never hear if anybody snuck in."

"So last night, how do you suppose the person who killed Ron got inside?"

He shrugs. "My guess is somebody knocked on the door and he tried to help them out."

"Like the Becker guy for example. If he was unhappy with the work, maybe he came back to voice that. Or maybe your boss completed the job and called him."

"Maybe."

"Or maybe somebody was waiting for him outside and forced him back in."

He shrugs. "I don't know what else to tell you, I really don't."

"That's okay," I tell him, "this is all helpful stuff. It's just building up a picture, you know? You need another drink there?"

"I'm still fine," he says. "I wish there was more I could add, but I really can't think of anything."

"You're doing good," Rebecca says, and gives him one of her biggest smiles. He smiles back at her.

"So all the staff has keys, right?"

"Yeah, because all of us have worked there at least six months. That's the rule—you gotta work there six months before you get a key. In fact the newest guy has been there two years. It's not exactly the kind of job with a high staff turnover, you know? But if you think it was one of us, well, you're heading in the wrong direction."

"So it's safe to say you know everybody fairly well," Kent says.

"Yeah, I do. I've been there ten years, right from the beginning. Other guys have come and gone over the years, but me and Ron, we're the core."

"Did you know Hailey?"

He takes another drink of Coke, then shakes the can so we can all hear it's nearly empty. "Actually, is it okay if I grab another one?" he asks. "It's kind of hot in here."

"Sure, no problem, but we're almost done here anyway," I say. "Just a couple of final questions. How well did you know Hailey?"

"She'd come into the workshop occasionally. I guess I could count the amount of times on one hand. And of course she came to my wedding, they both did, back before you know, before she was killed. She was at work functions too, like Christmas parties and summer barbecues."

"You liked her?"

"Sure, she seemed nice enough. We all liked her. She was always friendly to us. What happened to her, geez, I hate to think about it."

"And you're convinced Ron had nothing to do with that," I say.

"No chance at all."

"That's what we're starting to think too," I tell him.

He has the Coke halfway up to his mouth ready to drink the last few ounces then stops. "Excuse me?"

"We're saying we're open to the possibility that Ron was innocent," Kent says. "What happened last night, well of course that means we have to take another look at what happened seven years ago."

"Why's that?" he asks.

"In case the same person was involved."

"But what about the clothes in Ron's car?"

"What about them?" I ask.

"I mean, yeah, Ron's a great guy, one of the nicest, but you know, those clothes, well, they were in his car, right?"

"Right," I tell him.

"We think they were planted there," Kent says.

"Planted? Really? I thought that kind of thing only happens in TV shows."

"Not just TV," Kent says.

"They were ruled inadmissible or whatever the word is, right? That's why Ron never went to jail, right?"

"They were inadmissible," Kent says. "But not now."

He looks confused. He looks worried. "What do you mean?"

"See, the thing is, it's like you were saying," she tells him. "People plant things like the way they see it in TV, but it's never that simple."

"What we're about to tell you has to stay strictly between us, okay?" I say. "You can't go and tell your wife, or your friends or anybody else you work with. But you seem like a good guy, and you obviously really care about Ron. The thing is, the clothes we found had blood on them, and that's because the person wore them when he killed Hailey, whether that person was Ron or somebody else, the killer wore those clothes."

"They'll have DNA on them too," Kent says.

"DNA?"

I carry on. "See, we think whoever wore them would have sweated in them. So there'll be DNA in the armpits, around the collar, maybe all over the place. We think whoever wore them probably wore his clothes underneath them too in the hope his DNA wouldn't get anywhere on the shirt," I say.

"Seems like smart thinking, doesn't it?" Rebecca asks.

"Yeah, I guess."

"Yeah, you'd think so," I say, "only it's not that smart. The thing is, DNA gets everywhere. Whoever wore that shirt will be all over it. Ironically, if we'd been allowed to test it seven years ago we would have found out then somebody else had been wearing it."

"You'd have tested it for somebody else's DNA even though it was Ron's shirt and was in his car and had his wife's blood all over it?" he asks.

"Sure we would have," Kent says.

Chris goes pale. His mouth opens, but he doesn't end up saying anything, and after a few seconds it closes. "You could have arrested the right guy back then?"

"That's right," Kent says.

"What about now? Won't the DNA have degraded over time?" he asks.

"That's a good question," I say. "But the way we store things means that's not going to happen. Nope, that DNA is going to one hundred percent be there. And now that the clothes are admissible again we should send them out for testing."

"Hang on a second. Admissible again?"

"That's right," Kent says. "Now that Ron is dead, and now that we're no longer considering him an official suspect, it changes the conditions of the illegal search seven years ago."

"Changes them? Changes them how?"

"Well, it's too difficult to explain in lawyer speak," I tell him, "but I can try to boil it down. It sounds pretty insensitive, but basically we can do this now because Ron can't complain."

"You can do this because he can't complain?"

"On account of him being dead," Kent says.

"Jesus, I know he's dead, okay? It's just . . . just nothing," he says.

"We figure it's in his best interests," I say.

"No," Chris says.

"No?"

"If Ron is guilty, then it's not in his best interests at all. As it stands he's an innocent man, and if you go testing clothes you weren't allowed to test seven years ago, but are allowed to now, then you might change that."

"Change him from innocent to guilty?" I ask. "I thought he didn't do it?"

"That's not what I mean," he says. "I mean I remember what it was like seven years ago. You tried to railroad him back then, and it sounds like you're going to try and do the same again."

I take the last mouthful of coffee. "I see your point, Chris, but you don't have to worry about that. See, even you think he's innocent. You knew him much better than us, and hearing what you have to say, I really think getting those clothes tested is the way to go. I think later today or tomorrow we'll box them up and ship them to the lab. We might even get an answer this week. It's expensive, and we weren't going to do it, but hearing what you're saying, well, I think it's the next step."

He stares at the empty can of Coke, his hands wrapped around it.

"We think Hailey was having an affair," Kent says. "We're going to talk to all of Hailey's friends because one of them might know about it."

"And at the same time we'll ask everybody who knew Hailey and Ron to contribute DNA samples so we can compare them against the samples," I say.

"You can do that?" he asks. "Wouldn't you need a warrant or something?"

"Sure we would," Kent says, "but almost everybody is going to say sure, you can have my DNA, take as much of it as you want. Only one person is going to say no. Only one person is going to say we need a warrant. You want to guess who?"

"Whoever killed her," he says.

"Exactly," she says. "So we run all the DNA we can get hold of, and within a month or so we'll know who wore those clothes."

"Or sooner, once somebody won't volunteer their DNA," I point out.

"But is that fair?" he asks. "I mean, you're saying people who don't want to help are guilty."

"Fair? Probably not," I say, "and we know there'll always be some asshole who will hold out just to prove some kind of point, but that'll only slow things down a little. We'll follow all the holdouts and dig into their lives and see what comes up. But remember, this is just between us, okay? Last thing we need is this information getting out and the killer doing a runner."

"I need a break and a drink," Kent says, and then she points at Chris's drink. "You want a fresh one?"

"Huh? Oh, yeah, sure, thanks."

"Do you mind waiting here a few minutes alone?" I ask. "I need to use the bathroom."

"Huh? What? Yeah, yeah, whatever," he says.

"We'll be back in five minutes," I tell him, and I leave the folder on the table and we step out and close the door behind us.

CHAPTER SIXTY-FIVE

We go straight from the corridor and into the room next door. There's a surveillance camera in the interview room and it's pointing down towards Chris. He looks stressed. He leans forward and then leans back, he runs his hands over his head and grips them behind his neck and tucks his elbows in, then he looks up and his eyes are moving from left to right as he thinks about his options.

"It's him," I tell Kent. "I can feel it."

"You think five minutes will be long enough?" Kent asks me.

"To come up with a story? Yeah. We don't want to give him too long otherwise he might come up with a really good one."

He lets go of his neck and reaches forward and puts his first two fingers on the folder I left there, and then he swivels it around so it's facing him. It's an old trick, but a good trick, and it's good for a reason. Guilty men always look. Of course innocent people look sometimes too, but it's rare that guilty men can sit there and ignore it. Chris Watkins looks at the door, back at the folder, and the door one more time. What happens later today all depends on whether he opens that folder.

He opens the folder.

The top page is a printout of the photographs emailed earlier with the hairs. He looks at them, then uses his hands to judge the distance, and then he reaches behind his head as if remembering just how long his hair used to be back then.

"We got him," Kent says.

He goes to the next page, which is another photograph. This one of the shirt all laid out flat, the way it was folded out flat on a white table and photographed seven years ago. Kent has used a sharpie to draw two circles, one around each armpit, and then arrows from those circles go to the side of the page where she has written *Two DNA profiles. Both XY. Male. DNA from blood is XX. Female.* Chris looks at the photograph and he turns it one way and then another as if looking for his DNA. Then there are some crime-scene photographs of the room, and then one of Hailey, and this photo he turns over quickly. Then there is a *"witness statement"* from one of Hailey's nonexistent "friends" that we typed up that is dated seven years ago, saying she knew her friend was seeing somebody.

Then there is a memo written from the superintendent—though we actually wrote it half an hour ago—that sums up the position about the clothes by saying, *I can confirm these can now be used as evidence, but this will take some time and will be expensive, and hopefully both of those things can be avoided. What we need is the murder weapon used on Hailey McDonald. We have contacted the owners of the original crime scene, and they are allowing us to search their house, which is scheduled for nine a.m. tomorrow morning. If that weapon is there, we will find it, even if we have to dig up the entire garden. Then we can save time and money by not getting those clothes tested, then we can all learn from this experience and get it right next time.*

Chris closes the folder and pushes it back into place. We give him two more minutes, and then Kent grabs a can of Coke and we head back in.

"Sorry about that," I tell him.

Kent hands him the Coke. "Thanks," he says, and he rolls it across the back of his neck.

"Too hot in here?" I ask.

"A little, but I'll be okay." He opens the can and takes a big mouthful, then winces as he swallows. "I've been thinking," he says. "Ron was a good guy, he was, but he's dead now, and there's no need to keep secrets for a dead man, right? Dead men can't hurt you, and you can't hurt them."

"You're keeping a secret?" Kent asks.

He nods, and then shakes his head. "I can't believe I'm going to tell you this, but if it's going to come out, then it's going to come out." He starts flicking the tab on the Coke can with his finger. "Ron, Ron was a good guy, right? But things at home were stressed. Him and Hailey were fighting all the time. He said he hated her. Absolutely hated her. And they were going to get a divorce, right? Which meant she was going to get half of everything, and he said to me . . . Ah, shit," he says, "I don't want to tell you. I really don't."

"You need to," I tell him. "It could tell us what really happened."

"Well he said that classic line, right? Like marriage can be for life, but you only get ten years for murder. We were having a few drinks after work. He had just met Naomi, and he was saying he's going to lose half of everything he had, and if he just killed his wife and did the time he would come out of it financially better off. I just thought, you know, he was kidding, right? Blowing off steam."

I lean forward. I show him my *I'm annoyed* face. "Why didn't you tell us this back then?"

"Because back then I didn't think he had done it. People say shit all the time. My wife told me on the weekend she wanted to kill me. Sometimes I'll say I want to kill the bank manager, or the neighbor, or some idiot customer, but it means nothing."

"Just blowing off steam, as you said, right?" I say.

"Right."

"Which means you lied to us earlier," Kent says.

"I know. I know, and I'm sorry."

"Tell us about Ron," I say.

"Ron, well, there is this side to him that nobody else knew, right? Well, maybe Hailey knew, and maybe Naomi knows, but you'd have to ask her. But it was there, this dark side that would pop up on occasion, not much, but enough to know you should never mess with him. I asked him if he'd done it. This was two years ago, which was way after everything had settled down. We were in his office and it was a late Friday afternoon and work had closed up for the day. So we're in there and we're having a few drinks. He starts talking about how he hates everybody thinking he's a killer. So I'm getting drunker and drunker, and he starts talking about Hailey and starts saying what a bitch she was, so I say to him it really sounds like he did what the cops say he did. And that's when he said it."

"Said what?" I ask.

"He said she got what she deserved."

The room goes quiet then, except for a *din-dink* of his Coke can as he presses one side of it in, releases the tension, and it comes back out.

"You're saying he confessed to the crime," I say.

He shakes his head. "No, he didn't confess, but it sure as shit sounded that way."

"You should have come to the police."

"And then what, huh? I didn't want you guys arresting him because of some throwaway line he said when he was drunk. And even I knew Hailey could be a right pain in the ass when she wanted to be."

"So you did know her pretty well," I say.

"No, no, not that well, but he was always complaining about her, right? And the times she did come into work, well, I don't want to speak ill of the dead, but she could be a real bitch. I think what happened is she just pushed and pushed and pushed, and then he just snapped."

"And you kept this to yourself," Kent says. "All this key testimony that we could have used."

"I know," he says, and he hides his face in both his hands for a few seconds, then talks through them. "I screwed up. It doesn't matter now anyway, does it? If he did kill his wife, then justice was done. And he did kill his wife. I'm as sure of that as I'm as sure of anything, and I'll sign anything you put in front of me to say that, and I'll pay whatever price there is for not coming to you guys two years ago when he told me, but he did it. I know he did it."

I look at Kent, and Kent looks annoyed. "You made a serious mistake, you know that, right?" she asks him.

"Right."

"And there will be consequences," I say. "We don't know what, but you may face charges."

"I know. But at least you can save some money on those tests, right? That has to put me slightly back towards the good books."

"Why?"

"Because now you know he did it. No point in getting the clothes tested."

"Maybe," Kent says. "Or maybe we'll send those clothes out anyway."

"Always good to dot the i's and cross the t's," I tell him. "But in saying that, we have something else we're hoping might pan out."

"Yeah?"

"Yeah. And if it does, maybe it'll make us happy enough we can forget all about your screw up."

"Shit, okay, okay, anything I can do to help?"

"Nothing," I tell him. "Just go home and stay there the rest of the day." I push my chair back and stand up. "We'll be back in touch tomorrow morning when we know more. For now we're done here."

CHAPTER SIXTY-SIX

"You seem confident," Stevens says.

"I am confident."

"And if you're wrong?"

"Then I'm wrong. Still doesn't change the fact we're going to find more than one source of DNA on that shirt. I'm sure of it."

Stevens thinks about it for a few seconds. "DNA which we can't use. So now what?"

"So now we put one unmarked car at the old house. If we follow him, then we risk spooking him. Best just to have somebody waiting where he's going to go. But it won't be until tonight. I'll contact the current owners and see if I can get them to let us use the house."

"Then get it done. It'll be easier with their cooperation," he says. "There's something else. I just got word we've got a witness. The auto body shop next to McDonalds' workshop. He only just got into work, which is why we only just spoke to him. He says he was leaving work last night when he saw a bald guy waiting outside the front door around six o'clock. Says he saw Ron opening it up and letting him in. He says the sedan was parked right out front. He says he couldn't tell if the guy looked like the guy in the picture we're showing around because he had his back to him, but you know the best part about body shop workers and mechanics, right?"

Kent shakes her head, but I know the answer. "They know how to identify a car," I say.

"Exactly. We're looking for a dark blue Honda Accord. Says it would have been about ten years old. Is in pretty good condition, but there are some small dings and dents along the side that he saw. The other thing he said is the car had two brand new tires, maybe four if he had seen the other side. Said they looked like they'd just come off the rack. He said in reality they couldn't have been older than a week."

"Hutton said the burned-out car at Grover Hills had the spare wheel missing," Kent says.

"That's what I'm thinking," Stevens says. "So maybe the other car got two flat tires. Maybe this bald guy put his own spare on, and needed another. We're going to pull up a list of vehicles from the Transport Agency and start cross-referencing them with police, and also with family members of victims."

"A Honda Accord roughly ten years old? That's thousands of cars," I say.

"Maybe even more," he says, "but it's a starting point." He looks at his watch. "I've scheduled a media conference. We have enough that the public may be able to help us, and the media is breathing down our necks anyway. It starts in thirty minutes, and you're both part of it."

"I hate doing those things," I say.

"Do you also hate leading the investigation? Because you can't have one without the other, Detective."

"You're right," I tell him. "What I meant to say is I love doing them."

"Good. Get hold of whoever owns the McDonalds' old house and get surveillance sorted. I've assigned you another six detectives and I've already got them going from tire store to tire store with the sketch of the bald guy, and hopefully this guy paid for two tires on a credit card. Maybe we'll be lucky, huh?"

"Do we mention this at the media interview?"

"No," he says. "We don't want this guy scuffing them up. At the moment it's what makes that car different from every other Honda Accord out there. You been to see the medical examiner yet?"

"Not yet."

"Okay. As soon as the press conference is over, that's your next stop, okay?"

I go to my desk and set about figuring out the name and phone

number of the house McDonald used to live in, which takes two
minutes, and half of that is just waiting for my computer to come
on. I type in the address and the information comes up, and I'm expecting it to be another Williams, but it's not—the house is owned
and occupied by Lee and Nancy Charters. I make the call. Nancy
answers, and I identify myself and then she asks me if I'm calling
about what happened to Ron McDonald.

"You got there quickly," I tell her.

"It was all on the news," she says, and I can hear a small child in
the background, somebody going *fower, fower,* over and over, "and
I know we live in the house he used to live in. Lee, my husband, he
didn't want to buy the place because of what happened here, but
it was a good price and as I kept telling him, as long as you don't
believe in ghosts they can't hurt you. And we . . . Oh, shit," she
says. "I'm doing that thing again."

"What thing?" I ask.

"That thing where I always have to justify why we live here.
What can I help you with?"

I tell her. It's simple really. We want to put a couple of officers in
her house because we believe with the case making the news again,
there is risk of vandalism. "These things can happen sometimes."

"My husband is a used-car salesman," she says.

"That isn't going to make you any safer," I tell her.

She laughs. "My point is you can't be married to a used-car
salesman and not learn the fine art of knowing when somebody
is bullshitting you. So tell me, why do you really need our house?"

"I can't say."

"Are we in danger?"

"No."

"And it's just for today?"

"And tonight."

"Are you here to search the place? Last thing I need with a
fifteen-month-old baby here is an even bigger mess."

"No."

"Okay, well, if you're happy for a couple of guys to be here at dinnertime and bath time and sleepy time for a baby, then be my guest, but I warn you, it can be like a battle zone."

"I remember it well," I tell her.

I meet Kent downstairs in the conference room where the press interviews are held. There's a table running almost the width of the room at the front, it's raised up a few feet on a platform so everybody can get a better view. At the moment it's empty, except for a bunch of microphones clipped along the front of it. The room is already half-full of journalists, it sits thirty but in big cases you can get another twenty standing around the edges. I get the sense today will be like that.

I make my way to the front with Kent. The superintendent is standing in the corner talking to a couple of people, and when he finishes he comes over and we talk about what we're going to say to the media. Fifteen minutes later the room is almost full. He asks me if I'm ready, and I tell him I am. We climb onto the platform and we sit down behind the table and then it begins.

CHAPTER SIXTY-SEVEN

Schroder is sitting on the couch that he finds himself really beginning to like. It's comfortable, it was cheap, there are no holes in it. It's the best couch in the world. Warren is back too.

The radio is on and he's listening to the news, and the newsman tells him about the body found last night and there is nothing new there. Then the newsreader says something Schroder isn't expecting, and perhaps the newsreader wasn't expecting it either. But they are going to cross to a live press conference at the police department.

Schroder turns off the radio. Then he turns on the TV. It takes him five seconds to find the right channel. It's leading news. The conference looks like it has just started. Superintendent Stevens is talking. Stevens used to be his boss. The man was a pain in the ass, but he was fair, and that was what was most important. It was Stevens that fired him after he shot that old woman to save the young girl, and it was Stevens who helped cover that crime. At the time he was angry at losing his job, but grateful because it could have been worse. Now he wonders if they are kindred spirits.

He can't see Tate, so maybe . . . but then the camera angle changes. Tate is sitting to Stevens's left, and then to the left of Tate is Rebecca Kent, and the Old Him had a crush on Kent back when he knew how to have a crush. He guesses the Old Him had a crush on the Old Her. Stevens is talking. He confirms their belief that the killings on Saturday night are related to the killing last night. Peter Crowley, Stevens believes, is what the Five Minute Man would call collateral damage.

"Fuck you." He looks up at Warren. "Can you believe he said that?"

Warren doesn't answer.

"Fuck you too, Warren," he says.

A reporter asks if the cases are related to Dwight Smith, and Stevens says there will be time for questions at the end. Then he goes on to say that they are following several leads, and he holds up the sketch of the bald man that doesn't look like Schroder and, if anything, looks more like the dentist he used to have. Stevens tells the public this guy is a family member or a friend or a neighbor, and Schroder figures he is two of those, and perhaps still even all three as long as Warren can forgive him for swearing at him.

Stevens then asks for help from the public. They are looking for a dark blue Honda Accord, somewhere around ten years old, then holds up a generic photograph of the same make and model that Schroder is driving. He asks for calls from members of the public who saw this car near any of the crime scenes. The car could be a problem, right up there with the DNA found in the dog's mouth at the fire.

"We're dealing with a seriously dangerous individual," Stevens says. "Ballistics have proven the same gun was used in the deaths that occurred at Grover Hills as well as the death of Ron McDonald. The man who is using this gun is responsible for the death of Peter Crowley, and we also believe he was involved in the death of Dwight Smith. Do not approach this man. He believes he's on some kind of mission, and that means it's possible he will hurt anybody who stands in his way."

"So that's what this is? A mission?" somebody asks, a male voice coming from the crowd. "Does that mean he hasn't finished?"

"We will stop him," Stevens says, which doesn't answer the question. "Now, the man leading the investigation and who will answer your questions is Detective Inspector Theodore Tate. I'm sure many of you remember him, and I want to remind you to keep your questions relevant."

"Who's first?" Tate asks, and then most of the people in the room all seem to figure they are first, and questions come from every direction. "One at a time," Tate says, and then points into the crowd. The camera angle doesn't change, it stays on Tate as he listens to the question. His facial expression doesn't change.

"What would you say to the family members of the victims to ensure them all is being done that can be done?"

"I would tell them we are doing everything remotely possible, and everything by the book. We will—"

But then the reporter interrupts him. "But you were in a coma just a few months ago," he says. "And before that you were in jail. Seems to me the police force isn't doing the best it can, but loading the deck in the Five Minute Man's favor."

Before Tate can answer, Stevens goes back to the microphone. "Like I said, people, relevant questions. Not stupid ones."

"But—"

"You," he says, cutting off the same reporter and pointing to another one in the crowed, this time a woman. "I trust you'll stay on point?"

The camera angle doesn't show who asks the question, but this time it's a woman. "There are some people who think what the Five Minute Man is doing is a good thing. It's been a hot topic that the justice system in this country isn't hard enough, and the public voting the death penalty back in is proof of that. What would you say to those people?"

Tate glances at Stevens to make sure his boss isn't going to answer it, and Stevens straightens up, putting distance between him and the mic.

"I would remind them that half the country is against it," Tate says, "and I'd like everybody to think about where this would lead if we allowed people to run around playing judge and executioner. I know people out there have these Hollywood notions of a good man doing what he thinks is right, but—"

"And you, Detective? Where do you stand on that issue?"

"Innocent people are being hurt or killed, like Peter Crowley and Ron McDonald," Tate says. "I'm going to stop whoever is doing this."

There's a murmur in the crowd, then somebody asks the question that Schroder is thinking, and he knows Tate has said it deliberately. But what does it mean? "Are you saying Ron McDonald is an innocent man?"

"Of course that's what I'm saying," Tate says. "If he were a guilty man we would have prosecuted him seven years ago."

"You know that's not the general impression," the same reporter asks.

"I can't help what general impressions are, but the fact remains Ron McDonald was never charged with a crime, and therefore that makes him an innocent man."

"Are you saying he's just as innocent as he was seven years ago? Or have you found something to make him seem more innocent?"

"It's like I said," Tate says, "Ron McDonald was never charged. What I can tell you is that several interviews and a search conducted today have brought to light new evidence in the killing of Hailey McDonald."

"Does that mean you have a new primary suspect?" another reporter asks.

"What I'm saying is new evidence has come to light."

"Simplify it for us, Detective," another reporter asks. "In your opinion, did Ron McDonald kill his wife?"

"Ask me again tomorrow," Tate says, "because by then we'll know for sure."

There are more questions, some of them stupid, some of them to the point, and Tate answers some and brushes others aside, and Schroder sits through it all listening, listening, listening, but really what he is doing is thinking, thinking, thinking.

The conference carries on. Tate says the bald man may have been given a lift on Friday night, sometime after one o'clock in the morning, from the location of the train tracks. He says the bald man may have hitchhiked, and if somebody did pick him up, then he is to get in touch with the police. Kent doesn't talk, but Stevens takes over again and thanks the reporters for coming, promises they'll have more information for them tomorrow, then talks about Detective Inspector Wilson Hutton, whose loss will greatly affect the department, before reminding everybody just how dangerous the Five Minute Man is.

The conference ends.

Schroder switches off the TV.

He gets out his cell phone.

He calls Tate, imagining him still walking out of the room, imagining him reaching into his pocket while reporters are still trying to ask him questions.

"Detective Tate," he says, answering his phone.

"It's not going to work," Schroder says.

"What's not going to work?"

"You're trying to bait me. You're trying to make me think I killed an innocent man."

"Hang on a second," Tate says, and then there is a rustling sound and Schroder can picture the phone being dropped into a pocket, more voices, more footsteps, and then a closing door and silence. "I'm not trying to make you think anything."

"Bullshit."

"It's true. And the other thing that's true is Ron McDonald is an innocent man. You killed a good guy, Carl. You killed somebody who never harmed anybody, and tonight I'm going to prove it."

"You're lying."

"I'm not."

"I don't believe you."

"You will. This time tomorrow you will."

Tate hangs up. Schroder is left staring at his phone. His hand is shaking. He feels . . . emotional. He slips the phone into his pocket then looks up at Warren. "He's lying to me."

Maybe you're lying to yourself.

"Goddamn you, Warren," he says, and he takes his shoe off, reaches up, and splatters Warren into the shape of a fur ball. "Goddamn you for never being on my side," he says, and he hits him again, then again, and then again for good measure. Then he turns and throws his shoe at the couch. "Goddamn all of you."

CHAPTER SIXTY-EIGHT

I get off the phone. It feels good to have rattled Schroder. I get back out into the corridor. Reporters are still making their way to the stairwell and to the elevators. I find Kent in the task-force room on the fourth floor. A three-foot-square whiteboard has been put up in the corner and a grid drawn over it. In each square is a number.

"It's a pool," Kent says, "for tonight. I have twelve thirty." I realize then that the numbers are times, and that they are spaced ten minutes apart. Like she said, Kent has written her name in the twelve thirty slot. "It's for when Chris Watkins is going to show up tonight."

Most of the spaces are still free, meaning the grid has just been drawn, and what names are up there are between eleven and one.

"How much?" I ask.

"Ten bucks," she says, and points towards a container.

"And if he doesn't show up?"

"Then it's refunds all around."

I drop ten bucks into the container, then pick up the felt by the whiteboard and write my name in the two o'clock slot.

"You really think it'll be that late?" she asks.

"I have no idea, but two a.m. is as good a guess as any."

"I've heard phone calls are already coming in about the car. Lots of people seem to have seen it, or know somebody who owns one. We're probably going to be inundated with calls. The psychics are starting to call too."

I look at my watch. "It's only been ten minutes," I tell her.

"Yeah, but the psychics have known for fifteen."

"How we getting on with the guys canvassing the tire stores?"

"It's going to be a big job," she says. "It's not just tire shops—plenty of service stations change them too. Could take a week."

The tires are a worry. Could be later today they find a tire-store operator who remembers the car and the bald guy. Could be later today or tomorrow or next week, but it will happen. Could be they have surveillance, or that Schroder paid by credit card. Then what? Well then we have to bring him in for questioning. Then he tells us what he's been up to, and what I've been up to too. Then it's holding cells, prison cells, court, more prison cells, and the hangman's noose. Or lethal injection. Or whatever in the hell it's going to be—maybe that'll be decided by referendum too.

I can feel the net tightening around me.

"Are you okay, Theo?"

"Yeah. Just thinking."

"About?"

"About how good it's going to feel when we arrest Chris Watkins tonight."

"And until then? What's the plan?"

Well, the plan is to solve nothing. The plan is to keep pushing the investigation in a different direction, only that's impossible now. I can't stop the police from going from tire shop to tire shop. I can't say I'll help out and go from tire shop to tire shop too in the hope that I'll find the right one and can cover it up. I can't stop the list of Honda Accords being cross-referenced and, in a few days' time—or a week, or however long it takes to run through thousands of names—stop Schroder's name from coming up.

"Let's go check in with the medical examiner," I tell her.

We drive to the hospital together, and like always Kent drives. It's getting close to the middle of the afternoon and the sun is peaking and the temperature is peaking and I can't imagine having to wear a jacket again until next year. We park in the same spot as Saturday and sign in with the same security guard and take the same elevator down into the basement where the same shiny tools are lined up and a different selection of dead bodies are lined up too. Quite a few dead bodies. Including Wilson Hutton, who has a sheet covering his body right up to his neck. We walk over to him just as Tracey is coming out of her office.

"I'm really sorry for your loss," she says. "Hutton was a good man."

"What was wrong with him?" I ask.

"I don't know all the answers yet," she says, "but combining diet pills with way too much exercise when you were as big as him, well, it's not a good combination. I think his heart just gave out. Would you like a minute with him?"

"Sure."

She walks over to some blackened people that don't even look like people, but look like something that crash-landed from Mars and was thrown on the barbecue. We stay with Hutton for two more minutes, and Hutton reminds us how life can be so fickle, and we remind Hutton that we're going to miss him, and then we promise him we'll look after his city. My phone vibrates a few times and I keep ignoring it, hoping that it's not Schroder telling me he's chosen his next victim.

Then Tracey goes over her findings with us.

"It's grisly stuff," she says, then starts pointing to wounds that we can't see because of the amount of flesh that's burned away. The two bodies that were trapped under the car are in the best condition, but that's a comparative statement, like choosing to eat a really rotten tomato because it's in better condition than the one riddled with maggots.

Four victims. Bevin Collard. Taylor Collard. Matthew Roddick. Robin Walsh. All four men were shot in the head, but all four men were dead by that point anyway. Walsh had his Achilles tendon sliced open and was clubbed in the head before being shot. Roddick was shot in the throat, that bullet wasn't recovered because it was a through and through. The bullet to the head was a different story, and was recovered. His leg was also gashed open. Taylor Collard had his face opened up and the skull beneath it cracked open by a roof tile. And his brother, Bevin, was shot in the chest and the head, and had broken wrists, one broken arm, a broken collarbone, and a broken neck.

"Most likely from a fall," Tracey says, "and most likely from up-stairs to downstairs. Also, the brothers have nineteen broken ribs between them. My guess is they were used as a ramp to get the car up to the doorway. I don't know what in the hell happened out there," she says, "but it sure as hell wasn't pretty. These men really pissed off the wrong person."

"Any of them suffering from a dog bite?" Kent asks.

"Not that I've seen," Tracey sees, "but it's possible. The fire cre-ated a lot of damage, so there could be dog bites there, but I can't see them because the flesh has burned away. I heard about the dog and the DNA that was found. I've sent DNA to the lab from our victims here, so you'll know if there's a match soon enough."

"And Peter Crowley?" Kent asks. "What happened to him?"

"Peter died of blunt force trauma. Three blows to the head. I found green glass in the wound. I've sent it to forensics, but my guess is it's from a beer bottle. The bottle stood up to the first two blows, but shattered on the third. The brain started to bleed, it swelled up, and he probably lived ten or fifteen minutes before dying. He probably wouldn't even have been able to tell you his name at that point."

"Are there any crime-scene photos here?" Kent asks.

"Some," Tracey says.

"You get the ones we took of the position of his body?"

"They're here."

"Can I see them?"

Tracey disappears into her office.

"What are you thinking?" I ask.

"Peter wasn't supposed to die, right?"

"Right."

"Then you'll see in a moment."

Tracey comes back. She's holding a folder with the photographs of each of the bodies as they were found before being removed, and also the photos we took of Crowley. Kent twists the photographs of Crowley a little as if she can change the angle it was taken from. She looks at it for a good twenty seconds before handing it to me. "Look," she says. "You notice what isn't there?"

I take a look at the photograph, and the answer that pops into my mind is *Schroder*, but the answer I give is, "What?"

"Glass," she says. "He was hit with the bottle elsewhere, and dragged there. My guess is Peter was killed inside, and was dragged outside."

"Because the killer felt sorry about it," I say. "He was trying to help Peter, and he didn't want the guy getting all burned up."

"Exactly," Kent says.

"I know where you're going with this," Tracey says, "but between then and now he's been moved and touched and autopsied, and do you know how hard it is to get fingerprints off skin anyway?"

"Really hard," Kent says, "but sometimes it's possible. If our killer picked him up, there may be something."

"Or maybe he picked him up under the armpits and only touched his clothes," I say.

"True, but look at this," she says, then points at the photographs again. "Peter's eyes are closed. Maybe our bald guy didn't just drag him out before setting the building on fire, but maybe he used his fingers to close the dead man's eyes. Seems maybe the kind of thing he would do, especially if he never intended Peter to be hurt. I say we fingerprint the body, and I say we start with the eyes."

"I wish you'd thought of this yesterday," Tracey says.

"So do I. But it's possible, right?"

"Possible? Why don't you ask your best fingerprinting guy what he thinks, and he'll tell you that you'd be lucky to get even close to possible. Still, it's worth a shot," she says, and I feel the net tighten a little bit more.

CHAPTER SIXTY-NINE

We get out into the sun and the sun never feels as good as it does for those first few seconds when you're stepping out of a morgue.

"That's a good idea you had down there," I tell Kent.

"It might lead to nothing," she says, "but I have to tell you, I'm feeling confident. I'm going to call in and get somebody down here."

"Make sure you get the best," I say, but really I want Forrest Gump down here searching for prints.

I check my phone and see that I've been left a message from Superintendent Stevens asking me to call back right away. Which is what I do.

"You remember a guy by the name of Benson Barlow?" he asks.

I remember him. He's a psychiatrist who helped on a few cases over the last year. Schroder worked with him a few times, and I met the guy out at Grover Hills back when we were all learning all of Grover Hills's dark secrets. "Yeah. I remember him."

"He thinks he can help us."

Great. More help. Just what we need. "In what way?"

"He's just spent the last fifteen minutes down here. He said he's been following the case, and he watched the press conference, and somehow he's done what shrinks do and take everything he's learned and turned it into some kind of conjecture."

"And?"

"And for the last fifteen minutes he's been trying to convince us of one thing, and one thing only, and I'm somewhat inclined to believe him, especially after what we know about the missing cell phone."

"Which is?" I ask.

"Barlow knows who our killer is," he says, and in that moment my innards twist themselves to Hell and back, and my future heads that way too. My mouth goes dry and my tongue gets stuck to the roof of it. "You still there?" he asks.

"I'm just waiting for the reveal."

"He thinks we're looking for a cop. And not just any cop, but one who's been on the force for some time. One who's jaded, one who's sick and tired of playing the game. He thinks it's possible we're looking at somebody who retired. It lines up with everything we know, including the missing cell phone, and lines up with your partner's theory."

"He have any suspects?"

"Suspects? That's our job, Detective. But what I can tell you is I have a list of names of everybody at that crime scene last night, and it's being checked as we speak against what kind of car they drive in the hopes one of them owns a Honda Accord. If it's true, we're going to find him, or them. And soon."

"Lots of them could own Honda Accords," I say. "Even my dad owns a Honda Accord."

"Then we'll put your dad on the list," he says, and I'm not entirely sure that he's joking. "How did it go with the medical examiner?"

"We're working with something," I tell him.

"Okay, keep me updated. I've already put Barlow's profile into the mix. It might even shake things up."

I get off the phone and Kent has gotten off the phone, and she asks me who was calling and I tell her, and I feel sick, physically sick because I know putting Barlow's profile into the mix is sure to bring up Schroder's name. How can it not? A bald ex-detective who drives a dark blue Honda. I grab hold of the side of the car and Kent looks over at me and asks if I'm okay.

"I'm fine."

"You don't look fine," she says. "You need to sit down."

"I just need some fresh air."

"No, what you need to do is stop acting like a tough guy and sit down before you faint. It wasn't that long ago you were in a coma because of a head injury, Theo."

She gets the car unlocked and I sit down with my legs out the side and I take some deep breaths. A seagull is sitting on top of a car parked ten yards away. It stares at me with an all-knowing eye.

"I think coming out of the cold morgue and into the heat has thrown me a little," I say.

"You want some water?"

"I'm okay, it's passing," I say, and it is passing. Any dizziness I felt is moving into my legs that now feel like rubber.

"I'll be back in two minutes."

She disappears and I play the staring game with the seagull and then Kent returns with a fresh bottle of water and hands it to me, and I drink half of it in one go. What I really need is something stronger. It's been over a year since I last took a drink, since the night I got trashed and crashed my car. Some people can learn from an experience like that, and some people can't.

"I'm better, I promise," I tell her.

"Would you tell me if you weren't?"

"Of course I would."

"It's been a long day, and no doubt you're going to want to be at the house tonight for when Watkins shows up, right? How about I take you back to the station and you head home until then?"

I lift my legs into the car. "Sounds like a plan."

Kent starts the car and the seagull disappears. She drives us out of the parking lot and into traffic. "You need me there tonight?"

"Not really. It's all straightforward," I say, and even I don't need to be there, but I want to be. Of course I want to be—this is my case.

"Once I drop you off," she says, "I'm heading back down to the morgue. I want to be there when these fingerprints get lifted from our victim. I'm hopeful," she says. "You know, what we could do is have another pool with time slots. We could start picking times for when this case wraps up, because this thing is about to be closed."

CHAPTER SEVENTY

I update Kent about Barlow's theory as we drive, and then she drops me off at the station. I think about jumping into my car and speeding through the streets, racing to the morgue to get there ahead of Kent and the fingerprint technician, then using my sleeve to wipe away any prints left on Peter Crowley's skin, especially around the eyes. But I can't. There is only so much I can do to save Schroder and myself, and that's not part of it. The best I *can* do is hope any prints Schroder left on the victim didn't stick, or were wiped away during the autopsy.

I drive out to New Brighton. It's a suburb by the beach, most of the houses looking tired in the sun, and I park in front of a liquor store and a café and I take Schroder's cell phone and cross the road to the pier opposite. The pier is a lot of concrete and a lot of steel and it takes me a few hundred yards out over the water where some people are admiring the view and some people are fishing. I drop the phone between the bars and the big blue swallows it. Then I walk back to the car and go into the liquor store. The guy who serves me can see pretty quickly it's not Conversational Tuesday, and I point to a hip flask of whiskey. He takes the cash, puts the bottle into a bag and adds an empty cup in there too as if he's seen it all before and knows the drinking can't be put off for anything more than a few more seconds. I'm flattered he doesn't just think I'll drink it from the bottle.

But the drinking can be put off, and not just by a few seconds. When I get home I stuff the bottle under the seat where I'd been hiding the cell phone. It's tempting to drink it now, that way tomorrow's *From Coma Cop to Dirty Detective* headline won't bother me as much.

Bridget is waiting for me at the doorstep.

"That bad?" she asks.

"That bad," I tell her, and then I hug her tight and I close my eyes and I want to stay this way forever.

"I have something to show you." She leads me down to Emily's bedroom. "What do you think?"

In the bedroom is a crib. It's the same crib we had when Emily was a baby, back before she outgrew it and we gave it to Bridget's parents to look after on account of them having a lot more storage space. I didn't know they still had it, and the fact they did could say a lot. It could say they had held out hope their daughter would be okay one day, and would have a normal life. Or it could just mean they never cleaned out their garage. Seeing it there brings back a lot of memories, a lot of *really good* memories.

"This is going to be her room," she says.

I don't say anything.

"Are you okay?"

I nod. Yes, I'm okay, but I can't say it.

"And she'll always have Emily to look over her."

I keep nodding. *She'll have Emily to look over her, but not me. I'll be in jail.*

"It's going to be okay, Teddy," Bridget says, and she hugs me. Hugs me tight and breathes into my neck and I wrap my arms around her and close my eyes. "Really, it's going to be okay."

Only it's not going to be okay, not at all, and then there's the voice, the voice that says *You've done it before, you can do it again.* And that voice is talking about the dirty work required to take things from not okay to okay, dirty work that sees me leading Schroder through the woods and giving the Five Minute Man a taste of his own medicine. Dirty work required to protect my family.

Finally I listen to the voice. Finally I let my mind go there.

You can do it again, the voice says.

And the scary part is I'm pretty sure I can.

CHAPTER SEVENTY-ONE

At six o'clock Kent calls and says they weren't able to pull a clean print from Peter Crowley's body. She's disappointed. This makes the voice and the dirty, dark images of me and Schroder in the woods disappear, and those images weren't real anyway, and it also means for the moment that bottle hidden under the seat in my car can stay hidden. Yes, I've killed bad people, but Schroder isn't bad people. He's good people making bad mistakes. Schroder was my friend. She tells me nobody has called saying they picked up a hitchhiker on Friday night.

At eight o'clock I drop my wife off at her parents' house, kiss her good-bye and tell her I'll see her in the morning. I drive to the police station to switch cars because Chris Watkins would have seen my car last night when I parked outside the workshop. At eight forty-five, on my way to the house Ron McDonald used to live in, I get a phone call from Jerry Williams.

"You owe me," he says.

"You got something for me?"

"The hair you sent over this morning from Ron McDonald is a match to the single black hair I found in the shirt."

"That's good," I tell him.

"That's not all," he says. "We've got a mixed DNA profile on the shirt made up from three different profiles. Now, let me break it down for you. My guess is the shirt was washed before it was worn in commission of the crime. That shirt in the washing machine has picked up secondary DNA from other clothes and, despite what people think, DNA can survive a lot and, in this case, has survived the wash. The blood on the shirt matches the longest of the hairs we found, and is female. We have a second DNA sample that matches Ron McDonald's single black hair. And a third DNA sample that matches the remaining hair. This third DNA sample we found a lot of around the armpits, chest, and collar, and is also male."

"So somebody else definitely wore that shirt."

"Definitely? I can't state that. For all I know somebody picked up that shirt to wipe himself down. But if I were a betting man, then yes, I would bet the farm on it. Now, if you want those profiles compared to the criminal database, that is something I can't make go any faster."

"What about the DNA sample sent over from the vet?"

"We'll build up a profile tomorrow," he says, "but we might not be able to match it to anything for three or four weeks, and that's only if we have a matching sample in the system."

At nine o'clock I park two doors away from the house Ron McDonald used to live in back when Hailey McDonald used to live. There isn't a lot of life on the street. A teenage boy and a teenage girl holding hands, him leaning against a fence, her looking at him and smiling. There's a cat nibbling at a mince pie that's been dropped on the sidewalk, and from the trees a few dozen birds are watching it, as if they're forming a gang to get revenge on the cat for all the family members they've lost. I reach the house and knock on the door and a man in his late thirties wearing a pair of glasses that look like they came from the forties answers the door.

"I'm Detective Inspector Theodore Tate," I tell him.

"Lee Charters," he says, and offers his hand, along with a big used-car salesman smile. "You're the one my wife spoke to earlier today?"

"That's me."

He laughs. "I hear she gave you the *Don't bullshit a used-car salesman's wife* line."

"She did."

"She tries to use it on everybody," he says, and slaps me on the back. "Come on in. I'd offer you a beer, but I'm guessing you'd say no. I'm still going to offer anyway. My folks always said don't take beer from a stranger, but they never said anything about offering it."

"No thanks," I tell him.

"That your car I saw you pull up in?" he asks. "Or a police car?"

"Police car."

"What do you drive?"

"Something that's all I can afford."

"You'd be surprised what you can afford," he says, and hands me his card. "Why don't you come down and see me? We give a discount for law enforcement."

"Thanks," I tell him, and put the card into my pocket.

"You've got one colleague in the lounge, and the other in the study looking out over the backyard. If you need me for anything, I'll be in the kitchen. Nancy is still trying to get Lenny to get to sleep. Been one of those days, but you'll meet her soon enough." He slaps me on the shoulder again. "Let me know if you change your mind about that beer, okay?"

I head into the lounge. Detective Lance McCoy is here, a guy who I've worked with in the past, but not since being back on the force. We shake hands and he tells me so far there's nothing to report, and at the other end of the house is Officer England, who I don't think I've ever met. Officer England is armed with a Taser.

I look at my watch. It's five past nine. It's mostly dark outside, the streetlights taking more effect by the minute. I wonder who's going to win the pool. Maybe I'll win enough so I can put that law-enforcement discount into effect with Lee. Or hire a good lawyer.

"You look shot," McCoy says. "I got this covered if you wanna take a break," he says, and nods towards the chair. "It's not like there are a hundred angles here, and it's still pretty early."

I tell him I'm okay, and we talk about the case, and I tell him about the DNA. After a while Lee comes out and says they're off to bed, and I don't end up meeting the wife of the used-car sales-man. Ten thirty comes and goes, and I wonder whose name is on the board in the time slots that have slipped away.

Eleven o'clock.

Eleven thirty. I start thinking about the whiskey in my car, my car back at the station, and then I think of the beer that Lee offered me earlier. I'm fifteen yards from the kitchen, a few extra yards to the fridge. I could be there in ten seconds.

Eleven forty. Eleven fifty.

I guessed two a.m., but already I'm feeling like I'm wrong. Was I wrong? Or was I right and Watkins doesn't have access to the murder weapon? If he did kill Hailey McDonald, there's no reason he didn't drive out to the pier in New Brighton and watch the water swallow that knife up. Maybe Schroder's cell phone is sitting right next to it.

Midnight comes. Midnight goes. Kent picked twelve thirty.

But then twelve thirty comes. Her time slot hangs around for ten minutes. And then it's gone and a new time slot arrives. I stay by the window I've been camping at since I got here, a window that gives me a view to the left and the right, the curtains parted just enough for the view, and nobody comes. No moving shadows. No one coming to hide a murder weapon. Did we get it wrong?

One o'clock.

"This isn't looking so good," McCoy says.

One thirty. Three more time slots just slipped by.

"I'm busted," he says. "I had one twenty. You?"

"Two," I tell him.

"Good luck," he says.

Only my luck doesn't hold out. At one fifty, ten minutes before the time slot I guessed, Christopher Watkins, wearing a black pair of jeans, a black shirt, and a baseball cap—perhaps the same cap he wore seven years ago—steps into view. There is a small backpack over his shoulder. He's doing his best to keep a three-hundred-and-sixty-degree view by turning his body as he steps onto the front yard. He moves quickly to a large tree on the boundary line, and stands against it, watching and waiting and listening, and this he does for a minute before becoming satisfied the street is asleep. Then he moves towards the house. He's wearing a dark pair of gloves.

McCoy whispers into a handheld radio, letting the officer at the other end of the house know that Watkins is here, and to keep an eye out.

"How long do we give him?" McCoy asks.

"Let him place the weapon. I'd rather take him into custody when he's unarmed."

Watkins keeps moving. He makes his way to the garage and out of line from the lounge window. We move into the kitchen. The garage doesn't adjoin the house, there's a few yards between the two buildings, and from one of the kitchen windows we watch as he steps up to the side door. For a moment I think he's going to try and enter it, but instead he crouches down. He unzips his bag and takes out a handheld garden trowel. He puts the tip of it into the earth and removes two scoops of dirt and then he stops. His body stiffens and he turns towards the kitchen. He can't see us, surely he can't, but can he sense us?

He runs.

"Go," I shout, and before we get to the front door we can hear the baby at the other end of the house start crying, and at the same time the officer down there calls out a *sorry* before bursting into the lounge behind us while we get to the front door and get outside, but then there's the sound of a squeaking toy, a *fuck it* and a thud, and a crash from behind us.

Me and McCoy get outside. "Call it in," I say as we start running. Watkins has a thirty-yard lead and he's carrying his backpack in his left hand and trying to loop his right hand through the strap. We hit the sidewalk fast, my old man legs okay for the moment, McCoy tugging the cell phone from his pocket. I keep the same pace as McCoy, and together we keep the same pace as Watkins, and there is nowhere for him to go, no obstacle course or minefield or train he can jump past.

The thirty yards becomes twenty-five. McCoy starts talking into the cell phone.

Then Watkins stops running. It's almost like he hits a brick wall. He stops and turns towards us and he's given up on trying to put on the backpack. He's given up on everything. He can't outrun us. Backup is on the way. There is no flight here, but then I realize he's not thinking about flight anymore, but about fight. He reaches into his bag and pulls out a plastic bag, and inside that plastic bag is the knife.

We come to a stop. He looks at me and then at McCoy and starts to make a decision, figuring out which one of us to attack.

CHAPTER SEVENTY-TWO

I put my hands out in front of me. "Calm down, Chris. There's nothing to gain here. Put the knife down and let's think about this."

He doesn't calm down. Our Taser is back with Officer England and the child toy he tripped over. Which means the best thing right now is for us to stay out of Chris's reach. McCoy goes left and I go right, and Chris makes his decision, and goes towards McCoy.

"Chris," I shout, but he doesn't respond, just keeps going towards McCoy, the knife out in front of him, his elbow bent slightly. "Chris!"

But Chris isn't listening.

I move in behind him, and he hears me and turns towards me and swings the knife. It slices towards my face and I duck back and watch it race by, and then McCoy is behind him, grabbing him around the neck in a choke hold. A moment later Chris jabs the knife over his shoulder and McCoy turns his face away, only not far enough, and I watch the knife slide into the bottom of his ear, it moves upwards, slicing in deeper. Instead of letting him go, McCoy tightens his grip as blood starts squirting out from the wound. I jump onto Chris and grab hold of his wrist and push it out to the side, blood going everywhere. I fire a punch into the underside of his jaw. His head jolts backwards and crashes into the bottom of McCoy's chin, and the impact causes McCoy's ear to flop out to the side where the momentum tears it away. I don't see where it lands. He steps backwards and drags Chris, who is starting to struggle less. I grip his hand with both of mine and dig my thumbs as hard as I can into the underside of his wrist until he releases the knife, and then I punch him as hard as I can in the stomach. McCoy flips him around and throws him face down onto the ground, puts a knee in his back, and then I pull his hands around and get the cuffs onto him.

"Goddamn it," McCoy says, and he pushes himself a few feet away and sits down, touching his fingers to the side of his head and then looking at the blood. Chris Watkins rolls onto his side, his hands cuffed behind him, and brings his knees to his chest. He's gasping for air. "You move one more inch and I'm going to knock your teeth out," McCoy adds.

Chris must believe him, because he doesn't move another inch.

"You want to help me out here?" McCoy asks.

I look around the ground where we struggled. The knife is a chef's knife with a blade maybe eight inches long and a solid wooden handle. There's blood all over it. It's lying half on the sidewalk and half on the grass verge towards the road. McCoy's ear is a few inches away from it, sitting in a small pool of blood. It looks like a mushroom in sauce.

"I've got it under control," McCoy says, then nods back in the direction of the house. "Go get me some ice."

I run back towards the house. Everybody inside is awake now, the baby is screaming and the lights are on, and Officer England is on his side with his ankle pointing ninety degrees inwards, his face red and tight with every vein in his body trying to pop through his skin. Lee is leaning over him, trying to talk him through the pain.

"Backup is on the way," I tell both of them, then head into the kitchen. I open cupboards and find a plastic container with a lid, big enough to hold a couple of sandwiches. I fill it with ice from the freezer, and then I run back down the street to where McCoy is still sitting, part of me having expected to find he's stabbed Watkins or at the very least cut one of his ears off too. He's on the phone updating the officers racing to the scene. I pick up the severed ear and drop it into the bag of ice then have the urge to wipe my fingers on the lawn, and then actually do just that. I shake the container a little to make sure the ear gets completely covered, the ice rattling like dice.

"If this doesn't go back on right," McCoy says to Watkins, "I swear to God I'm going to cut your eyelids off."

"I want a lawyer," Watkins says.

"You're going to need one," I tell him, "because we know you killed Hailey McDonald, and right now you just tried to kill a police officer."

"I'm not saying anything else," he says, "just that I want a lawyer."

"How's England?" McCoy asks me.

"Probably rainy," I tell him.

"Ha ha," he says, and for a guy who just had his ear cut off, he seems extremely calm.

"His ankle is broken," I say. "It's on a ninety-degree angle. Looks like straightening it is going to hurt a hell of a lot more."

"Good thing I ordered us an ambulance."

The other police cars arrive before the ambulance does. There are just two patrol cars because the suspect is in custody. Watkins is helped into the back of one of them, and then he's driven away, where he'll go back to the station and insist again that he wants a lawyer. The ambulance arrives and the two paramedics start looking McCoy over, and I hand one of them the plastic container with the ear. McCoy is loaded into the back then has to wait five minutes while Officer England is loaded into the back too. Another car pulls up and another detective along with a forensic technician take some photographs of the knife, then it's slipped into an evidence bag and then the technician and the detective walk down to the house and take some more photographs, this one of the garden where Watkins started digging. The garden trowel is still there. It's put into the same kind of bag as the knife.

Then I'm the last one left at the scene. I thank Lee Charters for the use of his house, and he tells us to keep the container.

"Think of it as a reason to come buy your next car off me," he says.

Then I climb into my car, and head back down to the station.

CHAPTER SEVENTY-THREE

The station has only a quarter of the lights on and ten percent of the staff. Crime may not sleep, but the people cleaning up the mess sure need to. I make myself some coffee. It's four a.m. and I'm tired and want to go home. Watkins is in one of the interview rooms talking to a lawyer. Soon he'll be figuring out the best way to shave off a year or two for cooperating. He just has to mentally get there, that's all. Right now he'll be in a different headspace. He'll be trying to piece together a reason for why we caught him with a knife. He'll want a way out of this, a way that doesn't involve jail time, but that isn't going to happen. Stephen King couldn't come up with a reason why, at almost two in the morning, Christopher Watkins was in the yard where Ron McDonald used to live, innocently burying a knife that seven years ago was used to kill McDonald's wife.

I give Kent a call. She answers the phone sounding sleepy and I tell her what's happened and, still sounding sleepy, she asks how McCoy is. I tell her I haven't heard, then I think there might be a joke in there somewhere, about not having heard and about McCoy losing an ear, but I don't have the energy to figure it out. She tells me she's on her way.

I drink my coffee and I pace the task-force room, and I think about how some cases are simple and some are not. We've just taken thirty hours to solve a case that seven years ago we couldn't solve, and that makes it look easy. Kent arrives. She's wearing the same clothes she wore yesterday and she makes herself a coffee and then we head to the interrogation room. Kent is carrying a video camera and a tripod. I'm about to knock on the door when it opens anyway and a man in a suit smiles at us and identifies himself as

Ernest Grey. He shakes our hands, and then asks if we can have a word in the corridor. We tell him that's fine.

"It's four fifteen in the morning," he tells us. Ernest has a big, friendly smile and stands a little taller than me, he has mostly gray hair and it's floppy and tidy except for a few strands that are hanging over his forehead. He reminds me a little of my father. "Now, tell me if we're all on the same page here when I say we can deal with this tomorrow. This homicide you're going to try and charge him for is already seven years old. He's not going anywhere, the family won't mind waiting one more day. How about we reschedule this for a more reasonable time? Only thing I'd ask is you keep my client in his own detention cell."

I nod while he talks to us, even the bit where he said *try and charge him*. "I appreciate what you're saying, but we're here and ready to go," I tell him.

Now he's the one to nod. "Okay," he says, "but once my client looks like he's too tired to continue, I'm calling an end to it."

We all step into the room. Chris sits on the other side of the table where he also sat yesterday. He's a different beast from yesterday. His hands have blood on them. His lawyer sits next to him. Kent sets up the video camera and points it so it captures the four of us, then we sit down opposite the killer and the lawyer.

"Just before two a.m. this morning," I say, "you entered the front yard of Lee and Nancy Charters where you were caught trying to bury the murder weapon used in—"

Ernest Grey holds up his hand. The big smile is still there. "Let me stop you a moment there, Detective, because I can see where you're going with this." He looks at his watch. "Two and a half hours since my client was arrested. It is the middle of the night. Can you explain to me how you were able to get the knife tested for DNA in such a quick time and at such a strange hour?"

"It hasn't been tested," I tell him.

His eyebrows go up. "It hasn't? Sorry, I just thought I heard you say he was trying to bury the murder weapon. To what crime has this knife been linked?"

"Okay," I tell him. "How about this. Chris, you want to tell us what you were doing trying to bury a knife in the yard of Lee and Nancy Charters?"

"I wasn't trying to bury it," he says. "I found it there."

"You found it there?" Kent asks.

"Yes."

"A quick question," Ernest says, "because I think we can tidy up one of these issues right away. Can you tell me what my client said after you identified yourself as police officers?"

I don't answer him.

"Detective?"

"I think it was pretty obvious we were police officers," I tell him, knowing where he's leading us. "Especially since I interviewed your client twelve hours earlier."

"I see. So neither you nor Detective McCoy actually identified yourselves?" When I don't answer, he carries on. "So what I hear you saying is that anybody being chased down a street at two in the morning in the dark by two men should always assume those two men are police officers, even if they don't say anything?"

"Your client was found with a knife in his possession, which we believe we can link to the seven-year-old homicide of Hailey McDonald," I tell him.

"Yes, so you say, and we'll get back to that in a moment, but any charges you think you can lay against my client for assault·ing a police officer I'll have laughed out of court. You didn't identify yourselves. Chris here was acting in self-defense. Now, I hear you're running the shirt you found in the back of Ron McDonald's car for DNA. That bullshit might work on people who don't understand the law, but I do understand it, and those clothes are never coming back into evidence. Ever. Anything found from whatever DNA is found on those clothes can't be used. This attempt to manipulate my client earlier today is nothing but the police taking advantage of somebody who can't stand up for themselves."

"Settle down, Mr. Grey," Kent says. "Your client stabbed a

woman to death seven years ago and tonight he tried to do the same to a cop."

"No, seven years ago Ron McDonald stabbed his wife, and to-night my client tried to defend himself from two men he believed were a threat."

"Can your client explain why he was at the house?" Kent asks.

Grey looks at Watkins and nods at him, then Watkins shuffles in his chair and leans forward a little and rests his hands on the table.

"I was having an affair with Hailey," he says. "We'd been seeing each other for a few months."

"You were seeing her before Ron started his own affair," I say.

"Yeah."

"Did Ron know?"

He shakes his head. "No, he suspected she was having an affair, but he never knew who with, and he didn't really care. Especially after he met Naomi. He said their marriage was over anyway, and had been for a long time."

"Okay," I say. "So help me connect the dots here. How does that lead you to trying to bury a knife in the front yard of where they used to live?"

He shakes his head. "That's not how it happened," he says.

"So how did it happen?"

"I found the knife there."

"Explain that to us," I say.

"Tonight. I found it there. See, I knew you were going to search the house, right? I saw the report you left on the table yesterday. I saw—"

"That was very forgetful of you, Detective," Grey says, then wags his finger side to side. "A man more pessimistic than me would suspect you had left it there deliberately."

"Carry on, Chris," Kent says.

"Well, I saw the report, and I knew you guys were thinking Hailey was having an affair, and I knew that if you searched that old house you would find evidence of it. See, she used to leave a key out for me."

"A key?" I ask.

"Yeah. She would put it into a small plastic bag and she would hide it in the garden. That way on occasion I could call in sick at work and go to her house and let myself inside. She'd be waiting for me in the bath or the bedroom, you know, all ready for me."

"She left you a key," I say, "hidden in a plastic bag, buried in the garden."

"That's right."

"She did that rather than leaving her door unlocked," I say.

"Of course. Who leaves their door unlocked?"

"And she did that rather than answering the door," I say.

"Yeah. Part of the thrill was knowing I'd walk into the bedroom and we'd get started. Plus she didn't want people to risk seeing her naked when she answered the door. She was always naked for me."

"Why didn't she give you a key to keep?" I ask.

He shrugs. "I don't know and I never asked her. I just figured maybe she was seeing other people too. Maybe she wouldn't leave it out if there were other people coming over in case we all showed up at the same time."

"Okay, so what happened tonight?"

"Well, I knew you guys were going to find this key if it was still there, and that it would have my fingerprints on it, and I knew you guys were going to start taking all the DNA you could from people and I figured you'd probably take fingerprints too of anybody who knew her," he says, and again Ernest Grey is shaking his head, and he is wagging his finger back and forth in a *tsk tsk* gesture. "I just didn't want that key to be found, because I knew you'd think who-ever she'd been sleeping with was the one who killed her. So I went to where she used to hide it, and I started digging, and then I found the knife. It scared the hell out of me, because it confirmed right there and then that Ron had killed her, you know?"

"So rather than calling the police, or leaving it there, you de-cided to run?" I ask.

"Yeah. Because I sensed people were watching me. So then it was worse, right? Not only would people think I had done it because of the key, but then they would be really sure I had done it because suddenly I was holding the knife. I should have left it there. I don't know why I didn't, but when I thought people were watching me I just ran. I took the knife with me to protect myself. Then two dudes were chasing me, so I did what I could to defend myself."

He finishes talking and the room goes quiet. Chris is looking at Kent and he looks like he's about to cry. "I really loved her," he says. "I would never have done anything to hurt her."

Nobody else talks then. I look over at Ernest Grey, and he looks composed and relaxed, but his mouth is a little tight and he knows what I'm thinking and what Kent is thinking because he just heard the same story. He's thinking they are in a lot of trouble.

"That's the best you can do?" I ask him.

"What?"

"Detective," Grey says.

"That's really the best you can come up with," I say.

"That's what happened," Watkins says.

"Detective, that's enough," Grey says.

I start laughing. I can't help it. I really can't. Then Kent joins in. After the tension of the day, after McCoy losing his ear, after Hutton dying, all of that suddenly starts to disappear. I'm about to spend the rest of my life in jail, so why not get one more final laugh in if it's there to be had? "That is the most ridiculous story I have ever heard," I say, and I can barely get the words out. "And I've heard a lot of them."

"There is no way any jury is going to buy that," Kent says.

"He found the knife," Grey says, "and the only thing we know that knife was used for was an act of self-defense. Even if it was used seven years ago, any DNA from my client on that knife got there when he found it tonight."

I keep laughing.

"This interview is over," Grey says.

"Stop laughing at me," Chris says.

"Chris," Grey says, and puts a hand on his shoulder. "Don't say anything."

"This interview isn't over," I tell them, and I'm finally calming down, and so is Kent. "So far you've said nothing that gives us any reason not to charge you for the murder of Hailey McDonald."

"I didn't kill her," Chris says, his voice rising. "I loved her."

"You really expect us to believe the knife was buried in the exact same spot the key used to be buried in."

"Why not?" Grey says. "If one person thought it made an ideal hiding spot, why not another? And it would explain why the key may not be there when you go back to the scene—when Ron buried the knife, he found the key. Or perhaps any one of these other men who were potentially sleeping with the victim."

"Here's what I think," I say.

"No, here's what I think," Grey says. "You lied to my client this afternoon. You manipulated him into going to that scene because you sent that shirt out to a lab and something came back to point you in a different direction. You honed in on my client through illegal evidence, and that will get all of this thrown out in court."

"We invited your client in for questioning in the homicide of Ron McDonald," I tell him, "and during that questioning your client got it into his head that—"

"Because you left the folder behind!" Chris says.

"You were caught with the—" I say.

"Detectives," Grey says, raising his voice. "The fact of the matter is you've apprehended my client by the use of illegal means. You have no reason to hold him."

"We have every reason to—"

"This meeting is over," Grey says, and he stands up. "I am instructing my client to say nothing else. I suggest we let a judge point out to you that you're wrong. Let's do that first thing in the morning, huh? It'd be nice to get it out of the way then that way you can do something productive with the rest of your day rather than chasing men for things they didn't do."

"Sit back down, Mr. Grey," Kent says, "we've still got—"

"You heard my lawyer," Watkins says. "I've got nothing else to say."

"This is your last chance to help yourself," I tell him. "You tell us what happened, and maybe you can avoid the death penalty."

"What's he talking about?" Watkins asks.

"He's bullshitting you," Grey says.

"No, we're not," I say. "You know it's coming back, Chris, so what you want to ask yourself is do you want to be on our good side or on our bad side? Your lawyer can prance around and say anything he wants, but you know and I know what you did, and no jury is going to buy your story."

"And no jury is going to have to. This is going to be dismissed," Grey says. "All of it."

"It's not your lawyer getting the needle if he's wrong," I tell Watkins.

"The needle?"

"Or the gas, or the rope. We don't know what it's going to be," Kent says. "Could be a firing squad for all we know."

"That's enough," Grey says. "My client has nothing more to say."

"Is that right?" I ask Watkins.

Watkins nods. "Yeah, that's right."

"Well, we are charging you with the murder of Hailey McDonald, and the attempted murder of Detective Inspector Lance McCoy," I say, and I stand up. "If you're finished with your lawyer, then it's time to process you and put you in a holding cell."

"Don't say anything else," Grey says, "and I'll see you in the morning, okay?"

Watkins nods, the interview is over, and it's time for me to go home.

CHAPTER SEVENTY-FOUR

Out in the parking lot I stand with Kent and we talk about the interview. A newspaper truck drives past the entrance gates and I wonder what today's headline is going to be, but even more importantly I wonder about tomorrow's.

"You guys never identified yourselves?" Kent asks.

"No. I mean, we would have, but he just started running, then before we knew what was going on he came at us with a knife. There was just no time."

"Grey will say there is always time," she says, which is kind of like her saying *You should have found time*. And she's right. "But that story about the key and finding the knife, what do you think?"

"I think it's insane, but sometimes a jury buys insane."

"I'll come get you in the morning," she says. "About nine?"

"Sounds good."

We part ways and I head home, and without Bridget here it reminds me of all the other times I've come home late at night after investigating something, the house empty, my wife in a nursing home. I actually think about calling Schroder, or even going and banging on his door. It's five thirty and there's something about the idea of waking him up to tell him he screwed up that I enjoy, but not enough to go and do it. If killing an innocent man isn't enough to stop Schroder, I don't know what is.

Yes you do.

Yes. I do.

I set my alarm for eight thirty, and when it wakes me up almost three hours later I feel like I've been asleep for all of five minutes and, for the briefest of moments, I wonder if I didn't creep out to my car during the night and grab the bottle of whiskey. It sure as hell feels that way.

I jump into the shower and wake up a little, coffee wakes me some more, then I call my wife. We talk for ten minutes and I tell her things in the case are moving along quickly, and that things may wrap up today.

"When's Wilson's funeral?" she asks.

"Friday."

"Okay. I'll stay at my parents' today. You want to swing by and get me after work?"

"I'll see you then."

Kent honks the horn when she pulls up outside. I'm walking down to the car when my phone rings. It's Detective Travers.

"I got something," he says.

"What kind of something?"

"Where are you?" he asks, and he sounds excited.

"On the way to the station."

"So where are you right now?"

"Standing outside my house," I tell him, looking up and down the street in case he's here.

"Okay. You know where Tire Man Tim's Tires is?"

I picture the building, the location, just off the edge of town. "Yeah, I do."

"Then you should come down here," he says.

"Why don't you tell me over the phone?"

"Because it would ruin the surprise."

"I don't like surprises," I tell him.

"You'll like this one," he says, but I don't think I will. It's going to be Schroder caught on surveillance. It's going to be Schroder using his name and paying with a credit card. Travers hangs up. I head to my car, open the door, and slip the hip flask of whiskey into my jacket pocket. I head over to Kent.

"Good news?" Kent asks. "Has Watkins confessed?"

"It's something else," I tell her. "You know where Tire Man Tim's Tires is?"

"Yeah, I do."

"It was Travers on the phone. He said he's got a surprise for us."

"It must be where the bald guy bought the tires. This is exciting!" she says and she looks as excited as I feel awful. "We're getting close!"

I think of the hip flask. Today is all mapped out. The tires with fingerprints all over them. A new witness. The list of Honda Accords. My legs feel like jelly. I feel like I'm going to throw up.

"You still don't look so good," she says.

"I'm fine."

"You sure you want to do this?"

"I said I'm fine," I tell her, a little too forcefully.

"Whatever you say."

I take a last look at my house as we pull away. There are people on bikes and people out walking. They're soaking up the sun and eager to get to the other end of the day, where the five o'clock world ends. I imagine by then I'll be in an interrogation room, only this time on the opposite side of the table.

The tire shop has orange concrete block walls, the shade dulled by the passing of time and the passing of cars, exhaust dialing the orange back, same for the big black letters spelling out the name, which are now almost gray. The big bay doors have been rolled up, and inside are rows and rows of tires and tools, one car already hoisted up a few feet with the wheels missing, a couple of guys in black uniforms moving around in there, to the side of it all an attached office with a glass front wall for customers to pay and wait and to discuss finance options. Detective Travers is waiting for us out front, and by now my legs have regained strength. He's wearing a sharp blue shirt and sharp black pants that makes my own outfit look like somebody was once buried in it.

"We were lucky," he says, which makes my stomach drop even more, "but not lucky enough," he says, which goes someway to putting my stomach back into its rightful place. "This place was on the list, but at this rate we wouldn't have gotten to it for another two days. But Tom Headman, he's the owner—"

"Not Tim?" Kent asks.

"No, and don't ask me why," he says, "but that stuff about the car we released on the news yesterday was in the papers this morning, and that's where he saw it and recognized it. He phoned it in and said he serviced a car just like it on Sunday afternoon, putting on two brand new tires. So that's the good news. The bad news is there's no surveillance here, and the guy paid in cash. But more good news is that the tires he replaced are still here."

"He leave a name?" I ask.

"Yeah, he did," he says. "And that's the good part. You want to have a guess what his name is?"

I can feel the darkness rushing back. I can feel my legs beginning to sway. The only question is will Schroder take me down with him?

"Who?"

"It's you," he says. "Guy said his name was Theodore Tate."

It takes a moment to absorb the news. Theodore Tate. Not Carl Schroder. "Same name he gave the prison officer," I tell him. "You could have told me that on the phone."

"I wanted to tell you in person," he says.

I shake my head. "This is bullshit," I tell him.

"What?"

"You're full of shit and this isn't my first day on the force. You wanted me down here because you want Tom to take a look at me, right? You want to make sure it wasn't me who came in here on Sunday."

"Now, hang on a second—"

"Fuck you, Detective," I say.

"No, fuck you, Tate," he says, pointing his finger at me. "You would have done the same damn thing. There's a theory this killer is or was one of us, what was I supposed to do?"

Kent puts a hand on my shoulder and I have the urge to shake it off. "He's right," she says, "you would have done the same thing."

I shake my head. I know I'm overreacting, but I'm entitled to.

I'm having a stressful time. "Let's go and see Tom. Let's make sure this is my first time here," I tell him.

"Come on, Tate, don't be—"

"Whatever," I say, and I head towards the office.

"Howdy, Detective, I'm Tom," a man says, a man who must be Tom, and he offers me his hand and I shake it, and then he gives me a card. "Next time you need tires," he says, "come and see me."

"Let me guess, you give a law-enforcement discount?"

"I give everybody a discount," he says, "but law enforcement get the real savings." He hands a card to Kent too. I figure Travers already has one. "You guys do a hell of a job."

I put the card in my pocket. I feel calm again. No surveillance, no real name. Then I think about the tires that are here with Schroder's prints all over them from when he changed them at Grover Hills, and my heart starts to race. I just have to hope he wore gloves.

"So the guy paid with cash?" I ask.

"Yep."

"Any chance it's still here?"

He shakes his head. "Like I told your colleague, weekends are really busy. First thing we do Monday morning is take the profits to the bank. We keep a float, but that's always turning over. The guy paid in twenties, and those things come and go all day long. "

"So the two tires, they're here I've been told, which means they couldn't be fixed?" I ask.

"That's right," Tom says. "Not just the tires, but he left one of the spare wheels here. He was driving on two of them. One I patched up and put back into his car, the other he left behind."

"So what did he run over?"

"He hadn't run anything over," Tom says. "They'd been slashed. They were completely ruined. Like I said before you got here, they're out back in the scrap pile. They're all yours. You want me to give you a hand loading them up?"

"That's fine," Travers says. "There's a fingerprint technician already on the way. You just show me where they are and I'll take care of it."

"I'll get Neal to show you," he says. There's an open doorway between the office and the workshop, and Tom calls through it to one of the two men we saw earlier, this one a kid who is all of twenty years old who's pulling the tire off a rim. Neal looks up, sees Tom flagging him over, and then comes through. "Can you show the detective where the two slashed tires are that came in on the Honda?"

Neal starts nodding. He seems eager to please. He leads Travers back through the doorway and through the workshop.

"Did this man have to sign anything? Or touch anything?" Kent asks.

"Nothing. The guy just stood there watching the whole time. Didn't say much other than ask for two new tires and how much were they going to be. Stood there with his hands in his pockets in the workshop and watched. I remember he was wearing a long-sleeve shirt even though it was really hot, and the sleeve was all puffed up like his arm was bandaged beneath it. Only time he took his hands out of his pocket was when he paid, and also when he answered his cell phone. I was showing another customer around at the time, but he answered the phone with his name."

"Theodore Tate," I say, and how close did I come just then to saying *Carl Schroder.*

"Yeah, he looked at the display on his phone, and then flipped it open and said *Theo.*"

"When exactly was this?" I ask.

"I can't give you exactly," he says, "not on the phone call, but it wasn't long before he paid, and the receipt here says he paid at eleven fifty-seven.

"So this guy is still impersonating you on the phone," Kent tells me.

I nod. I think about the time line. Bridget saw him around then, didn't she? Is it possible that instead of him impersonating me on the phone, he looked at the display and thought it was me calling?

He wasn't saying *Theo*, as in *I'm Theo*. He was saying it because he thought it was me calling. As in *Hi, Theo*. I didn't call him, but if Bridget called from home, it still would have been my name flashing across his phone. It was the day after I showed her where Quentin James was buried. I think the following morning something inside her misfired. I think she called Schroder wanting his help. I think for some reason she took him out to the grave because the time line in her mind had gotten scrambled. That's how he found the body.

"How good a look did you get at the guy?" Kent asks.

"A really good look."

"So if we put you in front of a sketch artist, you'll be able to come up with something?"

"Sure, and it'll be something a hell of a lot more accurate than that sketch in this morning's paper," he says. "I mean, that sketch doesn't even have the scar."

I do my best not to cringe at those words.

"What scar?" Kent asks.

"Up here," he says, and taps the side of his head. "Looked like the guy had been shot."

CHAPTER SEVENTY-FIVE

We get back into the car. The dashboard tells us the temperature is the same as what it was ten minutes ago when we got here, but I tug at the top of my shirt and try to let some air in because it feels like the day has gotten fifty degrees hotter. It feels stuffy. So stuffy I'm struggling to breathe a little.

Kent says nothing and I say nothing and Tom Headman follows us in his car as we drive back to the station. We're more than half-way there when I break the silence.

"You can say it," I say.

She shakes her head.

"Come on, Rebecca. You can say it."

"I don't want to say it."

"Fingerprints are going to confirm it."

"We don't know that," she says.

"Yes we do," I say, because it's over now. It was over from the moment I found Kelly Summers's window had been forced open and said nothing. "We know we're looking for a cop."

"That's just a theory."

"We know Schroder isn't Schroder anymore. We know he's linked to the first two homicides. The first case was his and he knew all about Grover Hills."

"He saved my life. If it wasn't for him they'd still be scraping bits of me off the road."

I don't answer her.

"And you?" she asks. "You took him to Kelly Summers's house. Why don't you totally turn my world upside down and tell me you're the one who took the cell phone?"

"That wasn't me," I tell her.

"Promise me it wasn't, Tate. Please."

"It wasn't me. I promise," I say, and I don't know why the hell I'm still lying. It's over.

"So now what?" Kent asks.

"Now we keep it to ourselves. There's no point in making accusations until we know, right? Could be a lot of people out there who have been shot in the head. Let's run the prints and see what the sketch looks like."

"You've been to his house," she says. "You must know what kind of car he drives."

"I know."

"And?"

"And it's a dark blue Honda."

"An Accord?"

"I think so. Let's keep it to ourselves until we know for sure, okay?"

"And then?"

"And then we go and arrest him."

We get to the station. We head upstairs and Stevens comes looking for us and tells us we did a good job last night. He says me and McCoy screwed up by not identifying ourselves, but aside from that he's happy.

"He was there trying to bury the murder weapon," he says. "That weapon is out getting tested as we speak, and nobody doubts it's going to come back with Hailey McDonald's DNA all over it. Don't let his lawyer make you think this isn't going to make it to court. By the way, guess who won the pool?"

"Who?" I ask.

"I did," he says. "And I don't want crap like that taking place in this building again, okay? We're supposed to be professionals." He stops talking and stares at me for a few seconds. "You know, Detective, you don't look so good."

"I'm just tired," I say.

"Make sure you take a couple of days off when this is over, huh? We just lost one good man, and we sure as hell don't want to lose another."

Tom Headman steps off the elevator. He's being escorted by another officer. He sees us and he heads over, and we put him into an
interview room similar to the one we used last night, only a little
bigger and somewhat more comfortable. We get him set up with
the sketch artist and then we leave them to it.

We're back in the task-force room when my phone rings.

It's Detective Travers.

The tire has been printed.

They've found two sets of prints. One set will belong to Tom
because he's the one who stripped them from the rims and tossed
them into the scrap heap. The second will belong to the bald man.
The prints were found on the spare wheel he left behind. When he
put his fingers through the holes in the rims he left good prints in
the dirt and grease on the other side. Any prints on the tires were
unreadable.

"We're on our way back to run the prints," he says. "If this guy is
in the system then we're going to have him. If he's a cop, his prints
are going to be on file. This is almost over," he says, and he sounds
like a kid at Christmas. He hangs up and I turn to Kent.

"Travers found a good set of prints," I tell her.

"That's great," she says, but she doesn't sound thrilled. Of course
she doesn't. It's like she said—Schroder saved her life.

"I really don't feel well," I tell her.

"You want to go home?"

"Yeah, I think that's best," I say.

"I'll drop you off."

I shake my head. "Just give me the keys," I say. "I'll go home for
a few hours and come back after lunch."

She tilts her head slightly as she looks at me. "I know where
you're going," she says.

"I'm going home."

"If you say so," she says. "I just hope for your sake you're at home
lying down in about forty-five minutes because that's when all hell
is going to break loose."

"That's where I'll be."

"Good luck," she says. "I don't know whether you're going there to arrest him or warn him, but whatever it is, good luck."

"Thanks."

She hands me the keys. "Don't crash."

Don't crash. I think it might already be too late for that. I take the elevator and step out into the parking lot for the last time as a free man.

CHAPTER SEVENTY-SIX

I phone my wife, but there's no answer. She must be out somewhere with her parents. I think about leaving a message, but what is there to say? *Sorry, Babe, but you somehow showed Schroder where Quentin James is and now I'm going to jail?* The morning is still relatively young when I get to Schroder's house. It's ten thirty, but it feels like afternoon already. It feels like the longest day of my life.

You know what you have to do, don't you?

Yes. I know what I have to do. I have to give up. It's over now.

"Theo," Schroder says when he opens the door.

I hold up the bottle of whiskey. "Got some ice?" I ask him.

He looks me hard in the eye, looks at the whiskey, then back at me. His face softens. He sighs. "It's over, huh?"

"It is."

I follow him through to the kitchen. He grabs a couple of glasses and tosses a good helping of ice into each one, and an even healthier helping of whiskey on top. We sit at his kitchen table.

"How long do we have?"

"Not long. Thirty minutes maybe. Maybe not even that. Could be a little bit more."

"You told them?"

I shake my head. "No. If I told them I wouldn't be here."

"Then what?"

"Benson Barlow was in yesterday. He's convinced us we're looking for a cop."

"Did you try to convince them otherwise?"

"No, because your test with the cell phone came back to bite you in the ass. One of the officers saw it before I took it. So they know it's been taken. So they know it's a cop or somebody who's helping a cop."

"There are a lot of cops," he says. "You just have to make sure that—"

"It's too late to make sure of anything," I say, and I pick up my glass and I swirl it around, the amber liquid inside is like gold, it's heaven, and I take a sip and it's strong, so strong, and so, so good. "Maybe, maybe I could have done things different yesterday, but that was yesterday."

"And today?"

I take a bigger sip. Why did I ever give up? "And today there's a sketch of you," I tell him.

"There was a sketch of me yesterday too. I've seen it," he says. "It looks nothing like me."

"It's a new sketch from a new witness and it's being drawn right now."

"There are no witnesses," he says.

"Did you get the law-enforcement discount at Tim's Tires or didn't you tell Tom you used to be a cop?"

He takes a sip then winces as he swallows. I take another sip, and another, and it's good, damn good, and there's a rush here. The warmth is hitting my mind and expanding, and hello whiskey my old friend, thanks for dropping by. I take another sip, only they aren't sips anymore. I can feel myself smiling.

"He saw you, Carl. Jesus, he got a good look at you and this," I say, and I lean forward and tap his scar, "this may be invisible to a fifteen-year-old girl, but to Tom the Tim Tire Man or whatever the hell his name is, well, he's telling the sketch artist right now all about it."

"That's . . . unfortunate," he says.

"Ha. Yes, *unfortunate*. How *unfortunate* I killed people and how *unfortunate* I'm going to go to jail for it. Did you wear gloves when you took those wheels off your car, Carl?"

"No."

"That's what I figured," I say. "They lifted some prints off it. They're running them now. And they're going to come up with your name. And even then it wouldn't matter. They're running a list of Honda Accords against cops or retired cops. Your name is coming up no matter what."

"You were supposed to stop that kind of thing from happening."

I almost choke on the whiskey then. "Are you serious? Are you going to really sit there and blame me for how this is turning out? Top me up," I say, and slide my glass towards him. He picks the bottle up and gives me a refill. "You killed an innocent man."

"What, Ron McDonald? Come on, Theo, we both know that's—"

"Bullshit?" I ask. "No, what's bullshit is you saying this is bullshit. McDonald was innocent. We messed up, Carl, and we corrected that mistake last night. We've arrested Christopher Watkins for it."

"Who the hell is that?"

"He worked for Ron."

"The guy with the rattail?"

"That's him. He was having an affair with Hailey McDonald. We caught him last night trying to dispose of the murder weapon."

He doesn't say anything.

"Ron was innocent all along."

He still doesn't say anything.

"You screwed up, Carl."

"Shit," he says.

"That pretty much sums it up. It's case closed, Carl."

Schroder finishes off his glass, tops it back up, then tops mine up too. I can't stop asking myself why I ever gave up drinking. Right now I can't think of a good reason ever to have given it up. It tastes too damn good and makes me feel too damn good and damn, damn, damn . . . it makes everything look quite okay, and if there's whiskey in jail then jail won't be too bad at all.

"So now what?" he asks.

"What do you mean *So now what?*"

"I mean what's the plan?"

I shake my head. "You don't get it, do you? There is no plan. The plan is we're fucked. There is no plan, but to stay here and have a few drinks and wait for the police to come and arrest you. That's the plan. Then maybe we'll be cellmates, huh?"

"That's not much of a plan," Schroder says.

I look left and right and notice my vision lags by a split second. I'm getting drunk. "That's why I said there isn't a plan."

He pours the rest of the bottle into our glasses. That's the thing about hip-flask bottles—they don't hold anywhere near enough.

"Is there a liquor store nearby? We need more. We still have . . ." I say as I look at my watch, "the best part of twenty minutes."

"You're drunk," he says.

"No. Not drunk. Just resigned to the fact that because of you I'm not going to see my child grow up. That because of you innocent men have died."

"I'm sorry," he says.

"Yeah, I'm sorry too, you know? I get what you were trying to do, and yeah, you know what? Of course I took care of Quentin James. I shot that son of a bitch in the head. He took away my daughter. He took her away and now, and now you're taking away my other daughter." I realize I'm starting to cry. What in the hell is wrong with me?

"You were right," he says, "about me losing control."

"For a man so full of principle, for a man who really believes he's doing the right thing, I don't understand why you're here and not at Naomi McDonald's house right now."

"What do you mean?"

"Well that's the irony, isn't it?" I lean back in the chair, and for a second it feels like the chair has no back and I'm going to keep tipping, all the way to the ground. God I'm tired all of a sudden.

"She'll want her five minutes with the man that killed her husband—her completely innocent husband. That's what you believe, right? That everybody wants their five minutes?"

"That's what I believe."

"If you were a man of his word you'd be offering the same deal you offered the others. And you know what? I'd like to be there. I'd like to see exactly what karma looks like."

I take another drink. Schroder has both hands flat on the table, the glass between them, and he's staring at me. Hard. The room is starting to spin. I tilt the glass back and forth and watch the ice rattle. Cool, clear ice coated in cool, clear whiskey. I pop one of those cubes into my mouth and start sucking on it.

"You're right," he says.

"About what?" I ask, and I bite the ice cube and it cracks into a few pieces then starts dissolving pretty quickly.

"Then that's the plan," he says.

"What's the plan?"

"We go and see Naomi McDonald. You get to see me being a man of my word."

"Come on, Carl, I didn't really mean you should go there. I was just trying to make a point."

"It was a good point," he says.

"Let's just wait here for the police. It's over."

"It'll be over in fifteen minutes," he says.

"Because you have a plan."

"Yeah I do, Theo."

"So what, we drive there and you talk to McDonald's widow and what? Ask her to shoot you?"

"Why not? I have a gun."

"I'm not going with you."

He looks confused. "You just said you'd love to be there."

"Yeah, but I didn't mean it. Just like I didn't really mean you should go there."

"Come on, Theo, you're the one always saying the world is out of balance. You're the one who just said you wanted to know what karma looks like. Hell, I'm giving you that chance."

"I'm not going with you. I'm going to go and find a liquor store."

"I could threaten to shoot you."

"Yeah? You could. But you wouldn't."

"Don't be so sure, Theo. You've killed people too, remember. You're the Second Chance King, but maybe not anymore, huh? You've done the same shit I've done, why should I be the only one with a death sentence."

I point at him while rocking the glass side to side, the ice cubes getting smaller. "I'm not coming with you. And you know why? Because I can control myself, Carl."

"I'll tell you where Quentin James is."

I stop moving the glass. I look up at him.

"I can tell you exactly where he is, and nobody ever has to know. I'll keep your secret."

I finish off the rest of my drink in one long swallow. "And then what? The police are going to figure out I was helping you. The fact I'm here now tells them that."

"They may suspect it, but there's nothing to prove it. What do they have? Phone records? Is that about it? Hutton gave you a valid reason for calling me.

I think about it. There's still the problem of the shower curtain. If the police chase down that angle, they'll discover I beat them to it by days. But that's only if they chase the angle. . . .

"If I leave you here and the police show up in five minutes, you'll tell them where I am, won't you," he says.

"Probably."

"So come with me now. It'll be just like old times, right? The two of us wrapping up a case together. And there's something in that that feels right. There's some symmetry there. Together until the end. Tell me you don't feel it."

"I come with you now, and you tell me where Quentin James is."

"Yes."

"You keep all my secrets."

"I promise."

I reach across and grab his drink. He's barely touched it. I take two long swallows and then it's gone. "Okay," I say, and when I stand up the room spins even more, and I have to reach out to the table to stop from falling over. "Let's go."

CHAPTER SEVENTY-SEVEN

Schroder helps Tate out to the car. Ex-cop and current cop. Hell, a year ago it was the other way around. Tate was the one screwing things up. Schroder was doing good work, Schroder was the one headed for a promotion. He and Tate were worlds apart. He gets Tate into the front seat, and by the time he's moved around to the driver's side the man is asleep.

"Theo," he says, and shakes his shoulder, and Theo mumbles a little, but then nothing else.

The Evolved Him has come to the end of the road, that road paved with mistakes the recent versions of him made. The Final Him drives and thinks about calling his wife, but what would he say? He would tell her that he loves her, but what good would it do? It wouldn't change anything. It would just upset her. There would be questions and tears and, really, it's easier just not to call. The Old Him would. But the Old Him died. He switches off his cell phone and tosses it into the backseat.

He knows where Ron McDonald lives. Or lived. Of course he does. You don't plan on killing a man and not at least know where he works and where he lives. He drives there now, the sun slowly making its way higher as the temperature does the same, the police somewhere in the city looking for him or about to start looking, maybe knocking on his door this very second, maybe going and seeing his wife. The way it's going to go down—he can't believe it's all because of those tires getting slashed. All because Peter failed to find a pulse when there was one there.

"Don't blame the dead guy," he says, and then Tate mumbles something, turns his head and slumps it against the window. He starts to snore.

The McDonalds live in a neighborhood like any other, and he pays little attention to it, just watches the street names and then the letter boxes until he gets to where he is going, and this could be it. The final destination. And Tate, poor Tate is going to wake up in a world full of shit, but he'll get through it. All he has to do is say the right things and don't change his story. After all, Tate is the Second Chance King. Hell, Tate could probably waltz in there dragging the remains of Quentin James behind him, and people would still let him off with a warning and let him keep his job. He searches Tate's pockets and finds a pen and his notepad and tears out a page.

"I'm going to keep my promise," he says, because despite how annoyed he is that Tate gets to keep bouncing back, despite how annoyed he is that he's One Chance Carl, they did used to be friends. Great friends. They were together when Bridget gave Tate her number. He remembered laughing when Tate confessed to him how he had never gotten her name. He was there when Tate got the call and his life changed, his daughter gone, his wife only marginally better. They made a good team. Good cop and good cop, then it was good cop and bad private investigator, now it's bad ex-cop and Second Chance Cop. But none of this is Tate's fault. If anything, he's jealous. What he wouldn't do right now to swap positions. And Tate never killed anybody innocent.

He writes down the location of Quentin James's body, then slips the pen and pad and paper back into Tate's pocket. The instructions are simple. Tate is probably going to kick himself when he reads them.

There are no cars out front and none up the driveway and he makes his way to the front door and he knocks and nobody answers, and then he knocks again and nobody answers again, but he gives it another minute and gives it a third attempt. Then there are footsteps, then the door is slowly opened, then a woman holds her hand over her eyes to shield them from the glare. Her hair is a mess and her eyes are red and this woman is experiencing the remains of what is left when a hurricane comes through your life and destroys all the good bits.

"Yes?" she says.

"I don't know if you remember me," he says, "but my—"

"I remember you." She looks out at the street at the car and sees Tate in the passenger seat. "What's wrong with him?"

"Heat stroke."

She leans against the door frame and crosses her arms. "Why are you here?"

"I'm here to tell you I'm sorry about what happened to Ron."

She shakes her head. "No you're not. Seven years ago you tried to arrest him for murder. You're not sorry. You're just feeling guilty, and neither of those things will bring him back."

"I know. You're right. But I really am sorry, and he was innocent. I know that now."

She unfolds her arms so she can poke him in the chest. "I know that now and I knew that then," she says, "and I'm glad you know it now too. It doesn't change the fact that he's dead now, does it?"

"No."

She folds her arms again. "So what do you want from me? Just to apologize?"

"Have the police told you they found the man who killed Ron's first wife?"

"Yes. They were here a few hours ago."

"Then it's true," he says.

She looks confused. She frowns at him. "Of course it's true. I don't understand why you're here and not out there finding the person who killed my husband. You're the reason he's dead, you know. You and your narrow-mindedness," she says, and now she's pointing at him again, getting ready to poke him again. "You focused on my husband and because of that this madman was running around out there focused on him too."

"Can we go inside? There's something I need to discuss with you."

"No," she says. "No you can't. Say what you want to say and then leave, okay?"

"You're angry with me," he says.

She smirks at him then, her face pulling back a little. "Of course I'm angry with you."

"Would you kill me, if you could?"

"What?"

"Would you kill me because you blame me for what happened?" He can feel his heart thudding, he can feel the end coming, and he felt none of this over the last few days. Not even when the Collards locked him inside the mental institution. Right now he feels alive.

"Would I kill you?"

"Yes," he says. "That's what I'm asking."

She steps back and reaches out with her right hand and grabs the edge of the door, ready to slam it. "What the hell is wrong with you?"

"I killed your husband," he says.

"I know you did. You killed him by being a useless cop, and no doubt you would have killed others too if you'd stayed on the force."

He shakes his head. "You don't understand."

"No, I understand everything. You thought that—"

"No," he says, interrupting her, and he puts up his hand. "You don't understand. I killed your husband."

"So you said."

"I went to see him two nights ago because I thought he had killed Hailey."

She stops talking then. She looks at him and twists her head to the left as if she can eyeball him better from her right-hand side. She lets go of the door and straightens herself up. "What are you talking about?"

"I went to see him because he had to pay for what he had done. He told me he was innocent. I didn't believe him. I had a gun and I shot him in the stomach. It took him five minutes to bleed to death on the garage floor and I did nothing to help him."

"Is this some kind of joke? Some kind of sick . . . of sick . . . of SICK TWISTED JOKE!"

"I used this gun," he says, and he gets it out.

She looks at it, then at him. "YOU KILLED MY HUSBAND!"

"Yes."

She screams then, and she lunges at him, there's a flurry of fists and she strikes him over and over again, connecting with his face mostly, some to his neck and chest, a few to his arm. She knees him in the groin. But it's the blow to the side of the head that hurts the most, not on the outside, but somewhere deep on the inside, right around the area where his new best friend is hiding out, the bullet with his name on it. For a few moments he can see stars, bright colors, fireworks, he can see all of it. He holds the gun towards her, offering it to her. She digs her fingers at his eyes, he feels skin tearing up there, and then she stops. She collapses, landing on her ass, sitting on the path leading up to her front door.

He's still holding out the gun. The lights in his eyes start to fade, but the dull ache remains. Like a toothache in the middle of his skull. He crouches opposite her.

"It's loaded," he tells her, and the words are coming from somewhere else, perhaps somewhere as far away as the Old Him. This is the Old Him and the Evolved Him teaming up to the do the right thing. "All you have to do is say I attacked you. We fought. I pulled out a gun and it went off."

"What are you talking about?"

"You'll be in the news for a while. People will think you're a hero."

"You want me to shoot you?"

"All you have to do is keep saying it was self-defense."

She shakes her head. Tears are running down the side of her face and hanging from her chin. "You're wrong. You are absolutely wrong. Killing you wouldn't make me a hero. Ron was a hero. He survived what you put him through. He went to work every day and he came home every day and he loved me, he loved me more than anybody ever had. That made Ron the biggest hero in the world and that makes you the worst person in the world. Killing you doesn't make me a hero. Killing you just makes me as bad as you."

"I don't understand," he says. "Here," he says, and reaches forward so she can take the gun.

She shakes her head. "You messed up, and the same thing you judged Ron by you are now judging yourself by, and maybe I should respect you for that, but I don't, because I hate you too much. At least I can't call you a hypocrite, huh? But you've come here because you think you owe me the chance to put you down, you think it'll make me feel better and I sure as hell know it'll probably make you feel better, but you know what? Screw you, Detective. Get the hell out of here and take that gun with you, and live with what you've done. There is no redemption here for you, no ending. Why don't you drag your sorry ass down to the police station and turn yourself in?"

"I still . . ." he says, shaking his head, then stops shaking his head because the world sways a little, and he can almost feel the bullet jumping up and down a little. "Everybody wants their five minutes."

"Not everybody."

"Yes. Everybody."

"Then go and offer them to somebody else, because this everybody wants you to leave her the hell alone so she can get back to mourning what you took away from her. Part of me hopes you find what you're looking for. Part of me hopes you find somebody to put that gun to your head, but more of me wants you to live forever so you can always regret what you've done. Do I want you dead? No. I want you to sit in a cell every day and suffer for your sins. Hell, if there is any justice in this world, I'll still get to see you hang. Now get the hell off my yard."

CHAPTER SEVENTY-EIGHT

He leaves Naomi McDonald sitting on the pathway and heads back to his car, limping slightly from the knee to his balls, limping slightly because the world is on a slight angle, it's fractional, barely noticeable, but different somehow. The bullet has shifted. He's sure of it.

"It doesn't make sense," he tells Tate, only right now talking to Tate is just like talking to Warren. "All these years—I can't think of one person who wouldn't want to put a bullet into the brain of the man who killed their wife or husband. Not one person."

That's the spidering way, Tate says, but of course Tate doesn't say that, not really. All Tate does is stay slumped against the door, his head tilting forward now, breathing in the clean Christchurch air and replacing it with alcohol fumes.

"So where to now?"

I think you know, Tate doesn't say, but would if he weren't counting spiders. He would say, *Just because Naomi McDonald let you off the hook doesn't mean that others will.*

He reaches up to his eye and his fingers come away with a dab of blood. He starts the car and starts driving. After ten minutes he's in the same neighborhood he was in on Saturday afternoon, and now he starts taking the same streets. There are a few things that are different—the temperature, the fact that Peter Crowley is dead, having Tate asleep in the passenger seat. But there are things that are the same—not much traffic, a need to do something good. He reaches Peter Crowley's house and there are a couple of other cars here, probably grieving family members, hopefully no police. There's a bottle of water in the backseat and some painkillers in the glove compartment. He introduces the two things to each other and swallows the pills and hopes the headache that feels like a toothache is going to fade.

He knocks on the door, and Monica, the daughter, dressed the way Death would dress if Death were a fifteen-year-old girl, answers.

"You," she says.

"Is your mother here?"

She reaches up and wraps her hands around the back of her neck, then tugs gently at the hair back there. "You got my father killed, and she's not my mother."

"I know. I'm sorry."

She reaches up and slaps him, and the colors come back, the bright lights and fireworks and these are a warning from his new best friend. It's saying *Don't let people keep hitting you*, because that's what the doctor told him.

"I wish I could kill you," she says.

"I know you do," he says, but he's not here to let her have that responsibility. If she was twenty, maybe, but not fifteen. Otherwise he'd let her hit him over and over until the bullet inside did its work.

Then another woman comes to the doorway. Her photograph was in the paper. This is Peter Crowley's wife. Charlotte. She reminds him of his wife. Same haircut, same build, but sadder. Of course she's sadder. He can hear other voices from inside the house. "What's going on out here?" Charlotte asks, and then she sees Schroder, and then she says "Oh," as if everything in the world suddenly makes sense. "You're him, aren't you."

"Yes. My name is Carl Schroder," he says.

"What do you want with us, Mr. Schroder?"

"He killed my dad," Monica says.

"Please, Monica," Charlotte says, "let him speak."

"Fine," Monica says, "but I'm calling the police."

"Don't," Schroder says, and he puts his palm into the air and points it at them. "Not yet. Please, I just need five minutes of your time, and then you can call anybody you want, okay?"

"Five minutes?" Charlotte says.

"That's all."

"Don't give it to him," Monica says. "Let's just kick his ass."

"Please, Monica, let's hear what he has to say. Come inside," she says.

Monica complains, but only for a few seconds, and then he follows them inside and through to the kitchen. He can hear voices coming from another part of the house. Probably the lounge. "Can I get you a drink?" Charlotte asks.

"A water would be good, thank you." He looks at Monica who is glaring at him, then he looks back at Charlotte. "Can we talk alone?"

Charlotte gives it a few moments of thought, then nods. "Monica, go and talk to your grandparents, okay? I'll be through soon."

"I don't—"

"Please, please, Monica, please do this for me, okay? Please don't tell me I'm not your mother and you don't have to do what I tell you, because I know, okay? I know it because you've said it a hundred times already today."

Monica says nothing and turns from the kitchen. From the doorway she looks back at them. "But I'm calling the police."

"Monica—"

"That's fine," Schroder says. "Let her call them. We'll be done by the time they arrive."

Charlotte pours a water and hands him the glass. He pulls out the gun that he used to shoot four men in the head and one man in the stomach. Her eyes widen when she sees it, but go back to normal when he puts it on the kitchen counter and steps back.

"What do you want?" she asks.

"I want to give you your five minutes. That's what I was trying to do with Peter. I was trying to help him, but things got out of control."

She shakes her head a little, and then she must get it because she goes still. Her face changes a little. She gets it, but it's still confusing her. "You want me to shoot you?"

"Yes."

She nods. She looks at the gun and keeps on nodding.

"You've got it all wrong," she says. "I've had a few days to think about it. You know that saying about people who die doing what they loved? I never got it. Car racers crash and people say they died doing what they loved, but I always kept thinking it didn't make sense because they might have loved driving, they might have loved speeding around a track, but it wasn't the driving that killed them, it was the crashing, and how can you love crashing? Or like a rock climber falling to his death. He loved climbing rocks, but he didn't die climbing rocks—he died after a terrifying, long fall. He died when he splattered across the ground. He didn't love the falling. But now I get it. I loved my husband, I really did, but there was a part of him missing. I didn't know him before he lost his wife, so I can't tell you exactly what it was, but it didn't take a rocket scientist to see that part of him died right along with her. He tried his best. He was a good man, and he loved his daughter, and he loved me and my stepson as best he could, and he was always going to do right by us. But I wasn't Linda. Nobody was Linda. The biggest thing he loved in this world was the idea of something bad happening to those men who hurt her." She smiles, then she wipes some tears away from her face. "You've come to tell me you got my husband killed, and right now I'm clinging to that stupid saying, and I know I'll cling to it for years to come. My husband died doing what he loved. He died happy, and he died with you killing the men that broke him, and of all the ways to leave this world I think that's as good as any. I think Peter would have accepted that. Peter traded his own life for revenge, and in that he made sure those men couldn't ruin any other lives, and I will miss him, and I will always love him, but he died doing what he loved and who doesn't want to go out that way? Who?" she asks, and the silence falls around them, a few seconds turn into five, then into ten, and Schroder doesn't know how to answer her. He realizes the others in the house have gone quiet too. They're listening.

"Was Peter still alive when you killed those other men? Did he know?"

"Yes. Yes, he was, and he knew."

She crosses her arms, uses one hand to hold her elbow and the other to hold her chin. Her hands are starting to shake and the tears are close now, and this is his doing. The pain in this house, an empty space that can't be filled, this is because of him. "Were you by his side when he died?"

"I was."

"If you came here because you think I want vengeance, then you're wrong. You think getting my husband killed entitles me to the same five minutes you gave him, but it doesn't work that way. Not for me. Not in this house. Take that gun of yours and bury it, or turn yourself in to the police, because you're only going to get more good people killed if you're out there trying to make a difference. You are foolish and arrogant and you got Peter killed, but Peter was foolish and arrogant for going along with you. I'm angry about what happened, yes, but I forgive you Carl Schroder. So now I want you to leave and never come back, and I want you to take my forgiveness for getting my husband killed with you."

CHAPTER SEVENTY-NINE

"Have I been misinterpreting the world?" he asks Tate. Tate is still asleep. The long hours of the case, a fresh injection of alcohol after a year without it—Tate might sleep for the rest of the day. "Two mixed messages from two different women, neither wanting to see me dead. This last week—hell, the whole twenty years . . . I don't know. I don't know."

He remembers everything about the Kelly Summers case, including where she used to live, and also where her parents used to live. It's to her parents' place he now drives. The last time he came here, Kelly Summers was just out of hospital and he came to say they had caught the man who had done this bad thing to her. She had identified him, of course. It was her neighbor. Dwight Smith had not returned home, though. Instead he had run. He had headed north. The problem with New Zealand, or as was the good thing in this case, is that north cannot take you far. North, south, west or east all get you to an ocean in just a matter of hours. Any further you need a plane or a boat or a great set of lungs, and Smith had none of those. He had drained his bank accounts and made it as far as Nelson and then he had gotten into a fight with a pimp after he couldn't afford to pay the prostitute he had just spent fifteen minutes with. He had been found unconscious and admitted to hospital, and then the dots were connected.

The house is a small cottage in a big yard, a ten-foot hedge hiding it from the street, behind that hedge a thousand roses and dozens of lavender bushes and a whole heap of everything else that grows bright and strong, as if this family is using those colors to keep the darkness away. It's a gravel driveway that winds its way up to the house and there are four cars already parked here. One of them has writing along the side of it—it belongs to a funeral director. There's a wooden porch and Schroder steps up onto it, and he can see into the lounge where the chairs are full of people. He sees Kelly's dad look up, notice him, then the quizzical look as he tries to place the face. He gets up and comes to the front door.

"It's Detective Schroder, right?" he asks, and Roger Summers is in his late fifties, but looks fifteen years older, and of course he does—this is what a man like Dwight Smith will do to a family.

"Right," Schroder says.

"I'm touched that you've come to pay your respects," he says, "but this isn't the best time. The funeral is on Thursday and we would all appreciate it if you could come along."

"I need to talk to you and your wife. Please, it's important."

"Can't it wait?"

"No," Schroder says. "It really can't. It's about Kelly. Please."

Roger Summers nods. "There's an outdoor table around the back of the house. Head around and we'll see you there in a couple of minutes."

Schroder steps down from the porch and walks around the side of the house, more flowers and trees and bushes, more lavender being visited by dozens of bees, then a big backyard with a small pond that has a black cat sitting next to it, watching the fish. There's an outdoor table that would sit a dozen people, long and wooden and well made, and on a summer night where your daughter was still alive this would be a beautiful setting.

He sits and faces the sun and lets it burn his skin. One day that sun will burn out, life on this planet will disappear, and this—all of this will have been for nothing.

Roger appears then. He's carrying a pitcher of juice, the ice inside it rattling, condensation runs down the side of the glass, and his wife—and suddenly Schroder can't remember her name—follows, three glasses in her hand. They put them down and Schroder stands so they can all shake hands and the wife fills the three glasses.

"I'm sorry about Kelly," Schroder says.

"I know," the wife says. "We're all sorry."

They sit down. He takes a sip of the juice and it's like putting ice on the toothache in his head.

"Are you okay?" the woman asks.

"Yes," he says, and he's okay because this will be over soon, one way or the other. One way is with these people. The other involves the man asleep in his car.

"I liked her," he says.

"Everybody liked her," Roger says.

"She was one of those cases that always stayed with me. It's because of Kelly things have gone the way they have gone."

"What do you mean?" the wife asks.

"What kind of things?" Roger asks.

So he talks. And talks. And talks. The pressure in his head is building up, and if he can keep talking, if he can make room by getting rid of all these words, then the headache will go away. He goes back to the beginning. He says "I always wanted to be a cop, and earlier this year that was taken away from me." He tells them of the decision he was forced to make where he killed a woman, and about what kind of woman she was. "I shot her in cold blood, and if I hadn't done that, then the girl, the young girl would have died. I had to choose one life over another." He tells them how he lost his job over it, how the crime was covered up, he tells them of working for Jonas Jones, the psychic. "He's a slimy son of a bitch who's about as psychic as a weatherman." Then he talks about Joe Middleton, hunting him down, a hunt that ended with Schroder getting a bullet in the head. "When I came out of the coma I was lost. I wasn't who I used to be, and I didn't care."

Then he tells them about the referendum. The conversation. The *Why should*. He tells them how he learned Dwight Smith was free. He tells them how angry he was people came out of jail and got second chances. "Where's my second chance? Where?" As he tells them they sip their drinks and he can tell they are wondering where he is going with this, but they can also tell he is unloading, he is a man carrying a weight, and they are going to allow him to finish. They are good people. Which might very well go against him here. And as he talks, the sky—nothing but blue for the last few days—now has company in the form of several clouds on the horizon. Dark clouds. They are gathering out there.

He tells them about wanting to kill Dwight Smith. About following him from the service station. Breaking into Kelly's house. Kelly wanting her five minutes.

"We both knew," the woman says, "that our daughter couldn't have done it by herself. It was too much."

"Did she kill him? Did she at least do that much?" Roger asks.

"What do you want to hear?" Schroder says. "That she did?"

"Yes," he says. "I want her to have gotten revenge on that bastard."

"No," the woman says. "The idea that Kelly could kill somebody . . . No, that doesn't sit well with me at all."

"He deserved what he got," Roger says.

"I know," the woman says. "But Kelly . . . did she kill him?"

"Yes."

"Let me ask you, Detective," she says. "What kind of world do we live in when a young woman like Kelly has to kill a man?"

"My world," Schroder says. "I'm sorry I couldn't help her."

"Sorry?" the woman asks. "In what way?"

"She's dead because of me."

"I don't understand," the woman says.

So Schroder points it out for her. If he had called the police, then Kelly could still be alive. There would be no hiding the dead body. Cops would have gotten involved. People would have known all about it.

The parents sit in silence and they think about that, and they sip their juice, and he can hear the bees flying around the lavender and can feel beads of sweat running from his armpits down the side of his body and can feel the bullet inside his head, throbbing from the earlier blows, expanding in the heat, contracting from the cold juice, the bullet getting ready to do something.

"Is calling the police what she wanted?" Roger asks.

"No," he says, "but that doesn't matter. Your daughter died because of what I did, and you have the right to take your anger out on me."

Roger shakes his head. "We're not angry at you," he says.

"If it hadn't been for you," the woman says, "Kelly would have died on the bathroom floor. You didn't kill our daughter. Kelly didn't kill herself. Dwight Smith murdered her five years ago."

"It doesn't bring her back, but it does give us some kind of closure. Better she killed him than him hurting her again. Much better."

"I—"

Roger puts his hand up to stop him. "You're in pain," he says. "Any fool can see that. You're blaming yourself for what happened, but the way I see it, the world needs more people like you. It needs people to feel bad about the injustice, and it needs people to make a stand."

Schroder shakes his head and instantly regrets it. He's going to have to keep head movements to a minimum now until the bullet settles back down. "What I've been doing, it's a mistake. A huge mistake, and your daughter is dead and somebody has to pay for that."

"And somebody has paid for it," the woman says.

"I have to pay for it too."

They go quiet again, then Roger finishes his juice, picks up the pitcher, then puts it back down without pouring any more. "The way it sounds to me is you want somebody to punish you. You're feeling bad, and you think the solution is what?"

"The solution is you have the same five minutes with me that Kelly had with Dwight Smith."

"Is that really what you think?" Roger asks. "That we blame you? That we want to hurt you? That we want to kill you?"

"You should."

"No, we shouldn't," the woman says. "We owe you. Yes, our daughter is dead, and yes, right now we can function, but in a few days we won't be able to. In a few days they will have to carry us to the funeral because we won't be able to walk, but we don't blame you, Detective. Not at all. If blame is what you've come here to find, then you've come to the wrong place."

"You saved our daughter," Roger says, "and then she left this world and we will never recover from that, but we know she left on her own terms. We can't hate you for that, and we sure as hell can't punish you for it either. You took away from our daughter what would have been the last night of her life, a night that would have been the worst night of her life, and you gave her something she wanted—and that was to make that bastard pay. You gave our daughter a gift that I wish I could have given her, and if I had been a better man, a stronger man, I would have had the balls to do what you did. Even if I'd known he was out of jail, I'd have done nothing. So no, we don't blame you, Detective. How can I blame you for doing something that was my job to do? If anything I envy you. To me you are a hero. To me what this city needs is a lot more people like you."

CHAPTER EIGHTY

I'm back in the art museum with the large phone that has the little phones attached, the little phones making up the keypad, and all at once they start ringing. I try to reach out to them, but my arms don't move. In fact none of me is moving. The edges of the room are dark, but the middle is bright, too bright, and I want to look away, but I can't because my head won't move, my eyes won't move, and I have the kind of headache I used to get when I had to take a few hours off from drinking.

Then I remember that's what I was doing before going into the art museum.

Then somehow one of the phones is against my ear. It's Rebecca. She's found me in my dream.

"Tate? Where are you?"

I tell Kent about the headache, and the words form, but they don't make it out. They die somewhere in my throat and I swallow them back down. The big piece of modern art has gone, it's been replaced by a windshield, a road beyond it, some parked cars and houses and a bunch of lampposts and trees. I can taste whiskey. The sky is darker than I last saw it. There are clouds heading from the mountains to the west. The car is parked on the road outside a hedge.

"Theo? Are you there?"

I have the phone pressed against my ear. "Rebecca?"

"There have been two phone calls over the last thirty minutes," Rebecca says. "One from Naomi McDonald, and one from Monica Crowley. Schroder has been to see them. The police know, Theo. They know who they're looking for, and the print has been run and it's all confirmed. We're on our way to Schroder's house now. Where are you?"

"I'm in a car," I tell her.

"Where?"

"I . . . my head hurts," I tell her.

"Tate—"

"I was dreaming of modern art again," I tell her.

"Are you drunk?"

"Maybe. Why are you call . . . hang on a second . . ." I say, and the door to the car opens. "Hey, Schroder's here. Hey, Schroder! How the hell are you? Are we driving to a bar?"

Schroder reaches over and takes the phone off me. He switches it off and tosses it into the backseat.

"Hey, why the hell did you do that?" I ask him.

"We've got work to do."

I tell him to leave me alone, but the words are all lost at sea. They're drowning in the whiskey-induced headache. I feel like I did a few months ago just before slipping into the coma, that day where the headache got stronger and stronger and then disappeared, taking the world with it. Would they put a coma patient into jail? If so, would the years count? Would they hang a man in a coma?

"Would they?" I ask, and finally some words are appearing.

"Would they what?" Schroder asks.

"Hang a coma patient?"

"You're drunk."

"Where are we going?" I ask, because the street and the parked cars and the lampposts and trees are moving. We're passing them by.

"I did what you told me to do," he says.

I tighten my eyes and I can see some colors floating around. I'm thirsty. "I need some water," I tell him, and a moment later a bottle of it appears in my lap. I don't question where it came from. If I do, it might just disappear and turn out to be part of a dream. I drink half of it, then the other half, and it makes me feel a little better.

"Got any painkillers?" I ask, and the universe provides them too. With all the water gone, I have to end up dry swallowing them. Then Schroder takes a couple of painkillers too, chewing them down, and I guess he's got a hangover too.

I drowse as we drive. We're on the outskirts of town. Through neighborhoods and then heading north. The big, cruel sun beats down on the car and I'm sweating. I can feel the whiskey seeping out of my pores. The painkillers are starting to work.

"The police know," I tell him, waking up a little more. "That was Rebecca on the phone. She said . . ." I say, and then I really have to think about it. What did she say? "She said Naomi McDonald and Charlotte Crowley have . . . no, it wasn't Charlotte, it was Monica. She said Naomi and Monica called the police. She said you'd gone to see them."

"I gave them their five minutes," he tells me, rubbing at the side of his head.

"What?"

So he tells me more. First Ron McDonald's wife. Then Peter Crowley's wife. Then Kelly Summers's parents. He tells me all about it. The conversations. And as he tells me, we keep driving, and as we drive, I start to wake up more. We're heading north. Out of the city. Hotter out here because we're closer to the sun. But then the heat goes out of that sun. The clouds roll in and hide it away. Then the trees lining the paddocks start to sway.

"I went to all of them and none of them were angry enough at what I had done," he tells me.

"Are we going to the police now?" I ask.

"Does it look like we're going to the police?"

I look left and right and straight ahead. "No."

"When you killed Quentin James, how did it feel?"

I think back to that moment and all the moments that followed. "I didn't feel anything."

"Did it hurt?"

"Hurt? No. It didn't hurt."

His mouth turns down at the sides and he starts nodding. "Yeah, that's what I figured. It didn't hurt when I let Dwight Smith get killed, and it didn't hurt killing those assholes out at Grover Hills. It didn't feel wrong and it didn't feel right. I didn't feel anything. It's the bullet," he says, and he taps the side of his head the same way Tom from Tim's Tires tapped his when he said he knew how to describe the bald man. "The bullet switched off something inside of me."

"I know."

"But then Peter Crowley died, you know? He died, and then all that stuff that got switched off, well, some of it started to come back. I know I got him killed, but I didn't kill him, and there's a big enough difference between the two for me to feel bad, but not feel hurt. Does that make any sense?" he asks, and I can see him crying now. This man who feels nothing has tears rolling down his cheeks.

"It makes sense," I tell him, and the headache is almost gone now, but my mouth feels dry again. "Got another bottle of water?"

"That was the only one."

We drive along for another minute. He wipes his hands at his face, getting rid of the tears. A few drops of rain hit the windshield.

"Killing Ron McDonald," he says, and he keeps wiping his face, but the tears keep on coming, "that felt good. Ah, hell, Tate, I shot that guy in the stomach and he bled out and for the first time I didn't feel nothing, for the first time I felt great. I felt happy. I wanted to kill more people. The city is full of assholes who deserve to get shot."

"However flawed the justice system is, Carl, your way isn't any better. You're not out there like Batman, cleaning up a city. You're out there putting innocent people in harm's way, and those innocent people have died."

"I know that, goddamn it," he says, and he punches the steering wheel, then his face tightens up in pain, but I'm not sure why exactly, then he reaches up and massages his temple a little. He has a headache. Maybe a hangover headache, even though I don't think he drank much at all.

"Yeah, you know that now," I say.

"You're right. I felt good shooting that guy in the stomach, and

he cried when he died, Tate, he cried and he told me he was innocent, and that just made it all seem better. Then . . . then when
you called . . ." he says, and the tears are too much for him and he
has to pull over. We're well north of the city now, not too far from
the turnoff that would take us out to where Quentin James used to
be buried.

"It's okay," I tell him.

"It's not okay," he says. "It'll never be okay. I killed an innocent man, Theo. It's not like earlier in the year with that woman.
We had no choice there, and she was a monster anyway, but this
guy . . . this . . . Ah hell, it's all gone to shit. I've gone from feeling
nothing to feeling everything, and I want it to end, Tate. I want it
to be over."

He puts the car back into gear. We carry on driving. The rain
carries on raining. Harder now. Schroder puts on the wipers.

"Where are we going?"

"You'll see," he says.

"Let's turn around," I tell him. "Turn yourself in."

"Is that what you would do?" he asks.

"Yes."

"Really? You'll turn yourself in for killing Quentin James."

"Yes."

"Even though you'll never get to see your child grow up?"

"Yes."

"No," he says. "I don't believe you," he says, and he takes the
turnoff towards the woods that have played a big part over the last
few days, which can only mean we're going where I thought we
might be going. I just don't know why, but it doesn't feel like it's a
good reason. It's why I just lied to him that I would turn myself in.
Something is wrong here.

"I killed an innocent man," he says. "You killed the man who
killed your daughter. Naomi told me what a hero was, and that's
what you are, Theo. You've killed people, and I know Quentin
James isn't the only one, but—"

"There's nobody else," I say, "other than in self-defense."

"That's not true, and it doesn't matter because you're a hero to me. Would you really turn yourself in?" he asks, and before I can answer he carries on. "If I showed you where Quentin James was, and promised never to tell another living soul, would you turn yourself in?"

"Yes."

"Come on, Tate, be honest with me. There's nothing left but to be honest."

"Then no," I tell him. "He killed my daughter, and if I had the choice I wouldn't let him stop me from raising another one."

"We're almost at the end," he says, and we continue to drive, the houses petering out, the farms going on for acres and acres, and then the trees, the woods, and then we're pulling over in the exact same spot I pulled over with Bridget on Saturday, the same spot I pulled over the day I brought Quentin James out here to pay for what he did. Schroder gets out of the car and I do the same and the wind pushes at us and the rain slaps at us, and it feels like the weather doesn't want us out here. The world spins a little, but not like before. I got drunk quickly because I haven't had any alcohol in over a year, but I'm sobering up quickly too.

"What are we doing out here?" I ask him.

"We used to be so alike," he says. "Then you went one way and I went the other, but we've both been to the same places and seen the same things. Dark places and dark things. Hell, we were even in comas at the same time," he says, and he runs his hand over his bald head and wipes away the rain. "The thing is, Theo, we're always going to be the same, you and me. We believe in the same things. We're fighting the same fight. We've done the same things and you've been in my shoes and I've been in yours."

"And?"

"And that's why we're out here," he says, having to talk louder now. "We're one in the same. That test with the cell phone, that was silly and pointless, but it was a test and you passed. It meant you were on my side. Asking you about Quentin James, that was a test too, and that one you failed."

"What are you talking about?"

He takes the gun out of his pocket. "You're not prepared to take responsibility for your actions, Theo. Not like me. I offered those people their five minutes. They didn't want them, but that doesn't mean they still can't have them. I've done things on behalf of people, and I'll do this for them too. They deserve to see me dead."

"What are you going to do? Shoot yourself?"

"Why not? What's my future here? To be arrested? To be paraded around the courts and be made an example of, to maybe even be the first man to be executed under the new law? I don't want that for me or for my family. I've hurt them enough, and I've hurt too many others."

"Carl—"

"And you," he says. "I sure as hell don't see you offering yourself to the people you've hurt."

"What the hell are you getting at?" I ask, looking at the gun that is pointing at the ground, wondering where he's going to point it next. Or at who. But I already know. I felt worried in the car, but now it's worse. Now I'm scared.

"We're the same person, Theo. The same person. I killed an innocent man on Monday. When will you kill one, huh? Next Monday? Next year? The next bad guy you chase down, the next serial killer, will you kill him? Of course you will. What if the next one isn't the guy? It's going to happen, buddy, the same way it happened to me, and I can't let that happen."

"Let's go back to the police station and tell them everything."

"No," he says. "I still believe in what I was doing. I made some mistakes along the way, but I still believe in, in this . . . this mission. You and me, buddy, this here is the end of the line. These woods, right here, we're not going any further."

"We?"

He points the gun at me just like I knew he would. I should have started running the moment I got out of the car. "This is where it all started for you, and this is where it's all going to end," he says. "Symmetry. You said before you wanted to see what karma looks like? Well, now you're going to know. Come on," he says, and points the gun into the trees to show me where to start walking. "Let me show you where I put Quentin James and let's get this over with."

CHAPTER EIGHTY-ONE

We walk through the woods. The rain is hammering the trees. It sounds like a waterfall. It gets caught up in the leaves and branches, the drops running together and forming bigger drops that soak my clothes and roll down the back of my shirt. I keep moving because to not move is to get shot. To not move is to say good-bye to the world, whereas to keep moving means there's a chance. The longer I can stay alive, the more possibilities there will be. Maybe the cops will arrive. Maybe some people are mountain biking nearby. Maybe Schroder will step in a bear trap.

"Carl, come on, don't do this," I tell him. "Please, don't do this."

"Just keep walking, Theo."

I keep walking, but I also keep talking at the same time. Talking the walk and walking the talk. I'm heading towards Quentin James's empty grave because it's the only landmark out here I know, and Schroder doesn't say anything to correct me. I keep looking for branches I can hold and fling back at him, and there are some, but he's keeping his distance waiting for it. The day is getting colder. It's dropped ten degrees since we started our walk. The clouds are darker and—

A fork of lightning flashes overhead, it cuts the sky and disappears, a few moments later the rumbling thunder follows, it sounds like the empty belly of a giant. I pause to look at the sky and Schroder tells me to keep walking. There is more lightning and more thunder, one flash almost bright enough to blind me, one rumble so loud I feel it through the ground. Out here the world is ending. The rain, not to be outdone by the lightning, doubles its efforts. The ground around the trees pools with water. And still we walk, we walk and walk, and then we're there, Quentin James's grave, a place that three years ago I never thought I would need to see again, and now nobody can keep me away. The grave is empty, the walls are turning to mud and sliding inwards, at the bottom dirty water is pooling up.

"Where is he?" I ask, turning towards Schroder. "Where did you put him?"

"Check your pockets," he says.

So I check my pockets. I find a note inside one of them. It's from Schroder. It says "*Q. J. is twenty yards from where you left him to the north.*"

"Really?" I ask.

"Really. Now turn around and kneel down," he says.

"No."

"Seriously, Theo, do it. You can kneel down and we can talk, or I can shoot you right now and end this. Go with what you think are the better odds."

"We used to be friends," I tell him.

"And now we're both killers. Turn around and kneel. I won't ask again."

I turn around so I'm facing the grave. I kneel down. The ground soaks into my knees, into my trousers. My old man knees complain at the movement, but soon they'll be at peace.

"All that matters is that the world is about balance. About sym-metry," he says, and he has to talk louder now to be heard over the storm. "This is where you killed him, and it only makes sense that this is where justice is carried out."

"I thought you were carrying out justice for the people I haven't killed yet."

He doesn't answer.

"And, if I haven't killed them, then it's not justice at all, is it?"

"What is the biggest problem with being a cop?" he asks.

"Getting shot in the line of duty?"

"The biggest problem is we're reactive, Theo, not proactive. If you could arrest people before the crime, you would do it, wouldn't you? Only that's impossible. Except for right now. Right now it's possible because I know you're going to kill again."

"I'm not going to," I tell him. "Hell, even if you told me where Quentin James was and I got away with all of this, I would still give up being a cop. This isn't the life I want, not now, not with a baby on the way. Please, Carl, don't do this. Please don't do this."

He doesn't answer. I can feel him back there, can feel the gun pointing at me. Can feel him making the decision.

"Come on, Carl, please don't do this," I say. "I have a chance to make things right," I add, and I'm reminded of Quentin James out here, him telling me he would do better. This is the world finding balance. We are one gunshot away from symmetry. "Bridget is pregnant. Think about her. Think about what you're going to do to her. She can't go through this." He doesn't answer. The wind is howling through the trees. More lightning and more thunder. "Goddamn it, Carl, don't do this!"

When he doesn't answer again, I start to turn around. If he's going to shoot me, then he can shoot me while looking me in the eye. He can shoot me while . . .

Schroder is lying on the ground. He's on his side and his eyes are wide open, but they're not looking at me. They're not looking at anything. The gun is still in his hand, but the barrel is pointing into the ground, his wrist bent inwards, the other arm tucked beneath him. His mouth is sagging open, the tip of his tongue protruding.

"Carl?"

Carl doesn't answer. I move over towards him, grab hold of the gun, and then check for a pulse. There's nothing. I check twice more, once in the neck, once in the wrist.

Carl Schroder is dead.

The bullet inside his head has finally traveled its course.

CHAPTER EIGHTY-TWO

And just like that, the rain stops. It's as if a giant tap has been turned off. There's one more giant peal of thunder, but it's far in the distance, somewhere out to sea, and I don't see the flash of lightning it's chasing. Rain continues to drip from the branches.

I sit down and lean against the tree. I don't feel remotely drunk anymore. I think about my future. When I've thought things through, I make my way back to the car, my feet soaking and muddy, and as I walk I think some more. My phone is in the backseat and I grab it and switch it on and sit on the hood of the car as the clouds clear and the sun comes back out. Steam starts to rise off the tarmac.

I phone Kent.

"Jesus, Tate, where the hell are you?"

"I went to see Schroder," I tell her.

"Yeah, I know you did. *We* know you did. Where the hell are you now?"

"I went there to arrest him and he pulled a gun on me."

"What?"

"This sounds crazy," I say, which is what people say when they're about to lie their asses off, "but he forced me to drink. He knew about my problem and, well, he forced me to drink and then I passed out."

"He forced you?"

"Yeah. At gunpoint."

I tell her about the car rides of which she already knows. Then I tell her about the car ride out to where I am now, and I give her directions.

"And Schroder? Where is he now?"

"He's here," I tell her. "He's dead."

I hang up then because I don't want to talk anymore. Thirty minutes later I hear sirens. They get closer, then they're turned off, then cars are pulling up.

"What in the hell happened here?" Stevens asks, and he looks angry, angrier than I've ever seen him.

I spell it out for him. I went to make an arrest. The drinking. The trip into the woods. Schroder dropping dead as I knelt over a grave.

"Whose grave?" he asks.

"I don't know whether he dug it for me, or whether he dug it for somebody else. Also . . . he's done it before," I tell him.

"What?"

"Schroder. Dwight Smith wasn't his first. He said that Quentin James was his first."

"James? The man who ran over your daughter?"

"The very one. Carl said he took care of him for me. He said he did it because we were friends and partners and because he thinks I would have done the same for him."

"He say where the body was?"

"He said it was out here somewhere."

He looks at Rebecca. Other officers are getting out of their cars, but they're waiting for me to show them the way.

"Can we have some privacy here?" Stevens asks.

Everybody else moves away, leaving just him and me.

"This doesn't look good for you, Tate."

"In what way?"

"You warning him. You know somebody was helping him, and we've got phone records that show you calling him all the time, including the night Ron McDonald was murdered. There are some who think you were the one helping him."

"That's bullshit," I say. "He was going to shoot me in the head."

"We only have your word for that."

"What? Come on, why the hell else would we be out here? He was a changed man. When I came to arrest him, he really believed

I was the only one who knew what he had done. He thought he could hide the truth by shooting me."

"That's your story?"

"That's the way it happened, yes, and the medical examiner will back me up."

"Listen, Tate, I'm going to have to suspend you, okay? If there's any hint that—"

"That's okay," I tell him. "I don't want to do this anymore. This world, it's all about balance. I've done what I can for this city. Now I need to do what I can for my family. I quit," I tell him.

He nods. He looks like he might have been expecting this. "Are you sure about this?"

"Positive."

"You'll still be investigated, you know that, right?"

"I know that," I tell him.

"Show us where he is," he tells me, and then I lead them back into the woods, back towards Schroder, back to show them exactly what karma looks like.

ACKNOWLEDGMENTS

It's weird . . . scary weird, that this is book number eight. Scary weird to see the years flying by and to see that I've finally caught up in age with Tate. He was almost ten years older than me when I came up with the idea for his first novel. Now we're both saying goodbye to our thirties. I might make him ninety in the next book just so I can feel younger, and I might make him bald at forty-one so I can feel better about that too. It's not much of a guess as to where I got the idea for his old-man knees.

The novel was written on different sides of the world, the first half over the summer in New Zealand, then the second half over the summer in England. Then back to New Zealand for the following summer to edit it. I'm a summer guy. I try to avoid winter when I can. I've avoided a bunch of them over the last six or seven years. Bits of the novel were written in hotel rooms in the US, or France, or Germany—my mind never far from what Tate and Schroder were up to.

Like the seven books before it, *Five Minutes Alone* has been made better by the wonderful team at Atria. My editor, Sarah Branham, is amazing, and every year I'm so thankful to know I'm in good hands, that her feedback will always send me in the right direction. To the rest of the team—Judith Curr, Mellony Torres, Janice Fryer, Lisa Keim, Emily Bestler, Isolde Sauer, and all the others—thank you so much for giving me and my books a home.

Heading across the Atlantic and I'd like to say thanks once again to Jane Gregory of Gregory and Company—without Jane I'd be lost. Also Stephanie Glencross, Jane's in-house editor who also happens to be, in my opinion, the best editor in the UK. And

Claire Morris, who gets the books into other parts of the world, sometimes into places I've never heard of.

Of course I'd like to thank you as well, the reader. Over the years I've had some truly amazing emails and messages from many of you, and getting to travel and meet people at festivals and signings is the highlight of being a writer. I've said it before and I'll say it again . . . you guys are the reason I like to make bad things happen.

Paul Cleave
June 2014—Christchurch